I0739143

FREEWHEEL

#Honolululaw, #FamousTriathlete & a #Charity

Katharine M. Nohr

Green Bay, WI 54311

Freewheel by Katharine M. Nohr, © copyright 2017 by Katharine M. Nohr.
Passage from VO2 Max by Katharine M. Nohr, used by permission of the author.
Author Photo courtesy of Katharine M. Nohr.

This book is a work of fiction. All names, characters, places and events are products of the author's imagination or are used fictitiously, and any resemblance to actual persons, living or dead, or to actual places or businesses, is entirely coincidental.

All rights reserved. In accordance with the US Copyright Act of 1976, no part of this publication may be reproduced, distributed, or transmitted in any form or by any means, or stored in a database or retrieval system, without prior written permission of the publisher, Written Dreams Publishing, Green Bay, WI 54311. To contact the publisher, please visit their website at: writtendreams.com or by email at wdp@writtendreams.com.

This book is licensed for your personal enjoyment only. This book may not be re-sold. If you would like to share this book with another person, please purchase an additional copy for each recipient. If you're reading this book and did not purchase it, or it was not purchased for your use only, then please purchase your own copy. Thank you for respecting the hard work of this author.

Editor: Brittiany Koren
Cover Art Design and Layout: Devin McGuire and Eddie Vincent of ENC Graphic Services
Cover images © Shutterstock.com

Cover art designs for *Freewheel* by Katharine M. Nohr, *Death Nosh* by Mary Grace Murphy, and *Parts Unknown* by Toni Niesen are used by the permission of Written Dreams Publishing.

Category: Legal Mystery
Description: *Freewheel* takes readers for a spin in the real world of personal injury litigation, where the drama takes place outside the courtroom.
Hard Cover ISBN: 978-0-9987623-2-6
Paperback ISBN: 978-0-9987623-3-3
Ebook ISBN: 978-0-9987623-4-0

LOC: Catalog info applied for.
First Edition published by Written Dreams Publishing in March, 2017.

Green Bay, WI 54311

Advance Praise for *Freewheel*...

"Katharine Nohr's Freewheel is a fabulous mash-up of triathlon, law, and punchy characters. A great escape-to-the-beach or lazy summer day read."
—Meredith Atwood("Swim Bike Mom"),
Author, Triathlete and Blogger

"Set against the unbeatable tropical backdrop of Honolulu, attorney Zana West and a cast of memorable characters are once again entangled in a non-stop web of page-turning suspense in Katharine M. Nohr's Freewheel."
—Jill Marie Landis, Author of the Tiki Goddess Mysteries

"Freewheel is an entertaining read. Nohr captures the nature of the sometimes brutal competition of triathlon."
—Alice Duncan, Author of the Daisy Gumm Majesty series

"A convincing glimpse into a unique world, written with deft authority and insight."
—Doranna Durgin, Author of the Hunter Agency series

"Nohr has delivered another winner! Attorney Zana West is back in this sequel to Land Sharks, which opens with a gripping action scene, setting the stage for a refreshingly unique take on the legal thriller. The reader is privy to the inner workings of a Honolulu law firm, as well as the grueling life of a triathlete, while being given a deeply humanizing look into several characters' flawed personal lives. Tension mounts as they grapple with conflicting emotions, many of which are brought about miscommunication and misconceptions. The edge-of-your-seat action will keep readers turning pages as some very nasty characters must be outmaneuvered and the story races toward a satisfying finish line. I can't wait for the next in the Tri-Angles series!"
—Laurie Hanan, Author of fun Hawaiian mysteries

Praise for Katharine M. Nohr's
Land Sharks...

"Katherine Nohr's brilliant debut has it all: smart characters, crisp dialogue, a breathtaking setting, and an ingenious plot that will keep you turning the pages until sunrise."
—Doug Corleone, Author of *Robert Ludlum's The Janson Equation*

"With lots of twists and turns, and interesting characters involved in a triathlon, this book really drew me in. An excellent story that had me not wanting to stop flipping the pages. Great job, Katharine Nohr!"
—Siri Lindley, USA Triathlon Hall of Famer

"Move over John Grisham and make room for first time novelist Katharine M. Nohr and her cast of muscle toned, sun tanned characters chasing triathlon medals and courtroom victories. In this page turner of a thriller, Ms. Nohr takes us on a ride through the ultra competitive world of triathletes and trial lawyers, all the while weaving a story of mystery and romance. A thoroughly enjoyable, must read story for all audiences. Five stars."
—Teresa Tico, Film Producer

"I recommend this book to anyone who likes endurance sports, law, or just a good story. I am waiting to see what comes next from this author."
—Stefan Reinke, triathlon coach and Ironman triathlete

"More action than a transition area at the top of the bell curve! Who knew that triathletes were both meat and meat eaters?"
—Murphy Reinschreiber, Vice President of Operations, Conqur Endurance Group and triathlete agent

Freewheel's themes of the allure and memories of Paris were inspired by two special people in my life who have shared croissants, strode along the Seine and marveled at the Eiffel Tower with me. To *mon amour*, Bill Touth, whose stories of his year in France as a professional cyclist provided inspiration for this story.

To my friend, Lisa Moore Ghahremani, with whom one could never have a boring day as evidenced by our adventures in France in the 1990s. We will always have Paris.

Chapter 1

**@FreewheelMV Racing for $$$ today at #ParadiseTri.
The pressure is on BIG time. Will DESTROY
anyone who gets in my way!**

Ryan Peterson tugged at his swim cap with its bold number 2 and gave stink eye to his competitors, who flapped their arms—Michael Phelps' style—a few yards down Honolulu's Ala Moana beach.

"You've got this!" Coach Hal gave him a light pat on his well-defined bicep.

"I'm going to hunt them down one at a time and obliterate them," Ryan snarled. He spat into his goggles and bent down to wet them in the surf lapping on the shore.

He then launched his body into the choppy ocean to begin his warm-up before the Paradise Lagoons Triathlon, the only race offering $20,000 in prize money he sorely needed. At least during warm-up, he could keep pace with his most fierce competitors as they cut through the water with their carefully-honed freestyle strokes. As soon as the gun went off, they would leave him in their wake.

A shrill whistle sounded, signaling the men to take their places between two lifeguard-manned surfboards. Ryan positioned himself next to Jeff Paris, who donned his number 1 cap, glaring at him as they treaded water.

Ryan was well aware of the public opinion that he wouldn't have won the gold medal at the London Olympic Games if his competitors hadn't been injured or killed in the accident at the Olympic trials. Apparently, Jeff had recovered from his mental breakdown after watching a car mow down and kill his friend Vic Leavitt. He was now back in top form and was ranked one of the best triathletes in the world.

"Hold up," the race director said over the loud speaker. "Sorry folks, one of our orange buoys has broken loose. They're securing it and then I'll start the race."

Ryan turned his threatening stare to Terry Schubert, a twenty-two-year-old up-and-coming athlete who had just turned pro and had something to prove in this race. If he won, he would be the youngest athlete ever to win the Paradise Lagoons Triathlon. He would then be in the running for Mauna Kea Multi-Sport's Athlete of the Year, an honor bestowed on a new pro with the most potential for future glory.

"Two more minutes," the race director announced.

Ryan closed his eyes for some final pre-race visualization, a practice he had begun as a professional cyclist in France before he was "relieved of his duties" for a positive drug test after a Tour de France stage win. For the past three months, he had been visualizing a solid, relaxed but fast swim; a smooth and quick transition from swim to the bike leg of the triathlon; and then within a few miles of the bike leg, taking the lead from Jeff and Terry as he powerfully cycled past, leaving them in the dust for the rest of the race.

The way Ryan saw it, winning the $20,000 prize was his only choice. After he was falsely blamed in the international tabloid press for knocking his competitors out of the Olympic trials competition by some unnamed evil scheme, Ryan lost most of his sponsors. He was left with only a swimsuit sponsor that paid him for intermittent ads in specialty magazines, allowing him to eke out a meager living. After his funds ran out, he was forced to rent out all of the bedrooms of his house to pay the mortgage. He had been sleeping on a futon in a small office the size of a walk-in closet for months now. At twenty-nine-years old, if he didn't win this race, he would have to find a full-time job in a down economy with no post-high school education and only professional cycling and triathlons on his résumé.

"Athletes, take your places," the race director announced.

Ryan nodded to Sam Donahue, and then swam a few yards to position himself next to the other dominant cyclist who couldn't keep up with the top three guys in the water, either. Ryan and Sam had done this drill before. Their strategy was to draft off the feet of the faster swimmers in order to save some energy *if* they could keep up.

The starting gun blasted and Ryan launched into a rapid freestyle stroke, keeping his goggle-covered eyes open, looking for feet to draft off of. He soon fell into a rhythmic pace, being propelled by one of the top five in the field, Eric Low, who pulled him along for a half mile until Eric sped away.

Ryan kept his freestyle stroke long, and focused on breathing and form, intermittently looking up in order to sight so he wouldn't go off course. He swam hard the last 20 yards until his fingertips touched the sand, and then he sprang to his feet and sprinted through the calf deep water to the swim finishing chute, winding up the beach towards the swim-to-bike transition area—T1.

He was surprised Eric was still in sight, running with his bike towards the exit. Ryan wasn't as far behind the fast swimmers as he had been in previous races. He quickly located his bike.

But his white helmet was on the ground rather than balancing on the bike's aero bars as he had left it. *That's odd.*

His sunglasses had also fallen onto his towel. He didn't stop to consider how his carefully placed equipment had become strewn about. Every fraction of a second counted.

He put on his helmet, grabbed his bike off the rack and ran it towards the mount line on the perimeter of the transition area. It took about two minutes before Ryan passed Eric on the bike leg of the triathlon. He'd have to hunt down Jeff and Terry and pass them in order to take the lead, just as he had visualized.

Ryan pedaled hard through the streets of Waikiki, ignoring the curious tourist onlookers. He rode up Diamond Head alone and made his way to Kalanianaole Highway, where he passed Terry on the straight away. He could see Jeff in the distance ahead and crouched lower into the aero position on his bike, increasing his cadence. Ryan's only focus was passing Jeff.

As he was about to close the gap, he heard a cyclist coming up from behind. Ryan increased his cadence to sustain his lead, but felt the bicycle come up next to him on his left side—so close their handlebars touched, which momentarily made him lose his balance. He veered a few feet to the right, but was able to recover quickly.

To his surprise, the impact of the handlebars caused the other cyclist to lose control and Ryan heard the bike crash onto the pavement behind him. He glanced back and saw Terry on the ground. A Harley-Davidson motorcycle with its driver and a course official sped up to assist his competitor.

If Ryan stopped, he would not be able to catch Jeff so he made a quick decision to press on. Terry was in good hands and would promptly receive medical attention, if necessary. Ryan assumed that at most, Terry had fractured his collarbone, but he might also be fine, jump back on his bike and finish the race with only a few abrasions.

When Ryan had raced in the Tour de France, many cyclists had crashed, causing the Peloton to slow down so the fallen athletes could climb back onto their bikes with fresh road rash. Triathlon didn't operate by the same customs. Any delay could mean losing his chance at the prize money, which Ryan couldn't afford to risk with so few triathlons offering professional athletes a payday.

A few minutes after Terry fell, Ryan closed in on Jeff and had to focus all his energy into keeping up his speed against the head wind. Just as he was about 100 yards behind the leader, he shifted into a bigger gear without decreasing his cadence. Jeff wasn't as strong today, so it only took seconds before Ryan charged past him, taking the lead.

He focused on his own race now and kept his body as aerodynamic as possible. He would have to beat his opponent by at least two minutes on the bike in order to hold him off on the run.

After the turnaround, Ryan had the advantage of seeing where his competitors were positioned. He saw Sam and then Eric, but there was no sign of Jeff. *Did he have a flat tire?*

As Ryan rode back towards T2, he heard the sound of an ambulance. He didn't think much of it, but then realized it was possible they were picking Terry up from the course. Ryan forced his focus to the race and gaining as much of a lead as possible. Sam was a strong cyclist and there was no way Ryan was going to let him pass, because he wasn't sure he could outrun him.

After Ryan reached the transition area, he changed quickly into his running shoes, tossed off his helmet and took a swig of water before beginning the 10k run. He glanced behind, looking to see who might be on his heels, but it wasn't until his coach yelled out to him on mile two about his 56-second lead that he started to feel a bit more confident. The thought of prize money gave Ryan the energy to kick into high gear. He increased his pace, feeling his legs move fluidly as he pumped his arms and kept his body in an efficient running position.

As he reached the top of Diamond Head, he glanced behind his shoulder again and saw Eric at least 100 yards behind him. Eric was a slower runner and so if nothing went wrong, he could hold him off.

Ryan felt the wind pushing him forward and let his body relax as he moved swiftly, each step carrying him towards the finish line. He focused on his breathing and on the rhythm of his feet against the pavement.

As he approached within 150 yards of the finishing arch festooned with sponsor logos, the crowd became wild, yelling his name, encouraging him to finish strong. The shouting and whooping, along with Ryan's thoughts of the prize money made him forget about the pain he was feeling.

As he crossed over the finish line, hearing the announcer affirm he was the first place winner, Ryan's legs became jelly and he almost collapsed to the ground. A bikini-clad Polynesian beauty placed a purple orchid lei over his head and kissed him on his sweaty cheek. Cameras appeared in his face and someone handed him a towel with sponsorship logos on it.

"How does it feel to win the prize money?" the female television announcer asked Ryan as he was trying to catch his breath.

"Great. What can I say? I'm very happy," Ryan managed to respond.

"Did you realize you had such a big lead over your competitors?"

"Not really. I was just trying to run my own race," he said into the microphone, feeling sweat drip from his forehead.

"How do you feel about Terry Schubert?"

"I don't know. What about him?" Ryan asked, his eyes widened behind his sunglasses.

"Did you know he was taken away by ambulance?"

"Oh, that's terrible. I hope he's okay," Ryan said. In the heat of the race, he had forgotten their handlebars had touched, causing Terry to fall down. "If you'll excuse me, I need to hydrate and talk to my coach. Mahalo."

Hal was waiting for him to wind up the interview. As soon as they walked away from the finish line and ducked into the massage tent, Hal whispered into Ryan's ear, "Terry Schubert is dead."

Chapter Two

@ZLaw Tonight is #FightinginParadise gala event! If I trip on the red carpet, I'm buying new shoes. #Ecstatic

Zana West could count the number of times she had gotten pedicures on two toes. As she eased into the large massage chair at the salon and presented her calloused, athletic size nines to the pedicurist, she was sure the woman would be repulsed and might even refuse to work on her feet. She was relieved the Vietnamese woman wearing a "Linda" nametag dove right in and began her routine without so much as a verbal criticism, shake of her head or disappointed sigh.

"Would you like the super deluxe service?" Linda asked in her heavy Vietnamese accent.

"Yes, please," Zana said, not knowing what she was getting into. Now that she had managed to keep her job as an associate attorney at the law firm of Gravelle, Parsons & Dell for almost a year, she felt rich enough for a pedicure, even though she still didn't feel she could afford her own apartment.

"The super deluxe is fabulous here," the petite blonde haired woman sitting next to Zana said. "I love the leg and foot massage."

Zana smiled, noticing the woman's feet looked to be about size 6 and the subject of frequent professional attention. "It's been a long time since I've had a pedicure."

"Is it a special occasion?" the woman asked.

"Yes. My boyfriend is taking me to a gala tonight at the Royal Hawaiian Hotel," Zana said, beaming at the thought of dressing up in the Dolce & Gabana gown Jerry had bought for her to compliment his tux.

"What a treat," the woman said. "My name is Elizabeth Rowling. No relation to J.K., if you're wondering."

Zana chuckled. "I'm Zana West—no relation to Adam West—you know, Batman."

"Nice to meet you. I come here every week. They offer great services— waxing, massages, hairstyling…everything I need to keep my husband,"

Elizabeth said, flashing a multi-carat diamond ring. "We've been married for five years, and I try to look as good as when we first met."

Zana smiled. "Well, you look beautiful."

"How long have you been dating your boyfriend?"

"Only about six months. It's still a new relationship." Zana rubbed the back of her neck.

"By five months, my husband proposed and by eight months we were married," Elizabeth said, smiling warmly as she waved her hand in the air. "Oh, I don't mean to put pressure on you. Every relationship is different."

"I understand. Jerry is a great guy, but we're taking it slow," Zana said. She felt a tap on her foot. "Sorry," she told Linda, who was trying to get her to switch feet between the soaking tub and the work towel.

"What event are you going to tonight?" Elizabeth asked.

"The show 'Fighting in Paradise' is having a gala to kick off their fourth season. It's the last opportunity to have fun before they spend all of their time filming," Zana explained. "It's also a chance for the press to take photographs, and for the stars to get some publicity."

"Are you dating Jerry Hirano?" Elizabeth jumped up in her seat, causing the pedicurist to drop a tool.

She blushed. "Yes, Jerry's my boyfriend," Zana said, enjoying the sound of those words.

Elizabeth opened a magazine, wetting her finger as she turned through the pages. She then pointed to a picture. "Is this you?"

"Yeah, that photo was taken a few months ago." Zana looked at the image of her and Jerry walking hand in hand on the beach. It was the first tabloid picture she was in, and it had created quite a stir in her office and amongst her friends.

Elizabeth giggled. "Wow, can I have your autograph?"

"Really? I mean, I never get asked. But, sure," Zana said, pulling a pen from her purse. She scribbled her name on Elizabeth's magazine.

"What's it like to date Jerry Hirano?" Elizabeth gushed. "He's so good looking—and what an amazing body."

"He's lots of fun. Jerry's busy with his law practice and filming, so it's special when we get a night out like tonight." Linda carefully painted her toenails with a rich, red polish.

"I'll bet. I'm glad he's finally settled down. It wasn't long ago when every magazine picture I saw showed him with a different girl. I should have recognized you from the pictures I've seen lately. You've been in quite a few."

"Yeah, I'm starting to feel like the Duchess of Cambridge with all of the attention I've been getting."

"Would you like a design on your big toes?" Linda interrupted.

"Sure. A flower or rhinestones—whatever would look good for a formal evening. Something simple, please," Zana said.

"Well, it was nice talking with you Zana," Elizabeth said as she climbed from the chair and gingerly walked away with freshly painted toenails in her jeweled sandals. "I hope you enjoy your evening."

"I'm sure I will." Zana beamed.

***

After Zana returned home, she was careful as she slipped out of her well-worn rubber slippers before walking into the Kahala house where she was renting a room from another attorney at her office, Andrew Bergen and his girlfriend, Kelly. Even though they all hailed from the mainland, they strictly adhered to the Hawaii custom of no shoes inside the house.

She grabbed handfuls of Li Hing Mui and Iso Maki to snack on before heading to her bedroom to begin preparations for the evening event. After lingering in a plumeria flower-scented bubble bath, she blew out her straight, black silky hair and styled it in its usual Egyptian shape with bangs framing her emerald eyes. She didn't dare attempt an updo. Her cosmetology skills were rudimentary at best, because she had spent all her spare time since she could remember studying, working, triathlon training and otherwise scraping by. She had protested when Jerry presented her with the gown, which was still in its exquisite cover hanging in her closet where she had moved aside her Ross's Dress for Less clothes so none of them contaminated its seemingly magical aura.

Zana stared at her reflection in the floor length mirror. The red silk organza dress effortlessly draped her toned body. Its demur neckline plunge was the perfect style for her B cups and the delicate infinity diamond necklace Jerry had given her last week for this occasion.

She gently removed her new, sparkling Jimmy Choo heels out of their box. They had set her back a week's pay, but were worth it. They had never been worn outside. She slipped her newly pampered feet into them just as she heard a knock.

Jerry's eyes lit up when she opened the door. "Wow!" he exclaimed.

"Wow, yourself!" Zana said. He looked divine in his black Armani tux. Her heart skipped a beat as they embraced and then kissed passionately, as if seeing each other for the first time in weeks. She breathed in the familiar musky scent of his Polo cologne.

"Get a room," Andrew said as he and Kelly walked into the hallway from the kitchen. "Zana, you look amazing—even prettier than Jerry."

"Well, thanks bro." Jerry grinned.

"The paparazzi will be all over you two tonight," Kelly said, raising her iPhone. "Say cheese!" Jerry put his arm around his girlfriend and they smiled for the camera.

"We're going to have to run if we're going to get there for the red carpet," Jerry said.

"There's a red carpet?" Zana asked, suddenly feeling anxious.

"Yes—just for you, my dear," Jerry said, pulling her close. She was several inches taller than him in her stilettos, but he never seemed to mind so she felt comfortable wearing high heels when they went out.

"See you later," Zana said to her roommates as she and Jerry left through the front door. She was expecting to be transported in his red Ferrari and was surprised to see a stretch limo in the driveway with its tuxedo-clad driver standing next to it.

"OMG!" Zana said.

"Since you look like a princess, I wanted us to travel in style," Jerry said as the driver opened the door for them. "We can even have a glass of champagne on the way."

"You really know how to spoil me, Jerry Ho," Zana said, referring to Jerry's character in "Fighting in Paradise".

"Let's toast," Jerry said after the driver had poured them glasses of champagne and pulled the limo out of her neighborhood, only about ten minutes from the Royal Hawaiian Hotel where the event would be held. "To a beautiful lady and an amazing night ahead—cheers!"

"Cheers!" Zana raised her glass and clinked it against Jerry's. They snuggled close during the short drive, sipped champagne and took selfies.

As the limo rolled up to the hotel, Zana saw through the tinted glass that Jerry was right. There was a red carpet and paparazzi were out in full force waiting behind camera lenses as the cast arrived. Zana was relieved that her size nine feet emerged from the limo with freshly painted toes, but most of all, that Jerry gallantly helped her out of the vehicle and clung to her side as the cameras flashed.

She stood close to him as they posed for pictures and noticed his smile was as broad as hers. His eyes twinkled rather than blinked in response to the flashes of light. This was her first red carpet event and the first time she had ever been paired with a man wearing a tux, besides at her senior prom.

After they made their way down the red carpet to the famous pink hotel's grand entrance, other limos pulled up which allowed them to escape the cameras and join the festivities in the ballroom.

"I'm still seeing spots in my eyes," Zana said as Jerry led her to their table near the front of the room.

"Get used to it, sweetheart, it comes with the territory," Jerry said, winking at her. "I'm not great with names. If I don't introduce you to someone, don't take it personally—I probably just can't remember the person's name."

"Do you think that's a sign of old age?" Zana joked, following him through the maze of tables.

He nodded. "Yes. I'm sure it's early dementia, or maybe I've been hit in the head a few too many times."

"You could wear a helmet when you fight in the show." Zana paused at their table and Jerry pulled out her chair for her.

"Yeah, I'm sure that would increase viewership. They'd probably have to change the name to 'Nerds in Paradise'," Jerry said, sitting down.

"Have you got an idea for a new show?" a tall man with wavy red hair and stylish eyeglasses asked as he sat down next to Jerry.

"No, but I'll let you know when I do," Jerry said. "Probably when our ratings sink."

"Don't jinx us, especially tonight," Kenny said. "Who's this lovely lady?"

"Kenny, I'd like you to meet my girlfriend, Zana West," Jerry said. "Kenny is one of our producers."

"Nice to meet you, Zana. You do look familiar though. Have I seen you on the set?" Kenny reached out to shake her hand.

"It's a pleasure meeting you formally. I've seen you there, but you've always been working hard," Zana said. "This is such an amazing event. You should be very proud of the show."

"We wouldn't be doing half as well without Jerry. You're a lucky woman. I've never heard him refer to anyone as his girlfriend before." Kenny took a sip of wine.

Zana lifted an eyebrow. "Is that right, Jerry?"

"Hmm, yes, I think that's a first. You were worth the wait." Jerry draped an arm around her. "Where's your other half, Kenny?"

"He's around here somewhere." Kenny looked at the people milling around entrance doors. "Oh, there he is. Excuse me while I round him up. Preston is not a big fan of crowds."

"Do you know Kenny's husband, Preston Farnsworth, the third?" Jerry took a sip of water. "He's a partner at Bishop & Judd."

"You introduced me to him on an elevator shortly after we first met," Zana said.

"Preston's a character. He's quite different from Kenny, but I think they make a great couple. Kenny's the gregarious entertainer. Preston's serious and doesn't say much."

"Who else is sitting with us?" Zana asked as she watched Kenny lead Preston to the table. Both men were wearing tuxes, but Kenny's was made of a shiny material as was his bow tie, and Preston was wearing a more traditional tux, which looked like it had been rented even though she suspected it had been in the back of his closet.

"Hi Jerry," Preston said as the men shook hands.

"Preston, this is Zana West, Jerry's *girlfriend*," Kenny said. "Isn't she stunning?"

"It's a pleasure to see you again, young lady," Preston said, slightly bowing.

"Likewise," Zana said, firmly shaking his hand.

"I've got to greet some V.I.P.s. Have a seat next to Zana, darling," Kenny said to his husband and then scurried across the room.

Jerry's eyes followed Kenny as he approached several older men and their wives who had entered the ballroom. "Excuse me, I'm going to say hello to some of the producers. You two can get to know each other." Jerry squeezed Zana's bare shoulder and left her alone with Preston, who was sitting with perfect posture, staring straight ahead.

"Nice centerpiece," she stammered, referring to the white orchid arrangement. She desperately wanted to pull her phone out of her clutch and tweet about the event, but didn't think Preston would approve.

He nodded and turned to her. "Uh, what high school did you go to?"

Zana had lived in Hawaii long enough to know that this was the first question one asks when getting to know someone who grew up in the islands. The answer would tell you about their socio-economic background, how they were raised and something of their values.

"I grew up in California," Zana said, knowing this answer would render his question moot. "And, you?"

"Punahou," Preston said stiffly.

"Oh, President Obama's school. Were you his classmate?" Zana gulped her wine.

Preston laughed. "He's much younger, but I have met him a number of times. I'm not sure you know, but my father is a retired Hawaii Supreme Court Justice, my brother is a state senator, and two of my cousins are partners at my law firm."

"It sounds like the Farnsworth clan is powerful," Zana said, not sure how he expected her to respond.

He nodded. "We go back many generations in Hawaii."

A waiter had placed a glass of wine in front of him and after he took a few sips, his shoulders dropped and he leaned back into his chair.

"How long have you and Kenny been together?" she asked, pleased to see he was finally relaxing.

"Nine wonderful years." Preston smiled. "We were married shortly after gay marriage became legal in Hawaii."

"Congratulations!" Zana said as Jerry returned to his seat.

"They're about to start the program," he whispered into her ear and then kissed her neck. They shifted their chairs to face the stage.

"Aloha!" Kenny said into the microphone and the audience of the cast and crew of the show, media, sponsors, V.I.P.s and guests repeated, "Aloha!"

Kenny grinned. "We have a short program. Then everyone can enjoy dinner and our fabulous entertainment."

The lights went down low and three large screens with scenes from "Fighting in Paradise" appeared. Jerry was prominently featured in most as he used his martial arts skills to fight off Waikiki bad guys. The crowd applauded energetically as they watched Jerry rip off his shirt, kick, punch and block. Zana couldn't help but smile broadly as she observed the crowd's reaction to her boyfriend.

After the film clips were shown and the applause died down, Kenny sipped some water before he addressed the banquet room. "Our little show has created a big splash on this island. Mahalo for being here tonight to celebrate three seasons of 'Fighting in Paradise'. There are so many of you who deserve our thanks, but we would be here all night if I mentioned all of you by name. For now, I want to recognize the man who makes our show possible. If it weren't for this special person, we would not be on the air and we certainly wouldn't be celebrating in this beautiful hotel tonight. My sincere and everlasting gratitude goes to Bud Schubert, President and CEO of Schubert Enterprises, the sponsor of 'Fighting in Paradise' and the sponsor of this event. May I present to you, Bud Schubert," Kenny said, causing everyone in the room to rise in a standing ovation.

"Aloha and mahalo to our 'Fighting in Paradise' family," Bud said in his southern drawl after the applause died down. "These past few years have been challenging as the country has suffered economically. I'm pleased that Schubert Enterprises has survived and thrived due to hard work and diversity. One of the vehicles of its success has been this special T.V. show, starring Jerry Hirano. The people of Hawaii have embraced the show and turn to it for an escape when their lives are challenging. Sponsoring the show has certainly made Schubert Enterprises a household name and our developments, hotels and department stores have greatly profited because of it. We plan to continue our commitment during the next season and assist producer Kenneth Paxton in increasing its distribution to the mainland and internationally."

The audience gave a collective gasp and applause erupted, which Bud couldn't speak over.

Zana noticed tears welling in Kenny's eyes and how he clutched his husband the moment after the announcement was made. After they finally sat down after the second standing ovation, she felt Jerry's hand grab her bare knee exposed by the slit in her dress.

"On a more somber note, many of you know that my son, Terry, passed away about six months ago, competing in a triathlon. He was doing what he loved when he died and he always encouraged me to do the same," Bud said, dabbing his eyes with a handkerchief. "Because of this, I'm reminded that we have limited time on this earth and so I'm going to spend more of it with my wife and grandchildren. I plan to loosen the reigns a bit on my business and let my capable boards of directors and officers handle the daily operations so I can devote my energy to some special projects, and of course, spend more time on the golf course." He paused in response to a smattering of approving twitters from the audience. "I'm sure those special projects will include more visits to the 'Fighting in Paradise' set and so I look forward to seeing many of you more often."

The audience applauded again as Bud left the stage.

Although he was tall and distinguished with a full head of dark hair flecked with gray, Zana noticed his posture was stooped over so he looked older than his likely age. After the presentation was concluded, Jerry and Zana shared a piece of chocolate haupia pie with their coffee.

"You look as relieved as I am," Jerry said.

"You better believe it." Kenny sighed. "I've had some sleepless nights lately."

"Me, too. With our concerns about sponsorship and the network threatening to cancel, I've been wondering if I have to take on more legal cases," Jerry said as he sipped his cup of coffee.

"Things are looking up. With Bud behind us financially, we'll be fine. It sounds like he's going to help us with the extra boost to expand our distribution. That's what we've dreamed about." Kenny flashed his perfect white teeth as he smiled.

Zana's eyes widened. "I'm surprised you've been worried. I thought the show was really popular."

"It's hard to get much viewership competing with the networks. We're going head to head with 'The Big Rip-off' and 'America's Choice'. Our market share isn't too bad considering the competition, but we need to improve," Kenny said. "We're fortunate to have you on the show, Jerry. Without your popularity, we wouldn't exist."

"Thanks. I wish I could work on F.I.P. full time. With the cuts we made last year, I haven't been able to take much time off from my law practice," Jerry said.

Kenny put his hand on his shoulder. "From what Bud has told me, our budget should increase. You might be able to be a full-time actor in the next year or two."

"That would be my dream." Jerry grinned. "We'll have to keep Bud happy."

"You wouldn't miss practicing law?" Zana asked, surprised that he would be willing to give up the profession she was just starting.

"Let's see, I began practicing when I was twenty-six—so, it's been about seventeen years. That's enough for me," Jerry said. "We'll have to figure out how you can become a full-time triathlete."

She laughed. "I'd like to use my law degree first. If I could do what I want, I'd like to move to the sports agency group in my firm and represent athletes. It's not likely to happen until I have an athlete to represent. But I can hope."

"Why aren't you lawyers ever happy practicing law?" Kenny asked.

"Since we only went to law school because we couldn't get into medical school, we're never satisfied with what we're doing." Jerry grinned.

"Speak for yourself." Preston frowned.

"Or, maybe being a lawyer sucks and you just don't want to do it anymore," Kenny said.

"Yeah, that's another possible explanation," Jerry said, squeezing Zana's hand.

Chapter Three

@ZLaw #JerryHo has the sniffles. No complaints about vapor rubbing duties! ☺

Jerry woke up with a weird feeling in his throat. He hoped he wasn't catching a cold, but just in case, he mixed a glass of Airborne, took some vitamin C and Echinacea, and made a concoction of ginger and honey. He didn't necessarily believe these remedies would take the virus out of his system. But if he complained to anyone, he would be faced with an onslaught of cold remedy advice, as well as have to listen to friends and family speculate on how he contracted the illness. They would theorize he was sick from coming in and out of air conditioning rather than from uncovered sneezes or germy doorknobs.

It had been years since Jerry had stayed home because of a cold. It wasn't as if he never got sick. He did. He'd tough it out, coughing and sniffling through whatever he had to do. Today was different though. He felt emotionally exhausted from his long workdays and spending night after night with Zana. He wondered if getting sick was God's message to him to slow down and take a much-needed break.

As he lay on the couch watching the *Today* show, he texted his secretary: Good news! I'm out of your hair today. Home sick.

He texted Kenny next. So sorry. Home sick today. Can we film my scenes tomorrow?

Kenny's text popped up on his screen. Ok. Feel better.

Jerry sent a message to Zana. Under the weather at home today. CU tomorrow, Sweetheart. XOXO

Within seconds of pressing send, Zana's ringtone "Lady in Red" began playing and a picture of Zana wearing the Dolce and Gabana red dress at the gala appeared on his iPhone screen. He clicked the mute button on his T.V. remote before answering.

"Are you okay?" Zana asked, sounding breathless.

"I'm fine." Jerry reached down to pet his cat, Ming. "I might be coming down with something. You sound out of breath. Are you running?"

"Yeah—almost done," she said. "I'll bring you some chicken soup later."

"You know I would love to see you, sweetheart, but it won't help either of us if you get sick, too." Jerry flipped through the channels with his free hand. "Why don't you go for a swim or bike ride after work?"

"Are you sure? I don't want to abandon you when you're sick."

"There's a good chance I'm going to live," he said, smiling into the phone. "And, if I feel better, we can do something fun on Saturday night. What would you think of a romantic dinner at Chef Mavro's or Michel's?"

"Sounds fabulous," she said. "If you change your mind about tonight, call me and I can come over with all sorts of fun things like tissue, cough drops, and vapor rub which I'm willing to apply myself."

"The vapor rub does sound tempting, but I insist you work out tonight." Jerry coughed into the phone, hoping to further impress his girlfriend with the risk of germs. "If you really miss me, you can watch re-runs of 'Fighting in Paradise'."

"Okay. I'll miss you, Jer-bear," she said in a soft voice. "Now, get some sleep."

Jerry smiled after he hung up the phone. The last six months with Zana had been far more fulfilling than his habit of dating a new woman every few months. He hadn't planned to date so many, but he never met anyone who captured his interest for more than a few weeks—until he met Zana. She was not only gorgeous, but she was so bright—he found her sharp mind and quick wit to be entertaining and challenging. Plus, she was the only lawyer he knew who looked like a model. She was five foot eleven with a lean and muscular body from working out, and she was sexy. When they were together, he had a hard time keeping his hands off of her.

Jerry fluffed up a few pillows behind his head and clicked through hundreds of channels as he thought about her. She'd been staying overnight about four nights a week and they'd been seeing each other every spare moment since the day in court when they found out their attorney adversary, Rip Mansfield, was suspended from the practice of law.

Maybe it's time I come up for air. He adored Zana, but his stomach had been in knots the past few weeks. He no longer was free to have impromptu drinks with other cast mates or pop over to the gym for a few hours of weight training after filming. The late night dinners and overnights with her had cut into his sleep. His pants were feeling tighter, and Kenny and Mitch, the show's director, had exchanged looks when he'd taken off his shirt to shoot a scene last night. Zana complained about missing triathlon training and gaining five pounds. He guessed he had, too. Today, at least, he planned to chill and get his head together.

He finally settled on the Golf Channel. It was so relaxing to listen to the announcer's calm voice as the pro golfers hit balls down the fairways. Watching golf usually caused him to drift off to sleep on his couch and as soon as he got comfortable, his two Siamese cats, Ming and Miko, climbed on his chest and legs for a warm snooze. Shortly after Jerry and the cats had drifted off to sleep, his 'Hawaii 5-0' ring tone jolted him awake.

"Hey Jerry, what's up?" a female voice asked.

"Hi, not much," Jerry croaked. He sat up, disturbing the cats so he could sip some water. "I'm sorry, who is this?"

"It's Renee. I thought you'd recognize my voice. I've been on the mainland, but I'm back now."

"Oh, hi Renee. That's right you've been working in New York. I remember," Jerry said, settling against the pillows and scratching Miko's ears.

"My company transferred me back to Oahu. You're the first person I called—I just got in last night."

He swallowed hard. "Terrific. I hope you're enjoying the sunny weather. It must be cold in New York."

"I didn't call you to talk about the weather, Jerry. I've missed you."

"Thanks. I hope everything is going well for you," he said, not knowing what to say.

"Let's get together. Pick me up in that hot red Ferrari and let's go out like old times," Renee said.

"I'm sorry. I have a girlfriend now." The words felt strange on his lips.

"Oh, well—congratulations," she said, sounding disappointed. "I'm glad you're doing well. If anything changes, give me a call. I'll be around."

"Thanks. It was great hearing from you," Jerry said as he clicked off his phone, putting it on silent so he could get some rest.

He had been fielding calls from women he'd dated casually before Zana for months. The calls had gradually decreased after he changed his relationship status on Facebook and when the tabloids had photographed him with Zana identifying her as his girlfriend, a title they had never before used with his permission. Most of the women who phoned took the news well and were supportive, but some of them cried, revealing their feelings about him for the first time. He almost dropped his iPhone when Sports Illustrated swimsuit model Britt Olsen phoned to say how much she loved him. When they had called it quits six months ago, he felt little emotion and was sure she had slept with him for fun and temporary companionship. She and the others seemed to enjoy being seen in public with Jerry Ho, not to mention it fulfilled his teenage fantasies to be seen with so many beautiful women.

He thought back to a time when, as a scrawny, little kid, he attended public elementary school in Kalihi and endured bullying by a group of boys who called themselves the Ikaika Warriors. They would shove him into his locker, kick and punch him and give him wedgies. They even pulled him off of the toilet with his pants down and dragged him down the hall so most of his classmates saw him half naked. The principal punished the gang members, but nothing deterred them from picking on Jerry or several other undersized male classmates.

One day, he came home with a cut on his cheek from one of the beatings, and after his parents' interrogation, he reluctantly admitted the truth to them. His dad enrolled him into Kung Fu and Karate classes, not only to teach him how to defend himself, but to keep him busy after school every day—away from the bullies.

After a few weeks of training, a big Samoan guy—Ofato—pushed Jerry against his locker for a beating, but Jerry deflected his punches with newly learned basic blocks.

The following week when Ofato and other gang members cornered him as he was leaving the building, he counter-attacked with a flurry of punches and kicks, causing a few black eyes and cut lips. When he told his parents that he'd have to miss martial arts training for a week while he served his first and only detention sentence, Dad patted him on the back and Mom smiled.

The bullies soon moved their attention to other kids, but Jerry never lost interest in martial arts. He punched, kicked, and blocked his way to earn belts and compete in tournaments. His hero was Bruce Lee, and he embraced Lee's philosophy and the art of Jeet Kune Do. He strove to combine the best moves in various martial arts to become the greatest fighter he could be.

Sometimes, Jerry ran into the boys who had tormented him when he was a kid. Most of them still lived in Kalihi and other Honolulu neighborhoods, where they worked in gas stations, at Target, in construction, or drove tow trucks. A few of them had gone to college. One of the guys worked at an accounting office and another worked at a bank.

Now, after so many years had passed, the guys fawned over Jerry, impressed that he was a T.V. star. They commented on the "hot babes" they saw him with at different events. As Jerry lay on his couch, he realized he no longer had to prove anything to those guys, or anyone else.

Last week, his mother had touched him gently on the arm and said, "Jerry, I know you're having fun with that car, but it's time you grow up and be a man." He had scoffed at her suggestion, slamming his parents' front door behind him before walking the 100 feet to his cottage on their property. He wasn't really angry with her. His parents had always hoped he would get married and have children.

Jerry shifted under the weight of his cats and sighed. He was tired of calling women "sweetheart" so he didn't accidently blurt out the wrong name. On more than one occasion, he had started to drive to a previous date's house instead of the woman he was currently seeing. And, he had even messed up with Zana when he made mention of her mother, mistaking her with a previous girlfriend. Her eyes had become moist—probably from his misspeak and lingering sadness from losing her mom at such a young age. He vowed to be more careful.

Jerry closed his eyes and felt his body relax for the first time in weeks. As much as he needed a break, Zana penetrated his thoughts as she had since the moment he first laid eyes upon her cherry red lips and red shoes—that day in her office amid piles of documents. He smiled as he recalled the many dinners and lunches they had under the guise of investigating the Brad Jordan triathlon case. He had spent weeks stewing over whether she might be interested in him romantically.

After they finally kissed while watching mating whales on Maui, he felt hurt when she wouldn't answer his calls and texts. When she finally did, she refused to discuss anything with him other than work. It wasn't until Zana confided her jealousy after seeing him with witness Megan Alexander that he felt the crushing weight of her possessiveness. Despite this, he couldn't let her go.

As he lay on his couch, he felt an urge to call her. He missed her, but at the same time yearned to be free. Now that "Fighting in Paradise" had a solid sponsor and he didn't have to worry about the show's future, he felt less on edge. Breathing room away from Zana for a day would only make them stronger together. He wished they could work their schedules out so they saw each other only on weekends. He'd be able to better survive his fifteen-hour workdays, but it was hard for him to spend even a day away from his sexy, new girlfriend.

Pounding woke him up. The room was dark and he felt disoriented until he saw it was 7:45 on his phone. Ming and Miko were meowing, circling their empty food dish. He heard the pounding again and it took him a long moment to realize it was coming from the door. He pulled himself off the couch, rubbing his eyes with his fists.

"Hi sweetheart," Jerry croaked as he opened the door to Zana.

"I know you need to be alone, but I stopped by with some dinner for you in case you didn't feel up to cooking," Zana said as she walked in and put the bags of food on the counter. "I got you some chicken noodle and hot and sour soup so you'll have a choice. There's fresh squeezed orange juice, some multi-grain rolls, spicy meatballs, and chocolate chip cookies."

"Wow, Zana! You're the best," he said, putting his arm around her. "I'm sorry, I must have been sleeping for hours. I'm sure I look ragged."

"Not at all." Zana put her arms around him and pulled him into a tight hug.

Jerry breathed in the herbal scent of her hair.

"I tried to call first, but your phone must have been on silent." Zana gently pulled away and stepped into the kitchen. "I'll feed the cats and warm some food up for you. Then I'll leave so you can rest."

"You're the best girlfriend ever." Jerry followed a step behind her. "Did you get a workout in?"

"I ran six miles this morning and swam after work. It was a long day—I drafted a brief Frank wanted by five. I barely got it done. I'm a little nervous about what he's going to think about my arguments," Zana said as she scooped cat food into a dish.

Jerry felt a wave of dizziness so he leaned against the counter.

"I'm sorry, Jer Bear. I'm sure you'd rather not hear about work," she said and turned to him, holding the half empty cat food can in her hand. "Now, sit down and I'll feed you."

"That looks delicious, but I'll take the soup." Jerry scowled at the can in Zana's hand.

"Are you sure?" Zana pushed the can towards Jerry, who ducked out of the room and slumped onto the couch.

"Okay, meatballs and soup coming your way," Zana said. Miko meowed and walked away from the kitchen. "See. You offended Miko."

Jerry picked up the remote and flipped through the channels until he settled on "The Helen MacNamara Show".

"Here we go," Zana said, carrying a tray of food.

"Hey, there's a triathlete being interviewed by Helen," Jerry said, increasing the volume.

"Really?" Zana placed the tray on the coffee table and sat down next to Jerry.

He leaned towards the T.V. and asked, "Isn't that the gold medalist?"

"What have you been doing since the Olympics?" Helen asked Ryan Peterson who was dressed in black slacks and a blue polo shirt with the "Freewheel Movement" logo.

"I'm sure you know there was a lot of bad press about me, Helen. I was blamed for being connected with an accident that killed one of my competitors, Vic Leavitt," Ryan said.

"Were you charged with any crimes associated with that horrible accident, Ryan?" Helen asked.

"No, it was public opinion. Eventually, the truth came out and one of the athlete's girlfriend's admitted to crashing her car into the top contenders on the bike course—killing Vic," Ryan explained.

"I hadn't heard about this. Sounds like another Tanya Harding incident," Helen said.

"Yeah, there wasn't much national publicity and so I haven't been able to regain the sponsors I lost after the Olympics."

"So what have you been up to?" Helen asked.

"I've started the Freewheel Movement. My concern was that there are so many people struggling in this poor economy. They are out of work and either one paycheck away from homelessness, or already sleeping in their cars. I believe there's a better way to help them than with big government," Ryan said. "So I started a movement which encourages families or groups of friends to bring a needy person or family into their group to help them."

"What kind of help is given?"

"If the person or family is homeless, the group can help provide housing, food, household supplies, health insurance, mental health care, clothing—whatever they need. The movement is also designed to help isolated and elderly people by providing friendship, opportunities to socialize, or home visits," Ryan explained.

Zana nuzzled against Jerry and said, "I think I saw an ad about this."

Jerry nodded and increased the volume using the remote.

Ryan spoke while images of needy people with graphics of the website and phone number were shown. "It can cost nothing in the case of helping an isolated person, to perhaps one thousand dollars per month in the case of a needy person or family. The group gets to pick the person or family they want to bring into their circle," he said.

Helen and her guest reappeared on screen.

"How does someone find people to sponsor?"

"On FreewheelMovement.com. Once a group signs up and pays the hundred dollar administration fee, we use our connections with agencies in the donor's geographic area to find a person or family we believe will work well with them."

"It sounds like a needy Match.com," Helen quipped. "Do you have an example you can share with us?"

On cue, images of a family were shown with Ryan's voice-over.

"Last November, a large extended family in Los Angeles wanted to make a difference and were willing to commit to one thousand dollars each month to sponsor a single mother with three children who had been living in a van. She now has a studio apartment, and one of the sponsors is babysitting her two-year-old so she could go back to school and work at a fast food restaurant."

A close up of Helen was shown and she asked, "So, this young woman and her children can interact with the family?"

"Absolutely." Ryan beamed. "They even spent holidays together. The young woman feels like she's part of their family now and her older children are doing much better in school now that they have a more stable home."

"That's impressive. We're running out of time. It's been great having Olympic gold medalist in the men's triathlon, Ryan Peterson, on our show. Thank you, Ryan, and good luck," Helen said.

Jerry put the sound on mute and turned to Zana. "What a terrific organization. Sounds like such a simple and obvious idea."

"Yeah, it's amazing. Maybe Ryan will be able to get sponsors again," Zana said.

"Doesn't he live in Honolulu?" Jerry slurped the last of his soup.

"Yeah, I think he moved here several years ago. I've met him a few times biking and running."

Jerry yawned.

"I need to let you get some rest, honey, " Zana picked up the empty dishes from the coffee table and took them into the kitchen.

"You're a sweetie for bringing me dinner," Jerry said, following her and putting his hands on her waist. He was tempted to lead her to the bedroom, but felt a bit light-headed, so instead walked her to the door.

"How are you feeling?" Zana asked softly.

"Much better with your special attention. I'll call you tomorrow and we can plan something fun for the weekend," Jerry said. Momentarily forgetting he was sick, he kissed her tenderly on the mouth.

Chapter Four

@ZLaw As a matter of fact, I did go to #lawschool. Now, I question why…

Zana shielded her eyes with her hand as the sunlight penetrated through her office window, causing so much glare she could hardly make out the document she was drafting on her computer screen. Ordinarily, she would press a button to activate the electronic window shade, but the warm sun felt good on her skin, chilled by the frigid air conditioning.

She paused from the pile of medical records she was summarizing, closed her eyes and took a deep breath. She wished she had a sofa in her office where she could lay down for a short nap to recharge.

She yawned and shifted her weight against the well-worn leather chair, which had cradled dozens of young associates before her—most fired by her boss, Frank Gravelle. Yesterday, even though her door was shut, she heard him yelling at another associate about some typos in a document. Her roommate, Andrew, had been called into Frank's office to discuss his dissatisfaction with his billable hours that had dipped to 198 two months in a row. It was Frank who had assigned Andrew to spend most of his time helping a new associate, but he wasn't interested in excuses and threatened to fire him if he didn't exceed 200 hours per month in the future.

Zana was determined not to be the target of Frank's anger and so resumed her focus on the task at hand—summarizing medical records of an injured plaintiff. She jumped in her seat when the phone rang.

"Zana, this is Libby. Frank is headed to your office." Libby was Frank's secretary, who could gauge her boss's mood temperature the best.

"Mahalo," Zana said and hung up the landline with a shaky hand. *Great! Apparently, he's on the warpath today.*

Frank had been to her office dozens of times before, but she had never received such a dire warning. She straightened her body in her chair, bracing herself as if on an airplane before a crash landing. She looked at her ego wall and wondered if it had been a mistake to hang her diplomas and certificates of merit, rather than leave them on the floor next to an empty bankers box ready to pack up the moment she was canned.

Her door flung open and Frank barged in, hurling the brief she had written onto her desk. The papers became separated from their clip and scattered across the desk and onto the floor.

"Totally unacceptable!" Frank shouted so loud that Zana was sure all of the attorneys and staff on the floor had heard him.

"I'm sorry?" Zana said, not knowing how to respond.

"Your brief is an unorganized piece of shit. Did you even go to law school?" Frank asked, his face turning red as his voice and body shook with fury.

"I'll rewrite it," Zana said softly.

"You'll damn well rewrite it. Don't let me ever see such a mess again," Frank said, lowering his voice. He turned on his heel, stomped out of the office and slammed the door.

Zana looked at the papers strewn about the room in disbelief. She had worked for days on the motion and had done exhaustive legal research— even checking the law in other jurisdictions. She had spell checked, grammar checked, cite checked and even read it aloud in an attempt to catch any errors before printing it and delivering it personally to Frank. Tears welled in her eyes and were about to spill onto her cheeks when the door opened again.

"Are you okay?" Andrew asked.

"Not really." Zana slumped in her chair.

"I heard the commotion." Andrew sat down, facing his roommate.

"You've got that right." she wiped away a tear from her cheek.

"Do you want me to help you fix your brief?" he asked as she gathered the papers from her desk and floor, and put them in order.

"Are you sure you have time?"

"I'll work late. I don't want you dealing with this all by yourself." Andrew sighed. "I know what it's like."

"Has he yelled at you like that before?"

"At least four times—I've lost count." Andrew reached for the stack of papers. "Let me see."

Andrew read while Zana grabbed a tissue to blow her nose.

"Are you sure you gave him your final draft?" Andrew looked up from the document. "If you did, he's right. This is a mess."

"What?" Zana snatched the brief out of Andrew's hands. "Shit! I printed the wrong draft. You're right. I gave him a much earlier version. What should I do?"

"Print up the final draft and take it to his office and explain," Andrew said. "He'll still be a jerk about it, but at least you'll redeem yourself a little."

"Okay," Zana said as she turned to her computer to pull up the final document. "Maybe, you should read this first."

"Not necessary. Based on the great work you usually do, I'm sure it's good," Andrew said, turning towards the door. "Anytime you need a shoulder to cry on, you know where I am."

"If I do, I'll cry on Jerry's shoulder. But thanks for the offer," Zana said, cracking a smile.

"I think your sense of humor might be coming back, counselor," Andrew said as he walked out of the office.

Zana quickly put the correct brief together and walked past the rows of legal secretary cubicles to the other side of the building to Frank's office facing the ocean and Diamond Head.

"Is it okay if I knock?" Zana asked Libby as she approached Frank's closed door.

"Go ahead," Libby said.

Zana straightened her shoulders and plunged forward. "Frank, I'm sorry. I mistakenly gave you the wrong document. Here's the final draft," Zana said as she handed it across the desk with an unsteady hand.

"You've wasted my time. Don't let it happen again," Frank said gruffly and turned his attention away from her, signaling for her to leave.

After she returned to her office, Zana closed the door and leaned against it, letting out a deep breath. Her neck and shoulders felt tight and she wished she could duck out the door for a long stress-relieving run. Instead, she clicked her computer screen on and sat down. At least she could pretend to be working. She searched Active.com for Hawaii multi-sport. Triathlon season had ended, but there were usually some races fairly early in the year and if she signed up now, she'd have to start training soon.

She scrolled down the list, which included the same triathlons she had competed in for the last few years since she moved to Hawaii: The Bronzeman Triathlon, Pineapple Triathlon, Paradise Lagoons Triathlon, Hawaii Kai Triathlon, Kapolei International Triathlon, Ewa to Diamond Head Relay Triathlon, Aloha Charities Triathlon, and the Sparklers 4th of July Festival of Multi-Sport.

She noticed a new race—The Freewheel Movement International Triathlon. Zana clicked onto the website and discovered it was the first race of the season and was being held in multiple southern cities across the country on February ninth, the Sunday before Valentine's Day. The Hawaii race would start at Ala Moana Beach Park with race directors, Ryan Peterson, and the firm's former client, Ed Fairbanks. As Zana studied the race website, her cell phone rang.

"What's up?" Zana asked when she saw from her caller I.D. that it was her good friend, Shelby, who she trained with several times a week.

"Can you go for a fifty mile bike ride on Saturday morning?" Shelby asked.

"I'll probably have a firm meeting. Do you mind if we start the ride at ten-thirty?" Zana said, clicking onto the master firm calendar.

"I want to go before it gets hot. Can't you skip it?"

"It looks like Frank's tied up with a deposition, but the meeting is still on the calendar. You and Moana can go without me," Zana said.

"We'll start at eight," Shelby said. "I hope you can make it."

"Have you signed up for any races for next year?" Zana put her phone on speaker and clicked back to Active.com.

"A few. Are you going to do Freewheel?"

"I just noticed it." Zana clicked back to the Freewheel screen.

"We have to do that race. The winner of every age group gets a trip for two to Paris," Shelby squealed.

"Are you serious?" Zana frowned. Shelby was always making stuff up, and then laughed when she believed her.

"Yeah. You totally have to race. You could win a trip to Paris," Shelby said. "And, take me."

"I haven't won yet. There are some amazing women in our age group—Megan Alexander, Penny Feldman, and Trini Waimea to name a few."

"You're way faster than Trini. Megan and Penny are fierce, but if you train hard, you never know."

"I'll think about it. Frank is on the war path against me and I'd like to spend the little free time I have with Jerry," Zana said, looking out the window at the sunny sky.

"You're always with Jerry. I never see you anymore," Shelby complained.

"I know. If you were me, I know you'd do the same." Zana sighed. She wished she had time to see her friends, train *and* spend time with her boyfriend.

"I hope he's serious about you, Zana. The guy is such a ladies' man."

"He's a Zana man now." She smiled. The pile of medical records to summarize could wait a few more minutes. "What's going on with you?"

"Not a whole lot. I feel good about Honolulu Marathon. I'm hoping to run a 4:30, but you never know what could happen. My heel has been bothering me," Shelby said. "Hey, did I tell you that I went out with that guy I met at Moana's party?"

"Oh, yeah—Phil. How did it go?" Zana asked.

"It was fun. We had dinner at Irifuni—local style. Afterwards, we walked around Waikiki and talked," Shelby said.

"Are you going out with him again?"

"We're supposed to go to a movie on Sunday, but he hasn't called with any of the details yet."

Now hands free, Zana began deleting spam emails while talking. "Do you like him?"

"Not sure. He's cute, and he has a job and a car. And, he doesn't live with his parents," Shelby said.

"That's more than I can say about Jerry," Zana said, shifting in her seat.

"But, you said that Jerry doesn't actually live in his parents' house."

"No. He lives in a cottage, but it's still on their property. I always feel uncomfortable staying overnight. I'm sure they see my car in the driveway," Zana said.

"Have you talked to Jerry about moving to his own place?"

"I asked him once and he immediately changed the subject. Later, he said he loves living in the cottage and doesn't see any reason to move anytime soon." Zana opened an email from Macy's to check the sales.

"He at least makes up for it by driving a Ferrari, being super cute and a famous T.V. star," Shelby said.

"True dat," Zana said, skimming an email from a partner.

"I'm hoping Phil calls me, but if he doesn't—*c'est la vie.*"

Zana moved to Instagram, scanning photos. "He'll call. He'd be a fool not to."

"You never know. Maybe, he has some unfinished business with a girlfriend or something."

"Did you ask him if he's in a relationship?" Zana said, clicking to like a photo.

"I assumed he wasn't when he asked me out," Shelby said. "You're multi-tasking, aren't you?"

"As always," Zana admitted.

Shelby sighed. "Back to work. Hope to see you Saturday."

After their phone call, Zana took the elevator down the 27 floors to street level to pick up a turkey Panini at one of the restaurants next to her building. While eating her sandwich at her desk, she pulled up the Freewheel Movement International Triathlon website and explored. The course had a few hills, which would be challenging. The swim venue was ideal, because it was at Ala Moana Beach Park where she and her other triathlete friends did most of their training.

Do I stand a chance of winning my age group and a trip for two to Paris? She began studying the results for the Oahu races held the previous season. It would be tough to beat the women who consistently placed in the top third. Megan Alexander typically finished ten minutes faster than Zana, with the others close at her heels. Jerry and her friends would be encouraging, but she was sure her coaches would laugh at the possibility of a slightly above average age grouper coming from behind. This wasn't a movie where the underdog always seemed to win.

Zana clicked back to the Freewheel Movement website and its links to Paris. She watched a video clip of a breathtaking drone tour of the city, with a bird's eye view of the Eiffel Tower, Notre Dame, Arc de Triomphe and the Louvre. She had dreamed of going there since taking beginning French in middle school. The romantic city reminded her of youthful daydreams of walking along the Seine with her *amour* in Paris, and now, she imagined being there with Jerry. They would leave a lock of love with thousands of others on the Pont des Arts Bridge. When she closed her eyes, she imagined them gazing at a sunset view from the top of the Eiffel Tower, and Jerry dropping onto one knee to propose marriage. But, first she'd have to win her age group.

If she trained for the race, she would have to swim, bike and run for hours every day, with little time left to spend with him. There would be no time to continue her routine of hanging out at the "Fighting in Paradise" set after work like a groupie. She didn't want to risk her relationship with him for a slim shot at winning a Paris trip, but the chances of him coming up with the idea himself was remote. Jerry had a lifetime "all you can fly pass" on World Airlines he used for work trips to Japan, L.A., South Korea and Prague, but he had never suggested they take a vacation together.

Zana sighed and X'd out of the website. There was no way she'd give up precious time with her boyfriend to train.

She took the last bite of her Panini and then turned back to her computer. She forced herself to review and summarize medical records until she could risk slipping out of the office without being seen. At 5:15, she sped down the hall to the ladies room and on her way, pressed the elevator down button. She waited near the sink until she heard the ding signaling the elevator door had opened, and then raced out of the restroom door. She ducked into the empty lift, pressing the close button. Just as the doors were about to snap shut, her co-worker, Kim McCall slipped in.

"Made it," Kim said. He rubbed his hand on his shaved head and turned towards her. "Where are you going so early?"

"Coffee," Zana said, looking up at the numbers as they slowly made their way from the 27th floor down.

"I heard Frank gave you the business," Kim said, moving close to her.

She leaned against the wall to keep her distance. Then nodded, looking up at the slowly descending numbers.

"Is everything okay now?" He moved even closer.

"I hope so." Zana shifted her weight as the door opened. She hoped someone would enter and disrupt the conversation about the scene with Frank she didn't want to relive. The elevator paused at the tenth floor, but no one got in.

"Watch out. If you make just one more mistake you'll either be put on probation or fired, depending on Frank's mood," Kim warned.

"How do you know that?" She looked him in the eye.

"Since I've worked here, I've seen eleven associates get fired. Your office is a revolving door," Kim said.

"Oh, yeah?" Zana asked.

"Before you, there was Rodney Takahara, Ian Keller, and Diana, uhm—I can't remember her last name—and that's only while I've been here," Kim said. "All three were fired for mistakes. Frank blew his top, they packed up their boxes and were gone."

"I hope my office isn't bad luck or jinxed," Zana said before the elevator stopped and they both stepped out. He followed her to the escalator and to the street level.

"I'm sorry to break it to you, but you have the crappiest office in the firm," Kim said. "Maybe, you'll get a better office soon."

"How can I get a better office?" Zana asked, heading toward Starbucks.

She didn't really want another cup of coffee, but didn't want to be caught in a lie.

"Libby has an office sign up list. When they become available, the partners decide based on billable hours, seniority and the direction of the wind," Kim said, opening the door to Starbucks for her.

"How did you get your office?" Zana asked as they stepped into the long line of customers waiting to order.

"Frank was yelling at Ian when he was about to be fired. I happened to be talking to Libby and mentioned how much I liked his office. The next day, the office fairy granted my wish and I've been there ever since."

Zana stood in silence for a long moment. "What did Ian do wrong?"

"He turned in a disorganized brief."

Chapter Five

@FreewheelMV Check out our #FreewheelMovement website. We're helping one person at a time. #Charity

Ryan sat up straighter the moment the director signaled they were on the air. He took a deep breath after talk show host Danny Falcon introduced him. *Here goes.*

"What is a *Freewheel* anyway?" Danny asked.

"It's a clutch fitted in the rear hub of a bicycle that permits the rear wheel to run free from the rear sprocket when the pedals are stopped." Ryan sat up straighter in his guest chair.

"I'm not a car guy like my predecessor, but I appreciate an engine," Danny said.

"My legs are my engine," Ryan said. He waited for the zinger.

"What kind of fuel have you been using for your engine lately?" Danny smiled knowingly at him.

Ryan smirked. There it was. "No more doping for me. I've been clean since I left professional cycling. My fuel is healthy food and plenty of water."

"I've heard that before," Danny said, winking at Ryan.

"You can think whatever you want, but I'm done with doping. It's nice to win, but I'm okay with losing as long as the race is fair," Ryan said. The lines were well rehearsed, but he meant them.

"Since your Olympic gold medal in London, have you been winning races?" Danny took a sip of water from his "Evening Show" mug.

"I won the Paradise Lagoons Triathlon recently. Other than that, I haven't won first place in a triathlon," Ryan said. "If I were doping, I'd be doing better."

"Oh, I believe you." Danny chuckled. "You must have improved your bad boy image with the Freewheel Movement."

"That wasn't my intent, but the movement has gotten some favorable press." Ryan smiled at the topic shift. He was there to talk about his charity, not his failed pro cycling career.

"Is there any significance in the name, Freewheel?" Danny asked.

"I wanted to use a symbol that is circular to illustrate the concept of the movement. It's about people bringing others who are in need into their circle of family and friends," Ryan said, putting his hands in a circle to illustrate.

"How can people learn more about The Freewheel Movement?" Danny leaned forward in his chair.

"Our website is Freewheelmovement.com. We welcome anyone who wants to give back to their community to visit our site."

"Ryan Peterson, everyone. Thanks for stopping by. It's been a pleasure having you on the show tonight," Danny said before the network cut to a commercial.

Ryan was happy to leave the set, which felt more like a refrigerator than a living room on a stage before a live audience. Even though he had been on the talk show circuit for months, he still found it an uncomfortable way to spend an afternoon. Helen, Otis, Danny, and Javier had all asked about his doping, not because there was anything new to explain. No, they seemed to do it in order to get laughs or to increase viewer interest. Ryan had come clean years ago when he admitted to blood doping during the Tour de France and he had brought down a few big names with him. He wasn't proud of it and wished he could bury that part of his life forever.

As Ryan walked out of NBC Studios, a young man wearing a Michael Jordan T-shirt approached him.

"You're Ryan Peterson," the man said.

"Yes," Ryan said, used to attention from the public.

"Dude, I'm a big fan of yours. I just competed in my first triathlon. You were amazing in the Olympics," the man said.

"Thank you." Ryan smiled. He was relieved that the young man was a fan and didn't say anything accusatory, as so many people had after the tabloid press falsely blamed him for the Olympic trials accident.

"Will you pose for a selfie with me?" the man asked as he pulled out his smart phone.

"Sure," Ryan said, smiling. There were a few other people standing around them on the sidewalk in front of NBC Studios and Ryan assumed he had attracted a small group of fans. As soon as the picture was taken and the young man thanked him, a balding man with a beer belly threatening to pop the buttons off his shirt approached.

"Would you like a picture, too?" Ryan asked, smiling at the man.

"You've been served," the balding man said as he handed Ryan some papers.

"What?" Ryan felt a wave of dizziness. As he stood frozen, holding the papers, he blinked from the flash of waiting paparazzi cameras, poised to capture and cash in on his surprised look.

Here we go again.

After the balding man raced away, He wondered how he'd escape when he noticed the studio limo pull up. The driver stepped out and waved to him. Ryan shielded his face with the papers as he made a beeline for the car.

"I see this all the time," the driver said after Ryan had slipped into the back of the limo. "Where to?"

"Do you mind if we drive around for a while to get them off my tail?" He looked out the window and saw a few of the photographers hail cabs.

"No problem. Just relax and have a drink. Once I lose them, I can take you back to your hotel," the driver said, looking at Ryan through the rear view window and pulling into traffic.

Ryan selected a bottle of water from the mini-bar and looked at the document he was clutching. The lawsuit caption read: "The Estate of Terry Schubert vs. Ryan L. Peterson". It took a few seconds for him to register that he was being sued for causing the death of the triathlete at the Paradise Lagoons Triathlon. It said he was negligent while riding his bicycle, causing Schubert to fall and die from his injuries.

Ryan shook his head with disbelief as he read further. Plaintiff claimed he was negligent for riding too far to the left so that Schubert had insufficient room to pass him.

He pulled his iPhone out of his pocket and ordered Siri to call Charles Keaton, the attorney in New York who had represented him in several lawsuits that arose out of the doping scandal.

"Hi Chuck, it's Ryan Peterson."

"Hey Ryan. I haven't talked to you in years. From what I'm seeing on television, you're doing well," Charles said.

"Well I was. I just got served with a complaint. I'm being accused of causing the death of an athlete in a triathlon," Ryan said, letting loose his grip on the papers and they scattered to the floor.

"That's serious. What jurisdiction was the lawsuit filed in?" Charles asked.

"Hawaii."

"I'm only admitted to practice law in New York and New Jersey. You'll need to find a Hawaii lawyer."

"Do you have any suggestions?" Ryan asked. He stared out the window at the gridlock of yellow taxicabs.

"Maybe. Did you have homeowner's insurance at the time of the incident?" Charles asked.

"I think so."

"I suggest you call the insurance company and ask if you're covered for this. They'll probably provide you with an attorney and pay any judgment up to policy limits," Charles said.

"Sure, thanks. I'll call them," Ryan said, bending down to pick up the papers. "I really appreciate it."

"Now, stay out of trouble, son," Charles said in a fatherly voice.

"I'm trying," Ryan's voice cracked.

After he hung up the phone Ryan leaned back and closed his eyes, letting out a loud sigh.

"It sounds like you could use a drink, Mr. Peterson," the driver said, glancing at him through the rear view mirror.

"Thanks, but I don't drink." Even if he did, it wouldn't help him much in this situation. He was frustrated with having one big problem after another fall into his lap. After he was caught doping, it took him awhile before he would admit it. Now that he was on the talk show circuit to promote his charity, he was asked to admit his transgressions on international media almost daily.

Ryan stretched out his legs in the spacious limousine. He thought about the early days when he won almost every cycling race he entered in high school. He had no use for drugs then. At nineteen years old, he had moved to France with only a few words of French at his command. As a *domestique*, the lowliest position on a professional cycling team, he earned barely enough money to afford a rat-infested hovel and made due with days' old croissants. When faced with being cut from the team, he finally gave into the team doctor's ordered mystery injections to make his legs more powerful, increase his endurance and decrease recovery time. "All the cyclists are doing it," the doctor had said in broken English.

Ryan was able to keep his place on the team, and after marked improvement, moved up the ranks. He made it out of his grimy rattrap into a clean, modern furnished apartment where he could afford to keep the small refrigerator stocked with food and doping supplies hidden in Chinese take-out cartons and foil packets shaped like leftovers to fool inspectors.

Soon, the team relied on him and he was elevated to a leadership role with promise of one day being a star. After he won stage four in the Tour de France, he talked to the team doctor about racing clean, and they planned for him to taper off the performance enhancing drugs. But before Ryan was able to expel the banned substances from his body, USADA stopped unexpectedly by his apartment. Just the night before, he had thrown out the bottle of clean urine he always kept handy to switch with his tainted sample. He was finally caught. His suspension and the ensuing legal battle left him defeated and broke.

After moving back to the United States, Ryan thought his sports career was over until he competed in a triathlon for fun. Swimming was a challenge, but he made up for it with his explosive cycling, and his high school track experience served him well for the run. He started racing as an age grouper, but won so many races, it made sense to turn pro. In 2012, he qualified for a slot at the Olympic trials in Honolulu. He wasn't expected to make the Olympic team, because there were only two slots that would go to the top guys—Vic Leavitt, Brad Jordan or Jeff Paris.

In the race, Ryan lagged behind on the swim with little hope of catching up with his competitors whose lead was too great after the swim. Then, a freak accident occurred—a car entered the racecourse, killing Vic, rendering Brad paralyzed, and injuring Jeff. Ambulances attending to the victims almost blocked the course, but the race was still on and Ryan earned the coveted Olympic team berth. When he ultimately won the gold medal in the Men's triathlon in London, he was sure his bad luck was over—until all the tabloid headlines accused him of knocking out his US competitors at the Olympic trials. His sponsors quickly dropped him, and any chance for another comeback seemed over.

The idea for The Freewheel Movement came to Ryan in a dream. He couldn't get the concept for the charity out of his head. With little else to do with his time, he made it a reality. Ryan's life was finally on track—he was relaxed, happy and making enough money to live without roommates. He was able to fund his triathlon training and fly back and forth between Honolulu and L.A. and New York for talk show appearances to promote the charity.

Ryan opened his eyes and gazed out the limousine window. They were stuck in gridlock New York City traffic, but at least the paparazzi couldn't photograph him through the dark glass. He looked at the suit papers in his hands. His stomach ached as if he'd been punched in the gut. *How could anyone blame him for causing Schubert's death?* He had been racing his bike in a straight line on the course as fast as he could with the skill of a professional cyclist. It was Schubert's fault for passing too close and causing their handlebars to touch. It was a freak accident and certainly couldn't be blamed on him. Yet, Schubert's family wanted money, or possibly revenge.

Ryan sighed when his phone's ring tone sounded "Stronger" by Kanye West. It was his mother. He wasn't in the mood to talk, but answered so he could warn her about the newest media coverage.

"Hi Mom," Ryan said into the phone.

"How was the show, dear?" she said in her soothing voice.

"Fine. Nothing new," Ryan said, not knowing how to tell her that the negative press would begin again.

"Is something wrong? You sound upset, honey."

Ryan paused, trying to compose himself. "I just got served. I've been sued for a bike accident that wasn't my fault." He wiped tears from his cheek with the back of his hand.

"That's horrible. Everything will be okay, Ry. Take a deep breath." His mother always knew how to calm him down.

Ryan did as she said, taking a deep audible breath so she could hear his compliance through the phone.

"Did you meet any nice girls in New York?" she asked.

"Mom!" he winced.

"I can hope, can't I?"

"I'll call you tomorrow."

Just as he hit End on the phone call, the limo dropped him off at his hotel. Ryan had planned to stay in New York for a few more days, but now he felt anxious to get back to Hawaii and try to sort out his newest legal problem.

He headed straight to his room and called Friendly Isle Mutual. His agent said not to worry. His homeowner's policy would likely provide coverage and they'd hire an attorney to represent him. It made him feel a little better, but bad publicity worried him more than the cost of litigation. *Would this lawsuit destroy The Freewheel Movement?*

Ryan changed his flight to the morning so he would land in Honolulu in the afternoon. He planned to drive directly to F.I.M.'s downtown office to meet with the assigned claims adjuster, Alexia Moore. Maybe she would have some ideas about how to keep the lawsuit out of the public eye.

After Ryan took care of his business, he changed for a run in Central Park. After exiting The Baccarat Hotel, where he was staying, he dodged pedestrians as he made his way to the entrance of the park near Wollman Rink and the Central Park Zoo. It felt good to move his body and focus on the rhythm of his legs rather than the weight of his problems. He barely noticed the throngs of people choking portions of the path near the Metropolitan Museum of Art. He kicked his legs into high gear and sprinted past them, veering off the sidewalk and onto the grass. He then followed the six-mile path around the perimeter of the park, keeping his pace fast and only slowing down occasionally to avoid darting children or for a quick sip at a drinking fountain.

Ryan was soaked with sweat when he returned to the hotel. After a quick shower, he slipped into his Speedo for a swim workout in the small rectangle-shaped pool. He ignored the small children playing at one end and flip turned next to them with each lap until their mother hustled them out of the water.

Left alone, Ryan picked up the pace and swam long freestyle strokes for sixty minutes before he allowed himself a short soak in the hot tub. After drying off, he changed into some fresh gear and headed for the hotel gym to lift weights. The only way for Ryan to relax was to exercise, and his long training session left him blissfully tired and much more calm.

Ryan's post workout dinner was in the hotel restaurant where he sat alone enjoying the company of his Kindle. He planned on getting lost in the latest James Patterson novel, but half way through his salmon, brown rice and broccoli, a leggy red head wearing bright red lipstick stopped by his table.

"Hi there," she said in a soft, sultry voice.

"Hello," Ryan said, looking up from his Kindle.

"Would you like some company?" She put her hand on his shoulder.

Ryan leaned away from her. "No thank you," he said. He didn't like being rude, but the last thing he wanted was to spend time with a woman who might be on the clock.

"Would you like a drink, baby?" the woman persisted.

"I don't drink," Ryan said gruffly. He directed his attention back to his e-book.

"That's no fun. Are you a Mormon or something?" She leaned over and he looked up just as her cleavage came into view.

"No. I'm an athlete. Please—I'm not interested, okay?" Ryan said loudly.

"Okay. You don't have to be a jerk. Jeez!" the woman said and turned away.

Ryan watched her walk towards the bar in heels so high they caused her to wobble. The top-heavy young woman was wearing a short black skirt that could double as a tube top and a tiny black and white striped blouse that barely reached her navel. As he watched her walk away, he could hear his mother's voice in his head asking when he would settle down.

He scanned the room to see if anyone might have witnessed his encounter with the aggressive woman. The elegant dining room was almost empty save for a middle-aged couple sitting side by side in a booth, holding hands and sipping wine. *That's what I want.* Now that he was making money and finally had his house to himself, he was ready to meet a woman—maybe even his future wife. He didn't want to meet women on Tinder like his buddy, Greg, suggested, and he certainly wasn't interested in picking up a woman in a bar.

Ryan had watched his parents throughout their thirty-year marriage set an example of a couple who couldn't get enough of each other. As a child, he observed them kissing and hugging on a daily basis. They had the kind of marriage he had always envisioned, if he could only find the right partner. Ryan chuckled about the conversation he had with his mother the week before when he flew home to Newport Beach on his way to New York.

"Ryan, you know your father and I want you to be happy," his mother said.

"I know," Ryan said. "I am happy."

"We want you to have love in your life—you need a companion."

"I'll meet someone. Just be patient, Mom." Ryan sighed.

"We talked about it, and we just want you to know that we will accept you for who you are," she said.

"I know that."

"Do you have anything you want to tell us?"

"No. I really don't know what you're talking about."

"If you're gay, we're fine with it. We just want you to be happy," his mother said.

"Oh my God! Do you really think I'm gay?" Ryan asked, raising his voice. "Are you kidding?"

"You mean you're not?"

"What?" Ryan asked, and then started laughing. "No, Mom, I'm not gay. I'm just between girlfriends."

Ryan laughed to himself as he thought about his parents' anxiety about his singleness. He polished off the remaining bites of salmon as he considered what he wanted in a girlfriend and ultimately his wife. He would never admit it out loud, but he was looking for a woman who was like his mother—strong, yet sweet and caring. She had to be adventurous, have a good sense of humor, and be somewhat modest in her style. He was completely turned off by girls who showed a lot of skin in order to attract attention. Ryan was more attracted to the librarian-type hidden behind horned rimmed glasses than he was to a scantily clad sex kitten wrapped around a stripper pole. With all the bad press he was bound to get from the Schubert lawsuit, he doubted any decent woman would chance going out with him. Or, could he find a special someone who would appreciate and love him even if he couldn't keep his image out of the tabloids?

Chapter Six

@ZLaw New #triathlon case assignment. Being a #lawyer rocks!

As Alexia Moore bent down to pick up a stack of files by her desk, her waist long blonde hair swung forward and swept the floor. She flipped it behind her back and then noticed defense attorney, Brian Ching, watching her while he was talking with another adjuster at a nearby cubicle. Alexia frowned at Brian and he quickly turned away. She grabbed a cotton polka dot scarf from a hook on her cubicle wall and wrapped it around her neck to cover her décolletage.

Ever since she had escaped her abusive police detective husband to move to Honolulu, she had been careful to follow the rules of her rescuers. She never skipped a day of exercise, followed a strict vegetarian diet and kept weekly appointments at a salon to maintain her blonde tresses and artificially long lacquered nails. Transforming from the frumpy, overweight prisoner of an abusive husband to a breathtakingly beautiful and sexy career woman took constant work. As long as she kept her cover, it was worth it.

The more attractive Alexia became, the more she felt safe from Stan, who surely wouldn't recognize her now. He knew her only as a mousey brown-haired, part-time bank teller, who put up with his hard slaps across her face, body slams against the door and weekly threats to kill her if she didn't follow his orders. The chances of him looking for her in Honolulu were slim. They had never talked of visiting Hawaii during their marriage in Seattle, and on the few occasions they went on holiday, it was to Monroe Washington or St. George, Utah so Stan could race his dirt bike on motocross tracks. Their honeymoon had been a trip to Whistler, so he could ski and she could wait for him in the lodge. Even if she'd dare think about a tropical vacation, she knew better than to mention it out loud to her husband, who had been sweet to her before their wedding, but turned into a brute as soon as her name was officially changed to Elaine Finnegan on their marriage license.

Over the years, Stan's abuse and threats escalated until he started locking her up in their dank basement for any perceived violations of his many rules. She couldn't call the police, because they were his colleagues and would never believe her. After a particularly brutal beating which landed her in the hospital, a nurse slipped her the phone number of an underground agency who rescued abused wives of police officers and relocated them under assumed names—sort of like the Federal Government's Witness Security Program.

It had taken weeks to summon the courage to call them.

She had left her past behind and was flown to Honolulu in the dead of night a few years ago and given the name Alexia Desiree Moore, a claims adjuster job at F.I.M, and a strategy to keep her safe. She was warned that fifty per cent of the rescued women were found by their husbands, because of slip ups in maintaining their new identities. Alexia was determined to do everything in her power to hide behind the veneer of a blonde knock out, even though she still felt like plain Elaine inside.

Slowly, Alexia grew to love everything about Hawaii—the clean, warm and humid air, the tropical breezes, palm trees, pidgin English, street names of long Hawaiian words like Kalanianaole, plate lunches, rubber slippers, hula, slack key guitar, Diamond Head, and even being a haole from the mainland. It didn't bother her that she was a blonde surrounded by Asian and Polynesian faces—it made her feel exotic. Alexia often forgot she looked so different from everyone around her, because she felt Hawaiian in her heart.

Her changed appearance was not only due to her rigorous workout and dietary habits, but could also be attributed to increased self-confidence now that she was an ocean away from her abuser. However, she never felt completely free and continued to be jumpy, terrified her husband would suddenly appear at work or at home as played out in her frequent nightmares. She finally decided to see a psychiatrist to discuss her adjustment challenges. Dr. Tan prescribed Ambien for insomnia and put her on an anti-anxiety medication, which helped her adjust to her new life.

One of the initial challenges Alexia faced when she moved to Oahu was the aching loneliness, which initially seemed worse than Stan's successful efforts to isolate and estrange her from her friends and family. Instead of dwelling on her circumstances, she spent long hours working. In her free time, she was either at the gym or beauty salon. She ultimately lost 60 pounds, and delighted in buying size 2 clothes. She grew out her short, curly brown hair, and the most skilled colorist at the salon created a stunning ash blonde color with highlights, plus she underwent a silkening treatment every few months. An esthetician worked magic with Alexia's slightly oily skin and occasional acne problems, and a makeup artist helped complete the project of turning her into a stunning beauty.

Although she no longer had to use makeup to cover up bruises and black eyes caused by her husband's cruelty, she still bore the scars of his abuse somewhere deep in her soul and couldn't bear the thought of a romantic relationship. Men asked her out on a daily basis, whether she was at the grocery store or at work. Alexia wouldn't even register a guy's face or personality before she replied to his flirtatious pleas with a "no thank you".

It was fear that kept her from dating. She knew on an intellectual level that not every man was bad or capable of treating her like property, as her husband had. Yet, she couldn't bring herself to say yes to even the most kind-appearing men. Dr. Tan advised her to be patient. Eventually, the right man would come along and she wouldn't feel threatened. But after several years of counseling and no progression towards being able to even say yes to a single date, even Dr. Tan seemed to give up on her.

Now, Alexia positioned the scarf around her neck in an effort to cover up either the new her or the scared woman she'd left behind. She wasn't sure.

"Caron wants to see you," Hannah, another claims adjuster, said as she stopped by Alexia's cubicle.

"Mahalo, I'll be right there," Alexia said as she closed out a file on her computer.

Caron Rossi was the grouchy claims manager who never seemed to have anything positive to say to anyone. She had been with F.I.M. since the beginning of time and was reviled by plaintiffs' attorneys who tried to convince her to pay the value of their clients' claims. She had an uncanny way of convincing attorneys to settle for less than they would get from other companies, and so she was well liked by F.I.M.'s home office.

"You wanted to see me?" Alexia asked as she entered Caron's office and peered over the stack of files on her desk to get a glimpse of her boss, who was wearing a red suit that looked like it might have been fashionable in the 1950s.

"I'm assigning you a new file. The insured is Ryan Peterson—have you heard of him?" Caron barked.

Alexia moved some files off of a chair so she could sit down. "I'm not sure. He sounds kind of familiar," she said, stretching her neck to see Caron over the stack of files between them.

"Peterson won the gold medal for the US at the London Olympics for the Men's Triathlon," Caron said.

"Impressive. What's the case about?"

"Peterson was sued by the Estate of Terry Schubert for allegedly causing his death in the Paradise Lagoons Triathlon. Apparently, Terry Schubert passed him on the bike leg of the race and their bikes collided. Schubert hit his head on the ground and died shortly after." Caron looked down at the case file.

"Wasn't he wearing a helmet?" Alexia said, taking notes on a legal pad she had brought with her.

"The police and ambulance reports say he was, but somehow he sustained a head injury and died," Caron explained.

"So what does Peterson have to do with Schubert's death?"

"The estate claims that Peterson was cycling too far to the left, which didn't give Schubert enough space to execute his pass."

"I see." Alexia made a note to investigate the triathletes' lane positions. "What attorney did you assign to this case?"

"No one yet. What do you think about Zana West?" Caron asked.

"She'd be perfect, since she's a triathlete." Alexia glanced up from her notes. Caron usually assigned cases to male partners, not young female associates. "Zana did a terrific job on Brad Jordan's triathlon case."

"I agree. I'm thinking of assigning this case directly to Zana, rather than going through Frank." Caron adjusted her cat eye reading glasses.

"Won't he be upset?" Alexia asked. She had overheard Frank and Caron arguing over cases behind closed doors more than once.

"He might be." Caron leaned back in her chair and put her hands in a steeple position. "He's normally rough on young women associates, and I'm curious how he'd handle it if Zana got some power."

"Yeah, I just hope it's not at her expense," Alexia said, worried about the young attorney who had become a friend.

"I'll keep an eye on things," Caron said, leaning forward so she disappeared from Alexia's view. "Ryan Peterson is flying back from L.A. and will be dropping by the office with the complaint this afternoon. I told him that the case was being assigned to you. I suggest you meet with him and take his recorded statement."

"I'm available. Anything else we need to discuss?" Alexia asked, tiring of talking to her boss behind a wall of files.

"That's it," Caron said.

Alexia was concerned about assigning the case directly to Zana, rather than to her boss. On a few of Alexia's files, she had to input a new associate from Frank's firm every few months. One day over lunch with Zana, Alexia had asked her if she was afraid of being fired. Zana looked extremely uncomfortable and in a quiet voice had said that she was.

Alexia picked up the phone and pressed the number for Dell, Parsons & Gravelle. "Good morning," Alexia said when Zana answered her extension.

"Hi Alexia, what's up? If you're waiting for the deposition summary of Kerry Ito, I'll get it to you in a few hours," Zana said.

"No problem. Take your time," Alexia said, hearing the fear in Zana's voice that reminded her of how she used to talk to her abusive husband. Perhaps Zana's relationship with her boss was not unlike that of a battered wife.

"Thanks, I really appreciate your patience," Zana said.

Alexia paused, not sure she was doing the right thing. "I have a case to assign you."

"I can transfer you to Frank."

"No, this case is being assigned directly to you." Alexia picked up a rubber band from her desk and twisted it with her fingers.

"I don't understand," Zana said.

"The case involves an accident at a triathlon. Because you did such a great job on the Brad Jordan triathlon case, Caron wanted this case to be assigned directly to you—bypassing Frank, or any other partner in your firm," Alexia explained.

"Wow! I mean, thank you. Are you sure that's okay?"

"It better be. Caron insisted on it. We don't have any problem if Frank supervises you or if another attorney assists, but it will be your case, Zana."

"Mahalo," Zana said. "Who's opposing counsel?"

"I know you're disappointed it's not Rip Mansfield," Alexia said sarcastically, referring to the vile attorney who had represented Brad Jordan and was suspended from the practice of law because of unethical behavior. "The Estate of Terry Schubert is represented by Preston Farnsworth, the third."

There was a pause. "This is a wrongful death case?"

"That's right. You'll represent triathlete Ryan Peterson. Are you familiar with him?" Alexia put the rubber band back on her desk and clicked on her computer.

"Sure. I've met him and I've seen him on a few talk shows lately."

"It seems like everyone has heard of him except me. I guess I don't watch enough T.V.," Alexia said. "The only thing I know about him is that he won the gold medal in the Olympics, and didn't you tell me that he was blamed for Brad Jordan's accident?"

"Yeah, he was all over the tabloids. Now, he's getting a ton of press because of his charity," Zana said. "Why was he sued?"

"He was blamed for causing the death of another athlete in the Paradise Lagoons Triathlon. Have you heard about that accident?" Alexia asked as she deleted spam emails from her inbox.

"I volunteered at one of the water stations at that race in order to help out. I remember Schubert being taken away by ambulance."

Alexia turned her entire attention back to the call. "You didn't witness anything, did you?"

"No, I'm not a witness," Zana said. "Should I have a messenger pick up the file?"

"A copy is already being delivered to you," Alexia said. "I'm meeting with Mr. Peterson this afternoon. I'll let him know that you'll be calling to set up a meeting."

"Perfect."

"Zana." Alexia took a deep breath. "If Frank gives you any trouble about this assignment, let me know immediately."

"Okay…thanks," Zana said quietly.

After Alexia hung up the phone, it was time to get some lunch before her meeting with Peterson. She put on her sunglasses to shield her eyes from the afternoon sunshine as she left her office to head to the Bamboo Café where the counter girl already had her arugula lentil salad ready. She sat at her favorite umbrella-covered table and pulled the latest issue of *Marie Clare* from her tote bag. From her peripheral vision, she saw a man approach.

"Hi, gorgeous. Would you like some company?" the man asked. Alexia only saw his shiny brown leather shoes and the bottom of his khaki pants.

"No thank you." Alexia flipped her hair back and kept her attention on her magazine.

"Oh, come on. I see you here every day alone. I'd like to get to know you," the man said.

"No thank you."

"You haven't even looked up at me. How do you know you aren't interested?" he said impatiently.

"No thank you," Alexia said again in her deadpan voice. She was so accustomed to the begging and pleading of all types of men that she no longer found it necessary to consider them as individuals. She simply was not interested in jumping into the shark-infested waters of the dating pool, so she had made it a personal policy to decline every invitation. She used to provide excuses and look the men in their eyes, but the longer her blonde hair grew and the more fit her body became, the more desperate the men's entreaties were. Now, she only had energy for a series of "no thank you's" and the men eventually left her alone. It wasn't uncommon for them to mutter "bitch" under their breaths as they left with their tails between their legs, but Alexia didn't care as long as she stayed safe.

"Isn't there anything I can say that will make you change your mind?" the man asked, now standing over her, a little too close for her liking.

"No thank you," Alexia said calmly.

"Okay then. You look really pretty, but you're actually a bitch," the man said as he walked away.

Alexia nodded, continued to read her magazine and take bites of her salad. It wouldn't be long before the next one came along, but she refused to let the intrusion interrupt the only relaxing forty-five minutes of her busy day. When she returned to the office she planned to ask F.I.M.'s investigation unit to run a check on Ryan Peterson. She wanted a heads up on what the plaintiff's attorney would find out about him.

Chapter Seven

@FreewheelMV Crazy day: Flew the too friendly skies, but then met my dream woman. Do you believe in #love at first sight?

At LaGuardia, Ryan thumbed through a *Sports Illustrated* while waiting to board his plane. He hadn't wanted to fly back to Hawaii so soon, but wouldn't be able to sleep until he handed the complaint to the adjuster and heard some words of reassurance. The feeling of acid churning in his gut reminded him of the day in France when he opened his door to USADA agents and police officers who had charged him with doping violations. When the cuffs were slapped on his wrists he knew he was guilty. But now, he was absolutely certain he wasn't responsible for causing Schubert's death.

"Excuse me," a woman said.

"Huh?" Ryan looked up from the article he'd been staring at. He stepped back a few feet so he was no longer blocking an entire section of magazines. He grabbed a bottle of water and a small packet of almonds, and handed them to the cashier.

"Do you want the magazine?" the clerk asked, pointing at his hand.

"Sure," he said, buying it more out of guilt than interest.

He put the items in his backpack and made a beeline for his gate, which was surrounded by hundreds of tourists dressed in flip flops and shorts, prepared more for the beach than the chilly plane and New York's fall weather. He wore a Reyn Spooner Aloha shirt under his sweater and slacks in preparation for his downtown meeting. He would have preferred his usual jeans, but maybe he'd have less trouble with the insurance company if he dressed like a respectable Honolulu businessman.

Ryan ducked into Starbucks for a grande coffee he needed in order to survive the anticipated discomfort to his long legs folded up like an accordion for the long flight. He had made the reservation the day before and the only seat available was an economy middle seat in the back of the plane. After stirring honey into his coffee, he decided to wait in line to talk with a gate agent about a better seat. With all of the flying between Honolulu and the mainland lately, his frequent flyer status had been elevated.

"Good morning," Ryan said. "I know you're super busy, but I had to make this reservation at the last minute. Could you please check to see if you might have an aisle seat or bulkhead available?" Ryan gave the agent a smile and handed her his ticket. "Anything, but the middle seat."

"The flight's booked, but I'll take a look," the pretty brunette woman said, and after a few minutes of clicking her manicured nails on the keyboard she returned Ryan's smile. "Mr. Peterson, it looks like I can help you."

"Mahalo," Ryan said, relieved. If he could stretch his legs a bit, he might be able to fall asleep. He watched the agent tear up his ticket and grab another one off of the printer.

"Here you go," the agent handed him the new ticket. "Enjoy your flight!"

"Thank you so much, Miss," Ryan said.

He found an empty seat among the hundreds of people waiting to board. He then looked at the ticket and grinned when he saw his seat assignment was 3B. He was in First Class.

When he had won his Olympic gold medal, Ryan assumed from then on he'd be living the good life—until he flew home from London in coach. His economic situation was in free fall until his charity took off and the talk show circuit turned him from villain to hero. Now, he occasionally was upgraded to First Class and a studio limo was sometimes sent to fetch him from his hotel. However, most of the time he used his Uber app when traveling, shopped at Costco, drove a few extra miles to find the cheapest gas, and booked his economy plane tickets on Tuesday afternoons to get the best deals.

When the boarding announcement was made, Ryan stepped onto the red carpet reserved for First Class and elite airline status members. As he walked on the jet bridge, he yawned. He was looking forward to a delicious meal, a long nap and some peace and quiet before meeting the F.I.M. adjuster, who would grill him with questions and possibly even accuse him of causing the accident. The thought of the meeting made him feel nauseous.

He shoved his backpack into the overhead bin and made himself comfortable in the spacious leather chair. As soon as he was situated, a thirty-something year old brunette woman wearing a snakeskin patterned dress with matching snakeskin accessories asked to squeeze in so she could sit in the seat by the window next to him.

"Hi, my name is Olive," she said as she leaned forward to reach her purse under the seat, displaying ample cleavage and a partly covered nipple.

"Hi," Ryan said, wishing she would cover up her large fake breasts. She might be able to lure other men to bed using them as bait. But, he wasn't interested.

Olive stayed in a bent over, breast-revealing position as she talked to him. "This is going to be a long flight. I hope they've stocked up on the alcohol, cuz I need myself a drink. What's your name, handsome?"

"Ryan," he said, shifting in his seat so he was as far away from her as possible. If her breasts spilled out of her top, he didn't want them landing on his arm.

"Well Ryan, you're a hot guy. Why are you going to Hawaii all by your lonesome?" She leaned in closer.

He moved his arm closer to his body.

"I'm going home," Ryan said, hoping she would shut up after the plane took off.

"Aren't you lucky—living in Hawaii. I wish," she said.

"Champagne?" a flight attendant offered, coming by with a cart. Ryan shook his head, but Olive accepted a glass.

"I'm going to Hawaii to get my batteries recharged, if ya' know what I mean. I need a break from New York." Olive downed the flute of champagne in one gulp.

"Speaking of batteries, you'll have to excuse me," Ryan said as he put his headset on so he could listen to music instead of his seatmate's flirtatious banter. He could see from the corner of his eye that she stuck her lower lip out like a pouting child after he cut their conversation short. A few of his triathlete buddies would have been interested in her—but only as a "drive-by". She wouldn't be girlfriend material for them, either.

Ryan closed his eyes as the plane took off, trying to relax his body and stop ruminating on the lawsuit. He was surprised that when he woke up, the plane had leveled out, drink service was in progress and Olive was leaning against a man's seat a few rows up.

Ryan watched as the man, who was wearing a white polo shirt, a navy blazer, gray slacks, and a gold Rolex, focused his attention mostly on her chest. When a little turbulence jostled Olive, the man invited her to sit on his lap. The two were clearly going to end up in a tiny airplane bathroom together the way their hands were all over each other.

Ryan watched with curiosity. His guy friends teased him about being old-fashioned, but he had never been interested in what he called raunchy behavior. His mother had been dropping hints about grandchildren for years and Ryan was intent on ultimately having a family so he could fulfill both of their dreams, but he didn't have to do it with a woman who had loose morals. Ever since he was a child, he observed his father treat his mother as if she was a queen. He doted on her—holding doors open, helping her up when she was seated, taking out the garbage, washing dishes, buying her roses, and always asking her opinion before he made any decision. Comparing his friends' parents to his own, Ryan didn't see the teamwork, love and bonding. He wasn't surprised when one by one they divorced, leaving his friends with complicated lives filled with step-parents and step-siblings.

Ryan didn't want that. His plan was to find the right woman, get married and treat her and their children with love and respect for the next fifty years.

After enjoying his First Class lunch of a chicken Caesar salad, Ryan dozed again until the flight attendant announced that seats had to be restored to their upright positions and large electronics turned off and stowed before landing. Olive had traded seats with the elderly man who had been sitting next to her prey, and so for Ryan, the remaining moments of the flight were quiet.

His plan was to drive directly to F.I.M., meet with the adjuster, and return home as quickly as possible so he could get a workout in before bed. He could go for a long bike ride the next day before catching the red-eye back to New York. His talk show appearance with Javier Perez was scheduled for Friday, and he wanted to give himself enough time to get settled in his hotel room before he had to be on the set.

Ryan thought about his schedule and planning as he headed to the parking garage to pick up his car. He walked through baggage claim and watched Olive as she pulled an enormous magenta suitcase off of the baggage carousel. He walked outside just in time to see the man who she was groping climb into a car driven by a woman his age, presumably his wife or girlfriend. Ryan shook his head in disgust. He'd never understand why so many of his gender cheated. He felt sorry for the man's significant other, but suspected that she was not completely in the dark about his character.

The drive to F.I.M. was short. Traffic was light in the early afternoon and he found parking in their building's parking garage, hoping they would validate so he wouldn't have to pay $8.00 per hour.

With the complaint in hand, Ryan sat stiffly in a black industrial chair in the waiting room with its bulletproof glass surrounding the receptionist. He assumed that Alexia Moore and the other adjusters must be first class bitches to warrant such high security. He wondered whether he should expect a cavity search or metal detector scan before his meeting.

"Mr. Peterson, Ms. Moore is ready to see you now," the petite Japanese receptionist announced in her microphone from behind the thick glass. "You may enter through the door on the right."

As Ryan approached the door, he heard it click open. The most beautiful woman he had ever seen—or imagined—greeted him. She had long, blonde hair with wispy bangs, vivid blue eyes and a rosy complexion. It was obvious from her posture and fit body that she spent a lot of time in the gym. She wore a sleeveless blouse revealing the definition in her tanned arms and her knee length, black skirt showed off her shapely calves.

"I'm Alexia Moore," the gorgeous blonde woman said confidently as she reached her right hand out for him to shake.

He was tempted to grab Alexia's hand and kiss it, but she might take that the wrong way. He couldn't help but stare into her eyes, not breaking his gaze until she looked away.

"I'm Ryan Peterson. It's really a pleasure to meet you," he stammered, trying not to gush. He immediately noticed she wasn't wearing a wedding ring.

"Follow me, Mr. Peterson. Let's go into a conference room," she said.

"Call me Ryan, please," he said. He watched Alexia as she walked. Her body moved like a cat—strong and graceful.

"Have a seat," she said as they stepped into a conference room with windows facing what looked like a rooftop tropical garden. "Would you like some coffee or water?"

"No, thank you," Ryan said, trying to shift his concentration from Alexia to the lawsuit. He had never felt such intense, instant attraction to a woman before. He hoped he looked presentable after his long flight. He hadn't bothered to look in the mirror before their meeting, and hadn't felt the need to brush his teeth. He slid his tongue over his teeth, hoping to dislodge any lettuce leftover from his airplane meal.

"Let me take a look at the complaint," Alexia said, taking it from his hand. As she read through it, Ryan smoothed his hair and sat back in his chair to watch her. He noticed that when she was concentrating, her forehead crinkled a little. She held the papers with manicured nails, painted with purple nail polish that was almost black. Her earrings were gold and she wore a polka dot scarf wrapped sloppily around her neck, as if she was covering up her chest. He liked it. Her navy blouse accentuated her blue eyes and her waist long hair hung forward as she focused on the document in front of her. When Alexia was finished, she flipped her hair away from her face and set the complaint on the table.

"Just as I thought, we'll be providing you a defense under a reservation of rights. Do you understand what I mean by that?" she asked.

"I have no clue," Ryan said, without really hearing what this exquisite woman was saying.

"We will provide you with an attorney to defend this lawsuit. However, we still need to determine whether your policy provides coverage. You'll receive a letter which explains F.I.M.'s reservation of rights," Alexia explained. She pulled out a document from her file. "Is this your correct address?"

He looked at the paper and nodded.

"Let's discuss the allegations in the complaint," she said. "How did the accident happen, Mr. Peterson?"

"Ryan, please," he said, correcting her. "I was in the lead on the bike segment in the Paradise Lagoons Triathlon. Schubert, this other athlete, came from behind. He was trying to pass me, but his handle bar hit mine."

"Where were you riding?" Alexia asked.

"We were on Kalanianaole Highway."

"What I meant was, had you left enough room for Schubert to pass you?"

"I was riding on the right side of the road, if that's what you're asking," Ryan said, trying to sound pleasant and not defensive.

"Was he allowed to pass you?"

"Sure. He just passed too close and hit my handlebars." He shrugged his shoulders.

"Then, what happened?" Alexia leaned in towards him.

"My bike almost fell over, but I was able to recover. Schubert wasn't and fell down onto the road. I heard later that he hit his head and died."

"Didn't he have a helmet on?"

"That's the strange thing. The rules require us to wear helmets, and even though he was wearing one, he died anyway," Ryan said, looking down at his hands.

"What kind of helmet did he have—if you know?" Alexia asked, jotting notes on a legal pad.

"Interesting question. He was actually wearing my helmet."

"How is that possible?" Her blue eyes widened.

"I discovered a few weeks later that his name was on a sticker in my helmet. And then I realized that Terry must have grabbed my helmet in the transition area instead of his own." Ryan reached out and touched her arm as he explained.

"Your attorney will have to investigate this through discovery," Alexia said, moving her arm away. "I've assigned Zana West to represent you."

"That name sounds familiar," Ryan said.

"She's also a triathlete." Alexia flipped her hair back and when she did, Ryan breathed in the scent of mango.

"I'm sure I've met her. Isn't she a tall, pretty young woman with straight black hair with bangs?" He leaned in closer, hoping to catch more of her scent.

"That sounds like Zana," Alexia said. "You'll need to meet with her as soon as possible."

"I'm only here until tomorrow night—I've got to fly back to the mainland for a T.V. appearance," he said, hoping she'd be impressed.

Her face didn't register any emotion. "Are you still living on Oahu?"

"I am, but I've got an appearance on the Javier Perez Show on Friday. I might need to stay in New York for some other business, but I should be back on Oahu late next week," Ryan said, enjoying her intense eye contact. He wondered if there might be a mutual attraction.

"Zana can probably meet with you this afternoon or tomorrow. If you want to walk over to her office from here, I'll validate your parking. It's only a few blocks away," Alexia suggested.

"Good idea. What time are you off work today?" Ryan asked, hoping he could spend more time with her.

"Excuse me?" Alexia asked, sitting up straighter.

"Well, I was wondering if you'd like to join me for a drink after work," Ryan said. Although he didn't drink alcohol himself, he didn't mind being in the presence of an attractive woman in a bar.

"No, thank you," Alexia said flatly.

"Another time then," Ryan said, feeling his face flush. He turned towards the windows, hoping she wouldn't notice his disappointment. "Nice garden."

"Yes, it is," Alexia said, jotting down something on her legal pad. "Here's Zana West's office address. Do you know how to get to Bishop Street from here?"

"Sure, I'm familiar with downtown. Shall I come back and discuss this matter with you some more this afternoon or tomorrow?" He asked. If she wouldn't go out with him, at least he could get to know her better at her office.

"Not necessary. You'll deal directly with Zana from now on," she said. "I appreciate your coming here in person. The receptionist will make a copy of the complaint for my file and she'll e-mail it to your attorney. I'll also ask her to call Zana and let her know you're on your way to see her."

"Mahalo." Ryan swallowed hard. "You're beautiful, Alexia—I just wanted you to know that."

"Thanks." She reached out to shake his hand, but he leaned in for a hug, which she didn't return. She turned away and said, "Good luck with everything."

As Ryan walked to his attorney's office, he couldn't get Alexia out of his mind. He had never before set eyes on such an exquisite woman. Even though he had just met her, he felt that she was the woman of his dreams. As he approached his destination, he decided he wouldn't take no for an answer. He was going to be persistent with Alexia—she had to give him a chance.

Chapter Eight

@ZLaw Invited to the posh #Honolulu holiday #party of the year! Shall I wear #TrinaTurk, #KiniZamora or #AriSouth? Please weigh in on #shoes.

Bud Schubert bent over his garage workbench and his disassembled rifle. He slipped on his reading glasses and opened up the plastic toolbox where he kept his supplies to begin cleaning. His pals at the rifle range sometimes complained about this process, but he found it relaxing. He dampened a patch with solvent, attached it to the cleaning rod, and then pushed the patch through the barrel and out the muzzle, and then moved the dirty piece of cloth back through the chamber. Replacing the grimy patch with a fresh one, he repeated the process several times. He dampened a brush with solvent and pushed it through the barrel and out the muzzle, counting, until he repeated this action ten times. He then dampened another cleaning patch with solvent and threaded it onto the rod and pushed it through the barrel, from the chamber out the muzzle. Using new patches each time, he did this over and over again, patiently— humming while he worked.

This routine and his morning at the shooting range decreased Bud's stress level. In order to shoot well, his mind had to be calm, his breathing steady. He had to focus and be still. The only thing that mattered was squeezing the trigger, his breath and the target. Besides sleeping, it was the only way to keep his mind off of Terry's death.

The Paradise Lagoons Triathlon had been held on the same morning as a charity golf tournament, and even though Bud enjoyed seeing his boy compete in triathlons, he didn't want to disappoint the others in his foursome. At the second hole, his wife's ring tone stopped him mid-swing. In thirty-six years of marriage, she had never interrupted his golf game. He put down his club, fished in his golf bag and answered the call that would change his life forever. Terry was fighting for his life at Queen's Medical Center.

One of the guys in Bud's foursome, Rip Mansfield, insisted on racing him to the hospital in his Maserati. Now, as Bud threaded the cleaning rod through the barrel of his rifle, his mind flashed on the look on Sandy's face when he saw her rush towards him in the hospital waiting room. His wife's eyes were wide and her cheeks wet with tears. No words were needed. His son hadn't made it. They both collapsed onto the floor and sobbed in one inconsolable heap.

After they kissed their beloved son's body good-bye, they somehow made it home to break the news to their grandchildren who wanted to be triathletes, just like their uncle when they got older. Ten-year-old Caleb kicked his favorite toy truck and flung his transformer robot against the wall. Eight-year-old Chloe curled up into a ball and sucked her thumb—a habit she had given up several years before. Watching their pain was unbearable. When their daughter died of ovarian cancer when her children were still in diapers, Bud and Sandy stepped in to care for their grandchildren while their father was deployed to Iraq. His death in combat meant parenting young children full time again.

"Grandpa," Chloe said, interrupting Bud's thoughts as she walked into the garage.

"Punkin, you know the rules. You aren't allowed in here when I'm cleaning guns. It's too dangerous. Go inside right now," Bud said, instinctively checking to make sure there was no bullet in the rifle's chamber.

"But, Grandpa—your cell phone was ringing," Chloe said.

"That's okay. I'll listen to the message later. Under no circumstances are you to be in here when guns are not locked in the safe. Now, go inside, Chloe," Bud said, raising his voice.

Even though he never kept a loaded gun in the garage, his family knew better than to disturb him when he was working with weapons. Now that Terry was dead, he felt even more protective of his grandchildren and wife.

After Bud locked the clean rifle in the safe along with his other 15 rifles and half dozen pistols, he washed his hands in the laundry basin and then walked into the house through what his wife called the mudroom. He kicked off his work boots, replacing them with house slippers. He was not a fan of the no shoes in house rule after growing up in Texas where boots were worn everywhere except to bed, but he did it to keep her happy.

"Are you done in the garage?" Sandy asked as she broke eggs into a mixing bowl when Bud came into the kitchen.

"Yeah, what are you making?" he asked.

"Cupcakes for Caleb's swim meet tomorrow," Sandy said. "It's my turn."

"What's for dinner?" Bud asked as he always did—just to have something to say.

"I haven't gotten that far. What are you in the mood for?"

"I don't know. Whatever's easiest, I guess." He picked up his Blackberry from the counter and held it up to his ear to listen to the message.

"Hi Bud, this is Preston. Sorry to interrupt you on a Saturday, but I wanted to let you know that Peterson was served the complaint. There's an article about the lawsuit in this morning's paper, in case you haven't seen it yet. If you have any questions, call me," the message from his attorney said.

"Hmmph," Bud said as he put the phone down.

"What was that about?" Sandy asked, looking up from the mixing bowl.

"Nothing much. Did you read this morning's paper?"

"Not yet," she said. "Why?"

"I was just wondering," he said, hoping to shield his wife from the article. She wanted to grieve in private, rather than file a lawsuit and be faced with testifying before a jury about the loss of her son. After hearing that the accident was caused by dope head Ryan Peterson, Bud immediately went to Rip Mansfield for advice. As much as Rip wanted to help him in his quest to avenge his son's death, he had been disbarred from practicing law in Hawaii for what he said was a technicality. So, Bud contacted Kenny's significant other, Preston Farnsworth, III.

Bud stepped behind his wife and encircled her in his arms, kissing the top of her head. "I'm going to read the paper in the den and then I might take a nap—unless you have something you want me to do for you."

"Go ahead. I'm going to finish making this batter and then I have a few errands to run. Do you need anything from Costco?" Sandy brushed a strand of her freshly dyed auburn hair out of her face and turned to him.

"Preston and Kenny's party is in a few weeks—you might want to pick up some bottles of wine for us to take," Bud said.

"Oh, thanks for reminding me," Sandy said. "Anything else?"

"No—I'm good," he said, wiping a smudge of flour off her cheek. "Are you taking the kids?"

"Caleb's at Ethan's house. I'll pick him up on my way back. I'll take Chloe so you can get some rest," she said.

"Thanks, honey. I'll see you later this afternoon." Bud retreated to his home office with its well-worn brown leather couch and a flat screen T.V. for watching sports. After triathlon training, Terry used to hang out with him to watch football, basketball or baseball, depending on the season. His son was always famished after biking or running. They had gotten into the habit of eating popcorn mixed with arare crackers in large bowls and drinking Gatorade. Bud missed hearing his son cheer for his favorite teams and yell at the T.V. when an official made a bad call.

He hid the newspaper in the bottom drawer of his desk without opening it. He turned the T.V. on, but instead of watching the football game, he switched the channel to CNN with the volume down low. Then he lay on the couch and closed his eyes.

But he couldn't fall asleep. The lawsuit plagued his thoughts.

***

"I've decided on the mini lobster rolls and tarragon popovers with the wild mushroom crostini," Kenny said into his Bluetooth ear bud to his caterer while he typed on a keyboard attached to his iPad. He listened as she provided more menu suggestions for their annual Christmas party he was planning. "Okay, then—the endive salad with blood tomatoes. No onions. Preston's allergic." He tapped the ear bud to end the call.

Over the years, the list of guests had expanded so much that he and Preston had decided that this year's party would be limited to "Fighting in Paradise" cast, crew and sponsors, and some of the partners at Preston's firm. With significant others, the guest list would still exceed fifty people. They were planning on having a sit down dinner with tables set up in the back yard around their swimming pool.

As Kenny juggled his "Fighting in Paradise" schedule with party planning, he knew he was neglecting Preston, who wasn't interested in the details of the decorations or menu choices. Preston enjoyed the warmth of being surrounded by family and friends, but preferred the planning to be left to the professionals. Since Kenny's passion was creating events, he insisted on overseeing every detail. He spent months searching the Internet for new ideas and had more pinned on Pinterest than he knew what to do with.

"How's the planning, Kenneth?" Preston asked as he entered the large kitchen enclosed by floor-to-ceiling glass with an expanse of grass and sandy beach between it and the ocean. Preston brushed a wisp of red hair off of Kenny's forehead before bending down to give him a light kiss on the lips.

"Terrific!" Kenny beamed. "The menu is all set, and I've arranged for a photographer to take pictures of our guests that can be printed and given to them in a frame before they leave as a gift."

"What a creative idea. I like it better than last year's T-shirts," Preston said, pouring a glass of guava juice.

"The photographer came up with it. Have you met Derrick? He did an amazing job at Mindy and Carl's wedding," Kenny said in his usual rapid speech as he paced the floor.

"I vaguely remember meeting him," Preston said, before sipping the juice.

"You'll love the menu." Kenny paused at the window and gazed at the ocean for a moment before turning back to his husband. "Oh, I arranged for a violinist to entertain us for about an hour during dinner."

"Not Justin, I hope," Preston frowned.

Kenny shook his head. He knew better than to invite his ex to the party. "I've found a delightful young man who played for the Honolulu Symphony. I've also selected a slack key guitarist and a pianist."

"Sounds like quite a program."

"You'll love it." Kenny clicked his iPad and handed it to his partner. "Do you want to take a look at the guest list to make sure we haven't invited any enemies or committed any social *faux pas* by excluding anyone?"

Preston waved the tablet away. "I'm going to leave that up to you this time. As long as you're only inviting the folks from the show, sponsors and my partners, I'm sure it will be a nice mix of people." Preston rinsed his juice glass and placed it in the dishwasher.

"Is that your phone?" Preston asked as they heard a few lines from Frank Sinatra's "Fly Me to the Moon".

"Yes. Isn't it fabulous?" Kenny clicked his Bluetooth ear bud without waiting for his partner to respond. "Hello." Kenny continued pacing. "Okay, what time is he coming by?" Kenny nodded and told the caller that he'd "be there soon."

"Are you heading back to the set?"

"Yes—sorry, honey. I know you wanted to spend the evening together." Kenny put his arm affectionately around Preston's mid-back.

"I understand. I actually had to bring some work home tonight, so it's good you're going to the set," Preston said.

"Thanks for not making me feel guilty, Pres. There's a shrimp salad with balsamic vinaigrette dressing in the fridge for you."

"What's going on at the set tonight?" Preston opened the fridge and pulled out the salad.

"Bud's stopping by. Mitch wants me to babysit." Kenny laughed.

"Bud doesn't need much babysitting," Preston said.

"I know, but he's now our biggest sponsor. We need to give him the red carpet treatment."

"He's having a hard time dealing with his son's death. Coming by the studio probably helps him get his mind off—things," Preston said. "I'm sure you don't have anything to worry about."

"I know." Kenny grabbed his briefcase off the counter and slipped his iPad and his wallet into it. He then turned back to Preston and said, "I have an obligation to my cast and crew to keep our sponsor happy."

"You seem more calm now that the show is more financially secure," Preston said. "Don't be offended, but I think you're easier to be around."

Kenny smiled and cleaned his glasses with a dishtowel. "At least I don't have to spend so much money on Ambien. My psychologist must be wondering if I've dropped off the face of the earth."

"What time do you think you'll be home?"

"Hopefully, in a few hours," Kenny said, blowing Preston a kiss as he walked out the kitchen door to the garage.

As Kenny drove to the set in his silver Jaguar, he smiled to himself, thinking about how his life was finally coming together. Since their wedding, he felt more secure in Preston's commitment to their relationship, and now that they had a big sponsor for the show, he felt like the weight of the islands had been taken off of his shoulders.

After he parked his car and passed through security, he found Bud waiting for him.

"Good to see you, Ken," Bud said, greeting him with a firm handshake.

"How are you?" Kenny asked, trying not to cringe as Bud called him "Ken". He preferred Kenny or even Kenneth. He had always equated the name "Ken" to the doll.

"Okay," Bud said with not much enthusiasm.

"Are you staying to watch the filming?" Kenny asked, motioning to a director's chair.

"Sure." Bud sat down. "What scenes are you working on?"

Kenny excused himself and returned with a clipboard.

"We're filming some fight scenes with Jerry."

"I came on the right night, then," Bud smiled.

"We're lucky to have him," Kenny said, fidgeting with the clipboard. "It's not easy to find an excellent actor who's also a skilled MMA fighter. His fan base is growing so much, we're thinking about creating a Jerry Ho action figure."

"Good idea." Bud nodded.

"Would you like some coffee?" Kenny asked, scanning the set for an assistant.

"Sure."

"I'll be right back." Kenny couldn't ask the cameramen or grips who were busy setting up to fetch coffee, so he headed to the tiny kitchen himself. Zana West was seated about seven director's chairs away from Bud, looking intently at her iPhone as he walked past her.

"Hi Zana."

"Hey Kenny," she said, slipping her phone into her bag.

Kenny paused in front of her. "Did Jerry tell you about our fabulous party?"

"We wouldn't miss it."

"Excellent. I want to make our star happy and now that you're in his life, he's always smiling," Kenny grinned. "Of course, he has to do some serious acting to be a tough guy—you know, wipe that smile off his face. It's Emmy-worthy, really."

Zana laughed. "Thanks, Kenny. I appreciate your vote of confidence."

"Excuse me. My most important task as a producer is fetching coffee," Kenny said, rushing to the back room.

As he poured coffee in a "Fighting in Paradise" mug for their sponsor, he considered that without Jerry and Bud, the show would not be possible. Their party would be the perfect opportunity to thank them both and make sure they felt his appreciation. They could even have a V.I.P. table for special guests and their significant others. Before he took Bud the coffee, Kenny made a note on his iPhone to remember to buy some special gifts for his V.I.P. guests.

Chapter Nine

@ZLaw Is chin wagging a thing? My boss is not a fan, so I'll stick with texting. #Annoyed.

Frank Gravelle peered at the monthly accounting printout through his Long's Drugstore reading glasses, noting that six associates had billed less than 200 hours last month. A Post-it note affixed to the document excused associate Noah King for being sick with the flu for several days. *What was this? Elementary School?*

Frank ripped the note up and tossed it into the wastebasket under his desk. Despite his illness, King's billables were an almost respectable 199 hours. Frank squinted when he examined Zana West's hours. She was usually the top billing associate, logging in an impressive average of 212 hours per month, proving her dedication to the firm above anything else in life. *Not bad for a woman.* Frank blinked his eyes. *Had she only billed a paltry 192 hours last month?* It was time she received a stern warning. If she hadn't been the top billing associate for her first eight months at the firm, he would have sent her packing today.

In Frank's experience, female associates only lasted—at most—a few years before they turned their attention to getting married and making babies. Once their focus changed, he would immediately fire them for declining billable hours so he wouldn't be stuck paying their salaries under the Family Leave Act after their doctors ordered bed rest for the duration of their pregnancies, or some other foolishness. He canned the men when their hours dropped below an acceptable 200 hours per month, which was the only way he could be prepared to defend his firing practices against aggressive employment lawyers who always seemed to be nipping at his heels.

Frank put down the accounting printout and placed his glasses on his desk when he saw Caron Rossi's name on his phone's caller I.D.

"Good morning, Caron," Frank said into the phone.

"Hi, Frank. I'm assigning a case to Zana West," Caron said in her usual brusqueness. Frank was accustomed to her getting to the point immediately, which suited him. It was her no-nonsense style that had attracted her to him years ago. The large volume of litigation assignments she referred to the firm helped keep them in business. He considered her his most valuable client and trusted friend, even though they were ex-lovers. Their son, Lucas, who was now an associate at the firm, would always tie them together despite he and Caron being married to others.

"Thank you, Caron." Frank smiled and straightened the accounting sheets on his desk while cradling the landline phone under his strong chin.

"I want to make sure that you are clear about this. The case is being assigned directly to Zana and not to a partner," Caron said.

"Why would you do that?" Frank laughed at the absurdity of her statement. "True, Zana is a promising young attorney, but she doesn't have much experience."

"That's why I'm calling you. Zana did a terrific job on the Jordan case. I think she's the best match for another case involving the death of a triathlete."

"I see." Frank leaned back in his chair. He would have to hide his outrage that F.I.M. would assign a case to a mere associate, rather than to him or a competent partner of the firm. If this continued to happen, the power would shift. "Are you anticipating that a partner will supervise her?"

"Absolutely. I think she's the best match for this case, but any partner you assign to supervise is fine with me," Caron said.

Frank shifted the phone with his hand. "Okay."

"It's a high profile case. Gold medalist Ryan Peterson is the defendant and the athlete who died was Bud Schubert's son. Zana will represent Mr. Peterson."

"I *think* I've heard of him," Frank said, looking out the window at the view of Diamond Head.

"That proves my point. Zana knows Ryan and was at the race where the accident happened. She's also well-familiar with Ryan's career as a pro cyclist, triathlete and now as owner of the Freewheel Movement."

"The Free Will Movement? I'm sorry, but I'm not quite sure what that is."

Caron sighed. "Peterson started the Freewheel Movement. For God's sake, Frank, don't you ever watch anything on television except Fox News?"

"You know me too well, my friend," Frank said. "I appreciate your assignment of this case to my firm. I will supervise Zana myself. I'm sure you won't be disappointed in our work."

"Remember—it's Zana's case, Frank. But, thanks," she said. "On another matter, is Lucas keeping his billable hours up?"

"He's doing much better," Frank said. For his first six months at the firm, Lucas had barely billed 140 hours each month, but Frank was pleased he was now averaging between 170 and 185. After he had a heart-to-heart talk with his son and admitted he was his father, Lucas stopped playing video games in his office and began pulling his weight.

"I want Lucas to succeed on his own. Don't go easy on him because he's your son."

"Not at all. I'm just as much of a hard-ass to Lucas as I am to the other associates," Frank said with a laugh.

"I'm sure you are," Caron said in her brusque tone. "I've got to get back to work. Let's talk soon."

After Frank hung up the phone, he returned to his accounting printout, but couldn't concentrate after the news that an associate fresh out of law school—a woman, no less—had been assigned a wrongful death case from Caron. *Was Zana trying to poach his clients?* She was still so green. It hadn't been long since his investigator had checked out her background before he offered her a job. Of all of the firm's associates, Zana stood out because she came from the poorest background and had even been homeless at times during college and law school. While he admired her courage and fortitude to succeed despite many obstacles, he didn't trust her any more than he trusted other attorneys. He had overheard the secretaries talking about how Zana was dating Jerry Hirano, who was also an insurance defense attorney. Frank wondered if she was plotting to steal his clients, quit and then work for Hirano. He would need to keep a close eye on her.

Frank put the papers on his desk and marched down the hall to Zana's office. Without knocking on her closed door, he flung it open, catching her talking on her cell phone.

"Got to go," Zana said quickly, as she put it on her desk.

"Your personal calls are interfering with your billable hours," Frank said as he sat in a chair opposite her desk.

"I'm sorry," she said, offering no explanation.

"I expect your billable hours to exceed 200 this month, or you'll be fired."

"Okay," she said, her eyes wide.

"F.I.M. has assigned a wrongful death lawsuit—to you," Frank spat.

"Yes. Alexia Moore called me," she said, clicking her pen.

"Stop that!" He snapped. "It's annoying."

"Sorry." She put the pen down on her desk.

"I'll be closely supervising you," he said, and then he stared at Zana for a long moment.

"I appreciate that." She sat up straighter in her chair.

"F.I.M. is *my* client," Frank said in a voice far too loud for the tiny office. "No mess-ups."

"I understand," she said.

"And, don't think for a minute I'm not watching you. If you're fired or quit, the case stays with the firm. Do you hear me?" He raised his voice even louder.

"I understand," she said, softly.

"Now, get back to work." Frank rose from the chair. "Stop chin wagging on that phone."

"Yes, sir," Zana said much louder as he walked out the door.

After Frank returned to his office, he picked up his phone and pressed *1 to connect with his long time secretary, Libby.

"I want to see Noah King in my office immediately," he demanded.

"Sure," Libby said.

As Frank waited for Noah to arrive, he stared out the high rise window at a distant sailboat bobbing in the ocean he seldom took the time to enjoy. He noticed there were no clouds in the sunny sky. It had been years since he had been sailing and he couldn't remember the last time he'd been to the beach. Hawaii for him meant working six days a week, just as he would if he were in New York, Cleveland or Boston. His version of paradise was making money from the labor of ambitious young lawyers.

"Come in," he barked when he heard a timid knock.

"Hi Frank," Noah said as he slowly entered the room, standing close to the door. His right hand was visibly shaking and sweat beaded on his forehead, even though the air conditioner was on high. He wore a light pink shirt and black tie, which Frank's wife probably would've said was fashionable. Frank thought Noah looked feminine, which entered into his decision.

"Sit down." Frank motioned to a chair in front of his desk and waited until the associate was seated. "Noah, your billable hours were below 200 hours last month, which is unacceptable."

"I'm sorry. I had the flu for a week and had to take a day off. My doctor didn't want me to work with a fever, but I did anyway," Noah said, shifting in his seat.

"Clean out your desk immediately. HR will give you your termination packet. Thank you for your service to the firm, but I have to let you go," Frank said firmly.

"Can't you give me another chance?" Noah asked as his eyes welled up with tears.

"No. Now get out of here," Frank said, turning his chair in the direction of his phone.

Noah knocked the chair over in his rush to leave the office, slamming the door behind him.

Frank hadn't planned on firing Noah—he was an excellent associate. But, he had to send a message to Zana. She would surely find out that her colleague was fired for billing one hour short of the 200 hour per month minimum, since his office was two down from hers. She would feel pressure to resume her impressive billing numbers and firing Noah would likely frighten her enough so she wouldn't dare take advantage of being directly assigned a case from F.I.M. Human Resources always kept a list of qualified attorneys who they had interviewed and were eager to work for the firm. With the recession, applicants had increased significantly, so

Noah's replacement would likely be starting soon after he cleaned out his desk.

Within five minutes, Frank heard another knock on the door. Before he could pick up his phone and tell Libby to stop such disruptions, Lucas barged in.

"Dad, what's this about Noah being fired?" Lucas asked, slamming the door behind him.

Frank beamed whenever his son called him "Dad." He barely noticed the angry look on Lucas's face.

"That's none of your concern, son," Frank said, leaning back in his chair.

"I heard you fired him for billing only 199 hours last month. That's ridiculous," Lucas said, raising his voice. "You should fire me instead—I barely put in 170. It's not fair."

"I have my reasons." Frank rubbed his chin and paused. "It was not just Noah's billables."

"Don't tell me you're discriminating against him because he's gay." Lucas paced back and forth in front of his father's desk.

"Well, this is the first I'm hearing that. I guess that explains his pink shirts, but that's not why I fired him."

"I won't be surprised if the firm is slapped with a wrongful termination suit."

"It won't be the first," Frank said. "I don't understand why you're so upset about Noah."

"It doesn't seem fair. I want to pull my weight, but I'm having a hard time putting in the hours you demand." Lucas slumped into a chair. "You should have fired me. Noah just bought a condo and now he's not going to be able to make the mortgage payment."

"He's a bright guy. He'll land on his feet," Frank said.

"I don't understand why you can't be a human being for once," Lucas said, shaking his head. "You're a shark in an attorney's suit. Has anyone ever told you that?"

"Not yet. But I'll take it as a compliment. Look, son—the practice of law is not for the meek. I have to run this law firm like any business, and that requires me to play my employees like chess pieces. The reality is that associates are pawns and some have to be sacrificed in order to protect the King," Frank explained.

"I don't know anything about chess." Lucas stood up.

"Come over to the house and I'll teach you."

"I'm not interested in learning how to play your games, Frank," Lucas spat, before walking towards the door. "Now if you'll excuse me, I've got work to do."

Frank watched his son leave his office. Despite their argument, he was proud of him for sticking up for a colleague and risking his own job. Lucas had graduated from Stanford Law School last year and even though he could have landed an associate position at any firm, he moved back home and took a job at G, P & D—a large firm by Hawaii standards, but not the most prestigious on the island.

Caron had always told their son that Frank was a family friend, but Lucas had learned the truth years before when he overheard a conversation between his mother and Frank, and finally confessed he knew all along. Lucas had been angry at the cover up. His efforts to sabotage his status at the firm were forgiven by the partners, and in return, he stopped playing computer games in his office and gradually increased his billable hours.

"Libby, come into my office," Frank barked into his phone.

Within thirty seconds, his elegant secretary was standing before him. Over the years, Libby's hair had gradually turned grey, but she always kept it cut in a Dorothy Hamill wedge and dressed impeccably professional, wearing dresses with matching jackets.

"Yes, Frank," Libby said holding a pen and old-fashioned steno pad in hand.

"I'm assigning Lucas to assist Zana with the Ryan Peterson wrongful death lawsuit. I want you to monitor all e-mails regarding that case carefully. I'll need a printout of all communications by Friday, each week," he said as Libby took notes. "Do you understand?"

"Yes. Anything else?"

"No more disruptions today," he said. "Hold my calls and close my door on your way out."

Chapter Ten

@Zlaw Helicopter parents are bad enough, but helicopter bosses? You've got to be kidding me. #Meanboss

Zana paged through the Estate of Terry Schubert vs. Ryan Peterson file with as much concentration as she could muster while Frank stared at her from across the conference table, rubbing his chin. She suppressed a laugh as she envisioned her fellow associate's exaggerated imitations of their boss. They would repeat "billable hours" over and over again while rubbing their chins, reminding her of a scene from the movie *Intolerable Cruelty* where the aged partner breathing from an oxygen tank said those words as if they would be his last.

Finally, Frank stood up, rubbed his chin some more and walked towards the door.

"I'm afraid I've got to get to a deposition and Lucas is off island today," Frank said. "You'll have to meet with Mr. Peterson on your own. Do you think you can handle it?"

"Yes, sir," Zana said, trying not to sound sarcastic when she used the word "sir". He clearly didn't think she could handle it and would continue helicoptering the case until its conclusion. *Would Frank be acting like a parent dropping his eighteen-year-old off at a university dorm if Alexia had assigned the case directly to him?*

The conference room phone interrupted her thoughts. She pressed the speaker button.

"Mr. Peterson is here to see you," the receptionist announced.

Ryan sat on the modern white sofa reading the latest issue of *Men's Health* when Zana approached the newly remodeled reception area. She almost didn't recognize him without his running or biking gear. His Reyn Spooner Aloha shirt made him look more like an attorney or businessman than a pro triathlete and celebrity.

"Hi Ryan, I'm Zana," she said, reaching out her hand.

He ignored it and leaned forward to kiss her on the cheek, island style.

"We've met before--on a training ride." He then frowned and said, "I wish I was here under better circumstances."

"Let's go back to the conference room and talk." She gave him her most reassuring smile. "Would you like coffee, water, or guava juice?"

"No thanks," he said as he followed her into the small conference room.

"I was at the Paradise Lagoon race," she said as they sat down across from each other at the long table. "How did you guys manage to touch handle bars?"

"I have no idea. I was minding my own business and riding—really far to the right—when Terry tried to pass me and got too close." Ryan rubbed the back of his neck. "It was almost like he was trying to run me off the road."

"That's weird," she said, jotting notes on a legal pad. "Were there any witnesses?"

"It's possible. Except we were really far ahead of the pack," he said. "And, I didn't see any spectators on that stretch of the road."

"Was the race televised or filmed?" Zana asked, assuming the answer would be "no". Local triathlons seldom attracted audiences broader than the family members of the contestants.

"Good question," he said. "I'm not sure. If it was, maybe there's some explanation in the film footage about how Terry ended up wearing my helmet instead of his."

She looked up from her notes. "Interesting."

"I don't know why our helmets got switched," Ryan stammered.

She noticed the bags under his eyes, and there was a piece of what looked like lettuce stuck in his teeth.

"I wonder how he died if he was wearing a helmet," she said.

"Yeah, if they don't work, maybe we should go back to the old days of wearing hats while cycling," he said with a slight smile.

"Well, obviously your helmet didn't protect Terry. Did it fit him properly?" Zana made a note.

"I glanced back at him and didn't see anything unusual. If the helmet didn't fit his head, I probably would have noticed."

"When did you look at him? Think carefully." She watched him for about thirty seconds as he stared in the direction of the ceiling.

"I looked over my shoulder at some point to see who was behind me, and Terry was way back." Ryan paused. "I don't remember glancing at Terry right before the accident. I felt his handle bar hit mine, but I didn't look at him, because I was trying to gain control of my own bike."

Zana wrote his words down. "After you gained control, did you look back?"

He nodded. "I saw him on the ground."

"Did you notice anything?"

He again turned his attention to the ceiling for a few minutes.

"Oh, my God. His—my—helmet was on the ground near him. It must have come off his head somehow." His voice cracked and he leaned forward in his chair.

"How would it have come off his head?" she put her pen down.

"I don't know. Maybe, he didn't buckle the chin strap," he said softly.

Tears were welling up in his eyes. She handed him the box of tissues on the sideboard.

"Was there anything wrong with the chin strap that would have prevented him from buckling it?" Zana asked.

"No. I wore my helmet when I rode to the transition area the day before to drop off my bike. The chin strap worked fine." Ryan blew his nose into a tissue. "I even took a selfie."

He took his phone from his shirt pocket and pulled up a selfie showing himself grinning into the camera—his white bicycle helmet atop his head with the chin strap securely buckled around his chin. A palm tree and the ocean were in the background.

She studied the picture and forwarded it to her email.

"So, the question is…how did the helmet come off of Terry's head?" she asked.

He nodded and slipped the phone back into his pocket.

Zana spoke out loud while she made notes on her legal pad. "I'll focus on that question in discovery. We'll hire an expert to examine the helmet. I just got this assignment, and I don't know if anyone else took pictures."

"What if the chin strap was unbuckled? Will that get me off the hook?" Ryan asked.

"If Terry didn't buckle the chin strap, I'll argue that his death was proximately caused by his own negligence. I'll also argue that he was comparatively negligent more than 50 % when his bike collided with yours. If so, according to Hawaii law, his estate will not be able to collect money from you, even if you were negligent," she said. "We'll have to see what our investigation reveals."

Ryan tossed his used tissues in the wastebasket and pushed the box away. "This lawsuit sucks." He sighed. "My life was finally getting back on track. It's so depressing."

"I know it's hard not to focus on it. But, if you can, why don't you just leave things to me," Zana said, imitating what she'd heard Frank tell clients.

"That's easier said than done, but I'll try," Ryan said, tapping his knee up and down, making the conference table shake.

They sat in silence for a few moments and then he asked, "Are you doing the Turkey Triathlon Relay in a few weeks?"

"I didn't even know about it," she said, feeling her shoulders relax with the change of subject.

"It's sort of a word of mouth, informal event on Thanksgiving morning so everyone can burn some calories before eating stuffing and pie. It's a relay, so you need at least two people," he said, smiling for the first time since he arrived.

"Hmm. I wonder if my friend, Shelby, would be up for it," she said.

"I think I know her—she's that cute blonde who always wears pink cycling jerseys. It's just an eight hundred yard swim, a fifteen-mile bike ride and a 5k run. You have to predict your split and overall times. The winner whose actual times are closest to the predictions wins the sponsor's gift certificates."

"They don't give away a turkey?" Zana asked.

"They used to, but everyone had already bought their turkeys by Thanksgiving morning. You should do it," he said. "More importantly, are you going to compete in the Freewheel Movement Triathlon in March?"

"I doubt it. I try to spend my limited free time with my boyfriend." Zana shifted in her seat. "There's not much time left to train."

"You're missing out. I've got some great surprises planned," Ryan said.

Her eyes widened. "More than the age group winners receiving trips to Paris?"

"Much more than that." He smiled. "I hate to cut this meeting short, but I want to get a long workout in and it's getting kind of late. I thought I was only meeting with Alexia today."

"We can always meet when you have more time," Zana said, putting down her pen and placing her legal pad on top of the file.

"I'm glad you're my attorney instead of that stodgy guy who introduced himself while I was sitting in the waiting room," he said.

She stifled a laugh. "You mean Frank Gravelle?"

"I think so. He doesn't look like he even knows what a triathlon is. Was he born in the 1800s or something?" Ryan smirked. "He was actually wearing suspenders."

"He's my boss and will be supervising me on this case," she said. She was tempted to join Ryan in making fun of Frank, but feared there might be cameras or recording devices in the room. "I'm sure you'll see more of him."

"Well, at least I got to meet Alexia. She's amazing." His face lit up.

She nodded. "Yeah, I think all men drool over her a bit."

"Is she in a relationship?" Ryan asked, continuing to shake the table with his bouncing knee. "I was just wondering."

"I don't think so," Zana said, now curious about whether the two would be a good match. She had seen pictures of Ryan in magazines for years, and recently, he'd been on the talk show circuit for good reason. He not only had charisma and a photogenic face, but when he was rested, his blue eyes sparkled. "Why don't you ask her out?"

He scowled. "I already did. She shut me down."

"Keep trying. You never know—persistence may win her heart," she said, wondering if the lettuce stuck in Ryan's teeth had affected Alexia's decision.

"I don't want to bug her." He blushed.

"Maybe I'll put in a good word for you," Zana said, standing up to lead her client to the reception area.

"Please do. I would owe you big time," he said, following her out the conference room door. "I hope to see you at the relay. I'm dressing like a turkey."

"Are you kidding?" Zana stopped in her tracks and laughed.

"Maybe. I haven't quite decided if I'm going to wear a costume. There are a lot of athletes who dress up. Go for it. You've got to relax sometime," Ryan said as they continued walking together to the reception area. "If I had your job, I'd look as stressed out and as tense as you do."

"What a compliment." She frowned.

"You're beautiful, Zana. You just look a tad tense," he said, putting a hand on her shoulder. "I'll talk to you soon."

After Ryan left, Zana popped into the ladies room and looked in the mirror at her pale face. Her usually shiny, black hair looked stringy and dull. She noticed that, like her client, she had dark circles under her eyes and it looked like a small zit was forming on the side of her nose. With all of her late nights with Jerry and the long hours at the office, she hadn't been out in the sun much. Her days started before dawn and ended after dark and she'd apparently become as pale as Bella, the character in the *Twilight* vampire series. It was embarrassing that she had been living in Hawaii for several years now and looked far more ghostly than right-off-the-plane tourists catching their first rays of sun on Waikiki Beach.

After she returned to her office, she looked briefly out the window at the clear blue sky. Then, she slumped into her chair and clicked on her computer. Her stomach was still churning from Frank's behavior in the conference room. She was tempted to catch up with Facebook for a quick de-stress before diving back into work, but the small hula girl figurine on her desk was a quick reminder to buckle-down and bill hours. The tiny hula girl was all she had left from her mother whose death at a young age left Zana to fend for herself when her dad turned to drugs rather than dealing with his grief.

After running away from the foster home where she'd been sexually assaulted when she was in high school, Zana survived by couch surfing at friends' houses, sleeping in her old Buick, and when times were good, renting a room in someone's house. She had finally let go of some of her fear and anxiety after she won the Jordan triathlon case, and she and Jerry had cemented their relationship as more than friends and colleagues working on a case. But now, the gut churning and the tightening in her chest brought her back to her normal. She'd have to work long hours to avoid living out of her car again, and if she wanted to keep her relationship with Jerry, spending time with him was essential. There wouldn't be much time left over for triathlon training—or, for social media. And so, Zana dove back into work.

When she looked up from her computer, it was close to 5:30 p.m., the time when most normal people left their offices and headed home to their families. She'd logged only 9.1 billable hours for the day. She had a few more to go before she could leave. Now that she was under Frank's scrutiny, Zana wondered if she should do something outrageous and bill a record number of hours. *What would he think if she managed to bill 300 hours in a month?* The thought seemed ridiculous, but she wondered what it would take to make her feel job security. *How could she eliminate the constant gnawing feeling in her gut?*

"Hey, babe," Zana said as she picked up her iPhone vibrating in her purse.

"What are you up too, sweetheart?" Jerry asked.

"I'm just wondering how I can bill more hours, but I'm running on empty." She beamed at the sound of his voice.

"Coffee and food are the answer—you should take a Starbucks' break," he said.

"Do you have time to meet me?" She put the phone on speaker mode and applied lip gloss.

"We're headed out to Sandy Beach to do some filming tonight. I'm calling from my car," he said.

"You're filming at the beach in the dark?"

"Yeah. The script calls for a fight scene at the beach with a bonfire."

"I wish I could watch," she said, gazing out the window at the ever-present Dole pineapple in the distance.

"Even if you had time, it's a closed set tonight. The permit is only for three hours and they don't want any disruptions," Jerry said. "I've had an exhausting day of depositions. I'd rather go home and sleep."

"Sounds like you're the one who needs coffee."

"I'm sipping it as we speak." Jerry laughed. "So, I'll talk to you tomorrow?"

"I'll be up until ten, if you want to call me." She knew she probably wouldn't hear from him before she went to bed. He didn't leave the set until after ten and then he ate a late dinner, and if she wasn't with him, he sometimes worked out until 1 a.m. He went to sleep only a few hours before her alarm went off in the wee hours of the morning.

"Okay. Don't work too hard, sweetie," Jerry said softly.

"I'm sure I will. Goodnight, Jer-bear," she said in a tone she used only with him.

She wished he would say, "I love you," but they weren't there yet. They'd been dating for six months and it seemed weird to her that the only tender words they said to each other were generic. She didn't want to say those three words first for fear she would scare him off. *Shouldn't the guy be the first to say, "I love you?"* Both of her ex-boyfriends had said those words less than a month after they started dating. *Was there something wrong with her relationship with Jerry?*

Zana temporarily forgot about her tenuous job situation. She stared out the window, watching the sky grow darker as she ruminated on whether she might have misread his intentions. *Was he using her?* He had called to tell her she couldn't come to the set tonight. *Was he really working, or did he have a date with another woman?* Zana kicked the trashcan under her desk, causing it to spill over onto the floor. She bent over to pick up crumpled pieces of paper and the wrappers of three energy bars—her meals so far that day.

When she rose up and settled back into her chair, she resumed staring out the window. Now it was dark, and the floor to ceiling windows had become mirrors, showing the reflection of her slumped in her chair. It was 6:20. She could hear vacuuming in a distant office and the clang of wastebaskets being emptied by janitors. She hadn't accomplished anything more, so she decided to pack up her briefcase with Ryan's file and get a short run in at Ala Moana Beach Park before driving home.

As Zana walked down the hall, she passed Frank's open door. The light was off. He was probably home with his family while his minions slaved away in fear, making him piles of money.

"Are you headed home?" Andrew asked, stepping out of his office next to Frank's.

"I'm going for a run," she said, pleased to see that her housemate wasn't putting in a late night, either.

"I hear you've had a rough day."

"What did you hear?" Zana scowled.

"Frank told Libby to monitor you closely."

"Do you think he's going to fire me?" she asked.

"I hate to say this, since you're my friend," Andrew said, walking with her towards the elevator, "but if you're being closely watched, your job isn't any more secure than any other associate's."

"Thanks for the words of encouragement." Zana rolled her eyes.

"I'm afraid you're stuck working in this hell hole for a little while longer. Sorry, buddy," Andrew said as he pressed the elevator down button.

"Sorry, indeed."

Chapter Eleven

@FreewheelMV Did I miss something? Are men not supposed to send flowers anymore? Have #Cat #Memes replaced roses? I need the 411.

Alexia struggled to breathe, feeling the bed pillow pressed against her nose and mouth. She could feel him pressing the pillow more forcefully against her face until her air supply was cut off and she was gasping. The sound and feeling of her suffocating lungs jolted her wide awake.

She sat up in her twin bed and listened. The only noise was the ceiling fan whirring above her head to circulate stale air in the muggy room. Nightlights placed in each corner provided enough illumination so she could see that nothing appeared to have been disturbed. The windows were locked and painted shut from the inside for added protection from Stan, who she feared would find her and break into her tiny house, keeping his promise to kill her.

When Alexia was convinced that she was alone, she used the towel kept on her nightstand to wipe sweat from her face. There was no air conditioning. Tonight, she was drenched with sweat not only from the heat, but also from the vividness of her reoccurring nightmare.

Soon after she arrived on the island, she developed what the Internet told her was clinophobia—a fear of beds or going to bed. For the first few months in her Makiki house, as she lay in bed with eyes wide open in her dark room, she imagined every lump and shadow on the other side of her Queen-size bed was Stan. Even with the lights on, she still sensed his presence. When her co-worker, Tammy, mentioned that her son had moved to the mainland for college, Alexia swapped her queen for his twin bed so Tammy could host her visiting relatives, and Alexia could get more restful sleep. Although, the smaller bed eliminated the empty space, her continuing nightmares reminded her of the danger she was still in. Her police detective husband could find anyone.

Alexia's first shower of the day washed off the sweat from her sauna-like sleep conditions. She was usually in her workout gear by 4:30 a.m. and then sprinted the two miles to a nearby gym, staying on well-lit sidewalks. She wasn't afraid of strangers. She couldn't imagine any kidnapper or rapist being as brutal as Stan. The pepper spray she carried was to protect her from him if he jumped out of a bush or was waiting for her in the dark gym parking lot.

As she ran, her mind drifted to her meeting with Ryan Peterson the day before. Besides her husband, the scariest men were those after her heart. Meeting Ryan yesterday reminded her of how deceiving good looks and charisma could be. She obviously had bad judgment. Otherwise, she wouldn't have been fooled by Stan's charm and chivalry before they were married; she wouldn't have ignored his jealous rage when an ex-boyfriend asked her to friend him on Facebook.

Stan wasn't emotionally abusive until the moment they returned home from their honeymoon, and the beatings didn't start until his lies completely estranged her from friends and family.

One night, several years into their marriage, Alexia cooked him his favorite meal of barbequed steak and mashed potatoes. She broke the news of her pregnancy over hot apple pie. As soon as she finished her announcement, he grabbed her by the arm, pulled her to the top of the basement stairs and pushed her down. The pain of her miscarriage felt worse than her fractured collarbone.

Alexia looked at her watch when she reached Wilder Gym. It was a few minutes after five and the parking lot was empty. Most of the members lived in the adjacent high rises in Makiki. As she opened the door using her fob, she noticed the handful of regulars already doing bench presses, pull downs, squats, and running on treadmills. They politely nodded, but no one uttered a word before sunrise. It was almost as if they were working out in their sleep.

The gym was the only place Alexia felt safe. She grabbed a 15 pound dumb bell off the rack. It was arms, chest and back day so her routine began with pumping up her toned biceps in front of the floor-to-ceiling mirror. She liked looking at her reflection in the morning—the only time she was sans makeup with her hair pulled into a messy bun. Today, she was wearing her ratty gray T-shirt and baggy blue shorts. In the mirror, she almost recognized her true self and smiled. If someone called out "Alexia," she probably wouldn't answer. Here, she was still Elaine Metzker—the name she had before Stan stole her identity.

Alexia skillfully completed three sets of each exercise, doing 12 reps each, just as her trainer had taught her. She initially found gym workouts boring until she started to see and feel her body change. She became strong and dropped size after size, until she settled at size 2. She had moved to Honolulu with a suitcase full of size 16 clothes, which she happily donated to the Salvation Army as they became too large. The men started hitting on her when she reached size 8, and as her body became more fit, the attention increased exponentially. Alexia would have almost preferred to hide behind excess body weight, but her fear that Stan would track her down was incentive enough to become unrecognizably beautiful.

She completed her workout by wiping sweat off the treadmill after 60 minutes of running imaginary hills. Her soaked T-shirt felt cool against her skin as she ran home to shower again. She usually wore blue denim on casual Fridays, but decided to wear her new peach colored jeans, a white V-necked top and Nine West flats that felt as comfortable as bedroom slippers. When Alexia walked into the office at 7 a.m., she headed straight to the lunchroom where she poured herself a cup of coffee—freshly brewed by one of her co-workers.

She lingered for a few minutes, sipping coffee from her Gravelle, Parsons and Dell mug and reading the headlines from the Pacific Business News before heading to her cubicle to tackle the piles of work she had to get done by the end of the day—in order to avoid coming in on Saturday.

To Alexia's astonishment, a large bouquet of assorted tropical flowers was on her desk. Since she didn't have a boyfriend, she wondered which prospective suitor had ignored her rebuffs and spent $100.00 in an attempt to change her mind. The card was addressed to "Ms. A. Moore", and in neat handwriting, it read:

Alexia,

Meeting you was a special occasion. I hope these flowers brighten your day!

Aloha, Ryan

His phone number was below his name.

Stan used to follow up almost every cruel beating with a delivery of a dozen red roses and so their meaning became less romantic with time. On one occasion, he sent twelve dozen roses of all different colors to her hospital room where she was recovering from internal injuries from her latest tumble down the stairs, due to what Stan told her doctor was his wife's clumsiness. The scent of the flowers became unbearable and solidified her aversion to roses.

As much as Alexia detested receiving flowers, for some reason getting them from Ryan was not entirely despicable, partly because there was not one rose in the bouquet. She examined the anthuriums, ginger, birds of paradise, and orchids, and decided against dumping them in the trash as she usually did now.

"Who are the flowers from?" Tammy asked as she stopped by Alexia's cubicle.

Alexia sipped her coffee and leaned back in her chair. "No one important," she said.

"They must've cost a fortune," Tammy said, leaning into the bouquet to breathe in their scent.

Alexia nodded.

"I'll bet those are from that hunk who was in here yesterday," Tammy said, leaning against the cubicle partition.

"You mean, Mr. Peterson?" Alexia said softly. She didn't want her other co-workers to overhear.

"Yeah, that triathlete," Tammy said loudly. "I've seen him on T.V."

"How did you guess?" Alexia whispered, hoping her co-worker would do the same and lower her voice.

"I saw the way he looked at you," Tammy said in a more acceptable register. "He's smitten."

"That's an old-fashioned word." But she smiled. She moved some files onto the floor to make room for the arrangement.

"Okay—he's besotted. Better?"

"No. Even more old-fashioned," Alexia pointed out.

"You should go out with him," Tammy said, pulling out her phone to snap a picture of Alexia with the flowers. This caught Alexia off-guard as she usually didn't allow anyone to take her picture, but the flowers were beautiful and her face was caked with makeup, her hair was freshly dyed, and she bore almost no resemblance to her old, abused self.

"No way. I'm not going out with an insured." Alexia shook her head and moved back into position in front of her computer screen.

"There aren't any rules against it. Come on—have some fun. You never go out with anyone," Tammy said.

Alexia clicked on her computer and ignored her friend.

"You and that twin bed of yours. You really need to get laid." Tammy laughed.

"Shhhhh." Alexia hoped no one overheard. She whispered, "For someone who uses such old-fashioned words, you're really crude."

Tammy laughed again. "Don't change the subject. You're young and gorgeous. You should go out with the man."

"He's not my type."

"What is your type?"

"I've got to get to work." Alexia reached for her noise-cancelling headphones, hoping Tammy would get the hint.

"We'll talk about this later. If you don't go out with Ryan Peterson, I'm going to set you up on a blind date with my husband's cousin who has three chins."

"I'll pass," Alexia said, turning her attention to deleting e-mails. "I'm not interested in dating anyone, no matter how many chins they have."

Her Hawaiian bracelets clanking together, Tammy plopped back into her cubicle next door.

Alexia sighed. She hoped none of the other adjusters had overheard their conversation. She tried to focus her attention on work, but she could see the bright flowers from the corner of her eye. The vividness of the orange birds of paradise in contrast with the purple orchids was dramatic. She wondered whether to call Ryan and thank him, but she didn't want to open the door for a date. Her husband wasn't able to buy her forgiveness with roses, and she certainly wouldn't allow Ryan to purchase a date with a stunning floral arrangement.

After staring at the flowers for a few more moments, Alexia made up her mind to protect herself by not acknowledging the gift. Under no circumstances would she change her no dating policy. She was lucky to be alive in paradise. She would continue her solitude and routine. She smiled and dove into work.

She got into the rhythm of her job and made phone calls that yielded a few settlements lower than she expected. At the end of her workday, she was tempted to dump the flowers to prevent further distraction, but decided she had become strong enough to enjoy their beauty.

***

It had been several years since Ryan had sent flowers to a woman. He tried to order them on the Internet and phone without success. *What was the appropriate arrangement to send to a beautiful woman he'd only met once and who had turned him down? Did the occasion warrant roses, tulips or a spring bouquet?* He finally rode his bike to a flower shop a few miles away from his Kailua home and spent almost an hour with the florist as he created an arrangement so visually pleasing it would surely impress Alexia. Ryan imagined that she had been the recipient of many floral gifts, so he wanted his to stand out. He hoped she would change her mind about his invitation after this romantic gesture, or at the very least, she'd feel obligated to call with a thank you.

After Ryan confirmed the flowers had been delivered, he made sure his phone's ringer was on so he wouldn't miss her call or text. He checked his phone after he parked his car at the airport, after going through security, and before he boarded the red eye back to New York for his appearance on "The Javier Perez Show". His phone remained silent. As he sipped orange juice in first class before the plane took off, he stared at the tiny screen in his hand, toying with the thought of calling her. He swiped the screen, pressed the phone icon and pulled up F.I.M.'s claims department number and stared at it.

"Would you like more orange juice before we take off?" A pretty flame-haired flight attendant took his empty glass.

Ryan shook his head. "No, thank you."

"We're going to close the doors soon, so if you want to make a call, you've only got a couple of minutes," she said.

As much as he wanted to gauge the temperature of Alexia's feelings through her hopefully grateful phone voice, he didn't want to chance a mid-call interruption. He put his phone in airplane mode and slipped it in his backpack. He then binge watched episodes of "Breaking Bad," hoping to get his mind off her during the long flight.

The moment Ryan's plane landed at JFK International, he immediately turned his phone back on, frowning when he saw that the only calls he received were from his agent and a triathlon race director. It was 10:30 a.m. in New York and only 5:30 a.m. in Hawaii. The five-hour time difference protected him from his impulse to call her.

While waiting for a taxi, he deleted the F.I.M. number from his phone to prevent fatigue dialing. He wondered if he could ask Siri to block—at least momentarily—any future attempts he made to call her. Beauty required strategy.

He would have time for a short nap in his hotel room before an NBC Studio car picked him up. After waking, Ryan popped a Zantac, hoping it would take away the heartburn he usually felt shortly before a talk show interview. If the host only asked questions about the Freewheel Movement, he'd be fine, but the only reason he made such an appealing guest was his past doping, the Olympic trials accident scandal, and now the lawsuit blaming him for Terry's death. He steeled himself for the onslaught of questions.

While he waited for the medicine to kick in, he pulled up the contact list on his phone and called his attorney.

"Good morning, Zana West speaking."

"Hi Zana. It's Ryan Peterson." He wiped his sweaty hands on the bedspread.

"How can I help you?" Zana asked.

"I was wondering if you've obtained the photographs of my helmet yet." He paced while listening to her voice on his iPhone speaker.

"Not yet. It might take a few weeks," she said.

"No problem. I'm in New York for about four days. You can call me while I'm here if you have any questions," he said.

"Okay, thanks," she said.

"Have you talked to Alexia?" Ryan asked, using his most nonchalant voice.

"Not since before we met. Why?" Zana asked. "Did you send her flowers or something?"

"Uh huh." He nodded.

"No you didn't!" Her voice raised an octave.

He abruptly stopped pacing. "What do you mean? Is there something wrong with sending flowers to her?"

"Last I heard, Alexia doesn't like flowers or maybe she's allergic to them," Zana said.

Ryan slumped into the single chair in the room. "How do you know that?"

"About four months ago, I was meeting her for lunch and she was carrying a pretty decent-sized arrangement of roses and spring flowers, and she dumped it in the trash."

"That's strange, did she say why?" He rose from the chair and resumed pacing.

"I commented that the flowers were pretty, and she gave me a weird look and chucked them," Zana said.

"Maybe, they were from an ex-boyfriend," Ryan said, now worried that his bouquet had joined company with discarded packaging and rotting food in a dumpster.

"That's possible. The subject didn't come up at lunch," Zana said. "As much as Alexia and I are friendly, she's an employee of our firm's client so I try not to say anything inappropriate or too personal."

"Makes sense," he said.

"I'm sorry I can't be more helpful," she said. "If I hear anything, I'll let you know."

"Thanks." Ryan looked at his watch and frowned. He stepped into the bathroom for a quick shave and shower before being blasted in front of millions of television viewers. Maybe, there was another way to get Alexia's attention.

Chapter Twelve

**@ZLaw Early birds are overrated. But if I have to be one,
I'll take gummy worms. #Yawn!**

Zana awoke in the crook of Jerry's arm, trying not to move for fear of waking him. She then noticed a glowing light and realized Jerry was not only awake, but was intently focused on his Kindle.

She yawned. "What time is it?"

"Sorry. I tried to be quiet," he said.

"It's still dark. Do I need to get up and go to work, already?" Zana rubbed her eyes.

"Not yet. It's only two. Go back to sleep," he said softly. "I don't want you dozing at your desk."

"What are you doing up so late?" she asked, staring at his naked body, only partially covered by the sheet. He was wearing his tortoise shell reading glasses, which made him look bookishly sexy.

"I'm still wired. If you hadn't been here, I probably would have gone to 24 Hour Fitness and worked out."

"Don't let me stop you, Jer. I don't mind. I just need a few hours of sleep before going to the office." Zana wished she could take advantage of the naked man next to her. She moved her head onto her own pillow, turning her body away from him and the illuminated screen.

"It's too late already. I've got a client meeting at ten, so I've got to hit the hay." He clicked off his Kindle and placed his reading glasses on the nightstand.

"I feel bad. I don't want to get in the way of your workouts."

"We're on different time zones. It's not a big deal," Jerry said with an edge to his voice. And then he smiled at her. "You're actually a good influence on me. I need to go to bed at a decent time so I can get up early and work out."

"You know what they say about the early bird?" Zana turned towards him.

"He gets eaten?"

"No." She laughed.

"He wins the lottery?" He drew her in and wrapped his arms around her.

"No, silly."

"The early bird gets lots of billable hours, doesn't get fired, becomes partner of her law firm and lives happily ever after," Jerry said, as he kissed her neck.

"Yeah, that's exactly what they say about the early bird," she said. "How did you know?"

"A little bird told me," he said, moving out of their embrace. He pulled the sheet up to his chest and adjusted his pillow. "Let's get some sleep. I want to be an early bird, too—to make Frank happy."

Zana giggled in the dark and adjusted her own pillow before closing her eyes.

***

When Zana left Jerry's house that morning at 5:00 a.m., he was sound asleep. She got dressed in the clothes she had worn the night before, planning to go home, shower and change before she headed to work. She sometimes brought a change of clothes and makeup, but she had been so rushed the morning before, she didn't have time for meticulous planning and packing. She wished he would invite her to leave some of her belongings in a drawer and give her a little space in his closet, but despite her many hints, he'd never offered. The few times she had left a blouse or a hair brush, he had quickly returned them as if they were hot potatoes and would burn his hand if he didn't immediately pass them back to her.

When she got home, she was about to step into the bathroom when she saw a note taped to her bedroom door addressed to her. She unfolded the sheet of yellow lined legal sized paper, and read,

Hi Zana,

I tried to call you, but your phone must have been turned off. All of the litigation attorneys were called in to go back to the office at 3 a.m. to help with motions in limine and memoranda for Frank's trial. When you get this message, come in ASAP!

Andrew

"Shit!" Zana said out loud. She ran into her bedroom and quickly changed into some semi-wrinkled gray pants, a black long sleeved top and a dark gray jacket. Then dashed into the bathroom to brush her teeth and pull her hair into a high ponytail. She grabbed her makeup bag and stuffed it into her briefcase. At least she didn't have to go in wearing one of Jerry's shirts.

As she drove on the H-1 Freeway towards downtown, she noticed there were plenty of other cars on the road trying to beat the usual snarl of traffic as workers headed to their downtown or Waikiki jobs. She took a deep breath, desperately hoping she wouldn't be fired the minute after she walked into her office. She thought about calling Andrew for a heads up on the situation, but worried that Frank would overhear their conversation, didn't bother. It was probably better to show up and hope for the best.

The parking garage was virtually empty. She didn't see Andrew's car, but assumed he had parked on an upper floor. As Zana walked to the elevator, she decided that if she got fired this morning, she would behave as calmly as possible, pack up her belongings and walk out. She wanted to appear dignified so that in this small town where rumors spread as fast as an incoming tsunami, no one could say she wasn't a professional. Maybe, she could get a job working at the Attorney General's Office or at the Office of the Public Defender. She had heard there might be job openings and she had a few acquaintances working in those offices. Her salary would be lower, but she would probably be able to continue living with Andrew and Kelly.

As the elevator reached the 27th floor, Zana's heart raced. She imagined Frank yelling at her and could envision pitiful stares from staff and colleagues. Each attorney who witnessed her being canned would be relieved they weren't on the chopping block themselves.

The door was locked and Zana fumbled for the key card in her purse. She was surprised that the lights were turned off in the reception area. She clicked them on, assuming the litigation attorneys were either working in their offices or had convened in a conference room. She made her way down the hallway and noticed all offices had their lights off. She cautiously opened the large conference room door. It was dark and empty. Andrew wasn't in his office when she walked by his open door, either. Maybe they had finished their work and left, or gone out to breakfast at an all-night eatery.

She saw no sign of life before opening her office door. A large orange envelope with her name on it was placed prominently on her desk. Her hands shook as she opened and read the note inside.

GOTCHA, ZANA! IF YOU ARE READING THIS BEFORE 6 AM, YOU FELL FOR IT. HA HA!!

ANDREW

She laughed out loud and read the note a second time. She smiled and sat in her leather chair, letting her body relax as she imagined Andrew's meticulous planning of this practical joke designed to get even with her for her prank last month. She had told him the court had called with a message that his motion was going to be heard an hour earlier. He had rushed off to court to discover that she had pulled a fast one on him. Zana hadn't done it maliciously. Andrew had been complaining about getting to court only minutes before each appearance, because he never gave himself enough time to walk the half mile to the courthouse, go through security and take the elevators up to the fourth floor. She thought he would learn his lesson if he discovered how much more relaxing it would be to arrive early. Apparently, he had felt a counter move was in order.

As she turned on her computer, she realized the brilliance of Andrew's joke. She had been complaining about not getting in early enough and he had just given her a taste of her own medicine designed to give her a head start on the day. Despite narrowly escaping a massive coronary anticipating Frank's wrath, it felt good to be in the office before daybreak again.

She texted Andrew: **Asshole!** She then followed up with a smiley face emoticon text.

She shut her door, applied make up using a hand mirror and then headed across the street to Starbucks for a Grande latte and oatcake.

After returning to the deserted law firm, she settled in front of her computer to work on the Schubert vs. Peterson case. She first looked over the police report, which only listed her client as a witness. There were almost two thousand participants in the Paradise Lagoons Triathlon with thirty-five professionals vying for the prize money, according to the website. *How could there be no witnesses?* At the very least, she should be able to interview the first responders to the scene.

Zana analyzed the race results, which showed Ryan winning with a time of 1:50:36. Eric Low came in second place, clocking in at 1:51:09; Sam Donahue finished third with a time of 1:51:53; Jeff Paris was fourth at 1:52:46 and Jake Okuda came in fifth at 1:53:05. She then studied the top five triathletes' swim and bike splits to try to figure out who was closest behind Terry and Ryan before the accident.

She was deep in thought when her office phone rang.

"This is Zana West," she said into the landline receiver.

"I'm surprised you're in the office already," a male voice said.

"I did get here quite early," she said, not sure whose voice was on the other end of the phone line.

"I'm still in New York. Did you catch 'The Javier Perez Show' a few nights ago?"

She now recognized Ryan's voice. "I recorded it, but I haven't watched it yet. How did it go?"

"You'll have to judge for yourself. There were no surprises, and the audience gave me more than a smattering of applause," Ryan said.

"Sounds positive," Zana said. "I'm glad you called. I'm looking at the results from Paradise Lagoons Triathlon. I'm trying to figure out who might have witnessed the accident or seen something useful."

"Eric and Sam were on my tail—I'm sure you saw that they placed," Ryan said.

"I did. Jake Okuda came in fifth. Do you know him?" Zana asked.

After a brief pause, Ryan said, "I think he was here from Japan, but I'm not sure. I would probably recognize him if I saw him, but I don't know the name."

"Do you have Eric's, Sam's or Jeff's phone numbers by any chance?" Zana grabbed a pen and legal pad. "I'd like to call them each to find out what they saw, if anything."

"The numbers are on my phone. I'll e-mail them to you. You're wasting your time," Ryan said. "They said they didn't see anything."

Zana hoped they might remember something if pressed. "I'll call them anyway. Do you know how I can get in touch with Jake Okuda?"

"I have no idea," Ryan said. "So, what else is going on? Have you been to F.I.M. lately?"

"If you're wondering about Alexia, I haven't seen or talked to her for a while," Zana said. No other client called as much, so he clearly had an agenda. "When are you coming back to Honolulu?"

"I have some meetings here tomorrow, but I'll be back later in the week."

"We should probably meet again to work on your answers to interrogatories. I haven't sent them to you, because I knew you were out of town."

"Sounds good," Ryan said. "Put in a good word about me to Alexia, will you?"

"I'll do my best." She doubted the adjuster would appreciate her meddling in her love life, but maybe she could bring it up. Ryan seemed like quite a catch.

After she hung up, she finished drinking her latte. Then she called Eric Low, who said he was at work but could talk for a few minutes.

"Where were you when the accident between Terry and Ryan happened?" Zana asked.

"I'm not sure. Ryan was strong on the bike as usual—he blew past me after the swim," Eric said.

"Did you see Terry attempt to pass Ryan?"

"No. I didn't know there was an accident until I rode past Terry while he was on the ground," he said.

"What did you see?" Zana asked.

"Someone lying on the road, surrounded by police officers and race officials. I heard an ambulance. I slowed down a little bit, but I couldn't see who it was," Eric said. "To tell you the truth, I thought it was Ryan because his helmet was on the road."

"Why did you think it was his helmet?" Zana asked.

"I don't know," Eric admitted. "Maybe, his name was on it?"

"What color was it?" She took notes on a legal pad.

"White," he said. "Come to think of it, I remember seeing Ryan's race number on the helmet that I saw."

"Why would you know that?"

"He was number two," Eric said. "Numbers were assigned based on rankings. I was number five."

Zana pulled up the list of competitors and their race numbers to check Eric's memory. "Do you know if anyone witnessed the accident?"

"No one did," he said.

"Why are you so sure?" Zana asked.

"I talk to Jeff and Sam all the time. They didn't see the crash," Eric said. "Ryan was a pro cyclist—he's really fast. Jeff had a flat tire, and Ryan left Sam and I in the dust. We were way back."

"Can you think of anyone who might have seen something?"

"No. I wish I could help. No matter what anyone else says, Ryan is a nice guy," Eric said. "I know he has a lot of enemies, but I actually admire him—he's an amazing cyclist."

"Thanks for your help, Eric," Zana said.

"No problem. And just so you know, Ryan holds his line on the bike. He's not squirrely. I can't imagine him moving into Terry during a pass."

After Zana hung up the phone, she swiveled her chair to face the floor to ceiling window with its view of the Dole pineapple in the distance. She leaned back in her chair and chewed on the end of her pen. From what Ryan and Eric said, none of the top pro triathletes had seen the accident. *Were there any other witnesses?*

Nicki Minaj's "Starships" song—her phone's ring tone for Shelby—interrupted her thoughts.

"Hey," Shelby said. "Moana's birthday is coming up in a few weeks. I thought it would be fun to take her to out for dinner."

"To Alan Wong's?"

"No, we went there last year. What about Hau Tree Lanai?" Shelby said.

"That works for me." Zana swiveled her chair so it faced her computer. "I love that place."

"Okay, I'll ask Moana," Shelby said. "What are you up to today?"

"I'm trying to figure out why no one witnessed the accident between Terry Schubert and Ryan," Zana said, biting on the end of her pen.

"Did you look at the results to see who was behind him?" Shelby asked.

"Yeah—Eric, Sam, Jeff and a guy from Japan. *But*, they didn't see anything." Zana set her pen down and clicked back to the race results page on her computer.

"What about relays? You know how in those races they get the fastest swimmer, cyclist and runner together for a relay and they sometimes do almost as well as the top athletes?"

"Good point, Shelb." Zana clicked onto the relay results. "Maybe, there was a cyclist on a relay who saw the accident. I'll catch you later."

Shelby was right. The top finishing relay was comprised of one of the fastest swimmers in the state, Dustin Severson, whose swim split was faster than the pro triathletes' swim splits. The cyclist on the relay was a local time trial champion, Patrick Jarvis. His bike split was slower than Ryan's, but there was a chance he had seen the accident.

After making a few calls, Zana was able to find someone who had Patrick's cell phone number. Poised to take notes, she identified herself and asked if he had time to answer some questions.

"Sure. I remember that race," Patrick said. "What do you want to know?"

"Did you witness the accident between Terry Schubert and Ryan Peterson?"

"Yeah," Patrick said.

Zana dropped her pen. Bingo! "What did you see?"

"I was riding about eight bike lengths behind Ryan for a few miles, and then Terry passed me. I didn't want to get caught drafting so I dropped back to about three bike lengths behind Terry. After a few minutes, Terry kicked it into gear and was trying to pass Ryan," Patrick said.

Zana could feel her heart pounding in her chest when he paused.

"I don't know what happened, but their handlebars touched and Terry lost control and fell onto the road."

Zana wrote down his words. "Did Ryan do anything to contribute to the accident?"

"Not that I saw. He was riding straight."

Zana smiled and leaned back in her chair.

"When their handlebars touched, Ryan went farther to the right and he looked a little out of control, but he recovered and kept on riding," Patrick said.

"Did you see Terry do anything that contributed to the accident?" Zana asked.

"Well, he tried to pass Ryan. If he hadn't made the attempt, the accident wouldn't have happened."

"Did he ride into Ryan?" Zana asked.

"I guess so," he said. "It was an accident. I wouldn't want to blame either one of them."

"Did you see anything else that you think would be helpful for me to know about?" Zana asked.

"Terry was violating a safety rule."

"Oh?"

"His helmet chin strap was hanging loose—it didn't look like it was buckled," Patrick said, confirming the reason why the helmet had fallen off of Terry's head, causing his head injury and death.

Zana texted Shelby: You rock! Mahalo for the relay tip.

You owe me a lobster dinner. Shelby responded.

How 'bout a Big Mac, instead? Zana laughed.

Chapter Thirteen

@ZLaw Gobble Gobble! #HappyThanksgiving #TurkeyDay I'll wash my pumpkin pie down with wine.

Zana and Shelby pedaled their bikes towards Diamond Head, their silhouettes against the orange glow of the sunrise. The handmade sign announcing the Turkey Day Triathlon directed them to the makeshift transition area set up in the grass near the bandstand at Kapiolani Park. They had texted dozens of messages to each other the day before in an effort to guess how much time it would take for each of them to complete the swim, bike and run segments of the relay. They were hoping to win the race by guessing their split and overall times correctly, with Zana swimming and running and Shelby biking. After Shelby racked her bike in the transition area and Zana locked hers against the fence, they located the registration table.

"We haven't done this race before. What do you want us to do?" Shelby asked the two guys who were wearing "Gobble Gobble" T-shirts, sitting on folding chairs behind the table.

"List your names and time guesses for each segment of the race. I'm Mike by the way," one of the men said, and then he put his hand on the other guy's shoulder. "And, this is Rockstar."

"Oh, nice to meet you. I'm Zana and this is Shelby," Zana said, leaning against the table. "Is there an entry fee?"

"No. This is more of a workout than a race. We don't have any support at all. You're essentially on your own out there, but you do have to sign this liability waiver, since the race is sponsored by Kimo's Dive Shop," Mike said, handing the document to the women.

"Don't forget my company—Freewheel Bicycle Shop and Repairs is also a sponsor," Rockstar said, pointing to his company logo on a sign, which was a freewheel bicycle part.

"Oh, sorry," Mike said. "Freewheel is a new sponsor."

Zana studied the sign. "Isn't that Ryan Peterson's charity?"

"No. That asshole has nothing to do with *my* company." Rockstar raised his voice.

"Oh, sorry. It has a similar name and logo." Zana picked up a pen from the table and signed and dated the form, adding their time guesses that she and Shelby had agreed upon the day before.

"Yeah, tell me about it." Rockstar sighed loudly. Several athletes approached the table, debating what times they should guess.

"You really need to warm up in the water, Zana," Shelby said as they stepped away to walk back to the transition area where they had left their gear.

"Don't forget to take your watch off," Zana said.

"Oh, right." Shelby took her Ironman watch off and tucked it into her bike bag. "I don't want us to get disqualified. Your swim and run times are so predictable that we might have a chance of winning."

"I hope so. There aren't many people here," Zana said as she grabbed her cap and goggles.

"Hey, isn't that Megan Alexander over there?" Shelby asked as they left the transition area and went towards the beach.

"It sure looks like her," Zana said. "She's in amazing shape."

"She's so fast—light years ahead of anyone in our age group," Shelby said, keeping in step with Zana's long strides.

"I know," Zana said. "It hardly seems worth it to put the training in for the Freewheel Tri. She's going to win the Paris trip."

"You never know," Shelby said. "Maybe, she'll get a flat tire or something."

"It would take a lot more than her getting a flat tire for me to win. She'd have to get bitten by a shark, too."

Shelby laughed. "And hit by a bus."

"What are you ladies talking about? It sounds like you're planning on knocking someone off," a familiar voice said from behind them.

Zana turned to see her client. "Oh, hey Ryan."

"No, we're just depressed about Megan being in our age group." Shelby frowned. "We don't stand a chance to win."

"It's all about training. If you get serious, both of you could be contenders." Ryan placed a supportive hand on Shelby's shoulder.

"Well, Zana has a shot. I'm a horrible swimmer," Shelby said as they continued their walk to the beach with Ryan in step beside them.

"Welcome to my world," he said. "I guess you're doing the swim leg, Zana?"

"Yeah," she said, holding up the cap and goggles in her hand. "And the run. Who's in your relay?"

"I'm not doing the race; I'm helping out one of the sponsors," Ryan said.

"Must be the dive shop, because I understand that guy Rockstar is not a big fan of yours," Zana said, turning to look at her client.

"Oh, yeah." Ryan shrugged. "He can join the crowd. I'm lucky to have any fans with all of the trouble I seem to get myself into these days."

"Well, I'm a fan." Zana smiled.

Ryan laughed. "Well, you have to be—you're my attorney," he said as they stepped onto the sandy beach.

"Oh, that's right," Zana said. "Actually, I don't think you're half-bad."

"Tell that to Alexia." Ryan bent down to pick up a stone and toss it into the ocean.

"Zana, you better get in the water. I don't know what time it is, but you need to warm up," Shelby said.

"Relax," Ryan said. "This race is low key. We're going to be doing a group warm up—Gobble Gobble style—at the bandstand, and then everyone will go to the water together for a swim warm up."

"Are you kidding?" Zana rolled her eyes. "I guess we walked over here for nothing."

"Zana, I know you're a type A plus personality, but this is a fun morning. It's not a real race," he said, leading them back to the transition area. "I remember running the Helsinki Marathon years ago and before the race, everyone did aerobics to warm up. This will be similar. You'll see."

"That's totally awesome." Shelby smiled.

"You'll need some athletic shoes for the warm up, unless you want to do it in your bare feet," he said, looking down at Zana's feet.

"For the record, Ryan, I'm *not* a type A plus personality," Zana said, her brow furrowed. "I do like to have fun."

"The fact that you had to put that on the record proves my point," Ryan said, grinning.

"If you weren't my client, I'd sock you in the arm," Zana said as they approached the transition area.

"I hate to interrupt your attorney-client discussion, but does my tire look flat to you?" Shelby gestured to her bike racked alongside a few dozen other bikes.

Ryan reached down and pressed on the tire. "I'll change it for you, if you'd like."

"That would be great—I'm sure you can change a bicycle tire much faster than me, having been a pro cyclist and all." Shelby winked at Ryan.

He pulled the wheel off and in a few minutes expertly patched the hole in the tube. After he placed the repaired tube back in the tire, he tried using Shelby's small bicycle pump to inflate it.

"Your pump isn't working very well. Why don't you take this to Freewheel's truck over there," Ryan said, pointing to where Rockstar and two other guys with Gobble Gobble T-shirts were working on bikes under a small canopy covering. "I'd go myself, but as Zana said, Rockstar isn't a fan."

"I'll go with you," Zana said, following behind Shelby, who pushed her bike towards the canopy.

"Hurry, the warm up is going to start in about ten minutes," Ryan called after them.

They walked the remaining steps to the bicycle repair station and Shelby asked, "Excuse me, Rockstar, do you mind pumping my tire?"

"Sure. Hey Nick, can you pump this tire?" Rockstar took Shelby's bike from her and wheeled it a few feet towards one of his helpers, kneeling down pumping up another bicycle tire.

"Just curious, but why are you called Rockstar?" Zana asked.

"Well," he grinned, "my real name is Howard Hara. About ten years ago, I sang in a rock band. The name Howard doesn't exactly sound like Mick Jagger or Freddie Mercury, so my band started calling me Rockstar and the name stuck."

"Do you still sing?" Shelby asked.

"Nah." Rockstar shrugged his skinny shoulders and adjusted his hat. "I'm just a bike mechanic now."

"You seem to be doing okay for yourself," Zana said.

"Not really. The economy hit us really hard. My shop hasn't sold many new bikes in the past few years and we've been struggling." Rockstar pulled a tire off a rim.

"Oh, sorry to hear that," Zana said.

"You're all set," Nick said as he rolled Shelby's bike to her.

"Do I owe you anything?" Shelby asked.

"Just a kiss," Nick said, laughing. "Kidding!"

"We volunteer and sponsor events so we can get the name Freewheel out there," Rockstar said. "My shop is on Keeaumoku Street. You should stop by."

Zana gave him a look. "Isn't that where the strip clubs are?"

"Yeah." Nick raised his eyebrows. "It's a great location."

Shelby laughed. "Let's get over to the bandstand, Zana. It looks like they're about ready to start the warm up."

When Shelby and Zana reached the bandstand, about thirty people were doing aerobics moves and singing their own words to a familiar song:

> *"Oppa is Gobble style, Gobble style*
> *Oppa is Gobble style, Gobble style*
> *Oppa is Gobble style*
> *Eh— Juicy Turkey, Oppa is Gobble style*
> *Eh— Juicy Turkey oh oh oh oh"*

Shelby and Zana joined in, imitating the moves of the three fit young women leading the group on stage who were wearing Gobble Gobble T-shirts. Zana tried to conserve her energy, knowing she would be swimming 600 meters in a few minutes and then running a 5k after Shelby was done biking. Her split time estimates didn't take into account getting tired out from aerobic exercise before the race. When she looked around her, she noticed that everyone was smiling and laughing—having a great time. She wondered if Ryan was right. *Did her A plus personality make her boring? Maybe, that's why Jerry hadn't said I love you yet.*

"Eh, Juicy Turkey!" Shelby shouted and wiggled her hips to the music.

Zana tried to follow along, but couldn't focus as she ruminated on her relationship with Jerry. Once she locked into a problem, it was hard to shake it from her mind. This was going to bug her all day, and possibly, mess up her Thanksgiving. She was joining Moana's family for the holiday meal, since Jerry and his parents had flown to San Diego to spend the long weekend with his sister, Jenny, and her family. Zana had been invited, but couldn't go because Frank required all associates to work Friday and Saturday.

After the Gobble Gobble song, the triathletes collected their gear and headed to the water for a group warm up in the ocean—another unprecedented activity before a race. Zana wished she could do her pre-race swim alone and focus on getting her head right. Her shoulders felt tense as her mind swirled with insecurities about her relationship.

She thought back to the week before when she had slammed the door to her office after Frank had smugly refused her request to leave early on the Wednesday before Thanksgiving so she could spend the holiday in San Diego. He then circulated a memo to all associates announcing that they would be expected to put in a full day of work on Cold Turkey Day and gather for a meeting on Saturday morning. For the first time, she considered quitting, but then she remembered her student loans. Andrew's plans of going to New York to see his family had also been ruined. Usually, the firm was closed the Friday and Saturday after Thanksgiving. They both suspected that Zana's request for time off had given Frank an opportunity to make her life miserable at the expense of the other associates.

After the starting gun went off, Zana began her long freestyle strokes. She was still mulling over her problems and began veering off course away from the other swimmers. She didn't realize she'd run into the reef until her hand slammed against it, causing her to feel instant pain and jolt her face out of the water. Because it was more of a workout than a race, there were no lifeguards on watercraft monitoring the event. She lifted her right hand and grimaced at the gash oozing blood. She treaded water using her legs and her left arm, and wondered if she should continue swimming.

"Zana, are you okay?" a voice from behind her shouted.

She turned to see Ryan swimming towards her with his head up.

"What happened?" he asked as he reached her.

"I hit the coral really hard." Zana showed him her bleeding hand, which he examined while treading water next to her.

"Let's get you back to shore for medical attention," Ryan said. "I saw you charge off towards the coral and decided to swim out here to get you back on course. I don't have a board. Can you do some slow side strokes back to the beach?"

She nodded.

They began swimming slowly back to shore, facing each other as Zana held her bloody hand out of the water. "I hope Shelby isn't too pissed off at me."

"She'll be fine. This race is no big deal," Ryan said. "You might need to go to the ER to get your hand scrubbed. You don't want an infection."

"I'm sure it'll be fine," Zana said. "I'll wash the blood off with hydrogen peroxide and put some bacitracin cream on it."

"Your call," Ryan said as they approached the beach. "But if it gets bad, you have to promise me you'll go see a doctor."

"I will," Zana said. "You're more like Superman than the evil guy described in the tabloids."

"Where are the paparazzi when I'm doing a kind deed?" Ryan said as he helped her out of the water. "See, they're nowhere in sight. If I get caught doping or someone dies in a triathlon, they're swarming around me taking the most unflattering pictures."

"Well—you're my hero," Zana said as she inspected her hand. "Shelby is probably waiting in the transition area with her bike, wondering why I haven't finished such a short and easy swim. Let's give her the bad news."

"Zana," Shelby called, walking towards them on the beach. "What's going on? Are you alright?"

"Sorry." Zana held up her bloody hand and Ryan took off in a sprint towards the registration table.

Shelby gasped. "Oh, my God! Should I call an ambulance?"

"Not necessary." Zana felt a wave of dizziness and sat down on the sand. "It's worse than I thought."

As they examined her hand, Ryan returned with a first aid kit. After he put gloves on, he pressed gauze against the gash.

"Ryan, did you bring an SUV?" Shelby asked as she assisted by cutting tape.

Zana felt woozy when she saw the blood soak through the bandages.

"Yeah. Let's load your bikes and get Zana home," Ryan said.

Shelby shook her head. "She needs to go to the ER."

"But she doesn't want to," Ryan said.

"I'll go." Zana closed her eyes tightly. The wound was worse than she initially thought. At least, if she had it cleaned and dressed by a doctor, she would have a better chance of showing up to work the next day. It would look suspicious if she called in sick on a day when she and all of the other associates were forced to work because of her "audacity" to ask for an afternoon off.

Fifteen minutes later, the three sat in the hospital emergency department's reception area, waiting for Zana's turn, which was delayed because of a heart attack sufferer, a near drowning victim, and a few who sustained injuries from a car accident. A coral cut was apparently on the lowest rung of the triage ladder. Since they hadn't taken time to change, Zana and Ryan were both wearing their bathing suits and Gobble Gobble T-shirts, and

Shelby was wearing her pink biking jersey and black padded biking shorts. They focused on their smart phones, leaving the old magazines piled on the side tables untouched.

Zana read a text from Jerry, wishing her a happy Thanksgiving. She was able to use her left hand to text back, but decided to omit the fact that she was spending the day in the ER. He seldom had time to see his younger sister, nieces and nephew and she didn't want to be a disruption.

"You can go," Zana said after they had been waiting for over an hour. "I'll be fine by myself. I can take an Uber when I'm done."

"Are you sure?" Shelby asked. "I promised to help my sister make pumpkin pies."

"Go ahead and drive Shelby home, Ryan. I'm fine," Zana said, looking up from her phone.

"I can ride my bike," Shelby said. "I'll help Shauna and then come back."

"No need," Ryan said. "I'll stay with Zana and drive her home when she's finished."

"You really don't have to do that," Zana protested.

Ryan put his hand on her shoulder. "Shhh. Not another word. I'm a gentleman. I would never leave you here on your own."

After Ryan and Shelby left to get her bike from his SUV, Zana scrolled through Instagram. By the time a nurse wearing scrubs with a festive turkey print walked into the waiting room to check on some of the patients on the triage list, Ryan was back and sitting next to her.

"Ryan Peterson?" the nurse asked.

"Yes," he looked up. "Hey. How are you?"

"You're here again," the nurse said, tapping her clipboard with a pen.

"I know," he said. "I'm getting to be a regular."

"Do you get hurt a lot?" Zana lifted her eyebrows.

"No. Ryan has a habit of accompanying injured athletes here. We see him every month or two," the nurse said. "So what happened?"

Zana extended her hand. "Just a coral cut. Ryan insisted I come to the ER rather than try to clean it myself."

"Smart move. Once it gets infected, it can be nasty," the nurse said. "I'll take you back now. Ryan, are you going to come in here with your girlfriend, or do you want to stay out here?"

"Oh… Ryan's not my boyfriend," Zana said. She didn't think it was necessary to explain that he was actually her client. "Do you want to come back?"

"That's okay. I'll wait out here if you don't mind," he said and returned to his seat.

After Zana's hand was thoroughly cleaned, examined and dressed, Ryan drove her to her home.

"I'm so sorry. I probably screwed up your Thanksgiving plans today," Zana said when they were approaching Kahala.

"Not a problem." Ryan smiled. "I'm happy to help."

"I can ask Moana if you can come to her house for dinner. It's a big family. I'm sure they won't mind another person."

"That's nice of you to offer, but I think I'll go for a long bike ride and then talk to my parents on Skype. We've got some planning meetings for the Freewheel Movement Triathlon this weekend, so I decided to stay on Oahu," Ryan said.

"Okay. If you change your mind, text me."

"I noticed that you haven't signed up for the Freewheel Tri yet."

"I haven't decided whether I'm up for all that training." She furrowed her brow. "I'd like to spend time with Jerry."

"You can't put your life on hold for a guy who wasn't even here for you today," Ryan said as he pulled into the driveway. "You've got to live your own life."

"I know." Zana nodded. "Thanks for helping me out today. I really appreciate it."

Ryan unloaded her bike from the back of his SUV and gave her a warm hug.

She waved goodbye with her good hand and then entered the empty house. Her roommates must have already left to spend the holiday at Kelly's cousin's house and so Zana wrapped her injured hand in plastic and slipped into a hot bubble bath. As she was soaking, she wondered whether Ryan was right. Maybe, she should focus on training and let Jerry wait around for her. Before she could spend more time developing that thought, her iPhone resting on the toilet seat rang.

"Hi Jerry," Zana said, putting the phone on its speaker function and placing it back on the commode.

"I miss you, sweetheart!" Jerry said.

"I miss you, too." Zana smiled and sank back into the tub.

Chapter Fourteen

@FreewheelMV Plan B: Play it cool. Be #Antarctica

Bud's office was his sanctuary. His wife, Sandy, a card carrying PETA member, refused to set foot inside. She detested the beheaded animals mounted on almost every square inch of the room's walls, but wisely kept her complaints to herself. He had been hunting wild game since he was a boy, living on the two thousand acre cattle and hunting ranch in Lytle, Texas, which had been in his family for three generations. Bud grew up hunting white-tailed deer, wild turkey and feral hog.

While the couple dated as students at Southwestern University, Sandy seemed to support Bud's infrequent opportunities to hunt when he was not busy with his business school studies. Her passion for protecting animals began after they moved to Hawaii and his business ventures grew profitable enough, so she was able to quit working as a dental hygienist and be a full time mother. For the sake of their marriage, she tolerated Bud's bi-annual hunting trips to Alaska, Montana and Texas. He agreed to keep his trophies either at work or in his home office, and she agreed not to complain about them. This was one of the secrets to their long and happy marriage.

As Bud sat at his desk, which was as large as most people's dining room tables, he ignored the almost fifty pairs of eyes that seemed to watch over his business dealings from up on the walls. His focus was on the newspaper in front of him. The article quoted Harold Van de Carr, who had bought a large parcel of property from Schubert Enterprises last year, claiming failure to disclose drainage problems, which ultimately led to property damage from flooding. Bud slammed the newspaper on his desk after he read the part about Van de Carr threatening to file a lawsuit, and snatched the wireless phone out of its charger.

"I need you to take care of Harold Van de Carr," Bud said into the phone to his right hand man—Eddie.

"Done," Eddie said and hung up.

Bud refused to put up with nonsense. He had made his fortune and now spent his time and money protecting it, his company's reputation and his family. He had no tolerance for threats. He was well aware that some of his adversaries called him the J.R. Ewing of Honolulu, comparing him to the tough-negotiating, empire-building oil baron on his favorite show from the 1980s, *Dallas*. Bud didn't mind the comparison and often imitated the character's swagger, but rarely wore his boots and cowboy hat in Hawaii.

His attitude about his lawsuit against Ryan Peterson was fueled by the same venom he had when other people crossed him. Now that Bud was in his office, away from his wife and grandchildren, he could review his attorney's status reports. Before Preston Farnsworth, III was transferred to the litigation department of his law firm, he had handled most of Schubert Enterprise's business dealings. Now, Preston was brought on board to file and defend the company's lawsuits, which were many. He was trustworthy.

Bud wasn't a fan of his attorney's lifestyle, but felt that Preston was the perfect attorney to avenge his son's death. Several months before Terry died, he had confided to his father that he was gay. Bud's first reaction was anger and disbelief, but he soon realized that it wasn't Terry's choice—he was finally admitting the sexual orientation he was born with. As Bud reflected on the last few months of Terry's life, he remembered the time when they had hiked up to the top of Diamond Head, and as they enjoyed the spectacular view of Honolulu, he told his son that he accepted him just the way he was. He loved him no matter what.

Sandy, the rock in Bud's life, admitted that she had known Terry was gay for several years before he had the courage to tell his father the year before his death. When she saw Bud brooding while cleaning his rifle, she had ignored his rules and stomped into the garage to insist he fully support his son and not treat him any differently. He gave her a warm hug and as always, said, "Yes, dear."

Bud picked up the photograph on his desk of Terry wearing one of the many first place medals he won as a teenager. His chest tightened and he felt tears welling in his eyes. If it weren't for Sandy's strength of character and power of persuasion, he might have turned his back on Terry and missed out on his final months. He smiled at his son's picture and placed it gently on his desk. He sighed as he remembered Terry calling him his best friend when he chose to hang out with him, rather than join his friends one afternoon a few weeks before he passed away.

How dare that doper Ryan Peterson get away with murdering my son! Bud kicked the leg of the desk hard with his slippered foot and then screamed out in pain. "Fuck!" He scrunched up his face, grabbed the trophy of a whitetail deer off the wall and threw it with such force it slammed into an elk mounted above the television. Peterson would pay.

***

Ryan sipped coffee at an outside cafe table located adjacent to the F.I.M. building. He had arrived home from New York the day before and was hoping to accidentally run into Alexia. His eyes, shaded by Oakley sunglasses, read each section of the Honolulu Star Advertiser slowly, barely comprehending the meaning of the words. He hadn't thought of what he would say during his planned chance meeting, but he hoped his body language, sincerity, and maybe even his pheromones would win Alexia over and she'd agree to spend time with him.

Anyone walking by with blonde hair drew Ryan's attention from his newspaper. After nearly ninety minutes of false alarms, he was almost ready to give up when he saw her. She was wearing an emerald green jersey dress that hugged her shapely figure with that odd-looking polka dot cotton scarf draped around her neck, as if she was trying to cover up any visible cleavage. She passed him, heading in the direction of the sushi restaurant on the corner.

"Hey, Alexia," Ryan said loudly.

She didn't respond, so he leapt to his feet, walking quickly to catch up with her.

"Alexia," Ryan said again when he was a step behind her.

"Hello," she said without even turning her head to look at him.

"It's me—Ryan. Ryan Peterson."

"Oh, hi," Alexia said, slowing down and turning to him. "I didn't recognize you with sunglasses on."

"I just happened to be here to meet with a business colleague," Ryan said, realizing that when he said it out loud, his words sounded fraudulent.

"Oh, right." She fished in her purse and pulled out some Maui Jim sunglasses and slipped them on.

"I have tickets to Sei Bombay at the Blaisdell on Saturday. Would you like to join me?" Ryan asked. He hadn't actually bought any tickets, but saw an advertisement for the concert in today's paper. His friend who worked for a ticket broker could probably arrange for good seats.

"No thank you," Alexia said, resuming her quick pace and walking past the sushi restaurant.

"Why?" Ryan lengthened his stride. "Don't you like Sei Bombay?"

"I adore her," Alexia said. "She's one of my favorite singers."

"Then, why don't you want to go?" Ryan felt sweat beading on his forehead.

"I just don't."

"If I was one of your girlfriends and offered to go with you to the concert and pay for your ticket, would you say yes?" Ryan asked.

Alexia shrugged. "Yeah—in a heartbeat."

"Why don't you just pretend that I'm one of your girlfriends and we can go together. No strings attached," Ryan offered.

"I don't think that'll work." Alexia shook her head.

"I don't see why not. I won't make any moves on you. We can talk and enjoy the concert. If you want, you can meet me there," Ryan said. "I won't even buy you dinner. We'll just go to the concert and then you can go home, if that would make you feel more comfortable."

Alexia stopped in her tracks. She was silent for a few moments and then breathed, "Okay."

"Great!" Ryan beamed. "I'll meet you by the ticket kiosk outside the Blaisdell Arena at seven-thirty—the concert starts at eight," Ryan said.

"I'll see you then." Alexia frowned and walked away.

Ryan tossed the newspaper he was carrying into the trash and headed to his car. As he climbed into his Land Rover, he gave the woman who looked to be as old as his mother entering the car next to his a big smile. She looked a little embarrassed, perhaps misunderstanding its' meaning.

"You look happy," the woman said.

"I am. I finally talked a beautiful woman into going out with me," he said, pleased to tell anyone about his coup.

"That's wonderful. I hope you enjoy yourselves," the woman said politely before pulling her car door closed.

As soon as Ryan got home, he called his friend, who was able to sell him two tickets five rows from the stage for a steep price. Although Ryan was excited to spend an evening with Alexia, he felt more anxious than he had years ago when he scored a date with the head cheerleader for his first high school dance. This felt different, though. His feelings for Alexia seemed more real—almost serious. He might have met his future wife and if he blew this opportunity, another one might not come along. There was only one person he knew who could advise him.

"Hi Dad," Ryan said after his father answered the phone.

"Ryan—I wasn't expecting you to call so soon after Thanksgiving. What's going on?"

"I'm trying to make up for all of the time we've missed," Ryan said, feeling guilty for not calling home much in the past six months because he was too busy or not in the mood to talk.

"That's great, son. It seems like we see you a lot with all of your television appearances," his father said. "As I mentioned a few days ago, your mother and I have had to record them. We can't stay up to watch those late night shows."

"Yeah, I get it. Have you caught up on any more of the shows since Thanksgiving?" Ryan asked.

"Well, we watched that fellow Javier Perez. Your mother and I wish these talk show hosts would spend more time discussing your Freewheel Movement and less time on your past..." he paused, "...difficulties."

"I agree. My agent has made some effort to limit their questioning, but hasn't been successful."

"You need a new agent," his father said.

Ryan sat down on his couch and put his bare feet on the coffee table. "I agree. Actually, I am looking for a new agent. I would prefer to have a Hawaii agent who I can trust. I've gone through three in L.A., and they either don't understand the business of triathlon or they don't seem to be acting in my best interests."

"Son, I know you didn't call me to discuss your agent. What's wrong? I can tell from your voice that you want to talk about something."

"You know me too well." Ryan peeled the paper off of the water bottle he was drinking. "I met a girl."

"That's great, Ryan. When can we meet her?"

"It's not like that. Alexia is amazing, but she's turned me down every time I've asked her out until today. She finally agreed to go to a concert with me."

"How wonderful!"

From the sound of his dad's voice, Ryan imagined him jumping up and down.

"Not really. She wouldn't accept unless I promised we'd go as friends," Ryan said. "I adore her, but I don't know what to do."

"Play it cool, Ryan," his father said. "Knowing you, you've been giving her the full court press. Am I right?"

Ryan swallowed hard. "Yeah. I sent her flowers and I've asked her out a few times."

"Son, you're a famous athlete. There's no reason to grovel. Just calm down. Be yourself," his father advised. "If she senses you're relaxed at the concert, she might let her guard down."

"Good point. I have to admit, I'm overbearing at times." Ryan sighed.

"Maybe you need to be friends for a while so you earn her trust."

"Yeah, that's not a bad idea. The problem is that she's so dismissive. She declines every invitation as if she's on automatic pilot."

"She sounds like your mother when I first met her," his father said. "I know you've heard this story a thousand times, but it might be helpful for me to remind you that when I first met her, she was dating Bruce Livingston, our junior class president. He wasn't much to look at, but was really smart and her parents approved of him. I became obsessed with her. I even slipped notes in her locker and waited for her after class, hoping to walk her home."

"And then, on the day Bruce broke up with her to date Greta Faber, you consoled her. And then you and Mom became an item," Ryan said, recounting the details of the story he'd heard his parents tell many times before.

"There's more to the story. She turned me down flat for at least a month when I asked her out on dates. She was actually rude and dismissive. Just like your Alexia sounds," his father explained.

"How did you eventually win her over?" Ryan asked.

"I was relentless. Finally, she agreed to go to a school dance with me. My father told me to play it cool and not seem too eager. He was right. When I was more relaxed and wasn't so pushy, she was more interested."

"So, the secret is to play it cool, huh?"

"That's the secret," his father said.

"It's worth a try." Ryan sighed. "Nothing else has worked."

After he clicked off his phone, Ryan stepped into his garage half-filled with gym equipment. As he curled a 20 pound weight, he thought about his dad's advice. How could he "play it cool" with such a stunning woman? Since she had completely rebuffed his compliments and attention, it was worth trying another tactic—just as he would in a race if he fell behind his competitors. He despised relationship gamesmanship, but she was so elusive, what other choice did he have? He'd play it cool even if his first inclination was to hump her leg like a dog.

For the next few days, Ryan spent most of his time swimming, biking and running as he always did when he wasn't traveling to promote Freewheel. Whenever he was home, he worked on the movement's social media marketing, responded to e-mails, and returned phone calls. Now, he was also working with his agent to finalize a few sponsorship deals and a cameo appearance on "The Big Bang Theory" in a few weeks.

By the time Saturday arrived, he was ready to put his dad's advice to the test. He dressed play-it-cool casual—in jeans and a black T-shirt, and showed up at the ticket kiosk a couple minutes late so he wouldn't appear too eager. Alexia was waiting for him, wearing a short black skirt, a silky red top and a long necklace with a Christmas stocking pendant, a nod to the upcoming holiday.

"Hey, Ryan. I'm glad you're here." Alexia's face seemed to light up the moment she saw him. "I got here about fifteen minutes early and wondered if I'd gotten our meeting place or the time wrong."

"No, you got it right. How're you doing?" Ryan asked, feeling his heart race. He decided against kissing Alexia on the cheek in order to stay completely in the friend zone, and was surprised when she initiated a cheek kiss while standing on her tiptoes.

"I've seen a few people I know," Alexia said. "Everyone in Honolulu seems to be here."

"Shall we go inside?" Ryan said, still blushing after Alexia's kiss. He was tempted to put his hand on her back, but kept reciting his "be cool" mantra in his head, and instead, shoved his hands into his jeans pockets to avoid temptation. Ryan led the way to the short line of concert goers waiting to hand their tickets to Blaisdell employees who were randomly searching attendees' bags.

"I hope they don't search my bag—I didn't realize we couldn't pack heat," Alexia whispered into Ryan's ear.

"Are you kidding?" Ryan asked, alarmed.

"Jus' playin' with you," she said. "Did you think I was serious?"

He laughed and shook his head. She was not only beautiful, but had a sense of humor, too. "I don't know you well enough yet. You could be armed."

"There's a lot you don't know about me," she said, playfully putting her hand on his bicep as they walked towards their seats.

"Play it cool," Ryan said out loud and then realized that Alexia had heard what he intended as his silent mantra.

"What?" Alexia asked. "I'm sorry, what were you saying?"

"Nothing." He blushed.

"You said 'play it cool'. I'm not sure what you mean," she said. "I'll try not to be so hyper. I don't go out much, and so this is a treat for me."

"No, I didn't mean to tell you to play it cool," he stammered. "I was talking to myself."

"Okay," she shrugged. "Do you do that a lot?"

"No. Let's rewind to *before* I foolishly talked to myself," he said and then made an attempt to change the subject. "Have you seen Sei Bombay in concert before?"

"No."

"What's your favorite song of hers?" Ryan asked, hoping she would return to her playful mood.

"I like 'Runaway'."

"Isn't that the one with Jay-Z?"

She nodded.

"I love that song." He smiled. "I also like 'Ruby'."

"Are you kidding me? I can't stand that song. It's so annoying," she said, making a face. "Every time I hear it on the radio, I turn the channel."

"What don't you like about it?" Ryan asked as they made their way to their seats near the front.

"She repeats 'Ruby red' over and over again—it's annoying," she said as Ryan motioned her to her seat close to the stage.

"I agree, but if you listen to the rest of the words, it's not too bad," he said.

"If you say so," she said. "I'll try to listen to the words."

"Or, you can go to the concession area during that song," he said, tempted to reach out and put his hand on hers. Instead, he asked, "Would you like a beer or something to eat?"

"I've eaten and I don't drink alcohol."

"Me neither," Ryan said, surprised. "I rarely meet anyone else who doesn't drink. Is it because of your religion?"

"No, I work out a lot and it feels like empty, unhealthy calories so I just don't," Alexia explained.

"That's so cool. I don't drink for that very reason," he said, delighted they had found some common ground. "There are a lot of other professional athletes who don't drink alcohol. I used to put harmful substances in my body to give me an edge. Now, I'm more about not ingesting anything bad."

"Yeah, I heard about your PED issues," she said. "I hope you don't think I'm rude for bringing it up."

"If you didn't, that would be unusual. It seems like whatever I do, I'll always be known for what I did when I was twenty-two years old," he said.

"I'm sorry. I didn't mean to make you feel bad," Alexia said softly.

"That's okay. I'm used to it." He sighed. "It was a troubling time in my life that I'd like to put behind me. I wish I could somehow change my identity to be a different person. That would be the only way I could escape the poor choices I made when I was so young and didn't know any better."

"I totally know what you mean," Alexia said, looking Ryan squarely in the eyes for the first time.

He grinned, feeling a connection with her that he hadn't felt with a woman for a long time. If Alexia had agreed to a date, rather than spending the evening with him as a friend, he would put his arm around her and draw her close for a kiss. He was reluctant to make a misstep, especially since it seemed like he had broken down a wall between them.

Sei Bombay started the concert with the song "Ruby". Although Ryan whispered to Alexia that she could leave, she shook her head and gave him a big smile.

Chapter Fifteen

@ZLaw My friends think I'm a #cow. Stop being a cow? Or, get new friends? Hmmm…

After fourteen texts between them, the three friends finally decided on Brasserie du Vin for dinner to celebrate Moana's birthday. When she arrived, Zana found Shelby and Moana tapping away at their smart phones at one of the coveted umbrella shaded tables surrounded by exposed brick walls that looked more like Marseille than Honolulu's Chinatown. Half empty glasses of champagne and a partially eaten brie and fruit plate were on the white table cloth along with a small, black Alex and Ani handle bag stuffed with gold tissue paper.

Zana had hoped to be on time for once, but Frank was lurking in the hallway, talking to Libby. She didn't dare sneak past him. After he disappeared into his office, she staged her desk to look like she had popped over to Starbucks for a coffee to fuel a late night of legal research. She hid her gift and card for Moana in her largest handbag.

"Sorry I'm late," Zana said. "It's been a rough day."

"What else is new?" Shelby looked up from her phone. "I'm glad you made it. We were about to order our *moules frites* without you."

"Happy Birthday!" Zana hugged Moana and then fished into her bag for the gift.

"Mahalo!" Moana beamed.

Zana plopped into a chair and sighed loudly.

"You look like you could use a glass of champagne." Shelby signaled for the waiter.

Zana rolled her eyes. "I could use a bottle of champagne with a straw."

"A bottle?" the waiter, who looked more like a local guy from Kalihi than a Frenchman, asked when he approached.

"A glass of the happy hour champagne, please," Zana said.

"And three orders of *moules frites*," Shelby added.

"What happened?" Moana stashed her phone into her purse.

Zana leaned forward and talked in a low voice. "Remember Cole

Maddox? He's that super cute associate at my firm."

"I remember. We met him out drinking one night. You brought Cole and Prince Harry," Moana said, referring to the attorney with the flame red hair who looked like an heir to the British monarch.

"You mean Rex. That's right." Zana paused as the waiter placed a glass of champagne before her. "Cole was fired today."

"OMG!" Shelby said loudly, attracting stares from other patrons. "Why?"

"Shhhhh!" Zana looked around to see if she recognized anyone in the small courtyard. "His secretary sent a document for filing to the First Circuit Court in Honolulu that should have been sent to the Fifth Circuit Court on Kauai."

"How was that Cole's fault?" Moana asked.

"I have no idea," Zana said softly. "Each attorney is responsible for everything their secretary does."

"Did his secretary get fired?" Shelby asked.

"No. Bethany is such an airhead. I can't believe that her idiotic mistake got him canned," Zana grimaced. "I wonder if Frank was planning on firing him anyway, and her error gave him an excuse."

"Well, I hope you have a competent secretary," Shelby said, as she dipped a piece of baguette into a mixture of extra virgin olive oil and balsamic vinegar.

"Sylvia's anal about everything," Zana said. "She was out on sick leave quite a while for carpel tunnel surgery, but now that she's back and typing again, she produces her usual perfect work. She checks everything about five times before it goes out."

"That's good," Moana said. "I'm worried about you, Zana."

"I'll be all right." Zana sipped champagne.

"I'm worried about you, too," Shelby said as the waiter delivered their *moules frites*—mussels topped with French fries.

"It's not that bad. My hand is almost healed. I'll probably take the bandage off tomorrow," Zana said, holding up her hand.

"That's not what we mean, Zana." Moana put her fork down. "You work for Amanda Priestley in a Frank Gravelle suit."

Zana laughed at the reference from the movie, *The Devil Wears Prada*. "Good one. Don't worry about me. I just have to bill a lot of hours."

"I'm concerned about your relationship with Jerry," Shelby said.

"I don't know what you mean," Zana said, gulping the champagne now. "Everything is great. Please don't worry about me. I'm a big girl and fine taking care of myself."

"He has such a ladies' man reputation," Shelby said, carefully prying a mussel out of its' shell with a tiny fork. "He could be playing you."

Zana shook her head. "Jerry loves me. He wouldn't do that."

"Has he said so?" Shelby asked.

"Not yet—but, we've only been dating for six months." Zana popped a

French fry into her mouth and then said with her mouth full, "His actions show his love. I don't need words."

"He's getting the milk for free without having to buy the cow." Shelby gave Zana a knowing look.

"Excuse me?" Zana asked. "Am I the cow in this scenario?"

"'Why buy the cow when you can get the milk for free' refers to girls who put out without demanding commitment." Moana sighed.

"I know what it means." Zana shook her head. "Do you think any guy our age will date us if we refuse to have sex with him?"

"Very few. The problem is that you're way too easy for Jerry," Shelby said, pouring catsup onto her fries. "He might get bored."

"You think I'm boring?" Zana raised a brow.

"You're wonderful," Moana said. "It's just that Jerry is used to a rainbow of flavors and even though you're delicious chocolate chip mint, he enjoys some rocky road, strawberry cheesecake and mango sorbet."

Shelby nodded. "Have you agreed not to see other people?"

"Jerry's my boyfriend. We see each other almost every day," Zana said. "I have my own director's chair on the set. Kenny, the producer, gave it to me—sort of as a joke."

"Does it say Zana West on it?" Moana asked.

"No." Zana gulped the rest of her champagne. "It says Jerry's Other Half."

"So, any woman could sit in the chair." Shelby put her fork down next to her bowl filled with empty mussel shells. "Are you sure you're the only one who uses it?"

"That's ridiculous," Zana raised her voice.

Moana put her finger to her mouth to signal her friend to talk softly.

"Kenny bought the chair for me," Zana whispered.

"He bought it, but what does Jerry think about it?" Moana asked.

"Come on, you guys," Zana said. "Can we change the subject?"

"We can, but you might consider playing hard to get until Jerry says those three special words." Shelby put her hand on Zana's for a moment.

Zana blinked back tears at her friend's soft touch.

"I'll take it under advisement." Zana leaned back in her chair, took her hand back, and pushed her bowl full of mussel shells away from her. She managed a thin smile, but felt like running out of the restaurant. Not only was her friend, Cole, fired today, her best girlfriends had questioned her relationship. Even though it was less than a week since she had considered being less available to Jerry, it seemed different when others brought up the subject. She hated feeling defensive. She felt the urge to convince her girlfriends that she was in a lasting fairy tale relationship.

Shelby and Moana did as Zana asked and shifted the conversation away from her to their usual fall back talk of triathlon training. They discussed how many hours and miles they swam, biked and ran, future races, equipment, and other triathletes as they always did. Zana's non-triathlete friends usually yawned whenever they were privy to this non-stop talk, but her athlete friends were captivated. Multi-sport was their religion and lifestyle. If she didn't have the challenges of her budding legal career and her relationship with Jerry, she doubted their conversations would ever venture away from the sport. After having suffered from her friends' intrusive questioning, she was content with mind-numbing triathlon chatter and pretended to pay attention.

After Moana opened her presents—an Ironman hat from Zana and an Alex and Ani gold swimmer bracelet from Shelby—they shared a chocolate soufflé and drank cappuccinos before Zana said goodbye. She walked back to her office to straighten her desk and turn off the light. Afterwards, she decided to drive home rather than to Jerry's house to slip into his bed as she usually did. She couldn't help but wonder if her friends were right. Maybe, she needed to play games.

Before climbing into bed, Zana popped a Melatonin, hoping it would calm her and allow for quick sleep. She sat up against the pillows in bed checking her Facebook and Twitter feeds, and then, against her better judgment, texted him. Hey you...xoxox. She added a palm tree emoticon rather than a red heart. She set her phone on the nightstand and lay under her light duvet in the dark, waiting to hear the buzz of her phone signaling a text.

It only took a few minutes after Zana woke up the next morning to remember that she had fallen asleep waiting for his response. She grabbed her phone and stared at the tiny screen. There was no text from Jerry. She then checked to see if he had called or emailed. She slumped back against her pillows when she saw he hadn't communicated at all.

Zana bit down on her bottom lip. *Was she the only one driving their relationship?* She had voluntarily given up her evening workouts to hang out at the set almost every night. As she thought back over the last few months, Jerry hadn't invited her to the set but had suggested she spend her evenings training for the Freewheel Triathlon. She had also assumed he wanted her to come over to his house nearly every night and share his bed. On the nights she couldn't make it, he never complained. On the other hand, he called her everyday while he was in San Diego and seemed excited to see her when he got back. He had even brought her a small stuffed giraffe from the San Diego Zoo where he had taken his nieces and nephew.

As she lay in bed analyzing the state of their relationship, her iPhone alarm startled her. For a split second, she thought it was a text or call from Jerry and then she realized it was time to get ready for work. As she showered, blew dry her hair and applied makeup, she vowed not to call him. She was done following him around like a puppy dog.

The digital clock read 5:57 when she sat down at her desk that morning. She began researching the Paradise Lagoons Triathlon, Terry Schubert and Ryan Peterson in order to keep her mind off Jerry. She noted that the race's timing company was Sparkplug and the race director was Bob Kearns. She examined the list of sponsors on the website and saw the logo for Freewheel Bicycle Shop and Repair—Rockstar's company.

By 8:15 a.m., Zana's plan to lose herself in her work had succeeded. She hadn't thought of Jerry for several hours. She reached into her handbag for her phone and shook her head when she again saw no text or call from her boyfriend. She pulled up his number and almost pressed it to call, but then dropped it back into her bag as if it was radioactive. She thought of a guy she should talk to and asked Siri to connect them.

"Hi, Ryan?" Zana said when she heard the man's voice.

"Yes," Ryan said.

"This is Zana. How are you doing?"

"Good, good. Can't complain too much," Ryan said. "How's your hand?"

"It's much better. Thanks so much for your help. I'm actually calling about your case. Are you available to get together today to discuss it?" Zana asked, hoping they could meet so she could keep her mind off Jerry.

"I've got a long training day planned. Is your hand healed enough for you to go swimming?" Ryan asked.

Zana examined her hand. "Yeah, it's all healed. I took the bandage off this morning. There's only a small scar." Rex peaked his head in her partly opened door and she motioned him to sit down.

"How 'bout Ala Moana at the end of the day, maybe five-thirty?" Ryan asked.

"That's not the end of my day, but I can swim with you as long as we discuss your case," Zana said, tapping the meeting details into her computer calendar.

"No problem. We can synchronize our strokes and talk while we're swimming," Ryan laughed.

"Very funny. I'll meet you by the lifeguard stand at five-thirty."

After Zana hung up the phone, she turned her attention to Rex, who was slumped in one of her guest chairs.

"Are you okay?" Zana asked. Her co-worker's red hair was an uncombed mess. He wore a rumpled white dress shirt and his gray tie was loosened so it hung like a necklace.

"Not really," he said. "I know I have major eye baggage."

"Did you sleep in your office?" Zana asked.

Rex shook his head. "I went home for a little while. It looks like I'm next to get axed."

"Why do you say that?" Zana stood up to close her office door.

"The writing's on the wall. Bethany is also my secretary—if you know what I mean," he groaned.

"She made a mistake," she said, returning to her chair behind her desk. "It could've happened to anyone."

"No. Cole didn't trust her and checked everything she did, including the mail."

"Then how did a document get sent to the wrong court?"

"Cole has no idea. He checked the envelope before the document went out." He leaned forward. "We think Bethany changed the envelope in order to sabotage him."

"Do you have any proof?" Zana asked.

"No," Rex said and then lowered his voice. "Can you keep a secret?"

She sat up straighter. "Sure."

"Bethany is sleeping with one of the senior partners," he whispered.

"Who?" Zana asked, wide-eyed.

"I can't tell you." He swallowed hard. "Cole walked in on them in the partner's office late at night. We think Bethany and the partner hatched the scheme to get him fired."

"Then why do you think you're next?" Zana asked.

"It's more of a feeling than anything," he said. "She knows Cole and I are tight."

She chewed on the end of her pen. "Of course, he told you."

Rex nodded. "In less than a year of working here, Bethany became like the queen of the secretaries. She blows in late every day and it's all good. Tina was late to work twice and Frank fired her. That's got to tell you something."

"I'm so glad Sylvia's my secretary," she said. "No drama."

"You're lucky," he said, straightening his tie. "I better get back to work before I get the ax."

Zana was walking out the door to go to lunch not because she felt any hunger pangs, but because it was 1:30, and most of the restaurants in town stopped serving lunch at two. As she walked out the large glass double doors of the high rise, she heard Jerry's ringtone. Her mind told her to ignore the phone and let him leave a message, but her fast beating heart encouraged her to answer.

"Hello," she said more formally than she ever had when Jerry called.

"Where have you been, Zana? I fell asleep waiting for you," Jerry said.

"I've been working," she said, softening her voice after hearing his words.

"I meant last night." His voice had an edge. "I thought you were coming over."

"Oh, sorry. I decided to go home instead," she said as nonchalantly as possible.

"I felt lonely waking up without you."

"Well, that's nice to hear." She smiled for the first time all day.

"Can you come to the set after work?" Jerry asked. "I have a surprise for you."

"Sure, that would be great!" She felt a spring in her step as she made her way to Aloha Salads across the street.

"I can't wait to see you, sweetheart," he said. "I miss you."

They weren't exactly the three words she was hoping to hear, but they erased her hurt feelings and instantly restored hope in her for their relationship. She ate her salad at her desk while deciding on what outfit—still in their dry cleaning bags on the back of her door—she could change into. Rather than return to work, she busied herself with freshening her makeup and meticulously curling her hair. She slipped out of the office without checking her calendar.

Chapter Sixteen

@FreewheelMV Swimming in the girls' lane is like #swimming in the #Indie500 lane.

Ryan locked his bike securely to a rack near the Magic Island parking lot at Ala Moana Beach Park. He glanced at his Apple watch pleased to have almost a half hour before meeting Zana, allowing him enough time to run three miles around the park at a quick pace and stretch before their swim. After changing into his running shoes, he sprinted over to the lifeguard stand on the beach to stow his backpack filled with biking and swimming gear. The guard on duty kept a keen eye on his and other triathletes' gear during his afternoon shift.

As Ryan picked up his pace after a half mile warm up, he systematically passed walkers and joggers out for their daily exercise. He focused on his running form, pace and breathing until his concentration was broken when he reached the path adjacent to the beach with a smattering of sunbathers enjoying the warm rays of sun before it set. He scanned the glistening water filled with stand up paddlers, swimmers and kids playing inside the protective reef. There was a group of triathletes swimming freestyle in a pack. His running singlet, designed to wick away moisture was working double time in the island humidity and he looked forward to cooling off in the water when he swam with Zana—even though it would be a challenge to keep pace with her.

After Ryan finished his run, he took a long swig of water at the drinking fountain near the Magic Island bathrooms. He looked around, expecting to see his attorney amongst the other triathletes who had changed out of their work clothes. He stashed his running shoes in his backpack, grabbed his cap and goggles and began doing some yoga poses on the grass adjacent to the beach, keeping an eye out for Zana. He waved at a handful of triathletes as they made their way past him to the water. Some of them wore wetsuits to train for cold water triathlons, but most of them were in racing suits, readying for a 2,000 yard swim, from one end of the beach to the other and back.

Ryan watched the sun lowering over the water and wondered why Zana wasn't there thirty minutes after their planned meeting time. Anxious to cool off, he retrieved his backpack from under the lifeguard stand and fished for his phone to call her office.

"May I speak to Zana West, please?" Ryan asked.

"She's left for the day," the receptionist said after she put him on hold for a few minutes.

"I had an appointment with her at five-thirty and she's not here. I thought I had her cell phone number, but I don't," Ryan said, trying to keep his voice steady to hide his annoyance.

"Her assistant has also left for the day. Let me transfer you to Frank Gravelle's secretary," the receptionist said.

"Hello, Mr. Peterson, this is Libby."

"Hi Libby." Ryan switched the phone to the speaker mode so he could stretch his calves.

"Jasmin said that Ms. West is late for an appointment with you, is that correct?"

"Yes. We were supposed to meet at five-thirty. Could you please give me her cell number so I can contact her?" Ryan asked, now stretching his glutes.

"I apologize, Mr. Peterson. This is entirely unacceptable," Libby said. "I will attempt to contact Ms. West and have her call you immediately."

"Sure. Thank you. I hope she's alright," he said, wondering if his call had gotten Zana into trouble.

After he hung up with Libby, Ryan slipped on his biking jersey and strapped on his helmet. If he hurried, he would be able to catch the late masters swimming practice at the University of Hawaii pool. His phone rang as he was bending down to put on his bike shoes.

"Mr. Peterson, this is Libby. I've been unable to get in touch with Ms. West. I'm going to connect you with her boss, Frank Gravelle."

"That's not necessary," Ryan sighed. "I'll talk to her tomorrow."

"Mr. Gravelle insists on talking with you," Libby said.

Ryan shrugged. "Okay."

"Mr. Peterson—Frank Gravelle here. I understand that you're having problems with Zana West."

"No—you're mistaken," Ryan said, wishing her boss wasn't involved in what he was sure was a simple time mix-up.

"I understand that she didn't show up to a meeting with you," Frank said.

"It's entirely possible that I misunderstood the time of our meeting," Ryan said, wishing he hadn't called the firm.

"Ms. West's behavior is intolerable. I will have a stern word with her."

"That's not necessary. Please disregard my phone call. I'm certain that this was my fault," Ryan said, balancing the phone in one hand as he unlocked his bike.

"Mr. Peterson, I get the impression that you're no longer confident in Ms. West's ability to represent you," Frank said.

"Your impression is completely wrong." Ryan straddled his bike, wondering what it would take to get this guy off the phone so he could make it to swim practice on time.

"Clearly, Ms. West didn't show up to a meeting with you. I'm sure you don't appreciate her wasting your time."

"Mr. Gravelle, what I don't appreciate is your lack of support of your associate. I'm very pleased with having Ms. West as my attorney," Ryan said, raising his voice. "I'll have to take this up with my insurance company—they might not appreciate *your* behavior."

"I'm sure that isn't necessary," Frank said. "I'll leave word with Ms. West that you called."

"That's fine. Thank you," Ryan said and then clicked off his phone and began pedaling to UH.

As he rode through the early evening traffic, he skillfully dodged cars while thinking of his encounter with Frank Gravelle. He normally would drop it, but he yearned for any excuse to talk with Alexia. Ever since the concert, Ryan had been careful not to bother her. They had hugged goodbye, she had warmly thanked him for a fun evening and he hadn't called or heard from her since. His dad's play it cool strategy seemed to be working better than the full court press, but he hoped she would make the next move. Although Ryan had a lifetime of self-discipline as an athlete, it didn't translate well with his feelings towards Alexia and his efforts to maintain telephone silence.

He didn't have Alexia's cell number, so even if he did feel Frank's behavior warranted an immediate call, it would have to wait until work hours. When he imagined her responding to his call with the cold indifference of an adjuster assigned to his claim, he thought better of it and decided to stick with his previous plan of phoning her once every ten days. He had even started marking a red "X" on his calendar for each day he successfully refrained from contacting her.

Warm up had already begun when Ryan lowered his Speedo clad body into the fast lane of the 50-meter pool at the Aquatic Center at the University of Hawaii. He wasn't nearly as fast as the men who swam in the end lanes, but he had discovered that working out with the best athletes—whatever the sport—made him better. The only problem in the pool was that the guys were so fast they would lap him, which was embarrassing given his Olympic gold medal status.

"Ryan, hold up!" coach Gary ordered loudly.

Ryan heard his coach as he turned his head to breathe towards the end of his 200 meter freestyle warm up.

"Yeah?" Ryan said, moving to the corner of the lane so he could avoid being hit by swimmers flip turning at the wall.

"You've got to move down a few lanes," Gary said, as always, trying to convince Ryan that he didn't belong in the fast lane.

"No. I'm good."

"You have no choice. Move down or you're out of here," Gary said sternly with his hands on his hips.

"I don't see how I'm going to get any better if I swim with the girls," Ryan said.

"Your stroke is a mess. I need you to spend more time practicing technique and less time trying to prove that you can swim like Michael Phelps."

"Okay—okay," Ryan said before ducking under the lane line to the lane occupied by four of the fastest women in the pool. "Is this okay?"

"No—two more down," Gary motioned to a middle lane with only three women.

"If you say so— Jeez," Ryan said before ducking into the lane designated by his coach.

"I want you to work on your rotation tonight. You're swimming flat, like a bug," Gary said, demonstrating on dry land how he wanted Ryan's body to rotate.

"Okay," Ryan said.

"Do you understand what I'm showing you?"

"Yeah, it's not rocket science."

"Well—then, you should be able to do what I say for once," Gary said, raising his voice. "200 free—goep!"

Ryan followed Gary's instruction and kicked off the edge of the pool to begin his swim of four lengths. He tried to follow Gary's directions and focus on rotating his body. As he got into the rhythm, he noticed that he was swimming more efficiently. Maybe, Gary was right about not swimming with the fast men. With only three other swimmers in his lane, Ryan finally felt relaxed. He was able to focus on how his body moved through the water instead of trying to play catch up. As he reached the edge of the pool after a half dozen sets, he saw Zana's friend, Shelby.

"Hey, Shelby," Ryan said as he pulled his goggles off his eyes and placed them on his forehead so she might recognize him.

"Oh, hi Ryan. What are you doing in this lane? I thought you swam with the fast boys."

"Coach's orders," Ryan said. "Do you know where Zana is tonight?"

"She texted me that she was heading over to Jerry's house," Shelby said.

"Are you serious? She was supposed to meet me at Ala Moana at five-thirty," Ryan said as he leaned against the lane line.

"She must have forgotten. Did you call her on her cell phone?"

"I don't have her digits. I called her office," Ryan said, adjusting his swim cap. "Could you do me a big favor?"

"Sure."

"Can you text or call her tonight and warn her that her boss knows she missed an appointment with me? I don't want her to get in trouble."

"I'll do it right after I get out of the pool."

"What's all this chatter?" Gary asked, standing over them from the side of the pool.

"Sorry, Coach," Shelby said.

"Shelby, swim four hundred free and then warm down," Gary directed. "Ryan, how did it feel when you focused on your body rotation?"

"Awesome," Ryan said, looking up at his coach. "See, I do listen to you."

"It's about time. Now, I want you to swim two hundred free. Pay attention to your hand position and make sure your stroke doesn't cross the midline under water." Gary demonstrated the stroke with his arms.

"Got it," Ryan said. He put his goggles back on and pushed off the wall, focusing on following Gary's instructions for the first hundred. He was finally starting to feel more comfortable in the water. His body was more streamlined, moving so much faster with minimal effort. If only he had put his ego aside years before and listened to his coach.

The reason why the press had doubted his ability to win the gold medal at the Olympics without cheating was because his swim was so weak compared to his competitors. When Ryan looked at his gold medal in its Koa wood-framed case before he went to bed each night, there was a disconnect. It was hard to accept that he had earned it by beating out the two Germans who finished seconds behind him. Ryan knew in his heart that Vic Leavitt, who died in the Olympic trials accident, would have won if he wasn't hit by a car driven by Brad Jordan's evil girlfriend, Heather.

Whenever Ryan remembered the moment he crossed the finish line at the Honolulu Olympic trials, it was hard to hold back tears. Coach Hal had come running up to him and instead of congratulating him, broke the news of the horrible accident. Now, several years after that tragic day, as Ryan stroked through the water, his mind drifted to the more recent accident when Terry Schubert was killed. It felt like *déjà vu*. He was being falsely accused for yet another death.

"Your stroke is looking smooth and you have more extension in the water," Gary said after Ryan reached the end of the pool.

"Thanks," Ryan said as he tried to compose himself. He hadn't expected Gary to be kneeling down so close to his lane. His voice cracked when he said, "I'm amazed at my improvement in less than an hour."

"Are you okay?" Gary asked.

Ryan nodded.

"Almost everyone is out of the water already. Do you want to talk about it?" Gary asked.

"What's there to talk about?" He dunked his head under water for a few seconds, hoping he could avoid Gary's concern.

"I know about the lawsuit."

"You and everyone else." Ryan spit pool water out of his mouth.

"Terry was a good guy," Gary said.

Ryan nodded, trying to avoid eye contact with his coach.

"I know that you had nothing to do with causing Terry's death," Gary said in a low voice as he leaned closer.

"Tell that to the jury."

"I will," Gary said as he straightened up. "Make sure your attorney adds me to the witness list."

"I thought you were just giving me bullshit," Ryan said as he took off his cap and goggles. "What do you know?"

"Shhh," Gary whispered. "This is a small island. Let's just say that I've heard some things. I'd rather not discuss it right now."

"I'll call you tonight," Ryan said as he hopped out of the pool, not bothering with the ladder.

"I've got to get home. My wife and I have company," Gary said in a low voice. "I'd rather not talk about this with you. Do what I said and have your attorney add me to the witness list."

Ryan said in a low voice, "I will. They're probably going to take your deposition."

Gary nodded. Ryan watched as his coach grabbed his cell phone and keys from the pool office and locked the door before leaving through the men's locker room. Ryan sighed. At least someone believed him.

Chapter Seventeen

@Zlaw My Craigslist ad: #Lawyer seeks job—almost no experience, snarky attitude, arrives late, writes like crap and blows off meetings. Will work few hrs. for high pay.

Zana's iPhone vibrated repeatedly on the nightstand while Jerry moaned with pleasure on top of her. She gazed into his glistening eyes, ignoring the string of text message alerts. After tender lovemaking amidst sheets and clothing strewn across his king-sized bed that made a path to the bedroom door, they lie in each other's arms.

She was jolted awake by a sharp guttural snore in her ear, which continued more softly and steadily after he changed positions in his sleep. She carefully untangled her left arm and leg from his body—trying not to wake him, eased out of bed, and then tiptoed into the master bathroom to pee. She didn't dare flush the toilet. This was the first time she'd seen him sleep soundly in weeks.

As Zana was about to silently slide back into bed, she remembered the text message alerts. She'd left work early and there were probably dozens of new pressing work e-mails. She grabbed her phone in one hand and Jerry's rumpled T-shirt from the foot of the bed in the other, heading for the living room where she could have a glass of cold water and catch up with her digital life. She breathed in the scent of Polo cologne when she pulled his T-shirt over her head. She settled down on the couch, took a sip of water, and clicked on her phone. She read Shelby's text: U R in trouble. Frank knows u missed meeting with Ryan.

"Damnit! Shit!" Zana said loudly as she jumped up and began to pace. "Fuck!"

"What's going on?" Jerry croaked as he rushed into the room naked, holding his blue plaid boxer shorts in his hand.

"Oh, sorry I woke you," she sobbed.

"What's wrong, sweetheart?"

"I'm going to get fucking fired," she said, stomping her bare feet on the floor.

He encircled his arms around her. "What happened since we went to bed?"

"Look at this text from Shelby." Zana handed him her phone.

He studied the text. "What's this about? Did you have a meeting scheduled with Ryan?"

"We were supposed to swim at Ala Moana," she said, slumping down onto the sofa next to the sleeping cats. "I totally forgot."

"How does Frank know?" he asked as he gently re-positioned the cats so he could sit next to her.

"I have no idea." She rested her head on his bare shoulder.

"You need to call Shelby before you jump to any conclusions."

"It's 1 a.m.," Zana said, looking at the time on her phone. "She has to get up for a bike ride in four hours. I can't wake her up."

"You have to get up early as well. Any chance you can get some sleep and worry about this later?"

"No," she said, wiping a fresh tear from her eye. "You should sleep though. You're not the one getting fired tomorrow."

"It's Saturday. Wouldn't Frank wait until Monday if he really was going to fire you?"

"Frank doesn't take any days off from destroying people's lives," she said. "And, being the Scrooge he is, he would probably get even more excited about firing me so close to Christmas."

"Are you sure that leaving the firm would be all that bad, sweetheart?" Jerry asked as he brushed hair out of her eyes. "You're always stressed out."

"The economy sucks. I really need to work," she said, hoping he would profess his love and promise to take care of her.

He shrugged. "Yeah, it's not the best time to be looking for a new job. No firms hire in December." He rubbed her neck with his right hand and petted his cats with the left. "Everything will be okay. Let's go back to bed and try to get some sleep. We have Kenny and Preston's party tonight."

"Shoot. Well, maybe someone at the party will hire me." Zana grimaced. She moved away from Jerry's naked body and put her face in her hands.

"Let me tuck you into bed. Everything will be alright." He stood up and held out a hand for her.

"Go ahead. I'm heading home," she said, ignoring his hand and standing up on her own. "Where are my clothes?" She found her skirt on the floor next to the doorway to Jerry's bedroom and her blouse was serving as Ming and Miko's bedding on the couch. She nudged the cats away and picked up her black blouse now covered with cat hair.

"Do you need a lint brush?" Jerry smiled sheepishly. He then put his arms around her and pulled her close to his bare chest.

"It won't help," she said, tears streaming down her face.

"I'm sorry. I really need to get some sleep before flying out on Sunday," he said after she pulled away from his embrace and turned her back to him.

She didn't want him to see her so emotionally out of control.

"Remind me where you're going," she said through gritted teeth, trying to keep her voice steady.

"Remember my text? I'm headed to Rio—Kenny thought it would be a good idea if I practiced Capoeira with the locals before we feature it in some upcoming episodes. I told you about Paulo and Ricardo," Jerry said, as he gently placed his hand on her shoulder. "They have a Capoeira school in Ipanema. Kenny wants them to be on the show. I'll be back before Christmas."

Zana forced herself to count silently to ten in her head. *1-1000, 2-1000, 3-1000, 4-1000*. She didn't want to say anything to him that she'd regret. If she spoke her mind, it would be in a loud and bitchy voice. She was sick of him flying all over the world while she was stuck in the office. He always made his plans with no input from her. She realized that she'd lost track of her counting…*3-1000, 4-1000….*

"Zana—what's going on? You're so quiet," he said, slightly raising his voice.

"I've got to go." Zana glanced at the door. She was afraid of him looking into her eyes and seeing the hurt she was feeling from him flying off to Brazil when she was about to be fired from her job. He might recognize that she needed him. She didn't want him to see her love for him before he had declared his feelings to her.

"Okay. I'm picking you up at five-thirty. Call me if you need me," Jerry said. "Are you okay driving home?"

"I'm fine," she said, looking down. She hoped he would again insist that she stay with him for the rest of the night. She pulled his T-shirt over her head and tossed it onto the couch before putting on her own clothes.

"You don't seem okay," he said, pulling her towards him. He lifted her chin gently with his forefinger and looked at her with such concern that she felt breathless. "Talk to me, Zana."

"I love you," she said in a voice that was so soft she wasn't quite sure if it was audible.

"Hmmmm. You are so sweet," he said after his face registered something between discomfort and shock.

Zana went back to counting to herself after she realized what she had just done. Not only was she going to be fired from her job in a matter of hours, she had committed relationship suicide by opening up her big mouth. Now, she would not only lose her job, but had proof that Jerry didn't love her. She quickly buttoned her blouse and zipped up her skirt, leaving her panties somewhere in his room. She grabbed her purse, gave him a quick kiss on his lips and averted her eyes from his.

"I'll see you tonight," Zana said as she quickly walked out the door, making sure she had her car keys. He followed her, taking the keys from her hand so he could unlock and open the car door for her. After she slid into the seat, closed the door and started the car, he knocked on the window, which she opened electronically.

"You almost forgot your surprise," Jerry said and handed her the tiny box he'd given her on the set the night before. At first she'd thought it might be a ring, but then she opened it to find the small maneki-neko, a Japanese good luck charm. The tiny ceramic cat was beckoning with an upright paw. She nodded and took the gift, and tossed it into her handbag open on the seat next to her.

He leaned forward to give her a kiss, which she rigidly accepted. Zana forced a brief smile before she put her concentration into backing up without hitting the lion statues next to the entrance gate of Jerry's parents' house that stood less than 100 yards from his cottage.

She didn't start sobbing until she knew that Jerry was out of sight. She cried as she thought about losing her job. And then cried harder about her unrequited love. There was almost no traffic as she drove on dark side streets to Kahala. She ran the windshield wipers the entire time even though there was no rain and she hadn't bothered to turn her headlights on, even though a few cars flashed their high beams.

Zana managed to unzip her skirt and drop it to the floor before crawling into bed wearing her cat fur encrusted blouse. Despite her opinion that it would be impossible to fall asleep, she awoke with the sun streaming through her bedroom window.

At first she thought that someone had turned on the light in her room since she was unaccustomed to sleeping after sunrise. It took an instant to register that it was almost 7 a.m. and she would barely make it to work in time for the Saturday morning meeting. It took her another instant to recall that it didn't matter, since she was about to be fired.

After Zana showered and dressed, she headed to the kitchen and popped a half bagel into the toaster. She had no appetite, but the habit of making breakfast somehow felt comforting. She dipped a knife in the peanut butter jar when Andrew walked into the kitchen dressed in shorts and an ultimate Frisbee T-shirt.

"What's wrong?" Andrew asked as he poured himself a cup of coffee from the fresh pot that Zana made.

"Why do you ask?" she said without looking up from her bagel smearing.

"You're wearing black jeans and a polo shirt. You never dress like that—even on a Saturday," he said.

She mindlessly bit into her bagel and said with her mouth full, "I'm going to be fired today."

"What else is new?" He sipped his coffee. "What did you do this time?"

"I forgot a client meeting," she said.

He shrugged. "So, you'll re-schedule."

"Frank is on the war path about it."

"You're dead," Andrew said emphatically.

"Yeah—tell me about it," Zana sighed. "Do you have any boxes?"

"You can use the boxes I keep in my office for when I get canned."

"Thanks," she said. "Do you think I should have my stuff packed before Frank gives me the ax?"

"Maybe," he said, slipping a banana and bagel into a brown paper lunch sack. "It would allow you to leave quickly. I can help you carry the boxes to your car."

"We could use Libby's luggage cart," she said, taking a last bite and brushing crumbs off her shirt. "I think we can get it in one load."

"Okay," he said. "I've got to get going. Since you're being fired today, I'm probably safe so I need to get to the meeting on time."

"Thanks a lot." Zana rolled her eyes. He left through the garage door and she waited until she heard his car pull out of the driveway before she grabbed her handbag. She didn't bother with her briefcase, since there would be no work to bring home.

She was strangely numb about her impending doom. There was not a whole lot she could do about it. Today was going to stand out as one of the worst days of her life. She was going to be fired, and then she had to go to a party with her boyfriend who didn't love her and was leaving for Brazil the next day while she was stuck in Hawaii—an unemployed loser.

Zana took her time driving to work. Then, she drove round and round up each floor of the parking garage until she found the perfect space near the elevator so that moving boxes to her car could be done efficiently. It was after eight when she finally strolled into the office. She heard attorney voices coming from the conference room. Before opening the door, she took a deep breath. She'd been with the firm long enough to know that any attorney who was about to be fired would not be allowed in the meeting, and that Frank would excuse himself, escort her to her office and terminate her on the spot.

Just as she thought, everyone stopped talking as she walked into the room. She stood for an awkward moment in the doorway, waiting for her boss to order her out.

"Good morning, Zana," Frank said with what looked like a genuine smile. "Glad you could join us."

"Hello," she said wide-eyed.

"Sit down, we're going over the firm's calendar for the week," Frank said.

Zana slid into a seat next to Michael Lee, locking eyes with Andrew who was sitting next to Frank. Andrew raised his eyebrows and shrugged his shoulders.

***

"I guess you won't need those boxes after all," Andrew said, winking at Zana as they walked down the hall still in earshot of their colleagues after the meeting let out.

"Yeah—I have to admit that I'm a little disappointed," she said half joking.

"Oh, come on. You love it here," he said as he ducked into his office.

"Sure, I do." Zana headed to her office. She wasn't entirely sure if her job was secure, but Frank had been unusually friendly towards her during the meeting, not once criticizing, belittling or putting her on the spot. He had actually asked her opinion of the value of a case and praised her for her analysis. She was tempted to call Jerry with the good news, but to do so would only remind her that her feelings had progressed far more than his.

Once she settled at her desk, she saw Ryan's name on her caller I.D.

"Ryan, I am so sorry," Zana said as soon as he picked up.

"No problem. I hope you didn't get into trouble," Ryan said.

"Uh, strangely—no."

"I guess I put the fear of God into Frank."

She sat upright in her chair. "You? How did *you* do that?"

"I told him that if he gave you a hard time, I'd have a talk with the insurance carrier," he said. "Apparently, that's his weak spot. I take it my threat worked?"

"Yeah, he was actually *nice* to me—for a change," she said, clicking on her computer. "I owe you one. Can I buy your lunch?"

"Not necessary. But, I do have a favor of you to ask," Ryan said.

"Anything."

"You're friends with Alexia, right?"

"Yes," she looked out at the big Dole pineapple.

"Instead of taking me to lunch, could you go out to lunch with her and put in a good word for me?" Ryan asked. "I'm serious."

She smiled weakly. "Sure...I don't think it's necessary, but I'm happy to do it."

"I haven't talked to her since we went to the Sei Bombay concert," Ryan said. "Zana, I think I'm falling for her. You have no idea how miserable it feels to love someone who doesn't feel the same."

"Oh, you'd be surprised." Zana put her face in her hands and pressed the button to close the blinds. *That damn pineapple.*

Chapter Eighteen

@ZLaw The secret to packing light? Pack only tiny bikinis. Or, so I hear. #Travel

"You look amazing," Kenny said to Zana as he greeted her and Jerry at the front door. She was wearing a Trina Turk little black dress she had ordered online. Christian Louboutin peep-toe black pumps accentuated her long legs and elevated her to at least six foot two, making her a few inches taller than both men. She felt Jerry's hand on her waist guiding her as they walked into Kenny and Preston's Kahala beachfront mansion.

"Mahalo." Zana smiled. "Your house is beautiful."

"You'll love the kitchen—it's as big as my entire cottage," Jerry said.

"We've got to do something about your living arrangements, my friend," Kenny said as he led them through the entryway with its cream Italian marble floor enclosed by Koa framed windows. Zana admired the ten-foot ceiling-high Christmas tree, decorated with large magenta balls and white lights against a bamboo wall that was the focal point before they entered an expansive sunken living room with a dramatic view of the Pacific Ocean.

"What's wrong with my living arrangements?" Jerry raised an eyebrow.

"Oh nothing, if you don't mind living within listening distance of your parents." Kenny rolled his eyes. "Wouldn't you like to have more than two tiny bedrooms? I could find you a nice house on the beach."

Jerry laughed and squeezed Zana's hand. "Someday. I'll let you know when I'm ready and you can take me house shopping."

They joined the other guests who had arrived within fifteen minutes of the time engraved on the invitations. The others would arrive on "Hawaiian time" AKA fashionably late. Two waiters, wearing festive red and green Aloha shirts offered guests wine and pupus on serving trays. Zana recognized Preston Farnsworth, III, pale and skeletal as always, engrossed in a conversation with two men who she recognized as executive producers of "Fighting in Paradise". A few of the cameramen and their wives were admiring the view while sipping wine and eating ahi sashimi with chopsticks.

"Shall we?" Jerry led Zana to a cream colored love seat where they'd be able to watch the sunset, if they weren't directed to the dinner tables arranged on the beach front lawn within the next half hour. "Have you been to one of these beach front properties before, sweetie?"

"This is my first. They look so unpretentious from the street—I'm surprised this house is so gorgeous," she said as she focused on a large Wyland dolphin statue that seemed alive against the ocean backdrop.

He gave her hand another squeeze. "Would you ever want to live in one of these mansions?"

"I wouldn't complain," she said, not sure if Jerry was suggesting that a beach house might be in their future together. They hadn't discussed her "I love you" *faux pas* and he had apparently forgotten her fear about being fired, because he hadn't even asked about her morning at the office.

"It would be great waking up with you." He kissed her neck.

"Jerry, long time no see," said a petite Asian woman with long, shiny raven hair which she began playing with as soon as her eyes met Jerry's.

"Hey Annabelle." Jerry stood up and gave her a kiss on the cheek. "This is Zana West."

"Hi Zana, nice to meet you." Annabelle stepped forward offering her perfectly manicured right hand.

When Zana stood up to shake it, Annabelle was at least a foot shorter than her and tiny in comparison, making her feel self-conscious as she towered over the diminutive beauty.

"Hello," Zana said, wondering why Jerry had failed to identify her as his girlfriend. She had seen Annabelle on the set, but she had always worn her hair in a ball cap and baggy pants and a T-shirt. Now, dressed in a cocktail dress and heels, she was stunning.

"I work with Jerry on the show," Annabelle said to Zana and then smiled at Jerry. "Are you packed yet?"

He nodded. "All ready."

"Ready for what?" Zana asked, wondering what she was missing.

"We're headed to Rio tomorrow. They wear tiny bikinis down there, so I don't have to bring a very big suitcase." Annabelle giggled, then touched Jerry on the arm.

Zana felt her stomach churn. "I thought you were headed down there for work."

"We are," he said, putting his arm around his girlfriend. "Annabelle is the martial arts choreographer and in order to add the upcoming Capoeira moves into the show, she's going to be training with us in Rio."

"I've always wanted to go there. We're going to have a blast," Annabelle said, smiling flirtatiously at Jerry as she flipped her hair back.

"Excuse me," Zana said, as she walked away from Jerry and the choreographer. She couldn't stand to watch this woman flirt with her boyfriend for a second longer. She asked one of the waiters for directions to the nearest bathroom. After passing a baby grand piano where a man in a tux was playing "Greensleeves", she entered a hallway that led to a large guest bathroom decorated tastefully with purple, red and green reindeer. After locking the door, she put her face in her hands, but before she shed a tear she remembered her mascara wasn't waterproof so crying wasn't an option. She paced back and forth, trying to figure out her next move when there was a knock on the door.

"Are you okay, Zana?" Jerry called.

"I'm fine. Just using the restroom," she said, quickly flushing the toilet. "Just a second."

"I was worried about you, sweetheart," Jerry said as Zana flung open the door.

"Oh?"

"Don't pay any attention to Annabelle Wong. She's harmless."

"She looks like she wants to jump your bones," Zana said, surprised that she actually said out loud what she was thinking.

"Maybe so, but you're the only one I want to do that," he said, rising slightly on his toes to kiss her.

"Really?" Zana asked, relaxing her shoulders.

He put his hands on her waist. "Of course. You're so beautiful. All the men are staring at you tonight."

"Thanks." She smoothed her hair.

"You look like a model with those sky high shoes," Jerry said. "I'm a lucky guy."

"I'm going to miss you while you're in Rio," she said as they walked past the baby grand piano and back into the living room.

He grabbed her hand and led her outside where guests were now mingling. "Shall we find our table?"

"Sure," she said, disappointed that Jerry had missed his cue to say he would miss her. *Or, would he?* She wondered. She'd be lucky if he called her while he was traveling. Sure, he called while he was in San Diego with his family, but she'd felt sick with insecurity during his trips to Prague and South Korea a few months ago when he only texted every few days and never once called or answered her calls.

"Jerry and Zana, you're at one of our V.I.P. tables," Kenny said as they walked to the cluster of ten round tables covered in forest green tablecloths with votive candles and red and white poinsettia centerpieces. "Follow me."

They took their seats at an empty table with eight place settings. Zana noticed the place cards with the "Fighting in Paradise" logo with their names on them and small gold gift bags. She wanted to check to see if Annabelle was sitting with them, but didn't want Jerry to see her analyzing the nametags.

"Would you mind getting me a glass of wine, honey?" she asked.

"Sure, I'll be right back," he said as he stood up and walked towards a waiter.

Zana was relieved that Annabelle wasn't a V.I.P and wasn't assigned to their table. However, one of the place cards made her so uncomfortable she quickly moved it so the person would be sitting across the table rather than next to her.

"Here you go," Jerry said as he handed her a glass of white wine. "Is something wrong?"

"Bud Schubert is sitting at our table," Zana whispered.

"Is that a problem?" He sat down next to her.

"I have a wrongful death case against him—he's the plaintiff."

"He's our biggest sponsor. Did you expect that he wouldn't show up?" Jerry asked as he sipped his wine.

"Of course not. I just didn't think he'd be sitting with us," she whispered. "You know I can't talk with him unless his attorney is present."

"It's Preston's party. I'm sure that you're worried about nothing," he said, brushing a strand of hair away from her face.

"I wish there wasn't anything to worry about," Zana said, feeling anxiety about more than who would be joining them for dinner.

They sat alone at the table while Makana entertained the crowd, playing his guitar and singing a Hawaiian version of "O Holy Night".

"Please make your way to your tables, ladies and gentlemen," Kenny announced into a microphone.

"Hello," Preston said as he sat next to Jerry. Zana smiled at him and noticed Bud Schubert take his seat across from her where she had moved his place card. She kept her gaze on her plate when it was discovered that Sandy, his wife, wasn't sitting next to him. Preston promptly rearranged the cards so Sandy could join her husband, and everyone was seated, including another executive producer and his wife. Kenny's chair remained empty while he was helping direct guests to their tables.

"Nice party," Richard Marsland, one of the executive producers, said to Preston.

"Thanks, Rich," Preston said, "Do I need to make any introductions here? I think all of you know each other."

"I haven't met the young lady," Richard said.

"Oh, pardon me," Preston said. "May I introduce you to Zana West, an associate with the Gravelle, Parsons & Dell law firm."

"You're a very attractive attorney," Richard said. "Are you dating this character?"

"Mahalo, Rich. And yes, she's mine," Jerry said, putting his hand on Zana's bare knee under the table.

Bud pushed his chair away from the table. "You're the attorney representing that murderer, Ryan Peterson," he said, raising his voice and pointing at Zana.

"My client is Mr. Peterson," she said, not sure how to respond. She was startled by Bud's accusatory tone.

"Preston, this is completely unacceptable. How could you dare invite the enemy to this dinner—and, seat her at my table," Bud said loudly in his southern drawl, standing up and towering over the guests.

"Now, calm down, Bud. Zana is just doing her job representing a client," Preston said in a low voice as he stood near Bud. "She's here with her boyfriend."

"I'm not going to calm down. This is entirely inappropriate," Bud said, now shaking his fist. "This woman's client killed my son."

"Can we discuss this later? Please, Bud." Preston leaned into his client.

"What's going on?" Kenny asked as he approached the table.

"How can I sponsor a show with a star who's dating my son's killer's attorney?" Bud said, turning to Kenny with his fists clenched.

"Jerry and Zana, please come with me," Kenny said, leading them away from the table to another one that was mostly empty. "I'm sorry about this. I had no idea Bud would become so agitated."

"He's still grieving for his son." Zana's face felt flushed. She was more worried about Jerry's reaction than her own embarrassment. He hadn't said a word.

"Maybe, we should go," Jerry said softly.

"No, absolutely not," Kenny said. "You'll have fun. I've seated you with Annabelle."

It was now Zana's turn to become quiet. After Kenny left to help calm Bud down, Zana and Jerry sat in silence, both sipping water. They had left their wine glasses at the other table.

"Jer, I thought you were sitting with the big shots," Annabelle said as she sat down next to him. Zana noticed Annabelle move her chair so close to Jerry's that their thighs were probably touching under the table. She wondered if being with him meant always competing with beautiful women who didn't seem to care that he had girlfriend. It was like the reality show, *The Bachelor. Would she receive a rose at the end of the night or be sent home?*

While Annabelle entertained herself with what seemed to be a one-way conversation with Jerry, Zana noticed Bud Schubert having what looked like a heated conversation with Kenny and Preston. Jerry seemed to have disengaged with Annabelle, also watching Bud who was waving his arms as he spoke to the party hosts. They both stared at the three men in the distance until Annabelle excused herself to talk to a friend at a nearby table.

"You didn't tell me what happened at work today, Zana," Jerry said.

"Surprisingly, Frank treated me well. I still have a job," she said, turning her attention back to him.

"Well, at least one of us does," he snorted.

"What do you mean?"

"Look," Jerry said, gesturing to the sunken living room where they had been earlier. Bud Schubert and his wife were walking swiftly away from the party towards the foyer, with Kenny following a few paces behind.

"He's just angry. This will blow over," she said, not sure if she believed her own words.

"The star of 'Fighting in Paradise' is dating the attorney who represents the guy who killed the biggest sponsor's son. How is this going to blow over, Zana?" Jerry asked.

"Nothing has been proven yet. Give it time," she said, hoping he would calm down.

"I'll tell you what has to happen for it to blow over," he said. "Either they're going to fire me, or I'll have to break up with you."

"Maybe, the show could find another sponsor," she offered meekly.

"I don't think so—the economy sucks. We're damn lucky to have Bud Schubert. Without him, the show will be canceled in a heartbeat."

"They won't fire you." Zana swallowed hard. "Who would replace you?"

"One of at least a dozen good-looking guys who are a lot younger than me," Jerry said. "Do you know how hard it is for an Asian guy in his forties to get a lead role in a T.V. show?"

"Jerry, you're the star," Annabelle interjected as she returned to the table. "They would be foolish not to keep you. I'd do *anything* necessary to keep you on the show."

"Thanks, Annabelle," he said in a tone that Zana thought sounded almost tender. "I really can't handle this. I need to leave."

"Okay," Zana said, standing up with Jerry. She put her hand on his shoulder, wishing he would return the gesture. It was clear that one of his choices was breaking up with her if he wanted to keep his job. She couldn't bear the thought of him pondering his dilemma while traveling with bikini-clad Annabelle to Rio.

They stood in silence while the valet retrieved Jerry's Ferrari.

"Do you mind if I just take you home?" Jerry asked after they pulled out of the circular driveway. "My flight leaves early tomorrow morning and I don't think I'll be good company tonight."

"Okay, if that's what you want," she said. She started counting to ten on their drive to her place so she wouldn't say anything she would regret. Once she reached ten, she started counting over and over again until he pulled his car into her driveway.

After he dropped her home with a too short kiss, she slumped on the living room sofa in the dark. She made a mental list of what she might do to remedy the situation. One by one, she dismissed her options. The only hope was to quickly settle Ryan's case, but how?

Chapter Nineteen

@ZLaw Living at the office is not so bad. All the blasting cold air from the A/C I could ever want and a stunning view of the Dole pineapple. #BillableHours

"What are you doing here so late, Zana?" Lucas asked as they passed in the firm hallway. In one hand, she carried a take-out salad and in the other, a Starbucks coffee.

Zana smirked. "I live here."

"Don't we all?" Lucas shrugged, turned on his heel and followed her back to her office. "No—seriously. Didn't you get here at four o'clock this morning?"

"Yeah, but that doesn't mean I ever get to leave." Zana unpacked her salad, the dressing on the side, chopsticks, a napkin, and a multi-grain roll while Lucas sat across from her and surveyed the piles of documents strewn across her desk.

"Is Jerry out of town or something?" Lucas probed.

"Let's talk about the Schubert case," Zana said as she poured part of the dressing on her salad and took a bite using chopsticks.

Lucas nodded. He wore an Aloha shirt with red and green wreaths. It reminded her of what she was missing with Jerry out of the country—holiday parties, shopping together, and decorating for Christmas. She yearned to take the Waikiki Trolley tour downtown for a romantic evening of colorful lights and strolling amongst hundreds of others at the Honolulu Hale display of Christmas trees. Her roommates had described the trees there creatively decorated by city and county department employees. Kelly said her favorite last year was the one adorned with Smurfs.

"So what's going on with your investigation?" Lucas asked, pen poised over a legal pad.

Zana paused to finish chewing her roll and then clicked on her computer screen. "I was able to get the phone number of Jake Okuda, the athlete who placed fifth in the Paradise Lagoons Triathlon."

"That was fast," Lucas said. "What did you do—sleep with the race director?"

"Not even." Zana grimaced. "I just asked him."

"Sure you did," Lucas said with eyebrows raised.

Zana ignored his comment. He had behaved surprisingly civil and had been fairly industrious since their deposition trip to Minnesota months ago, but he was an attorney-boy just like the others. His mind seemed to be only a half-thought away from sex at all times and, on occasion, she still caught him playing computer games instead of working. Since he was Frank's son, she dare not fully trust him. *Who knew what he might reveal over the dinner table?* And so she kept most of their conversations focused on work.

"I also got the names of the race officials and all of the course motorcycle drivers as well," she said.

"Sweet!" Lucas took notes on his legal pad. "Have you called anyone yet?"

"I was waiting until after dark when they're home from training." She took a bite of salad and then washed it down with coffee.

"That's why you're here so late," Lucas said.

At least, he didn't guess the real reason. She pushed her Styrofoam container away, pulling the landline closer. After dialing the number, she pressed the speakerphone function so Lucas could hear the conversation. "May I speak with Jake Okuda?"

"This is he," the man who answered said in what sounded like a Japanese accent.

"This is Zana West. I'm an attorney, representing Ryan Peterson," she said.

"Okay," Jake said.

"Do you remember the Paradise Lagoons Triathlon last year?"

"I think so. I race a lot."

"Do you remember the accident with Terry Schubert?" Zana asked, looking at the phone speaker as if she was questioning a witness in person.

There was a pause on the other end. "That was so sad. Yes. He was a great athlete."

Zana made a note on a yellow legal pad. "Do you remember *anything* that might be helpful to us?"

"Why are you asking?"

"Ryan Peterson is a defendant in a lawsuit brought by Terry Schubert's father," Zana explained. "I'm trying to get as much information as possible."

"Someone's knocking at my door, I've got to go."

"Can I call you later?" Zana pressed.

"I didn't see it—I already told that to the police," Jake said. "I don't want to get involved."

"You don't have to," she said, hearing the impatience in her own voice.

"Just a moment," he said.

Zana and Lucas stared at the phone for what seemed like several minutes.

"Sorry," Jake finally said. "I don't remember anything."

Zana sighed. "Ryan Peterson is being blamed for Terry's death. I'm sure you can appreciate my need to find out what really happened."

"The only thing I remember…," Jake's voice cracked and then he paused, "…when Terry passed me on the bike, at first I thought he was Ryan. And then I noticed it was Terry. I counted the guys ahead of me—Jeff, Ryan, Terry, Eric, and Sam—I was in sixth place."

Zana's fingers sped across her computer keys, taking down everything he said. "And then what happened?"

"Like the other guys, I needed the prize money. We bust our butts and barely make a living. It's not like golf or tennis," Jake said. "It really sucks."

"Yeah, that's rough." Zana nodded. "Do you remember anything else?"

"Nothing," Jake said. "I never passed any of the guys. I only came in fifth place because Terry died."

"Thank you for talking with me, Jake. Let me know if anything else comes to mind," Zana said, and hung up the phone.

She leaned back in her seat, put her hands in a steeple position and closed her eyes for a few moments. "Do you think he's covering something up?"

Lucas shrugged and after a few moments, said, "Next."

Zana leaned forward in her chair and looked up the number of another prospective witness and pressed in the digits. "Is this Sam?"

"Yes—who's this?" Sam asked.

"It's Zana."

"Long time no talk," Sam said. "You caught me at a bad time. I just walked in the door after flying home from Western Australia. I did an Ironman there."

"Congratulations!" Zana said. "How did you do?"

"Not bad. I came in third overall. I had a flat tire, but otherwise it was a good race," Sam said.

"You must be exhausted. Do you have enough energy for a few questions?"

"You attorneys—so inquisitive," Sam said. "Go ahead, but I've got to multi-task while I talk. I need to make a protein shake—I'm starving."

Zana heard some clanking through the phone. "No problem. Do you remember the Paradise Lagoons Triathlon—the race where Terry Schubert died?"

"I race about once a week during the season. It's hard to keep them all straight."

Zana took a long swig of lukewarm coffee. "Do you remember anything about Schubert's death?"

"I didn't witness it, if that's what you're asking. Terry passed me, and then Ryan. They were faster than I was that day," Sam said.

Zana typed his words on her computer's keyboard. "Why do you think

Terry passed you first?"

"I saw them," he said. "I guess I noticed Terry's helmet."

"Was there something distinguishable about it?" she asked, continuing to type.

"Yeah, we did a Century bike ride together a few weeks before. We had florescent green stickers on our helmets from it. Terry's sticker was still on his."

Zana took her fingers off the keyboard and locked eyes with Lucas. "Are you saying that you saw the helmet with the sticker on it pass you first?"

"Yeah. I thought Terry was going to win the prize money." Sam paused. "I remember thinking it was unfair, since his family is rich."

"Did you notice anything about Ryan's helmet?" Zana asked.

"I assumed he was going to be disqualified," Sam said.

She sat upright in her chair. "Why?"

"His chin strap was dangling," Sam said. "It wasn't fastened. I remember thinking that if Ryan gets disqualified, then I would place and win at least *some* money."

Her fingers flew across the keyboard. "What colored clothing was Ryan or Terry wearing during that race?"

"Zana—I'm not a chick," Sam said. "I don't notice those things."

Lucas started to laugh and Zana shot him a look.

"I'm sure they were wearing tri-suits with sponsor decals," Sam said.

Zana paused and thought for a moment.

"Did you notice any of the sponsors on either of their tri-suits?" she asked.

"It's been a long time—how would I remember that?"

"Humor me. Can you remember any logos?" Zana checked her iPhone for texts while she waited for Sam to respond.

He finally said, "I was behind Ryan for a few miles. I think he had the Schubert Real Estate logo—wait a minute." Sam paused. "Why would Ryan be wearing the Schubert logo? Do you think I mistook Terry for Ryan?"

"What do you think?" she asked.

"Did Terry die because he didn't buckle his chin strap?"

"I don't know." Zana was hesitant to get into a discussion with a witness. She had her own opinions, but couldn't hash them over with Sam, because she planned to call him as a witness at trial.

"I find it hard to believe. Pro triathletes buckle their chinstraps. It's automatic," Sam said. "You know that."

"Of course." Zana shrugged and looked at Lucas, who was studying a cuticle.

"I'm sorry, I've got to turn on my blender so I'll have to hang up," Sam said.

"No problem. Mahalo for your time. You'll hear from us." After Zana hung up the phone, Lucas yelped and pumped his fist.

"What's that for?" Zana asked.

"Isn't that the smoking gun?" Lucas grinned.

"All we know is that Ryan and Terry somehow had their helmets switched. We also know that for some reason Terry didn't fasten the chin strap on Ryan's helmet," Zana said.

"Why didn't he buckle it?"

"That's what I want to know," Zana said, turning to her computer. She pulled up colored pictures of the helmet Terry was wearing at the time of the crash and Lucas stood up to peer at them over her shoulder. "I wish I could see the buckle better."

"Yeah, it's not very easy to see from these photos," Lucas said, leaning forward. "It looks like whoever took the pictures didn't want the buckle to stand out, since it's black and they were taken on a black background."

"I'll schedule an inspection of the helmet and bring an expert with me," Zana said.

Lucas sat down again. "Is there any such thing as a bicycle helmet buckle expert?"

"I'm not sure. I'll Google it," Zana said.

Lucas looked at his wristwatch. "It's almost nine; I've got to get out of here."

"Hot date?" Zana asked.

"With my pillow," Lucas said.

"Sexy." Zana raised her eyebrows.

"What about you? Where's Mr. T.V. star?"

"Out of the country," she snapped, turning back to her computer so Lucas wouldn't see that the mention of Jerry caused her eyes to become moist. She had received a lame text from him yesterday about their getting a lot of work done, but she was still waiting for a call.

"I'll see ya' tomorrow," Lucas said as he walked out the door. "Don't work too late."

***

Lucas reported to his father's office five minutes before the scheduled time. He still wanted to impress Frank with high billable hours and punctuality, mostly out of guilt for behaving like an arrogant fuck up during the first few months of his employment. After his deposition trip with Zana to Minnesota, he had decided to come clean and admit to his mother, claims manager Caron Rossi, and Frank that he had known since the fourth grade that Frank was his father. The past six months had been a mixture of what felt like normal father and son outings to catch up for lost time, and pressure at the firm to perform up to Frank's expectations. Lucas was flattered that his father had assigned him to work with Zana on the Schubert case, especially when Frank told him that he needed someone he trusted to keep an eye on Zana.

"You're here early—that's what I like to see." Frank smiled.

Lucas was surprised to see his father in good spirits for a change. He assumed Frank had been more irritable than usual because of staff screw-ups and billable hours not being up to snuff, but he wondered if his father might still be upset at his mother for assigning a file directly to an associate. *Did Frank think he was losing his edge?*

"I aim to please." Lucas sat down.

"I have some good news for you, son," Frank said.

"Oh?"

"Now that Charles has been appointed to serve as a judge, he's moving out of his corner office after thirty years," Frank said, rubbing his chin.

"Are you going to give me his office?" Lucas grinned.

"No, Lucas," Frank said. "We've offered Charles' office to Michael Lee. But that leaves Michael's office empty. It's a large office with a view of the ocean and Diamond Head. Are you interested?"

"Oh, my gosh—are you kidding me?"

"No, I never kid." Frank leaned back in his chair.

"Won't it be a problem for the other attorneys?" Lucas rubbed his chin. It wasn't fair, but if his father wanted to give him a posh office, why should he turn it down?

"Let me worry about them. I'm the partner in charge of office allocation and I want my son to have a nicer office."

"Thanks Dad," Lucas said, still not comfortable calling him anything other than Frank. He tried to keep his composure. If he were with his friends or his mother, he'd be doing a happy dance. Instead, he sat up straight and tried to shift his focus back to work.

"Don't give it another thought. I'll let Libby know you're moving offices. She'll coordinate any needs for new furniture you might have," Frank said. "Now, tell me. What's going on with the Schubert case?"

"Zana's going down some harebrained path," Lucas said, knowing how to brighten his father's day.

"Oh? What path is that?" Frank smiled.

"She was here late last night calling some triathletes who said they saw Schubert and Peterson before the accident. Apparently, they switched helmets and one of them saw Schubert's chin strap hanging."

"If he didn't fasten the helmet, his own actions would be a proximate cause of his own death." Frank rubbed his chin. "Isn't that right, son?"

"I think Zana's going on a wild goose chase with liability," Lucas said.

"Why do you say that?"

"Zana and the witness both said that pro triathletes would never risk disqualification by not fastening their helmets. I don't think there's any concrete proof that Terry Schubert's helmet was not buckled."

"What's your evaluation of the case?" Frank picked up a pen and poised it over a legal pad.

"I think it's worth over one million dollars," Lucas said, rubbing his chin again. "The guy died. He was a promising pro triathlete."

"From what I hear, pro triathletes don't make much money," Frank said.

"It doesn't matter." Lucas shook his head. "Preston Farnsworth is going to hire an economist who will do his black magic and come up with numbers that will persuade the jury to give Terry's grieving family big bucks."

"Do you think F.I.M. should make an offer to settle?" Frank asked, crinkling his forehead.

Lucas nodded. "Yes. Absolutely. I think it's a disservice to our client not to offer policy limits of one million."

"Well," Frank said, pausing. "My hands are tied here. I can't step in and convince your mom to offer policy limits. This is Zana's case."

"Can't you just tell Zana what she needs to do?" Lucas leaned forward.

"I'm not sure I want to. If she screws this one up, F.I.M. won't give her any more cases and I'll have a good reason to fire her."

"When did you ever need a good reason?" Lucas asked, raising his eyebrows.

Chapter Twenty

@ZLaw If I were Rocky, I'd go into a butcher's refrigerator and punch meat with my bare fists. #Grrrrrrr!

Kenny sat across from Preston at the Hawaii Kai Starbucks as they each read the day's news on their iPads. They had broken their usual Sunday morning routine of coffee and Apple Store browsing at Kahala Mall for the scenic drive to the marina where they would take a walk after the caffeine kicked in. It was refreshing to enjoy their only free morning together in peace. So far, there hadn't been any interruptions by friends or colleagues stopping by their table to exchange pleasantries or gossip.

"Did you know there's a hurricane heading our way?" Kenny said with a furrowed brow.

"It's nothing to worry about. I've been tracking it. It's heading over cold waters," Preston said, sipping coffee from a ceramic mug rather than the usual paper cup. "By Wednesday, it'll be a tropical storm at most."

Kenny leaned forward. "Speaking of hurricanes, Bud's on the warpath about Jerry and Zana."

"How is Jerry's sex life any of his business?" Preston said. "When we started dating, there were plenty of detractors—remember?"

Kenny nodded. "He's threatening to pull his company's sponsorship."

"What can *you* do?"

"I told Bud that she's Jerry's flavor of the month," Kenny said, putting his iPad down on the table. "It's true. The guy goes through girlfriends like you go through Merkur razors."

Preston chuckled. "What did Bud say to that?"

"He still wasn't happy, but it seemed to placate him a bit," Kenny said, bouncing his knee under the table.

"Stop it." Preston put his hand on his partner's thigh. "Kenneth, you haven't told me everything about this situation. Am I right?"

"You know me too well." Kenny stretched out his legs.

"What did you do this time?" Preston shook his head and set his tablet down.

"I sent Jerry to Rio with Annabelle." Kenny smiled at his ingenious plot. *How could the star of "Fighting in Paradise" resist one of Waikiki's top bikini models who also happens to be a black belt in both Tae Kwon Do and Kung Fu?* "When it comes to Jerry, she's like a bitch in heat."

"So that's why you re-seated Jerry and Zana with Annabelle." Preston pursed his lips.

"There were open chairs at that table, but it didn't hurt that Annabelle is even more flirtatious than Jerry, which is saying a lot. I decided to play it up to Bud," Kenny said. "Jerry and Zana's relationship isn't going to survive the Rio trip."

"And people say attorneys are snakes," Preston said, shaking his head. "This is dastardly. I actually feel sorry for Zana, and she's my adversary."

Kenny took it as a compliment and smiled. "I've been thinking about sending Jerry and Annabelle to Bali together directly from Rio to study Indonesian Martial arts for a few weeks."

"He would never agree. I'm sure he can't be away from his law practice for long," Preston said.

"Jerry's firm is usually slow this time of year. I think I could talk him into a Bali trip."

"Kenneth, I think you're going a bit too far with this. Jerry can fly Zana out to be with him, and I'm sure he would like to spend the holidays with his family."

"I know. A guy can scheme, can't he?" Kenny flashed his most devious smile.

***

The rain was so heavy Zana could barely see the pineapple in the distance from her office window. She hadn't been able to get outside to work out for days and could feel her muscles atrophying with each passing hour. She clicked on a weather website and read that forecasters blamed global warming for the unusual post-season hurricane, which had been downgraded to a tropical storm now raging through the island chain. A flash flood warning was in effect for all islands.

Zana sighed. The wait for cardio equipment at the YMCA was at least forty minutes in the early morning and evening and during the busy hours a strict time limit had been placed on each machine.

At 10 a.m., she feigned a coffee run and headed over to the Y, hoping a machine would be free. Surprisingly, there were four open treadmills so she had her pick. She climbed on, programmed it for a hill workout and picked an upbeat playlist on her iPhone. A Beyoncé song was playing when her phone rang.

"Hey, Alexia," Zana said into the head set after she saw the claims adjuster's name pop up on the screen.

"Sorry to bother you, but Caron insisted I call. We're missing the filed answer to complaint for the Schubert case," Alexia said.

"I'll have Sylvia email it to you," Zana said. "I'm not sure why you don't have it."

"Where are you? You sound out of breath."

"The Y. There are actually some open treadmills," Zana said.

"You are so lucky. I've only been able to lift free weights. My gym has been packed," Alexia said.

"If you want to be my guest and come now, I'll save a machine."

"I'll be right there," Alexia said and hung up the phone.

After she made arrangements with the front desk to have a guest, Zana cranked up the speed and adjusted the grade on the machine for hills. After about 15 minutes, Alexia showed up wearing black running shorts and a pink running bra. She carried a bottle of water and a towel. She climbed on the treadmill next to Zana and began jogging at a slow pace.

Zana popped her earbuds out and put her phone and headset in an empty drink holder. "I hope this rain will stop soon. I'd rather run on the beach."

"I know what you mean. I was hoping to go for a hike." Alexia adjusted the settings on the machine to increase her pace.

"I love hiking, but triathlon training gets in the way."

"It's a great workout. You could substitute hiking for a long run."

Zana nodded.

Alexia drank from her water bottle while keeping up her pace. "How's the Schubert case coming along?"

"I've been following up on some leads in the investigation. I'm quite certain that Ryan had no fault in Terry's death, but I'm still trying to prove it," Zana said.

"Let me know what you find out." They ran next to each other in silence for a few minutes. Then Alexia said, "I went to a concert with Ryan."

"You did?" Zana feigned surprise. She knew about the concert, but didn't think Ryan would appreciate it if she told Alexia that he talked about her.

"Yeah. We saw Sei Bombay."

"How was it?" Zana slowed down so it was easier to talk.

"It was fantastic!" Alexia said, also slowing down.

"I love her, but I'm not a fan of her song 'Ruby'." Zana wrinkled her nose.

"Me neither, but for some reason, it wasn't as bad in person." Alexia looked at Zana as she jogged. "It was a weird evening, but I had fun."

"Why was it weird?"

"When I first met Ryan, he was so aggressive about trying to get me to go out with him. When I finally agreed, he was kind of standoffish."

"He's quite the gentleman," Zana said.

Alexia nodded.

Zana wished Jerry would take a few lessons from her client about how to treat her. Ryan had no trouble picking up the phone to call her when he was out of town. "Any woman who dates him would be lucky," she said.

"Why do you say that?" Alexia wiped her face with a small white towel.

"Since I've known him, he constantly goes out of his way to help me. He really goes the extra mile."

"Like what has he done?"

"I sliced my hand up on the coral while swimming in a triathlon on Thanksgiving morning. Ryan swam out and rescued me." Zana pointed to the scar. "He gave up his entire holiday to be with me in the emergency room. Did you know that he is constantly helping athletes who get hurt?"

"I had no idea. Most guys I've known *send* women to the emergency room," Alexia said and then wiped her forehead again with the towel.

"Ryan's a catch," Zana said. "You're lucky to have gone on a date with him."

"It wasn't really a date." Alexia frowned. They both ran for a few minutes in silence and then she said, "Maybe, I should go on a real date with him."

Before Zana could respond, Alexia hopped off the treadmill and said, "I've got to get back to the office. Thanks for the guest pass. Keep me updated on the case."

"Talk to you soon," Zana said. She noticed the men momentarily stop exercising to watch Alexia as she walked past the long row of cardio machines, her long blonde ponytail swaying behind her.

Zana increased her speed and programed another sixty minutes. She would work late.

***

After she finished her run and showered, Zana braved the heavy rain and stopped by Starbucks for a latte and sandwich before heading back to the office. While she waited for her order, she felt a tap on her arm.

"Are you stalking me?" Zana asked when she saw Ryan standing there with a coffee in one hand and a dripping umbrella in the other.

"Yes, Zana. As a matter of fact I am," he said. "I was at your office waiting for you *forever* and decided I needed a caffeine fix."

"You should have asked my secretary to call me," she said, picking up her order.

"That would have been nice, but I've been down that road before and ended up on the phone with Frank," Ryan said, making a face. "I played it low key for a change. Do you have time to sit down for a few minutes?"

She nodded and they found an empty table.

"I'm freaked out about my deposition next week," he said.

"You'll be fine." It was the first deposition of a client she would be handling on her own, and she felt her stomach churn every time it was discussed. "I'll prep you during our meeting on Tuesday. In the meantime, I'll email you a link to a deposition preparation video you can watch as many times as you'd like."

"Mahalo." Ryan slumped in his chair. "Maybe, we should change the subject."

"Just so you know, I was at the Y running on the treadmill," she said before biting into her sandwich.

"I'm glad to hear it, you've got a lot of training to do," he said. "I saw that you signed up for the Freewheel Tri."

"Yeah, I thought I'd give it a go," she said. "Jerry's out of town and it's about time I focused on something else."

"Work hard, and you'll give Megan a run for her money." Ryan sipped his coffee.

"I feel sort of like Rocky, except I won't have any steps to climb when I finish the race," she laughed.

"I think you're more like a Rockette, with those long legs," he said, gesturing to her legs that were stretched into the aisle.

"LOL." Zana smiled. "Oh, I forgot to tell you. Guess who I was running next to at the gym?"

"Who?"

"Come on, you've got to guess," she said, sipping her latte.

"Jeff Paris?"

"No."

"Frank Gravelle?"

"No!" Zana laughed. "Alexia was there."

"Are you kidding? Did you talk to her?" Ryan leaned in.

"Now, don't have a coronary. I told her what an amazing man you are. Your own mother would not have praised you as much as I did," she said.

"Thank you so much." He grinned. "You are the bestest attorney ever!"

"I'll put that on my C.V. I'm sure Frank will be impressed. I have a feeling that Alexia will go out with you again."

"Are you joking?" Ryan's eyes widened.

"You might want to wait a few days to call her," she said. "Give her a chance to let my praise sink in."

"Okay, I'll play it cool," he said, standing up. "I have a radio interview. Thanks again, Zana."

After Ryan left, she finished her sandwich. She was about to head out the door when the sky seemed to open up and sheets of water poured from the sky. Her flimsy umbrella would provide little protection so she returned to her seat to wait out the weather. Zana scrolled through her emails, which were mostly about pending discovery. She accepted an invitation to friend one of Shelby's triathlon buddies on Facebook and then clicked on the newsfeed to pass the time. She seldom looked at her friends' posts, because she had little interest in their pictures of food, pets and sentimental quotations. After watching a few cute dog and cat videos, she punched in Jerry's name, which she hadn't thought to do since his posts from the "Fighting in Paradise" gala.

Her jaw dropped when saw the new pictures he'd posted. She tucked her phone back in her bag and looked around the café to make sure no one she knew witnessed the tears forming in her eyes. Then she bolted out the door without bothering to open her umbrella. She ran across the street, not looking to see if it was safe to do so and ignored the blaring horn of the car that screeched to a halt to avoid hitting her. She splashed through water pooling on the sidewalk and sprinted into the building, sliding on the wet marble floor, knocking over a Caution: Wet Floor sign. By the time Zana reached the elevator, her hair and clothes were soaking wet, dripping a puddle onto the floor. She used her fob to let herself into the back entrance near the bathroom in order to reach her office without passing the receptionist, and walked past Sylvia's cubicle as quietly as possible.

"You're back," Sylvia said. "I need you to sign…"

"I've got to take a call," Zana interrupted, and slipped into her office. She didn't notice the frigid air conditioner's impact on her drenched clothes and bee-lined to her P.C. so she could see Jerry's new Facebook posts on the large screen.

The first picture showed Jerry and Annabelle drinking wine, sitting next to each other in a restaurant. She wondered whether the photographer was someone across from them, or a standing waiter. Either way, she felt her stomach knot up at the sight of their smiling faces and their bodies so close together their shoulders were touching.

The next two images showed the two of them at the beach. In one photo, Jerry was standing in the water with only his chiseled bare chest showing and Annabelle was a few steps in front and to the side of him, revealing her almost naked body covered by a skimpy red thong and tiny bikini top which only covered one nipple. She looked like sex on a stick. The next picture showed Annabelle's exposed rear end and the red strip between her butt cheeks. She was facing Jerry, who wore a Cheshire cat smile. His eyes seemed to be looking at her chest rather than the camera. It wasn't clear who had taken the pictures, but the captions said "Fun in the sun," "Party time in Rio," and "It's Hot in Rio." There were 47 likes, which was surprising, because Jerry wasn't exactly active on Facebook. Zana couldn't believe some of the comments. "Lucky dude!" "It looks like you're having fun, Jerry!" "Who's the hot chick, Jerry Ho?" "You lucky S.O.B." "Guess you're moving to Rio" and "Skinny dipping…ooh la la!"

Zana suddenly felt a chill and her teeth began chattering uncontrollably. She slipped off her wet shoes, pulled her knees to her chest and closed her eyes. After a half hour or so, she clicked off the computer and changed into a dry set of clothes hanging on the back of her door.

She pushed away her time sheet. She wasn't going to be able to work until evening as she intended. Instead, she took out a fresh legal pad and pen. She had to come up with a plan.

She grabbed a handful of tissues and leaned back in her chair. As she wiped her tear- and rainwater-stained face, her thoughts went straight to

Jerry. *Was he really having sex with Annabelle?* She looked at her phone to see his last text, which was his usual "I miss you" message from that morning. But there were no calls. Ryan had it right. It was time for her to play it cool.

She swiveled her chair so it was level with the Dole pineapple in the distance and chewed the end of her pen while she stared at nothing in particular. She only knew one thing for sure. She couldn't continue giving up her dreams in order to spend time with a guy who may have already moved on. It was time for her to pursue her own goals. She wrote on the page:

> *GOALS:*
> *1. Win age group in Paradise Lagoons Triathlon*
> *2. Transfer to the sports agency section at G, P & D*

She then folded the page and put it in her purse, wiped the tears from her eyes, and headed back to the gym for the evening spinning class.

Chapter Twenty-one

@ZLaw The force was with the Depo Twins today. The power of matching outfits. #DepositionFashion

When Bud heard the newspaper smack against the house, he leapt up from the couch but just as he flung open the front door, Sandy grabbed his arm.

"No!" Sandy said, pulling her husband towards her. "I'll call them and complain. There's no need to attack a twelve-year-old boy."

Bud scowled. "Let me get the paper."

She released his arm so he could walk outside in his robe and slippers to retrieve the folded and rubber-banded newspaper from the Hibiscus bushes flanking the house. *Why couldn't the paperboy simply place the damn paper on the porch?* He ignored his wife's disapproving look, marched into his office and slammed the door.

He slumped on the couch and pulled out the sports section, but his focus was drawn to the only paper on his desk—the deposition notice. He planned to tell Sandy he was going to a meeting rather than upset her with the news of Ryan Peterson's scheduled deposition in a few hours. Preston told him not to attend, but how could he focus on work, playing golf or shoot at the gun range knowing his son's killer was being questioned today?

"Are you going to a Texas funeral?" Sandy asked when Bud reached for the garage doorknob, hoping to slip out without her noticing. He was wearing a black shirt and slacks with a matching cowboy hat.

"I'm late for a meeting," Bud said his rehearsed line. He grabbed his black suit jacket hanging from a hook in the mudroom in preparation for the air-conditioned conference room. When he draped it over his arm, he felt hard metal.

"We're in Hawaii. Maybe, you should change into something with some Aloha spirit. You have a closet full of Hawaiian shirts." She followed him into the garage.

"No time," Bud said, managing a half smile and kissing her on the lips goodbye. He climbed into his Ford F-150 truck. A floral print shirt wouldn't send the right message to his adversaries, and would do nothing in his quest to collect all available insurance money and drain every last cent from Ryan Peterson's accounts.

Shortly after Terry's death, Bud contacted his friend at the Honolulu Prosecutor's office, Herman Kim, and tried to convince him to indict Peterson for criminal charges, but was told there wasn't enough evidence to support homicide, manslaughter or negligent homicide convictions. Herman suggested a civil action instead. Bud preferred the meanest son-of-a-bitch attorney he knew, Rip Mansfield, as his advocate. But, Rip was still suspended from the practice of law so he decided to go with Preston who had known Terry and seemed passionate about his cause.

The last time Rip was part of his foursome, Bud told him about Peterson's deposition. The mention of Zana West's name caused Rip's face to contort with so much rage he sliced the ball near the tenth hole so it dropped into the bunker. If Bud were a competitive golfer, he'd have discovered the secret to distracting his golf buddy. Rip's sudden tirade upon hearing Zana's name resulted in a broken club and a double bogey. Throughout the remaining eight holes, Rip called her every profane name Bud had heard of and some he hadn't. Later, when Bud thought about her, the same expressions came to mind.

How could Jerry Hirano, the star of the show he was pumping hundreds of thousands of dollars into be dating her? After his golf game, Bud had contacted his accountant about withdrawing sponsorship money from "Fighting in Paradise," but was advised the contract wasn't up for renewal for months. News of Jerry's short attention span when it came to women gave Bud some hope of continuing sponsorship. He'd wait and see.

Preston, smartly dressed in a navy suit and burgundy bow tie, was sitting behind his imposing Koa wood desk in his office with its view of Iolani Palace and Diamond Head. Bud was pleased he'd trusted his instincts and wore a jacket. The oldest and largest law firm in Honolulu, led by many of the famed "old boys' network", was not the place for dressing casually.

Preston rose and gave Bud a hearty handshake. The two men stood well over six feet tall—an imposing pair in a city with a large Asian population. The attorney then motioned his client to sit down.

"Preston, I'm curious about something," Bud said, leaning back in the chair.

"What's that?"

"I golf with Rip Mansfield," he said. "Are you familiar with him?"

"Sure," Preston said. "He's an infamous Honolulu attorney."

"Well, I understand he was suspended from the practice of law." Bud adjusted his cowboy hat.

"That's what I hear."

"Did his suspension have anything to do with Zana West?"

Preston shifted in his seat. "Why do you ask?"

"He was absolutely beside himself when I mentioned her name," Bud said.

"I'm not one to gossip, but I heard that he was suspended because of his behavior in a case against her," Preston frowned. "Apparently, there's a videotape of Mansfield admitting to telling his client what to say at his deposition."

"And, that came out because of Zana?" Bud asked.

"I hear she's quite resourceful for a young associate," Preston said, picking up a glass paperweight etched with the scales of justice and holding it in his hands. "I never underestimate opposing counsel. It's easy to become complacent after so many years of practicing law. These young attorneys have so much energy and they're so comfortable with technology."

"Well, she sounds like a snake to me," Bud said. "I don't trust her as far as I could throw her. Her representation of that murderer Peterson tells me a lot about her character."

"Now, now," Preston said, dropping the paperweight onto his desk with a thud. "Ryan Peterson was certainly negligent, but the evidence doesn't support a charge of homicide."

"I disagree. Texas has it right. I've never understood this liberal state without the death penalty." Bud squinted his eyes. "Peterson deserves to die."

Preston shook his head. "Bud, this kind of talk is inappropriate. I suggest you calm down. Be patient and let the legal system work."

"Okay, okay." Bud sighed.

Preston's secretary walked in the room without knocking. "They're ready for you," she said.

"Thank you, Kulani." Preston stood up. "Let's get this over with."

The two men were silent as they walked down the hall to the large conference room with a glass wall separating it from the imposing reception area.

Bud felt queasy when he saw Ryan Peterson and his attorneys sitting down at the conference table as they approached the room. Taking heed of Preston's advice, he shifted his focus past his adversaries to the expansive view of the ocean with Aloha Tower and a cruise ship in the forefront. He followed Preston's lead and sat next to his attorney, across from Zana. He stretched his long legs under the table until he felt something—then he realized he'd probably stepped on her high-heeled foot. Her face didn't register any emotion, but he felt her leg retreat. The last thing he wanted to do was play footsie with the enemy.

***

Earlier that morning, Zana was checking emails and sipping a latte when her phone rang. She saw it was her client before picking up.

"Are you sure I shouldn't wear a suit and tie?" Ryan asked.

Zana laughed. "I can't imagine you in anything other than your talk show uniform." Ryan always wore a black T-shirt and jeans whenever he appeared on television. When they met the day before to prepare for his deposition, he had pleaded with her to allow him to wear his usual clothing, but she had insisted he wear a collared shirt and slacks.

"What about plaid pants?" Ryan asked.

She smiled. "I'm going to hang up now."

"Okay, I'm just giving you crap. I'm on my way."

"Behave, or I'll tell Alexia." Zana sipped her latte.

"You wouldn't dare tell her I'm wearing a florescent pink shirt and orange pants. See ya soon!" he hung up before she could respond.

She leaned back in her chair and grinned. Even though she'd only been practicing law for a short time, Ryan was her favorite client and made the long hours and stress worth it. If only she could convince Preston and Bud Schubert to accept a low ball offer of settlement. Maybe, if Ryan did an outstanding job at his deposition, they would be convinced the case wasn't worth much.

She heard a soft tap on the door before Lucas walked in, carrying a legal pad.

"Sorry I can't attend the entire deposition with you." He sat down across from her.

"That's okay," she said. "Insurance companies are not interested in paying for two attorneys anyway."

"Frank wants me to take the deposition of a witness in a car accident case this afternoon," he said as he clicked his pen.

She nodded. "I'm happy you're getting some experience."

"Yeah, it beats being stuck in my office researching, summarizing medical records and responding to document productions."

Zana wanted to add playing video games to his list, but she'd only caught him doing it a few times lately and so it seemed her coworker had changed his slothful ways as promised.

"I can work on last minute prep and be there for the first few hours," Lucas said.

"Sure." She would rather go to the deposition with reinforcements, even if it was with another new associate. At least he had the cache of being a partner's son and had an imposing physical presence.

"Mr. Peterson is in conference room two," Jasmin, the receptionist announced from the phone speaker.

Zana grabbed her legal pad and laptop, and followed Lucas down the hallway.

"Good morning, Ryan," she said as they shook hands. If Lucas weren't standing next to her, she would have given her client a hug.

Lucas laughed. "Did you get the memo, Ryan?"

"I'm sorry, I'm not sure I understand," Ryan said.

"You two are dressed alike. Was that planned?" Lucas asked, referring to Ryan and Zana's black pants, olive green shirts and black jackets.

"Zana told me not to dress like Simon Cowell, as I usually do," Ryan said.

She scowled. "Believe me, this wasn't planned." They each pulled out a chair and sat at the conference table.

"It's not a big deal. I kind of like it—you're depo twins," Lucas said.

"Let's just focus on the case. I could change my blouse, but I don't think it matters that we both have great taste. What do you think, Ryan?" Zana asked.

"I don't care, either. You never know. Maybe, the twinsy outfits will help us settle the case," Ryan smirked.

"I doubt it will help, but at least it's something to cut the tension and it shows we're on the same team," she said. "Did you review the documents I e-mailed to you?"

"Yeah, there wasn't much to review," Ryan said, fidgeting with his near empty coffee cup.

"You look nervous," Zana said, noticing that her client was wearing one black and one brown sock.

"You would be, too, if you were accused of murdering someone. I had nothing to do with Terry's death," Ryan said. "I actually liked the guy."

"Have you ever had your deposition taken before?" Lucas asked.

"I think so. I got questioned about doping when I was riding with the team, but I don't remember a court reporter being there. I was in Paris and USADA attorneys grilled me in French. They wanted to know the names of doctors and other athletes involved," he said. "I came clean. I told them everything they wanted to know, but now I have more enemies than you can imagine."

Lucas frowned. "Well, at least you've had some experience being questioned in a hostile environment."

"This might be a little like that," Zana said, not really knowing everything she needed to discuss with Ryan, having not represented a client in a deposition yet on her own. Even though Frank treated her more like a well-educated secretary than an attorney, she sort of wished he were there so she could follow his lead.

"Do you think my experience on talk shows will help?" Ryan asked. "You'd be surprised how tough Helen, Javier and Danny were when they grilled me. Hawaii Morning was even worse."

"Oh, totally," Zana said. "You handle yourself well. I would avoid your amusing anecdotes, though. You've not been invited to the deposition to entertain us—just tell the truth."

"Well said," Lucas piped in. "Shall we head over there?"

Ryan and Zana followed his lead to the high rise next door. She could see sailboats dotting the sparkling ocean and Aloha Tower through the floor to ceiling windows the moment she stepped out of the elevator into the reception area of Bishop & Judd. Her knees felt weak when she saw Sue, the court reporter sitting at the end of the longest conference table she'd ever seen, visible through the glass wall.

Preston's no-nonsense secretary, Kulani, led them to the large room, pointing out the coffee and water available on a credenza and instructing them to sit in the chairs facing the ocean view—no doubt, a ploy to distract Ryan during his testimony.

Preston and his client soon joined them. The attorney greeted them with an outstretched hand to shake and Bud slumped solemnly into a chair across from her, not even tipping his black cowboy hat, which he adjusted to partly cover his eyes. Zana was startled when she felt Bud's foot touch hers, seemingly on purpose.

She yanked her foot away and shifted her legs under the table. *Was this his brand of sexual harassment?*

Ryan was seated directly across the table from Preston who would be asking the questions. Preston waited for Zana to open her laptop to view the Real Time transcription of the proceedings, and for Sue to swear Ryan in before questioning him.

Q. (Preston Farnsworth, III) You were terminated from your pro cycling team, correct?

A. (Ryan Peterson) Yes.

Q. On what grounds?

A. Use of banned substances.

Q. After you were fired, you started competing in triathlons, isn't that true?

A. Yes.

Q. Isn't it true that you competed in the Olympic trials in Honolulu in 2012?

A. Yes.

Q. Your primary competitors in that event were Vic Leavitt, Jeff Paris, and Brad Jordan, correct?

A. I'd say so. Yes.

Q. Leavitt was killed, and Paris and Jordan were injured so they couldn't continue the race, is that right?

A. Uh huh.

Q. Is that a yes?

A. I'm sorry. Yes.

Q. We need to get a clear transcript. Make sure you say yes or no rather than uh huh.

A. Okay. Yes.

Q. You won the Olympic trials because your main competition was wiped out. Is that a true statement?

Zana West: Objection. Calls for speculation. Irrelevant. Argumentative.

Q. Do you understand my question, Mr. Peterson?

A. Yes, I think so. I won the race.

Q. Would you have won if your competition weren't eliminated because of death or injury?

West: Objection. Calls for speculation.

A. I don't know.

Q. You competed in the Paradise Lagoons Triathlon, is that correct?

A. Yes.

Q. Was there prize money at stake?

A. Yes.

Q. How much?

A. Twenty thousand dollars.

Q. You needed to win that prize money very badly, didn't you?

A. Yes. Pro triathletes don't have many opportunities to make money.

Q. Who were your main competitors in that race?

A. Jeff Paris, Terry Schubert, Sam Donahue and a few others.

When Ryan mentioned Terry's name, Zana noticed Bud shift in his seat. She then saw him wipe his cheek with his hand, and open his jacket. She thought he was reaching in his pocket for some tissue, but saw what she was sure was a gun.

"Let's take a break," Zana blurted.

"We can take a break when I finish this line of questioning, counselor," Preston said, looking at her sternly.

"No, we can't. I need to speak with you in your office," she demanded, standing up. "Now!"

Preston shrugged. "Alright." He shuffled his notes and then turned them over. His client blew his nose loudly.

Zana whispered in Lucas' ear, directing him to take Ryan out of the building. Rather than use the elevators, they should run down the stairs and go immediately to the security office in the parking garage. She waited until Lucas led their client away, and then she motioned for Preston to follow her.

"Call security and have them come up here right away," Zana said in a low voice to the receptionist as she led opposing counsel past the front desk and to his office.

"What's this all about?" Preston asked gruffly after she shut the door behind them.

"Your client has a gun," her voice cracked.

"No he doesn't," Preston said.

"I saw it."

"You must be mistaken."

They stood facing each other between his desk and the door.

"He opened his jacket. Mr. Schubert needs to immediately be escorted out of here, or I'm calling the police," she said, her face flushing with anger and fear. "This isn't Texas."

Preston shook his head and said, "No need."

"Bud Schubert has called my client a murderer. I'm concerned that he intends to harm Mr. Peterson and possibly myself," Zana stammered. "We can talk about how to proceed safely in the future. Please, get your client out of here immediately before he hurts someone."

Zana walked with Preston to the reception area where three security guards were standing.

"What's the problem?" a large Samoan man wearing a white shirt with the security company logo asked.

"Please make sure that the man wearing the black cowboy hat is escorted out. He's armed," Zana said, hands on hips.

"He already left," the smaller security guard said.

Chapter Twenty-Two

@FreewheelMV Taking a break from Twitter for a while to go under cover. Just call me #007.

Alexia's alarm sounded at 4:15 a.m. Instead of jumping out of bed, walking across the room and turning it off as she always did, she covered her head with a pillow to drown out the shrill noise. She drifted off to sleep and when she woke again, daylight was shining through the windows. Beads of sweat formed on her lip and forehead as she climbed out of bed and crept through the small, airless house, checking the doors and windows to make sure they were still locked.

She paused in front of the full-length mirror and checked her appearance, comparing what she looked like now versus when she was under Stan's control. Her long, blonde hair was silky straight with no dark roots showing, her skin was bright and clear from weekly facials, her nails were acrylic and painted pastel green, and when she lifted up her T-shirt, she could see her abdominal muscles. Even if she pinched her skin, she couldn't produce any fat. Her eyes were drawn to the tattoo of a slinky black cat on her right hip, symbolic of her freedom from Stan, who despised and even tortured cats. She recognized her old self when she looked into her brown eyes in the mirror, but with blue contacts, false eyelashes and heavy makeup, she bore no resemblance to her former battered self. Her short brown hair, uneven complexion, pudgy body and frumpy clothes were a distant memory. Even though her husband was not likely to recognize her now, she couldn't shake the constant fear of waking up to him pointing a loaded pistol in her face.

Alexia had only slept through her alarm one other time when she'd caught the flu. She paced the floor. Was she blowing her cover? Not once since she walked off the plane to start her new life in Hawaii had she ever let her guard down. Constantly feeling like a hunted animal allowed her to stay one step ahead of Stan, who would make good on his promise to kill her if she ever left him. Whenever an excuse to skip a workout crept into her consciousness, she remembered the words of her rescuers who insisted that her survival depended on her constant efforts to maintain her altered appearance. He would be looking for the out of shape woman he married, not the blonde bombshell she had become.

Since it was too late to go to the gym and still be on time for work, Alexia quickly did 50 pushups and 30 burpees. She could go for a long run after work, so she'd not impacted her fitness level with one slip. Nevertheless, Alexia felt on edge. While she filled her blender with smoothie ingredients for breakfast, she tried to figure out why she'd been feeling anxious for the past few weeks. She was fine before the concert with Ryan. But after Zana raved about how incredible he was, for some strange reason, he had been on her mind constantly. *Did she have a crush on this guy?* The last time she had felt this way was when she met Stan years ago, but those feelings went away after his first beating.

As Alexia sipped her smoothie, she let herself daydream about going on a date with Ryan—sitting across a dinner table from him, feeling his hand reach for hers, their lips kissing and their bodies entwined together. The more she imagined being with him, the more anxious she became about her silent phone. He had only called her once since the concert to ask how she was doing, and then quickly made an excuse to end the call. She shook her head, hoping to erase those thoughts so she could focus on a long day of work. It was Friday and if she were going to finish in time for a run, she'd have to get moving.

She spent the day in court for a settlement conference on a premises liability case. By the time she returned to the office at the end of the workday, her co-workers were chattering about their plans for the weekend—kids' soccer games, romantic dates, meeting up with friends, concerts, movies, and camping. The only thing she had to look forward to was her manicure and weekly hike alone.

After work, she drove to Kapiolani Park where most of the serious triathletes and runners trained. From there, she ran up Diamond Head, through Kahala, past the golf course and then down Monsarrat Avenue and back to her car, hoping she might accidentally bump into Ryan. He was nowhere to be seen. When her calves were fully stretched and she could think of no other excuse to linger, Alexia grabbed her phone and on impulse called him.

"Hello," he said after a few rings.

"Hi Ryan, it's Alexia," she stammered, hearing traffic noises and what sounded like music coming through the phone.

"Hey, nice hearing from you," he said.

"How are you?" She wiped sweat off her forehead with a small white towel.

"Well, not so great, to tell you the truth."

"Why? What's wrong?" she asked, alarmed that something bad might have happened to him while she was waiting for him to call for the past few weeks.

"I'm driving to the airport," he said. "I'll be away for a while."

"Where are you going?"

"I'm so sorry, but I can't tell you—or anyone," Ryan said, his voice catching.

"Are you ill? Is someone in your family sick?" Alexia paced next to her car.

"It's nothing like that," he said. "You probably wouldn't understand, but there's someone who wants to kill me and I need to get lost for a while."

"Believe me, I understand." She leaned against her car. "Who's after you?"

"Has Zana told you what happened at my deposition yesterday?"

"No, not yet. I was in a settlement conference all day, so even if she tried to reach me, I was in court."

"Bud Schubert brought a gun to the deposition," Ryan said. "He's publicly talked about killing me, and Zana thinks I should flee the state without saying a word to anyone."

"I won't tell a soul." She closed her eyes, her unsteady hand holding the phone to her ear.

"I'm sorry I'm so freaked out about this." Ryan paused for a long moment and then said in a shaky voice, "I'm sure you can't relate."

"You'd be surprised." Alexia sighed. "I understand all too well."

"Really?" Ryan asked. "Well, you're an adjuster—you probably get death threats all the time."

"Yeah," she swallowed. "That's it. When will you be back?"

"I'm not sure."

"I had such a great time at the concert. I wonder if we can get together again." She held her breath.

"I would love to see you, Alexia," Ryan said. "I just don't know when I can return. Zana convinced me not to risk my life by staying here."

"Ryan," Alexia said, she wanted to try to put her feelings into words, but her mind went blank.

"Yes?"

"Be safe."

***

As Jerry disembarked from the plane at the Honolulu International Airport, the weight of the humid air made him instantly regret his decision not to change into shorts. The contrast between the heat and the chilly first class cabin was so remarkable that he immediately ducked into the restroom near Gate 10 to change clothes and brush his teeth before meeting Kenny at baggage claim. When Kenny had called last week about extending their time in Rio and adding on two weeks in Indonesia, Jerry had refused. There was no way he was going to miss spending Christmas at home with his parents and Zana, and he certainly couldn't leave his law office unmanned for such a long time, despite his capable staff. He had been reviewing emails and keeping up with work remotely, but he couldn't put off several depositions any longer. It was time to come home.

It had been close to midnight in Rio when Jerry made up his mind to catch the first available flight back to Hawaii. There was a 6 a.m. flight to Houston the next morning with some seats available, and he was able to fly through San Francisco so his time in the air was less than 20 hours. He spent the rest of the night packing, since he would have plenty of time to sleep on the plane.

In order to avoid any unnecessary drama, he decided to wait until he was on the plane to text Annabelle about his departure. The last thing he wanted was to have her tag along, which would disrupt his sleep time on the plane and might also interfere with his long awaited reunion with Zana. He decided to wait until he got to Honolulu to surprise his girlfriend. It had been weeks since they'd been together and he missed her.

After many grueling hours on several planes, a long wait in the customs line in San Francisco, his plane had finally touched down in Honolulu amid cheers of excitement from arriving tourists. He wheeled his carryon bag, but he also had checked in a large black suitcase filled with Christmas presents for his family and Zana from Rio, along with his clothes and a few martial arts souvenirs for himself. As Jerry waited for his luggage at baggage claim, Kenny texted that he was circling the terminal. A handful of people also waiting for their luggage recognized Jerry, even though he wore a black ball cap and sunglasses. After long flights, he was usually exhausted and not in the mood to talk to anyone, and certainly not interested in posing for selfies. He posed for a few, but was relieved when his suitcase was the first to slide down onto the luggage carousel so he could ditch his fans and catch a ride with Kenny without more delay.

"Howdy stranger," Kenny said as he gave Jerry an affectionate hug and opened the trunk of his Jaguar for Jerry's large bag. "Do you have a body in there?"

"If you hadn't extended my stay so long, I would just have my carry-ons," Jerry said as he deposited his 20-inch roller board and briefcase in the back seat.

"If I had known you were stuck in baggage claim, I would have parked. Next time, let me know. I can't have my star fending for himself," Kenny said, snapping the trunk closed.

As Kenny negotiated his way through the cars waiting for passenger pick up curb space, Jerry pulled his iPhone out of his pocket and tapped some keys.

"What are you doing?" Kenny asked.

"Texting Zana to let her know I'm here."

"You mean, she doesn't know you're back?" Kenny turned to Jerry.

"I wanted to surprise her."

"With a text?"

"Yeah, I guess that's really lame," Jerry said, putting his phone back in his pocket.

Kenny smiled. "I'm glad you're back. I need you at the studio to go over some scripts."

Jerry sighed. "I'm sure you don't mean now."

"Sorry, Jerry. I know you're tired from flying. We'll just pop over to the studio for a few minutes. The writers are there now," Kenny said as he maneuvered his car into the H-1 Freeway traffic.

"Can we make it quick?" Jerry said. "I can't wait to see Zana."

"I can imagine. We'll go over a few of your lines, and then I can drop you and all your luggage off at home," Kenny said, smiling. "How's Annabelle?"

Jerry rolled his eyes. "That chick can be a pain in the ass—if you want to know the truth."

"How so?"

"I couldn't shake her. She tagged along with me everywhere I went," Jerry looked at the downtown high rises as they inched along in traffic. "It was almost as if she was paid to try to get in my pants."

"Hmmm. I'm sure that she's just another one of your many admirers," Kenny said as he looked straight ahead at traffic. "Was she successful?"

"I'm not even going to answer that," Jerry said, taking off his ball cap and running his hand through his hair. "Is it possible that you sent me to Rio with horny Annabelle to try to break up my relationship with Zana?"

"Is this cross-examination? You and Preston—I tell you. It's like I'm always in a deposition. I guess that's what I get for surrounding myself with land sharks." Kenny laughed. "You'll like the new format for next season. It's going to position us well for future syndication and hopefully, being sold to a major network."

"I get it. You're evading my question because the answer is yes. I realize I'm not a rocket scientist, but you have to give me a little more credit in the brains department."

"I don't know what you mean."

"Just take me home." Jerry leaned his head against the window and closed his eyes.

"We have to go over some scripts."

"Are you sure that this isn't just another ruse to keep me away from Zana so our precious Bud Schubert doesn't have another conniption?" Jerry asked.

"I don't know what you're talking about, Jerry. You've been away for weeks and there's so much work to do with the writers. I didn't want to bother you with it when you were in Rio, but now we need to get this taken care of," Kenny said as they approached the exit for the studio.

Jerry shook his head. There was no reasoning with the producer, who had become a more demanding taskmaster now that the show was on the brink of profitability. He looked at the time on his phone. It was already almost 11 p.m. in Rio. As much as he could hardly wait to see Zana, he could feel the weight of fatigue.

As Kenny finally pulled into his reserved parking space at the studio, Jerry didn't want to extract his head from the headrest.

"You look tired," Kenny said.

"You think?" Jerry asked, not even trying to hide his irritability.

"I promise—this will only take a few minutes." Kenny walked around the car and opened Jerry's door. He reached into the Jaguar and put a hand on Jerry's bicep in an effort to pry him out of the car.

Jerry kept his sunglasses on as he followed him into the studio. Just as Kenny had promised, the three writers were there—pounding away at their respective laptops at the conference room table, littered with empty Starbucks cups and sandwich wrappers.

"Hey—welcome back, Jerry," Peggy said as she looked up from her work. Her frizzy red hair was pulled back into a ponytail and she wore glasses on the end of her nose.

"How do you say *hello* in Portuguese?" Russ asked, giving Jerry a friendly slap on the arm.

"Oi, *tudo bem*," Jerry said, slumping into a chair next to Peggy.

"No, I don't think that's right," Gregor said. "I think hello is *ola* in Portuguese."

"I just got back from Brazil, not Portugal. I don't know many phrases, but at least I can say hi and good afternoon in Brazilian Portuguese," Jerry said.

"So, maybe there's a language you don't speak, Gregor," Russ said.

"I'm sure it's *ola* in Portuguese. We learned all the European languages…" Gregor said in his slight Austrian accent.

"Yeah, we know—you speak seven languages," Russ said, rolling his eyes. "*Sprechen Sie* Brazilian Portuguese?"

"You can't even pronounce German," Gregor said, laughing.

"Guys…I'm beat. I just want to get on with it and go home," Jerry said, resting his head on the table, still wearing his sunglasses.

"We're good," Peggy said.

"I brought Jerry here so he could go over some of his dialogue with you," Kenny said, leaning against the wall.

"It's looking good," Russ said.

"What?" Peggy turned to look at her boss. "Do you think there are problems, Kenny?"

"Jerry hasn't worked with you in weeks. I thought you might need to have him run some lines," Kenny said.

"No need," Gregor said. "Do you mind if we get back to work?"

"That sounds like a great idea," Jerry said, and promptly stood up and walked toward the door.

"*Tchau*, Jerry," Gregor said.

"That's Italian," Russ said. "Jeez."

"No, that's right. *Tchau,*" Jerry said.

He was in no mood to make small talk with Kenny during the ten-minute drive to his house. He wondered if it would be better to wait until he had some sleep before discussing anything serious with his boss.

"You're quiet," Kenny said after they pulled into Jerry's driveway.

"Uh huh." Jerry nodded and pulled out his carry-on bags. He waited for Kenny to pop the trunk before retrieving his large suitcase.

"What's going on?" Kenny asked.

"Are you going to fire me from the show if I stay with Zana?" Jerry took off his sunglasses and looked Kenny in the eyes.

"I'll be honest with you, Jerry," Kenny said, placing his hand on the actor's shoulder. "Bud is ready to pull his money out."

"Is my job on the line?"

"Let me put it this way," Kenny said. "We can't continue the show without Bud's money, but we *can* re-cast your role."

"Thanks for picking me up," Jerry said, and stalked off into his house.

Chapter Twenty-Three

@ZLaw Surrounded by trees, tinsel, elves, jolly Santas, twinkly lights, but I'm just not feelin' it. #Scrooge

"Smile," Kelly said as she aimed her smart phone at Zana posing in front of the huge shirtless Santa Claus and mu'u mu'u clad Mrs. Claus, who seemed to be standing guard in front of Honolulu Hale. Zana's face reverted to a frown as soon as she heard the click. She should be in a joyous mood, seeing the Hawaiian-style oversized Christmas decorations up close for the first time.

"No more moping," Kelly commanded. "You can think about Jerry later. See, people from all over the world are here."

"She's not kidding," Andrew said, grabbing Kelly's hand as they shuffled towards the building entrance with the crowd of tourists and locals wearing shorts and sundresses. A horse drawn carriage rode by as the passengers snapped pictures of Santa's elves and the giant blocks that spelled Mele Kalikimaka (Merry Christmas). The Waikiki Trolley stopped to drop off another load of couples and families mesmerized by the multicolored lights flashing in time to Hawaiian Christmas carols sung by a boys choir, accompanied by hula dancers and ukulele players.

Zana followed her roommates into the building, which housed the city attorneys and the Honolulu mayor. She had been there once before to vote in a primary election. The business of state government seemed temporarily abandoned and replaced by the festive atmosphere, heavy with the scent of pine trees and the sounds of hundreds of voices echoing in the large open area at least a few stories high. Visitors, with smart phones up to their faces, viewed dozens of Christmas trees festively decorated by the city and county departments, and maneuvered to take selfies in front of their favorites. Children squealed with delight when their turn came to sit on Santa's lap in a colorful North Pole display.

Zana used her elbows to push her way between the fire department's tropical aquarium themed tree and waste management's Harry Potter Christmas creation. She tried to focus on the decorations, but then she saw The Bus's *Wicked* tree, with good and bad witch decorations from the Broadway musical she had seen with Jerry. Zana sighed. She couldn't stop ruminating about her boyfriend, who was not answering any of her phone calls—so frequent she feared she met the criteria for stalking under some state statutes.

"Here," Kelly said as she handed Zana her phone to take a picture of her and Andrew in front of the Department of Transportation's tree, which was decorated in the movie, *Frozen* theme.

"Act cold," Zana directed and her friends huddled together with teeth chattering in what they called freezing weather. The temperature *had* dipped below eighty degrees.

After Kelly took her phone back, she immediately stopped to post the picture on Facebook while Zana and Andrew watched.

"I don't understand why you have to post that picture right now. Can't it wait?" Zana asked, trying not to sound too irritable, but she could hear the whininess in her own voice.

"How else will Kelly look like she's having a fabulous life if she doesn't contemporaneously post all of the cool things she does on Facebook?" Andrew asked, steering his girlfriend closer to the wall to avoid being run over by the crowd.

Zana squeezed past a large family and stood next to him. "I think you can have a really great life without posting anything."

"The question is: does anything you do really count if you don't put it on Facebook?" Kelly asked, looking up from her phone.

"It doesn't. If it's not on Facebook, it didn't happen," Andrew said.

"That's ridiculous." Zana frowned.

"No. It's reality. The only way to be interesting nowadays is to lead an exciting virtual life," Andrew said.

Zana stood with her hands on her hips. "Are you saying the calories don't count if I don't post my food on Facebook?"

"What I'm saying is, that your life doesn't count if it's not on Facebook," Andrew said.

"Don't you think that's really bleak?" Zana asked.

"Not my problem. I post everything on Facebook," he said.

"Shut up—you do not," Zana said, punching Andrew hard on the arm.

He laughed. "Okay, ya' got me. Can't pull anything over on you."

"You'll be sorry when I'm gone." Zana rolled her eyes.

She then excused herself and made her way through the tightly packed bodies crowded around the Department of Parks and Recreation tree, decorated in a *Snow White and the Seven Dwarfs* theme. As she gazed at the tree, she held her phone in her hand. The crowd's noise drowned out the sound of the audio alerts, so even if the theme song from "Fighting in Paradise" played, she wouldn't hear it. She leaned against a small patch of wall and scrutinized the last series of texts between them.

Z: Hey Jer-Bear. I Miss You. When will you be home?
J: XOX
Z: XOXO
J: XOXOX
Z: Where are you, J. Bear?
J: XOX
Z: XOXO

Zana scowled. Jerry's Xs and Os that had once sent shivers of excitement up and down her spine were now simply annoying. As her expectations had increased, she found it unacceptable for him not to communicate with her. For weeks, she had envisioned walking through Honolulu Hale hand-in-hand with Jerry, the way Kelly and Andrew did tonight. And now, she was the third wheel. She felt a lump in her throat as she imagined Christmas alone. She stared at the frosted tree with its Snow White, Grumpy, Sleepy, Bashful and the other dwarfs marching across its branches. She reached out and touched Sleepy, the dwarf she most related to with her long days of work and heavy schedule of triathlon training in preparation for the Freewheel Triathlon. She yawned, wishing she could ditch her roommates and go to bed early. Unfortunately, Andrew had driven and would likely want to drag them to a bar for drinks before going home.

"Oh, there you are," Kelly said, sidling up to her.

"We've been trying to find you for about ten minutes," Andrew said.

"I've been here with the dwarfs," Zana said.

"Well, Snow White, we're thirsty," he said, putting his arm around his girlfriend. "Where shall we go for cocktails?"

"I'm not in the mood," Zana said. "Do you mind taking me home? You two can go out by yourselves without me tagging along."

"No word from Prince Charming?" Andrew asked.

Zana shook her head. "Not much."

"Let's stop at the Fighting Café for a glass of wine," Andrew said. "It's on our way home and then we can all make it an early night."

"I'm not sure Zana's in the mood to be surrounded by pictures of Jerry," Kelly said, referring to the décor of the Fighting Café, which had "Fighting in Paradise" pictures and memorabilia covering the walls.

Zana gulped. "It's okay. At least I'll get to see pictures of him."

"When is he coming back from Rio?" Andrew asked.

"He hasn't said," Zana shrugged. "Last he texted was that he was in Ipanema and working long days in a capoeira studio on choreography."

"With that Annabelle chick," Kelly added as they made their way back to Andrew's car. "I'm sure he's missing you terribly, Zana."

Zana shrugged. "I wouldn't know."

"Let's get out of here," Andrew said, leading the women through the crowd.

During the car ride, Zana pulled out her phone and grinned when she saw a new text from Jerry. Instead of generic Xs and Os, this one said I miss you. She tapped her response: Me too. ;(

Maybe, he was thinking about her. She smiled.

The café was crowded, but a few parties were leaving just as they arrived and it was only a short wait before they were seated. The hostess escorted the three to a booth near the entrance. Despite Zana's attempt to make small talk with the hostess, who was usually friendly, she ignored Zana and gave her a bitchy look. *She's just busy.*

The café had recently added an extensive wine menu. As Zana studied it to decide whether to order a chardonnay or a pinot grigio, she heard a familiar voice. She turned to look towards it, and then she saw him. Jerry was following Kenny toward the front entrance. *Were her eyes playing tricks on her? He was supposed to be in Brazil.*

She felt a wave of dizziness wash over her and grabbed the table to steady herself. He dropped back and waited until Kenny was outside before he approached their table.

"Sweetheart, it's so great to see you," Jerry said, with an expression that looked to Zana as if he'd been caught cheating.

If the restaurant wasn't full of people staring at them with their smart phones poised, she would have slapped him in the face and told him off. Months of dating him in the public eye had taught her to think before she spoke. She stared at him and waited a few beats.

She then stood up, towering over him in her three-inch heels. "What's going on, Jerry?"

"Let's talk in the back," he whispered into her ear.

She felt her stomach churn at the intimacy of his tone and the touch of his hand on her bare arm. She nodded and followed him through the café, down a hallway, past the restrooms and out a doorway that led to the alley. The smell of rotting garbage from the dumpster overpowered her senses and she instinctively plugged her nose with her fingers and briefly closed her eyes, hoping her queasy stomach would settle.

A few restaurant employees leaning against the building having their smoke break greeted Jerry, as if dodging into the back alley was his habit.

"Do you mind if we have some privacy to talk out here, guys?" Jerry asked them.

"No problem," the two young men said. They took one more drag of their cigarettes and then stomped them out on the pavement before heading back into the café.

Zana waited until the door snapped shut before she said in a low voice, "What the hell is going on?"

"I wanted to call you when I got back, Zana," Jerry said, wiping sweat off his forehead with the back of his hand.

"Well, why the fuck didn't you?" Zana said, hands on hips.

"Okay, I understand the language. I've got some things I need to work out." Jerry leaned against the wall.

"With Annabelle?"

"Not with her." Jerry's eyes widened. "What are you talking about?"

"Aren't you sleeping with her?" Zana spat, and then tears streamed down her cheeks. "I saw your Facebook pictures."

"I'm *not* sleeping with Annabelle. Jeez," Jerry said, raising his voice. He then whispered, "Kenny is doing everything he can to keep me away from you."

"What?" Zana searched his eyes to see if he was telling the truth.

Jerry sighed, and then put his face in his hands. "I don't know what to do."

"Does this have anything to do with Bud Schubert?" Zana whispered.

"Of course it does. If I'm seen with you, I'll be fired from the show," Jerry said, kicking an empty plastic water bottle that hadn't made it into the dumpster.

"This is all because I represent Ryan Peterson?"

He nodded.

Her knees felt weak so she grabbed onto his arm, and when he reached out to steady her, she could see the hurt in his eyes.

"I'll withdraw as his counsel," Zana said. "Our relationship is more important than my representing Ryan."

"I can't let you do that," Jerry said, reaching out to caress her face. "You know Frank will fire you on the spot."

"Yeah, he would. This totally sucks." Zana looked at the ground.

"Tell me about it," Jerry said. He pulled her towards him and kissed her deeply. He held her tight in his embrace for another minute. "I really miss you, Zana."

She breathed in the scent of his cologne and momentarily forgot they were standing feet away from rancid garbage. She whispered into his ear, "Can we be discreet and see each other privately?"

"Nothing I do is private. I'm sure we only have a minute or two before Kenny or the paparazzi find us," Jerry said, enveloping her closer in his arms. "I've got to get back to Kenny—I'm sure he has no idea where I am."

Zana held onto him firmly. "What should we do, Jer-Bear?"

"I'll think of something." He then put his hands on her arms and looked her in the eyes. "People need to think we're broken up, Zana. Do you understand?"

She nodded, feeling the dizziness return. He wiped a tear from her cheek with his fingers.

"I'm going to have to be seen in public with other people, but that doesn't mean I don't want to be with you. I need you to know that."

"Can you at least text me?" she whispered in his ear as they held each other closely.

"I will. I'll have to be discreet though. I know this is going to be tough, especially over the holidays," Jerry said, swallowing hard. "Know that I'm thinking of you. Always."

She nodded, as more tears streamed down her cheeks.

He held her even tighter. After a few minutes, he looked her in the eyes and said, "Okay, sweet heart?"

"We have no choice," she said, barely audible.

He gave her one last kiss on the lips and then released her.

Her knees buckled and she grabbed onto the wall. As he turned to go inside, she saw tears in his eyes.

"Wait five minutes before you go back inside, okay?" Jerry croaked. "If Kenny came back into the restaurant, I don't want him to see you."

The moment he disappeared through the door, Zana wretched onto the grimy concrete and then dropped to her knees, sobbing. She heard the door swing open and a bus boy with cigarette in hand appeared, but then retreated back into the café when he saw her.

She heard the ding of a new text message from her purse. Hoping it was from Jerry, she pulled her phone out and sighed when she saw it was from Andrew, wondering where she was.

She texted back: I'll meet you at your car.

Andrew responded: 5 minutes.

When Zana reached the car, her roommates were already there waiting.

"Oh, my God! Are you okay?" Kelly asked.

Zana shrugged. She hadn't looked in a mirror, but was sure her mascara had not held up to the barrage of tears.

"What was that all about?" Kelly asked as soon as they were seated in the car, with her boyfriend driving and Zana in the backseat.

"It's complicated," Zana said, looking out the window to avoid eye contact.

"I knew it—Jerry's sleeping with Annabelle," Andrew said.

"Andrew!" Kelly said harshly.

Zana gulped. "No, he's not cheating on me."

"Then, why didn't you know he was back in Honolulu?" Kelly asked.

"Let's just say that there's kind of a Romeo and Juliet scenario going on," Zana said, slumping further down into her seat.

"His parents forbid your relationship?" Andrew asked, looking at her through the rear view mirror.

"If his parents' names were Bud and Kenny, the answer would be yes," Zana said.

"Ah, I got it." He nodded.

Zana leaned against the window. "Could you please not tell a soul about this?"

"Why is it such a big secret?" Kelly asked, reaching a hand back to pat Zana's knee.

"Did you notice that when Jerry had a pimple on his chin or when he had a bandage on his finger, they were front page news?" Zana asked.

"What if we want to make some money selling this big story?" Andrew grinned at Zana through the rear view mirror.

Zana shook her head. "Not funny. Just keep our secret. Will you? Please?"

"Okay, fine." Andrew started the car and pulled onto the road. "No tabloids."

"Absolutely," Kelly said, putting a firm hand on Andrew's arm. "You know you can count on us."

Zana nodded and they rode the five minutes to their house in silence. After Andrew parked in the garage, Zana followed her roommates into the house and headed straight to the refrigerator for the magnum bottle of Chardonnay she had opened the day before. She poured an extra-large glass and settled on the sofa, hugging a pillow while sipping wine in the dark room. The only solution was to somehow convince Bud Schubert of Ryan's innocence. *But how?*

Kelly interrupted her thoughts by turning on a lamp and sitting next to her.

"We're planning a traditional Hawaiian Christmas dinner at home. It's just going to be the two of us, and maybe a few of my friends from work. I hope you can join us."

"Yes. I would love to, Kelly," Zana said and smiled weakly.

Chapter Twenty-Four

@ZLaw Enjoying my work-cation. All quiet on the office front. Do you like my selfie? And, yes—that is the Dole Pineapple in the background. #Bored

Zana walked through the silent hallways, past cubicles with computers turned off, chairs tucked in and files neatly stacked. The attorneys' offices were dark and many still had Christmas cards taped to their doors. There wasn't another soul at the firm, even though it was 10 a.m. on a Wednesday. December twenty-sixth was usually like any other day, except this year. Shortly after noon on Christmas Eve, Frank had made a surprise and uncharacteristically humane announcement that the billable hour requirement was only 100 hours for December and every additional hour would be credited to the next year.

Within minutes almost all of the attorneys and staff had packed up their things, wished each other "Mele Kalikimaka" and rushed out the door to spend the remainder of the year with their families.

Zana hadn't joined in the mass exodus, but remained at her computer to finish up a medical records summary. On his way out, Andrew stopped by her office, sat down and nervously drummed his knee and tapped his fingers on the arm of the chair.

"Calm down," she said, abandoning her work and turning to him.

"It's easy for you to say. What if she says no?" He had dark circles under his eyes and his hair looked more unruly than usual.

"Kelly loves you. She'd be a fool not to marry you." This was at least the third time in the past few days they'd had the same conversation. She tried to act like it didn't bother her—she wanted to support her friend. But her heart ached after Jerry's appearance and their imposed separation the night before.

"What if she doesn't get along with my family?" Andrew frowned.

Zana sighed. "Who wouldn't love Kelly?"

"Are you sure she'll like the ring?" Andrew's leg picked up speed as it nervously shook, causing her desk to vibrate.

"It's gorgeous." She leaned towards him. "Have you decided on how you're going to pop the question?" The romance of Andrew's proposal made her temporarily forget her own troubles. Her roommates were headed to New York and images of a Central Park or Empire State Building engagement popped into her head.

"I made a reservation for dinner on New Year's Eve," Andrew said. He grinned and his leg stopped bouncing. "I'll ask her at midnight after a kiss and champagne toast."

"Perfect," Zana said flatly and then pasted a smile on her face. She wished she were spending New Year's Eve with Jerry, but instead would probably spend it home alone, watching the ball drop on T.V.

"I'm sorry. This must be hard for you," he said. "You can date other people, you know."

She shook her head. She was afraid she'd start crying if she spoke.

"I'm going to take off." He stood up. "Why don't you take advantage of this week and take a stay-cation?"

Zana swallowed. "No. I'm trying to figure out a way to get Ryan off the hook."

"You're exhausted—take some time off," Andrew said. "Work will always be here, but Frank may never again give you the holidays off."

"I know. I promise, I'll only work half days. I have lots of training to do before Freewheel," Zana said.

"We're having prime rib tonight, so don't be late," Andrew said before joining the crowd of staff and attorneys waiting their turns for the elevators.

Zana had made it home in time for their delicious Christmas Eve dinner and spent the next morning opening presents with her roommates, wondering what Jerry was doing. As soon as she could politely excuse herself, she hopped on her bike and rode more than sixty miles. She focused on keeping her cadence up as she pedaled her way down Kalanianaole Highway, through Hawaii Kai, along the coast, through Waimanalo, and didn't turn around until she had reached Kaaawa.

By the time she made it home and helped Kelly prepare dinner, she was exhausted and hopeful that after a glass of wine, she'd finally get some sleep.

Now, Zana sat in her silent office. The rhythm of tapping fingers on keyboards and voices in the hallways discussing cases was absent. She'd taken her roommates to the airport early that morning so they could catch their flight to New York. Kelly had given her a long hug and reassured her that soon Jerry would be back in her life.

But, she wasn't so sure. The next time she saw Kelly, she would have a ring on her finger and be consumed with wedding planning. Zana wanted Andrew and Kelly to be happy, but worried about where she would live after they were newlyweds.

A text from Moana interrupted her thoughts.

Still waiting for you to let us know about New Year's Eve…

Zana looked out the window at the pineapple. She was torn between joining her friends for drinks and going to bed early so she could start the New Year with a pre-dawn morning run or long bike ride.

I promise—I'll let you know soon. Zana texted.

You have no choice. We'll kidnap you if we have to. Moana texted back.

Ordinarily, Zana would be amused by her friend's plan, but the thought of New Year's Eve without Jerry made it hard for her to breathe. She swallowed, feeling a painful tightness in her throat and texted a smiley face, an emotion she couldn't reproduce, and tucked her phone back into her purse. She fished around for some gum, but felt an unusual square object. She pulled her bag up to inspect and saw the small box that looked more like it should contain an engagement ring, rather than a tiny good luck cat. She opened the box and examined the maneki-neko closely for the first time.

Maybe if she carried it everywhere she went, she'd have the good luck he wished for her. She smiled and zipped the cat into an inside pocket of her purse.

She returned to her computer and her almost empty email inbox. No one else seemed to be working. Plaintiffs' attorneys would wait to file lawsuits and schedule depositions after the holidays, and most of the claims adjusters were taking the remainder of their vacation days. As she deleted a few new spam emails, a calendar reminder popped up. William Kent, PhD, the helmet expert she'd hired would be meeting her shortly for an arranged inspection of the helmet Terry Schubert had been wearing at the time of his death. Preston had been willing to arrange the meeting, because Kenny was busy on the set.

"Dr. Kent, it's so nice to meet you," Zana said as they shook hands in the downstairs lobby of Ali'i Place, the building where Preston's large law firm was spread over three floors.

"Thanks for asking me to work on this case. It's been awhile since I had a bike helmet matter," Dr. Kent said. He was heavyset and was wearing olive pants that clashed with the green in his un-tucked Christmas themed Reyn's Aloha shirt.

"I want to move forward with this case, and I appreciate you making yourself available during the holidays," Zana said, pressing the elevator button to the 23rd floor.

"No trouble at all," Dr. Kent said. "My wife wanted me out of her hair today. This was a good excuse for me to get out of the house."

After Zana and Dr. Kent were escorted to a small conference room, a paralegal entered with a bike helmet she placed on the table.

"Will Preston be joining us?" Zana asked.

"He's with a client. If he finishes before you're done, he'll probably come by," the young woman said. "My name is Vicki. Just press sixteen on the phone if you need anything."

After she left the room, Dr. Kent immediately began taking pictures with a Nikon digital camera. He positioned the helmet next to a ruler so the photographs would have scale. After about fifteen minutes of fastidious photographing and note jotting, the expert witness placed his camera back into its case and turned to Zana.

"Do you see this edge?" he said, pointing to the chinstrap.

"Sure," Zana said, squinting her eyes and bending over the helmet.

"The strap was cut," Dr. Kent said. "Probably by a sharp knife or scissors."

"Could it have broken from wear?" she asked.

"That's unlikely. There's minimal fraying," Dr. Kent said as he pulled out a magnifying glass to further examine it. "It's clean. It appears that the chin strap was intentionally cut."

"While Terry was on the bike?" Zana raised her eyebrows.

"From my review of the witness's statements, I would surmise that the chinstrap was cut sometime between the time Ryan brought the helmet to the transition area and the time the athletes got on their bikes after the swim," Dr. Kent said.

"I wonder who cut it." Zana examined the chinstrap closely.

"I'll have to leave that for your investigation," Dr. Kent said, crinkling his forehead. "I can tell you that the strap was not worn out, causing it to break. It's a fairly new helmet. I can also opine that the chinstrap could not have been fastened. Had Schubert been wearing a helmet with a fastened chinstrap, he might be alive today. It appears that the cut strap ultimately led to his death."

Zana smiled at her expert witness. If someone other than Ryan cut the chinstrap he would surely be off the hook. She wished she could call Jerry and let him know, but he hadn't texted her once since their tearful goodbye, and so she decided against it.

After she thanked Dr. Kent and returned to her office, she saw there was an email from Alexia, asking for status on several cases, including the Schubert matter. Zana responded, explaining what Dr. Kent had concluded.

Alexia must have been sitting at her computer, because she emailed back within a few minutes:

Hey Zana:

I hope you had a Merry Christmas. It's pretty quiet here, but there's plenty of work to do. That's interesting about the chinstrap being cut. My bet is that Plaintiff will claim that Ryan cut the strap and then purposely switched his helmet with Terry's. They'll argue that he caused the accident, knowing Terry would die if he fell to the ground without a secured helmet. I know it sounds ridiculous, but I've seen it all before.

Alexia

Zana immediately wrote back, wondering if she should just call Alexia and have a conversation.

Hi Alexia,

You're probably right.

FYI: Preston noticed the deposition of a witness, Kyle Conner. Ryan told me that Conner, T.J. Watanabe, and Beck and Yvonne Holmes were renting rooms in his house at the time of the incident, but he didn't say much else. Kyle and T.J. are on Plaintiff's witness list, but T.J.'s address is unknown. I can't imagine they have much to say. According to Ryan, they didn't attend the triathlon. Kyle Conner's deposition is tomorrow—I'll summarize his testimony. Also—Plaintiff noticed Coach Gary Moretti's deposition. Ryan asked me to put him on our witness list.

Zana

Less than two minutes after Zana pressed "send", her phone rang. It was Alexia.

"Hey, Alexia. How can I help you?" Zana said. Even though she tried to sound like an attorney on the phone, to her own ear, she sounded like a fast food drive-thru employee.

"You mentioned in your email that Ryan told you that the witnesses were renting rooms in his place." Alexia paused. "Is he back?"

"I don't think so," Zana said. "I haven't heard from him since he left."

"Okay, well. Let me know when he returns," Alexia said.

"I sure will. I'll also email an update for you after the deposition tomorrow," Zana said. "When Ryan comes back, if I were you, I'd go out with him."

"Uhm— We'll see," Alexia said. "Happy New Year!"

Zana could hear an edge to Alexia's voice so she wondered if she'd crossed the line by continuing to urge her to go out with Ryan. The adjuster was the most private person she had ever met. Every time she asked an innocent question about her past, Alexia would immediately change the subject. If they were on the phone, she would quickly end the conversation. She wondered whether Alexia was hiding something or just trying to keep up her professional image. Zana didn't have much time to contemplate this, because she needed to prepare for tomorrow's deposition. She had no idea what the witness would say and worried she was in for a disappointing surprise.

She Googled Kyle Conner, searched court documents on the Ho'ohiki website, and called their investigator to request a quick criminal background check.

***

The next day, Zana made sure to arrive at Preston's office fifteen minutes early. This would be the first deposition she had attended completely on her own, but since she was assigned the case, she felt no need to seek supervision from Frank. Lucas had gone to Maui with his Stanford Law School buddies for a few days and no one else was around to question whether she was prepared to handle discovery on her own. After her research the day before, she felt ready.

The court reporter, Wendy, had already set up her machine. Zana hunted for an outlet for her own laptop and was still setting up when an unshaven, gum-chewing, backpack toting man who looked to be in his early twenties was led into the room by Preston, who was followed closely by Bud Schubert. This time, Bud was wearing an Aloha shirt, no jacket and fairly snug, TSA friendly, beige pants that wouldn't easily conceal a firearm. She had insisted a retired police officer attend. When Preston reconvened Ryan's deposition, more security measures would be necessary.

Ordinarily, Zana would shake hands with everyone in the room, but this time, she didn't acknowledge Schubert. *Why should she be civil to the man who was responsible for destroying her relationship?*

"Have a seat, Kyle," Preston said, motioning to the chair across from him and next to the court reporter. Schubert took a seat next to his attorney.

"Swear in the witness," Preston said, nodding to Wendy.

"Please raise your right hand. Do you swear to tell the truth in today's proceedings?" Wendy asked.

Kyle stiffly raised his hand and bobbed his head forward. "Sure."

After asking Kyle some preliminary questions, which revealed that he was twenty-three years old, worked at Zippy's Restaurant as a line cook, was single and living with roommates in Kalihi, Preston handed the witness a tissue.

"For your gum," Preston said when Kyle looked confused.

"Okay," Kyle said as he pulled the gum out of his mouth with his hand, placed it in the tissue and then made a small ball and tossed it several feet into a wastebasket. "Scored!" he said loudly as he raised his hands in victory.

Zana rolled her eyes and hoped the others didn't notice.

"Let's resume," Preston said, shaking his head. "Do you know Ryan Peterson?"

"Yeah, that dude was my landlord," Kyle testified.

"How did he come to be your landlord?" Preston asked.

"Ryan was hurting for money, so he put an ad on Craigslist to rent out rooms in his house," Kyle said, drumming the table with his fingers.

"Did you rent one of the rooms?" Preston asked.

"Yeah, and so did my buddy, T.J."

"T.J. Watanabe?"

"Maybe. I'm not sure about his last name."

"Where did Ryan Peterson sleep when you lived in the house?" Preston asked.

"There was a tiny office—I guess that's what you'd call it. He had a futon in there," Kyle said. "A couple slept in the master bedroom upstairs. T.J. and me slept in bedrooms downstairs."

"What were the names of the couple in the master bedroom?"

Kyle looked up towards the ceiling and then said, "Sorry, I can't remember. Her name could have been Yvonne."

"Don't guess. Just tell us what you know and remember," Preston said.

"I don't remember. It was a while ago," Kyle said.

"How did you know that Ryan was 'hurting for money'?" Preston leaned in.

"He said so. He was always complaining about being broke. He was desperate," Kyle said. "He would even eat some of our food from the refrigerator."

"How do you know that?"

"I saw him, dude," Kyle said. "He drank some of the milk I bought for my cereal. It pissed me off."

Preston flinched when the witness called him "dude" and then asked, "Did you know that Ryan was competing in the Paradise Lagoons Triathlon last March?"

"Yeah, he was training all the time. Always biking and running every day."

"Did he talk about the race?" Preston asked.

"Constantly. He said that he wouldn't let anyone get in his way," Kyle said. "He was determined to win the prize money so he could kick our sorry asses out the door."

"Did he call you 'sorry asses'?" Preston asked.

Kyle nodded. "Yeah, he was always giving us shit. He wouldn't let us smoke in our rooms. No parties either, and we paid six hundred dollars apiece in rent."

"Did he ever talk about Terry Schubert?" Preston asked.

"I think so. He would watch videos in the living room of some guys racing. Terry and another dude, Jeff, were a few of them he mentioned."

"What did he say about them?" Preston straightened his bowtie.

"It would piss me off, because I was playing video games on the T.V. Ryan would make me turn my game off so he could watch these boring videos," Kyle said.

"Did Ryan say anything about Terry Schubert when he watched the videos?"

"Fighting words. He'd say that he would kill them, or something like that. He was intent on winning. He said he was going to win—no matter what he needed to do," Kyle said, now clicking a pen over and over again while he talked.

Preston grabbed the pen away from the witness and asked, "Ryan Peterson used the words 'kill them'?"

"Yeah, 'kill 'em' or 'beat 'em'. I don't know—he wanted to pulverize them. He was determined," Kyle said. "He said that there's nothin' that would stand in his way."

"Did you hear about Terry Schubert's death?"

"Not until you called me," Kyle said.

Preston frowned. "What happened after the Paradise Lagoons Triathlon?"

"Ryan made a lot of money so he kicked us all out of the house," Kyle said. "He was really happy to get his bedroom back from that couple. I think her name was Yvonne or Yvette."

"Thank you, Mr. Conner," Preston said. "Nothing further."

It was Zana's turn to ask questions and so she consulted the notes on her computer for a few minutes while everyone in the room silently waited for her. She had never asked questions before in a deposition.

She took a deep breath and asked, "What did you say or do in response to Ryan's kicking you out?"

"We were pissed," Kyle said.

"The question was not how you felt, but rather what did you say or do in response to Ryan's kicking you out?"

"We left," Kyle said. "What else could we do?"

"Did you do anything to Ryan, because of your anger that he kicked you out?"

"We trashed the place," Kyle said.

Zana leaned back in her chair and looked the witness in the eye. "What do you mean by that?"

"We cut his sofa and sprayed red paint on his walls and stereo," Kyle said, putting his hand to his mouth.

"Anything else?"

"We broke some flower pots outside," Kyle said through his hand.

"Anything else?" Zana repeated.

The witness paused and looked at Preston, as if to get his permission to respond. Preston nodded.

"We slashed the tires of his bikes," Kyle said. "That's all."

"Are you still angry at Ryan?" Zana asked, leaning towards the witness.

"Yeah, he kicked us out before the end of the month. The guy really pissed us off," Kyle spat. "I had to find a new place to live."

"Isn't it true that Ryan filed a restraining order against you and T.J. Watanabe a week before the Paradise Lagoons Triathlon?" Zana asked.

"Yeah, the guy's a jerk," Kyle said.

"Isn't it true that you assaulted Ryan because he called the police when he caught you dealing drugs in his house?" Zana asked.

"That's what Ryan says, but it's not true," Kyle said. "We were just smokin' some weed. We gave some extra to our friends. No need for him to call the cops.”

“You punched him, correct?” Zana asked, looking the witness in the eyes.

“Not that hard,” Kyle said.

“No further questions,” Zana said.

She took a deep breath and noticed Bud looking at her through narrowed eyes with his arms crossed.

Chapter Twenty-Five

@ZLaw #HappyNewYear! Kidnapped by so-called friends. Remember: karma is a bitch.

"Are you sure you want to wear a white shirt, Pres?" Kenny asked as he tucked in his own shirt. He was standing next to Preston in front of the mirrored wall on the far side of their bedroom-sized closet.

"Do you like the black shirt better with this bow tie?" Preston asked.

"Yeah, I think it'll work best with your complexion," Kenny said, reaching for the shirt hanging on the mechanical circular clothes rack that operated like one found in a dry cleaner's shop. Preston replaced the white shirt with the black one, and Kenny nodded with approval.

"I wish we were staying home tonight," Kenny said, slumping down on the plush forest green bench next to the wall of cedar shelves, displaying their neatly stacked T-shirts, sweaters and rows of shoes.

"That's not like you," Preston said as he turned to Kenny. "You love going out on New Year's Eve. What's going on?"

Kenny sighed. "I'm tired."

"That's never stopped you before. You're always up for a party." Preston sat next to his partner on the bench. "What's *really* going on?"

"To tell you the truth, I'm not in the mood to deal with the Bud and Jerry show," Kenny said. "Jerry's dailies have no life since he broke up with Zana."

"He's a professional. I'm sure he'll get back on track soon."

"Maybe." Kenny shrugged. "I wish you'd settle the case."

Preston put his arm around him. "I'm working on it. We may be able to get the carrier to pay policy limits after the last deposition. Our witness testified that Ryan planned to kill anyone who got in his way of winning the triathlon."

"Wow!" Kenny sat up straight. "It sounds like the insurance company should pay or Ryan is going to lose everything."

"You'd think so, but Friendly Isle Mutual is notorious for holding tight to their money. Another carrier would have paid a long time ago, but I think we have a fight on our hands," Preston said, rising from the bench.

He opened a cedar drawer where he found a lint brush and used it to pick up a few specks on his black shirt. "Hopefully, Jerry will cheer up."

"Yeah, I'm sick of watching him mope around. He hardly says a word to anyone—you'd think he lost his best friend," Kenny said.

"He did. Kenneth, honey, I don't like the way you interfered with his relationship with Zana," Preston said.

Kenny rose and stood on tiptoes to adjust Preston's bow tie.

"It wasn't my doing. I can't help that Bud doesn't appreciate the star of the show dating the attorney who's representing his son's killer." Kenny turned away from Preston and looked at his reflection one last time before they went out.

Preston scowled. "It sounds too much like a bad soap opera. I'll have another talk with my client." He then looked down at Kenny and smiled. "Let's go out and enjoy the evening. You'll feel better once you're surrounded by friends with delicious food and drink."

Kenny smiled back at him in the mirrored reflection. "We look good." He grabbed his partner's hand and led him to the garage.

"Shall we take your car?" Preston asked.

Kenny nodded. "Sure. If we weren't dressed up, I'd suggest walking to the hotel. It's such a beautiful night."

"That would be good in theory, but I imagine that after a few drinks, you wouldn't want to walk home," Preston said.

"So you're the designated driver?"

"You bet. I'll keep it to one glass of champagne." Preston slid behind the steering wheel for the short drive to the Kahala Hotel.

"You're a better man than I." Kenny looked towards the ocean as they pulled out of the driveway. The sky was orange and blue as the sun dropped towards the sparkling sea. He watched a few sailboats in the distance. The tranquil setting was interrupted by the sound of a low flying helicopter, a common occurrence lately whenever they went to an event with the cast of "Fighting in Paradise". He wondered why the paparazzi didn't just use drones to snap their valuable photographs.

As Preston handed the car key to the valet attendant, Jerry's red Ferrari pulled in behind them.

"Well, speak of the devil," Preston quipped. "Who's that lovely woman with him?"

"It's Jennifer," Kenny said as they walked toward the grand entrance.

"He didn't waste any time," Preston said in a low voice.

"It's his sister," Kenny said, squeezing his partner's arm. "She's here for the holidays."

Just as Jerry opened the door for his petite but shapely sister, who looked less Asian than her brother, with her light brown curls and big, brown eyes, several paparazzi sprung into action. Rapid-fire flashes of light illuminated the dark circular driveway of the hotel as Jennifer blinked and shaded her eyes with her jeweled clutch.

Kenny and Preston ducked past the photographers into the opulent hotel lobby where a handful of the cast and crew were gathered.

"Hello gentlemen," Annabelle said as she approached them, wearing a black shimmery gown with a v-neckline, which reached to her belly button, revealing a good portion of each breast so even Preston and Kenny couldn't help but stare.

"You might want to cover up, dear," Preston said. "This is a family event."

"This is couture," Annabelle beamed. "Besides, everyone's seen them before." She laughed while gesturing to her almost bare breasts.

"Jerry's here," Kenny pointed toward the T.V. star, now surrounded by photographers and television cameras. Preston poked him in the ribs with his elbow.

Without saying another word, Annabelle turned on her Jimmy Choo and made a beeline in Jerry's direction.

***

Lucas was only mildly disappointed that he was spending New Year's Eve watching T.V. with his mother, who had begged him to come over to keep her company after her new husband, Roger, had to take last night's red eye to be with his ailing father on the mainland. If she hadn't called, Lucas would probably be hanging out with some of the guys from the firm, talking about cases and billable hours, and checking out the women.

"It's a shame we live in the same city and I only see you on holidays— just like when you were in law school," Caron said, as she munched on popcorn while sitting on the couch in front of the 60 inch T.V. screen tuned into the New Year's Eve special of the ball dropping in New York City.

"That's not true, Mom. I see you." Lucas adjusted the Lazy Boy so that he was lying down as flat as the chair would allow.

"Maybe when you stop by the office to pick up a file," she said. "I saw you in court a few times."

"I'll do better. I promise, Mom. Would you be happier if I came over for dinner once a week?"

"That would be nice. But, you should call first," she said, sipping a Michelob Ultra. "Roger and I don't always cook. We've been taking some neighbor island trips on weekends lately."

"That's great. It sounds like you're finally getting away from the office." Lucas reached for a handful of popcorn. "Growing up, I remember you would work every Saturday and bring work home on Sundays. You never relaxed."

"I can't do that anymore. I'm getting too old." She sighed.

They silently watched the T.V. for a few minutes.

Caron looked up at her son and said, "Frank told me he gave you

Michael Lee's office."

He nodded and smiled. "Yeah, it's an amazing space. It's mine as long as I don't screw up."

"Frank tells me you're doing well."

"Better." Lucas's gut churned when he thought of his subpar billable hours. "You should come by and see the view. I even have a couch and small refrigerator." By the look on his mother's face, he could see that he didn't need to add the words— "while I still have it."

"How are the other associates handling your new digs?"

"Libby advised me to be discreet. I'm not sure they realize I've moved out of the low rent district."

"She's a wise woman," she said, grabbing another handful of popcorn.

"Yeah, she told me that envious associates could make my life a lot more difficult and talked me out of having a party to celebrate," Lucas said with his mouth full. "The weird thing is that I'm working on one of your cases with Zana and I'm not sure she's even aware that I moved."

"You may want to keep it that way," Caron said, decreasing the T.V. volume with the remote control. "Which case are you working on with her?"

"Schubert vs. Peterson."

"That's Alexia Moore's case," she said. "So, what do you think?"

"F.I.M. should just pay policy limits," he said, adjusting the Lazy Boy so he was sitting more upright. "Zana emailed me notes from the last deposition. Peterson was telling people he would kill anyone who got in his way at the triathlon. That guy would be horrible in front of a jury. He was caught doping in the Tour de France and he was a suspect in the Olympic trials case. You should cut your losses."

Her eye widened. "Is that what Zana thinks, too?"

He shook his head. "Nah, it's almost like she worships Ryan or something. She doesn't think he caused the accident. She keeps trying to find new evidence that will exonerate him."

"I hope she finds something. One million dollars is a tremendous amount of money to pay on the case," she said. "F.I.M. is doing a little better now that the economy is improving, but we can't afford to pay a lot of high claims."

"What alternative do you have?" he asked. "If you don't meet Plaintiff's demand for policy limits and a jury comes back with a multi-million dollar verdict against Ryan Peterson, he could sue F.I.M. for bad faith for failing to settle when you could have for policy limits."

Lucas could see the color drain from his mother's face.

"Are you okay?" he asked, leaning towards her.

"I need to keep my job—at least for a few more years." She twisted her wedding band.

"Sorry." He patted her hand. He seldom saw his mother get emotional about claims. "I'm sure the case will settle."

She sighed. "Can we talk about something besides work?"

He nodded and made his chair flat again. He considered his options. *Protect mother by helping Zana succeed on the Schubert case? Or, sabotage Zana and make Frank proud—and, keep his swank office?*

***

It was well after 7 p.m. when Zana rushed through the front door of the Waikiki Yacht Club where she was meeting Shelby and Moana for their New Year's Eve celebration.

"I'm a guest," Zana said breathlessly as she approached the reception desk.

"I've been watching for you." Shelby gave her friend a hug. "You're late."

"I know. My training went longer than planned."

"What are you wearing?" Shelby asked, referring to Zana's pale floral cotton dress and wedge sandals. "It's New Year's Eve. You look like you're going to church or something."

"I know. I've been busy training for Freewheel Tri and haven't had time to drop off my clothes to the dry cleaners or do laundry."

"Or do something with your hair," Shelby said, pointing to Zana's messy ponytail. "It doesn't even look like you got ready in front of a mirror. What did you do, shower at the beach and change in the parking lot?" Shelby laughed.

"Yeah. Sorry, I went for a swim and didn't have time to go home first," Zana said, undoing her ponytail, smoothing her hair and then putting it back into the elastic band. "It's not like I'm going to see anyone."

"You mean, you're not going to see *Jerry*. You've got to get over him, Zana. I'm sure he's not going to wait until you settle your case to have sex, and neither should you," Shelby said, standing next to her friend in the entrance way. "Now, let's join Moana and our dates at the table."

"Dates? You didn't tell me there were dates." Zana's eyes widened.

"Moana and I have dates. If you would have let us fix you up, you would have one, too," Shelby said as she led Zana to their table at the far end of the restaurant section of the club.

Zana sighed. "I don't want to be the fifth wheel. I'm going home."

"No, you're not. Enjoy the evening with us. You'll have fun."

"For a little while. I've got to get to bed early, I'm biking seventy miles tomorrow morning," Zana said as they approached the table with Moana and two young men, wearing matching cardboard top hats, dress shirts and slacks.

"This is Jack and Liam," Shelby said as the men stood up and shook Zana's hand.

"Hey girl," Moana said. "What's with the wrinkly dress? When you were with Jerry, you were all Gucci or Prada, not Walmart."

Zana smirked. "I know. Shelby already got on my case. This morning at four a.m. when I packed my workout bag, I totally forgot it was New Year's Eve. This was wadded up in my trunk," she said as she sat in a chair at the head of the table. Shelby and Jack sat on one side facing Moana and Liam, who were across from them. "Am I witnessing first dates here?"

"Not really, Shelby and I met Liam and Jack while we were biking a few weeks ago," Moana said.

"Oh, are you triathletes, too?" Zana perked up.

"No, we were walking our dogs, and Moana and Shelby stopped at the park to refill their water bottles," Liam said, looking lovingly at his date.

"That's nice," Zana said, taking a sip of water. "What do you do for work?"

"Liam's a carpenter and I'm a gate agent at the airport," Jack said, puffing out his chest.

"Oh, that's cool," Zana said. She then summoned the waitress and ordered a glass of Chardonnay.

"So, how's training for Freewheel going?" Moana asked.

"Good. I biked forty miles this morning and then decided to make it a brick and ran four miles. My calves are killing me," Zana said, becoming animated. "Since we were meeting at the Yacht Club, I couldn't resist a sunset swim and I ended up swimming a mile."

"You looked great on the bike on Saturday. I think you've got a shot at beating Megan this time," Shelby said, leaning in.

"No way. Did you see her time for the Norman Tamanaha run? She was first place overall for women," Zana said. "I'll be lucky if I get third."

Moana shook her head. "You'll smoke her in the water."

"She's super-fast," Zana said, smiling at the waitress who had set her glass of wine on the table. "How's your training going, Moana? I haven't seen you for a few days."

"Yeah, I feel guilty. I took a day off, because of work. Then Liam and I went to a play last night," Moana said, glancing at her date.

"Are you biking tomorrow?" Zana asked.

"Excuse me," Liam said, setting his beer down on the table with a thud. "Do you ladies ever talk about anything except triathlons? Moana just said that we went to a play and you didn't even ask her what we saw."

"Oh, sorry," Zana said, her face turning crimson. She took a long sip of wine. "What did you see?"

"Uhm…uh…what did we see, Liam?" Moana asked, turning to him.

Liam rolled his eyes, took a swig of beer and looked at the ocean.

"I'm so sorry. I didn't mean to blow in here and ruin your fun evening. I need to go home and get to bed," Zana said, gulping her wine.

"Aren't you staying for the fireworks?" Shelby asked.

"No, not tonight. I've seen them before. Have a great evening," Zana said as she stood up. She pulled a twenty-dollar bill out of her wallet and put it on the table. "Nice to meet you guys."

As she walked to her car, she was relieved that she didn't have to continue trying to make small talk with her friends' loser dates. *Well, they aren't really losers. They just didn't want to talk non-stop about triathlons. Was Jerry bored of it, too?*

As she drove home, she wondered what it would have been like if the girls set her up with a blind date. *Could she have fun?* Now that she was in love with Jerry, average guys had lost their appeal. She had no interest in socializing unless she was with him, and the only moments she could take a break from thinking about him was when she was focused on work. While she trained, she thought of him with every swim stroke, bicycle pedal and run step. She wondered what he was doing tonight and wished they could welcome the New Year with a romantic kiss.

Zana made it home and changed into an oversized "Fighting in Paradise" T-shirt and cotton pajama bottoms with swim, bike and run patterned fabric. By the time she poured herself another glass of Chardonnay, it was already time for the early local news. As she sunk into the couch cushions, she watched clips of the ball in New York's Times Square dropping to welcome in the New Year and crowds celebrating all over the world. Hawaii's time zone made it one of the last to celebrate and there were three more hours to go until midnight.

She sat up straight when the station shifted to live news footage of a party at the Kahala Hotel. Her heart nearly skipped a beat when a camera zoomed in on Jerry, wearing a tux and a huge grin on his face. When the shot widened and she saw his arms around two beautiful women, one who she didn't recognize, she dropped her wine glass, causing it to shatter on the tile floor. The other woman was Annabelle, with one hand on Jerry's rear end and her breasts almost completely exposed in the dress she wore.

The newscaster reported, "Jerry Hirano is celebrating New Year's Eve with his date at the Kahala Hotel." Zana's grip tightened on the remote control and she felt bile rise in her mouth. Her phone binged. As she grabbed it, she hoped it was Jerry telling her that what she had just seen and heard wasn't true.

Through tears in her eyes, she saw the text from Andrew: She said yes! We're engaged!! ☺

Chapter Twenty-Six

@ZLaw Fresh start for the year: 1) Yelled at by a dog-daddy; 2) Left in the dust on Heart Break Hill; and 3) Ex-boyfriends suck! I want a #do-over!

The smoke from New Year's fireworks was still lingering in the pre-dawn air as Zana pulled her SUV into a space near a stone memorial. There were already a half dozen trucks and SUVs parked on the side of the road next to the small, lush patch of grass filled with large shade trees, re-named the Operation Red Wings Medal of Honor Park in 2008. Triangle Park, as the triathletes still called it, was the perfect place to begin long training rides and runs with its ample roadside parking and proximity to the bike lanes of Kalanianaole Highway.

She leaned her bike against the memorial as she carefully loaded water bottles and checked the tires. She noticed other athletes quietly preparing their gear, keeping any talk to barely audible whispers, because the neighborhood was asleep. The ground was still littered with red papers from firecrackers, reminding her of the need to wear earplugs and take Ambien the night before in an effort to sleep away her heart pounding, crushing jealousy.

As she reached for her bicycle pump from the back of her vehicle, a thundering voice broke the silence.

"What the fuck are you doing?"

She turned to see Liam, Moana's New Year's Eve date, still wearing the same clothes and his silly cardboard top hat, approaching with a small, fluffy white dog on a leash.

"Shhhh…" She put her finger to her lips. The other athletes had stopped what they were doing and were looking their way.

He approached her and with his hands on hips, said in a low voice, "Get your god-damned bike off the memorial. Who do you think you are?"

She flinched from his harsh words and stared at him, not knowing what to say.

"You triathletes think you're heroes or something. You all think you're better than everyone else," he spat. "This memorial your fucking bike is leaning against honors the *real* heroes."

With head down, Zana snatched her bike off the stone monument and obediently leaned it against her car.

"If you stopped obsessing about triathlons for a moment, pulled your head out of your ass and read these plaques, you'd learn that this park honors a SEAL team ambushed during an operation and attempted rescue in which nineteen soldiers and sailors died." Liam became more animated and louder as he spoke. His dog lifted its leg on the memorial and he yanked on its leash. "Bad dog!"

"Oh, sorry," Zana mumbled, tossed the pump back in her car, locked up, and sped off on her bike without looking back at him. The guy obviously had some serious issues with triathletes. She doubted things would work out with him and Moana, who would not likely give up the sport.

As she pedaled down Diamond Head Road in the dark, she thought about Liam's words. She wished she were as courageous as Navy SEALs. It seemed that all she'd been doing lately was ruminating about Jerry. She needed to wipe out the images of him and his New Year's Eve "date" and move forward with her life. It had been almost a month since she and Jerry had spent time together. If he really wanted to be with her, he wouldn't let anyone get in his way. It was time to stop making excuses for his behavior.

She slowed her bike and looked up at the sky, still hazy from fireworks. While riding on the dark road adjacent to the golf course, she could ordinarily see millions of shiny stars putting her problems in perspective. She could still make out the moon through the haze, and despite Liam's outburst and the knot in her stomach, she smiled.

On New Year's Eve, almost fifteen years ago when she was living on the street after escaping her last foster home, a man had approached her and promised her an apartment, nice clothes and money if she worked for him. Before he had finished his offer, she had turned on her heel and ran away as fast as she could. She refused to be a streetwalker like a few of the other homeless teen girls she knew.

Even though her parents had spent most of their meager earnings on new bikes and race fees for themselves, she had been taught the difference between right and wrong. Since she was a little girl, her parents always told her she was a winner. Her father often quoted his favorite coach, Vince Lombardi, telling her, "Winning is a habit, Zana. Unfortunately, so is losing."

On New Year's Day so long ago, she remembered waking up in the abandoned car she had called home for a few months. She decided that day to go for a long run. On about mile seven, she had stopped and looked up at the smoggy California sky and decided that nothing would get in her way. She would find a way to finish high school and go to college. She would be somebody—a winner.

Now, she breathed in the faint smoky post-celebration air and thought of how far she had come. Wearing grimy clothes, eating food she had scrounged out of the garbage and studying by flashlight in the old car or wherever she could get some rest, she had managed to graduate in the top of her high school class. With scholarships, grants and multiple part-time jobs, she had managed to finish college in five years and then went to law school. If her mother were still alive, she would surely call her a winner.

It was time to stop obsessing about Jerry and focus on her plan. Her New Year's resolutions should include goals she at least had a shot at accomplishing. If she were to win her age group in the Freewheel Movement Triathlon, she'd have to train harder than she had ever done in her life. She took one last swig of water and settled onto her aero bars, and with a determined gaze at the road ahead, pedaled faster.

As the sky became light, she saw a group of four cyclists riding in the distance. She increased her cadence with the hope of catching up with them to join their pace line. It would be easier to finish her planned 70-mile ride if she took turns leading and blocking other cyclists from the wind for part of the way.

After several miles of sprinting towards the group on Kalanianaole Highway, Zana finally approached the back wheel of the last bike.

She focused all of her attention on the bicycle in front of her so she could stay close on its wheel without crashing. When she glanced at her Garmin Edge bike computer, their pace was 27 miles per hour. They rode past Niu Valley adjacent to light highway traffic. Zana could hear her breathing and the rhythm of her pedal strokes as they swiftly moved toward Hawaii Kai. She had no idea how long the other cyclists planned to ride, but felt that keeping up with them and taking her turn in the lead would give her the confidence she needed in the upcoming race.

When the group arrived in Hawaii Kai, they took a back road into the Portlock neighborhood, slowing down so they could drink from their water bottles. They rode abreast of one another and talked while they caught their breath. Zana hadn't yet noticed the identity of any of the cyclists, but now as they relaxed and chatted, she got a closer look. One of them was Megan Alexander.

A thin cyclist, wearing an orange and blue bike jersey, interrupted her thoughts. "I've seen you around. I'm Cal." He drank from his water bottle, sitting back on his saddle.

She smiled at him and said, "Yeah, I think I saw you in a few triathlons. I'm Zana."

"Oh, I'm not a triathlete, but I occasionally compete in some tri relays," he said.

She took a swig from her water bottle. "I'm a triathlete."

"I can see from your bike," he said, referring to her bike's triathlon configuration as opposed to a road bike set up. "You're doing a good job keeping up with us."

"Yeah, you're looking strong." The compliment came from Megan, who pulled up next to Zana, riding with one hand on a handlebar and another holding a water bottle.

"Thanks," Zana smiled at her fiercest competitor.

"How far are you riding today?" Cal asked.

Zana sat up in her saddle. "I'm hoping to do seventy miles."

"Are you training for an Ironman?" Megan asked.

"No, Freewheel."

"Why would you go so long?" Megan asked. "I'm training for that race and I'm only doing twenty-five to thirty-five mile tempo rides."

"Yeah, going *that* long isn't going to help you much in the shorter, faster races," Cal chimed in.

"Makes sense," Zana said, now questioning her training.

"My coach doesn't want me to ride long until I get closer to Ironman," Megan said. "Why don't you ride thirty miles with us today and you'll see that it's a really good workout."

Zana nodded. "Okay, thanks." *Why was her nemesis giving her coaching tips?* Her father had always told her *to keep her friends close and her enemies closer*. This was probably what he meant.

After the group took a short break, they resumed their pace line along Lunalilo Home Road. When they turned right onto what the triathletes called Heartbreak Hill, they broke out of their line and powered up the steep incline separately. Zana lost steam halfway up and fell behind the three men and Megan. By the time she made it to the top, the other four cyclists had reached the bottom of the hill. She zoomed down, turned right and caught up with the others, who were now going at a relaxed pace. She pulled up next to Cal, matching his pedal strokes.

"I noticed that your gear was too high and your cadence was too slow on the climb for your fitness level," he said.

"Oh?"

Cal slowed his bike down even more as he explained, "You might be able to keep up with us if you shifted into a lower gear and increased your cadence."

"Thanks. I'll try it." Zana felt her face flush. She wasn't used to riding with expert cyclists who had to wait for her. She wondered if she should drop back or abandon their group by going a different route. But winning her age group would require pushing through any pain or embarrassment and keeping pace with Megan.

"You'll get it. It just takes practice and lots of hill training," Megan said, pulling up next to her so they were riding three abreast on the empty street.

Zana nodded, noting that Megan was much nicer than she had previously thought. She wondered if Megan knew of her role as an attorney in the lawsuit that had put her twin sister, Heather, in prison for killing Brad Jordan and Vic Leavitt. If Megan knew of Zana's involvement in that case, she didn't say so. Instead, she smiled at her and encouraged her on their way to Sandy Beach along the scenic coastal highway.

On the ride back to Triangle Park, several other cyclists joined their pace line, which moved at an even faster clip than they had on their way to Hawaii Kai. Zana felt energized that she was able to keep up with this group of top triathletes and cyclists. Once they reached the neighborhood close to their destination, the group again slowed down to drink.

"Great job, Zana," Cal said.

"Thanks. I really appreciate your help today," Zana said, taking a swig from her water bottle.

"We're going to Fighting Café for breakfast. Do you want to join us?"

"No thanks. I appreciate the offer, but I'm going for a swim," Zana said. She could feel her stomach growling. If he had mentioned any other restaurant besides Fighting Café, she would have happily joined them. There was no way she was going to subject herself to photographs of Jerry and the possibility of running into him and Annabelle wearing one of his shirts after an overnighter.

"Are you coming, Megan?" Cal asked.

"I'm meeting with my coach for a run," Megan said. "Next time."

Zana rode to her SUV, leaning her bike against it. As she stretched her calves, she saw Megan approach a tall, extraordinarily fit man wearing running gear and leaning against the rock memorial.

"How was your ride?" the coach asked.

"Not bad. We kept the pace fairly easy, but it was a decent workout," Megan said.

"Download your data and email it to me, and I'll see for myself," Coach said, looking at his iPad. "I've been checking your competitors' stats."

"Am I going to win Freewheel?" Megan said, stretching her right arm behind her head.

"You've got it in the bag. Trini and Penny are your only competition and I'm not impressed with their splits," Coach said.

"Great news!" Megan beamed, switching arms. "I can't wait to go to Paris."

Coach looked up and smiled. "You can pack your beret and striped shirt."

"Whew hoo!" Megan jumped in the air and after landing, asked, "So, how far are we running?"

"Eight miles. Let's do some hills," Coach said. "How do your legs feel?"

"Not bad. I'm going to change into my running gear. Give me five," Megan said, turning to jog back to her vehicle.

Zana focused on stretching, hoping that Megan and her coach didn't realize she had listened to their conversation. Her legs felt trashed. They were so wobbly after what she felt was the most challenging bike ride she had ever experienced. She couldn't imagine running eight miles. She now understood why Megan was so helpful and supportive—she didn't consider her to be a threat.

***

Zana pulled her SUV up to baggage claim H where Andrew and Kelly were standing with their thumbs out as if they were hitchhiking.

"Congratulations!" Zana said, helping Andrew put their luggage in the back of the SUV as fast as possible so she wouldn't get ticketed for dawdling in the loading zone. Andrew climbed in next to Zana, and Kelly slid into the back seat.

"When's the big day?" Zana asked as she was pulling away from the curb.

"Do you think it would be too cliché to get married in June?" Kelly asked.

"You can get married whenever you want," Zana said, focusing on the road ahead. "So what's the scoop? Big or small wedding? I need details."

"I want to get married in Frank's office, but Kelly prefers the beach," Andrew said. "What do you think?"

Zana laughed. "Frank's office sounds romantic as hell. Will he be your best man?"

"I just threw up a little in my mouth," Andrew said. "We're actually trying to find a way to avoid inviting any partners of the firm. We're thinking about a small wedding on the beach on Maui."

"Partners are capable of getting on a plane and flying there," Zana said, glancing at her roommate.

"They won't be invited." Andrew adjusted his sunglasses.

"I don't want to have a stressed out groom on our wedding day," Kelly said. "If there are partners there, Andrew will probably ditch me at the altar."

"I would never do that, sweet pea," Andrew said, looking back at his fiancé.

"On another topic—I hate to break it to you Andrew, but we've got to go back to work tomorrow," Zana said, eyes on the road.

"Don't remind me. It makes me sick to my stomach thinking about it," Andrew said. "I hope you took some time off over the holidays."

Zana nodded. "I worked shorter days. The triathlon case is heating up. I've met with our expert and depositions have started."

"Do I detect a tan?" Kelly asked, leaning forward in her seat to look at her roommate. "When I last saw you, you looked even more pasty white than Andrew's relatives in New York."

Zana winked at her in the rearview mirror. "Yeah—my vampire lifestyle was interrupted and I actually saw the light of day this past week. Since I saw you last, I've managed to train every day in the sun."

"Good for you. Did you have a hot date for New Year's Eve?" Andrew asked.

"Shhh," Kelly said, putting her hand on Andrew's shoulder.

"It's okay. We're over," Zana said in a quiet voice.

"You never know. Maybe, when the Peterson case gets sorted out, you two can get back together," Kelly said. "There's always hope."

"Maybe, you shouldn't give her false hope, Kelly," he said.

"If you're meant to be together, somehow you'll find a way," Kelly said.

Zana put her blinker on to change lanes. "I need to focus on training for Freewheel right now and stop thinking about him."

"That makes sense. It looks like he's moving on with his life as well," Andrew said.

"Why do you say that?" Zana asked, turning slightly to look at him.

"Oh, I guess you didn't see the cover of We Magazine," he said.

"No, was he on the cover?" Zana felt queasy.

"It's a stupid tabloid," Kelly said. "Andrew, let's change the subject."

Zana wasn't in the mood to hear more bad news, but it was probably better to get it over with now. "You should tell me before I hear it from someone else."

Andrew gulped. "Okay, the story was that Annabelle is pregnant with Jerry's child."

"Are you kidding me?" Zana asked, trying to focus on driving on the H-1 Freeway.

"I'm sure it's not true." Kelly placed her hand on her friend's shoulder.

"I don't know," he said. "The *National Enquirer* had the same story."

"Do you really think that Annabelle would wear a dress on New Year's Eve with a plunging neckline down to her belly button with her boobs sticking out if she were pregnant?" Kelly asked.

"Yes," both Andrew and Zana said at the same time.

Chapter Twenty-Seven

@FreewheelMV I'm back, mates! Are you ready for the #FreewheelMovement #Triathlon? Top winner in each age group scores a trip to #Paris! *C'est Magnifique!*

Zana used chopsticks to eat salad, the only food on her training diet amongst the fried and breaded offerings at the catered luncheon in the firm's large conference room. Andrew, Michael, Kim, and a handful of new male associates had been able to break away from work for the weekly G, P & D hosted buffet, which had begun years ago for team building. In order to emphasize this goal, a series of teamwork posters with rowers, skydivers and the Blue Angels were tacked up above the food table.

"That's a big pile of macaroni salad you've got there," Zana commented after Andrew sat down with his heaping plate of food. "You won't be able to fit into your tux for the wedding."

"There'll be more of me for Kelly to love," Andrew said, patting his Aloha shirt clad belly. "How do you have energy eating like an anorexic?"

"Anorexics don't eat." Zana grimaced. "I just ate a 320 calorie protein bar at my desk."

"Yum!" Andrew said. "With all that swimming, biking and running, you've earned the right to pig out. If I did all that exercise, you couldn't get me out of the donut shop."

Zana laughed. "Yeah, a lot of triathletes use their training as an excuse to overeat, but the added weight slows them down. Freewheel Movement tri is about ten days away so I need to be careful."

A new male associate leaned towards her and asked, "Are you doing that race?"

"Yeah," Zana said, searching her memory for the associate's name. "I'm so sorry, I know we were introduced, but I can't remember your name."

"This is Dennis Pang," Andrew said. "Sorry, Dennis, this place is kind of a revolving door and Zana has a hard time remembering *my* name and I'm her roommate."

Zana gave him stink eye and then turned her attention to the new associate.

"That's okay," Dennis said. "I just heard about the triathlon on the morning news. The race director—that guy who was doping in the Tour de France—was talking about giving away trips to Paris to the winners."

"You saw Ryan Peterson on the news this morning?" Zana dropped her chopsticks on her plate.

"Yeah. Channel eight," Dennis said. "Why?"

"He's not supposed to be in Hawaii." Zana rose from her chair and tossed her half eaten salad into the trashcan.

She marched out of the room, her face twisted in a deep frown. *How does an even more lowly associate than me know more about my client than I do?* Thoughts boiled in her head and it felt like steam was blowing out her ears. *Didn't I tell him to call me first when he got back? Didn't I tell him to stay away until I gave him the all clear? Would he have listened to me if I were a man?*

On her way back to her office, Zana ripped a Christmas card off Frank's office door. *It's practically February, for God's sake!* She pulled off another one and tossed them to the floor, not bothering to see if someone was watching. She stomped to her office and flung open the door.

"Howdy stranger," Ryan said from his seated position in one of her guest chairs.

Zana stared at him. "You're back." She turned away when he attempted to kiss her cheek and slowly walked around the desk to her chair. Even though he was a fellow triathlete, he was a client so she took a deep breath and managed a thin smile.

"You know I had to come back to get ready for the race," he said. "It's not going to run itself."

"Of course," she said, letting her shoulders relax. She had to agree with his logic. "Well, it's good to see you. How've you been?"

"Great!" Ryan beamed. "I was so stressed out when I left. This lawsuit was like the camel that broke the straw's back."

"Or, something like that," she said, breaking into a genuine smile. "Where did you go?"

"If you were going under cover, where would you go?"

She shrugged.

"Down under—natch," he said. "I went to Australia, which is an amazing place to train this time of year. I have a cousin there and some triathlete friends. We had a blast."

"Good to hear," she said. She was surprised at the physical change in Ryan since the last time she saw him. He looked well rested, relaxed and tan.

"That's not even the good part," he said. "I raced in the January Fest Triathlon, which drew a small international field of triathletes from colder climes."

"Did you win?"

"Yes, but that's not the point. It's summer in Australia now so there were some American, European and Japanese athletes. One of the guys from Japan was Jinsei Okuda."

"Should I know the name?" Zana asked.

Ryan nodded. "He goes by Jake when he's racing in the US."

"Jake Okuda? Oh—he was the guy who was in the top five in Paradise Lagoons Triathlon. I talked to him already and he said he didn't see anything," Zana relaxed her shoulders.

"I didn't want to cause any problems with the case so I asked one of the other triathletes who's a police officer in New Zealand if he would ask Okuda some questions."

"Smart, but did he change his story?"

Ryan nodded and so Zana grabbed a pen and wrote Okuda's name on the top of a legal pad.

"Like he told you, he didn't see anything," Ryan said. "But he said he now remembers a Japanese television show with crews on motorcycles during the race."

Zana sat up straight in her chair. "How can we contact the station?"

"No need. Jinsei had a copy of the footage on his iPad. He e-mailed it to the New Zealand cop who forwarded it to me," Ryan said.

"Okay, and why am I not hearing this until now?" She furrowed her brow.

"Take a look." He pulled a tablet out of his messenger bag and turned it towards her. The screen came to life, showing scenes from the triathlon. "I'll fast forward this a bit." He positioned himself so they could both see it.

The scene showed Jake Okuda biking in his aero bar position. It then showed the top cyclists, with Ryan in the lead and Terry closing the gap. A close-up of Terry showed his helmet chinstrap dangling down.

Ryan paused the video. "Are you sure you want to see this? It's gruesome."

She stared at the tablet and nodded her head.

He pressed play and the screen showed Terry attempting to pass him, and then their bikes' handlebars colliding. Terry's bicycle wobbled momentarily as he tried to regain his balance, and then crashed. As his body hit the road, his helmet tumbled off and his unprotected head smashed against the asphalt. A shrill scream sounded and a voice shouted to call 9-1-1. Ryan clicked off the video.

Zana abruptly turned to look out the window, hoping Ryan wouldn't see her pained expression. The video was more graphic than she'd expected. Despite Bud Schubert's threatening behavior, this was his son.

"See, I didn't do anything wrong," Ryan said, interrupting the silence.

"Well, Terry didn't have his chinstrap fastened," Zana said, slowly turning to face her client. "But, it's hard to see why your handlebars collided. The camera was on a motorcycle riding to your left and the angle

190

made it so Terry's body was in the way."

"I held my line. It wasn't my fault that Terry hit me," Ryan said.

"I know. This is helpful." She straightened a few files on her desk. "I just don't know if it will convince Bud Schubert that you weren't at fault."

Ryan slumped in his chair. "I'll email it to you so you can pass it on to opposing counsel."

"Good idea." She nodded. "Don't be discouraged; we still have hope."

He put his face in his hands. "What hope do I have?"

"While you were out of the country, I retained an expert to examine the helmet. It's his opinion that the chinstrap was cut. If we can find out who cut it, maybe we can find out who's responsible for Terry's death," she said.

"Did you get fingerprints?" Ryan looked up and then slipped his tablet back into his bag.

"We did. After our expert issued his report, we requested to have the helmet dusted."

"And?"

"Nothing. The only fingerprints on the helmet were yours and Terry's," she said.

"So, it looks like I'm the one who cut the chinstrap and switched my helmet with Terry's." He sighed. "And then, I turned into him with my handlebars when he was trying to pass me so I could knock him out of the race and win the prize money."

"I hate to tell you this, but your former tenant, Kyle Conner, testified that you said you'd do anything to win—even kill your opponents."

"That douche bag. He's such a liar," Ryan said, raising his voice. "You should have seen the place after Kyle and T.J. trashed it. He's still trying to get even with me for kicking him out, calling the cops and flushing his weed down the toilet."

"Did you ever use fighting words when you were talking about your opponents?" She rested her face on her hands with her elbows on her desk.

"Yeah—probably." He shrugged. "Don't you use fighting words when you're talking about kicking Megan Alexander's ass in the Freewheel tri?"

"Maybe, but not out loud," she said. "I would never threaten to kill her—even to myself."

"I guess it's a guy thing," He said. "What's next?"

"Well, we have some more depositions scheduled." Zana consulted the calendar on her computer. "Gary Moretti's depo is scheduled for January 31st. Would you like to attend?"

"Yes, but…" Ryan grimaced and leaned forward. "There's something else I need to show you."

"What's that?" She leaned forward towards him, steeling herself for another gruesome video. Instead, he handed her his phone with texts from a Hawaii phone number that read:

I'm going to kill you, Peterson!

Watch your back!

I didn't get you this first time, but that doesn't mean it's over.

"Oh my God!" Zana looked up at her client and handed him back the phone. "Are these from Bud Schubert?"

"I think so. The Australian police couldn't find the source," he said, rubbing the back of his neck. "Maybe Schubert used a disposable phone."

"You should have listened to me and stayed away," she said, biting her lip. "It's too dangerous for you to be here."

"You sound like my parents." He sat up straighter in his chair. "I have to live my life. Besides, the Freewheel Tri can't go forward without me."

"I don't think you should go to Gary's depo."

Ryan shook his head. "He's my coach. If Bud fires a shot at me, hopefully he'll go to jail and leave me alone."

Zana put her hands in a steeple position. "I'll talk to Preston about having the deposition in the court's conference room so his client will have to go through security."

"That should work. I'm not sure you know, but Gary was also Terry Schubert's swim coach since he was a kid. My guess is that anything Coach Gary says Bud will believe."

"Do you know what he's going to say?" She leaned forward.

"I have no idea. He just told me to make sure he's on the witness list," Ryan said.

Zana paused, not sure she wanted to know the answer to her next question. "Did you ever tell Coach Gary that you wanted to kill Terry or any other opponents?"

"Well, yeah. I didn't keep my ambitions a secret. If that's what you're getting at." Ryan turned his gaze out the window.

"Uhm, were you ever accused of being violent when you were using performance enhancing drugs when you were a pro cyclist?"

"Yeah, it's called 'roid rage," Ryan's voice cracked.

***

Alexia was waiting at the Kapiolani Park bandstand and was already stretching her calves when Zana arrived after work. As soon as Ryan had left her office, Zana had called the adjuster and suggested a run around Diamond Head.

After they made small talk about work, Zana broke the news. "Ryan's back."

Alexia stopped in her tracks. "Why didn't you tell me?"

"He dropped by my office today," Zana said, and then continued running with Alexia by her side. She noticed that her friend was actually smiling. She then realized that Alexia always had a serious expression on her face and her eyes often looked fearful. When she had asked her about it at lunch one day, Alexia had changed the subject.

"Do you think I should call him?" Alexia asked as they began the climb up Diamond Head.

Zana thought as she ran up the steep incline. After they reached the top, she said, "I have a better idea. Let's plan a group activity."

"I'm not sure I want to be stuck in the friend zone."

She turned to look at Alexia and asked, "Are you saying that you're actually interested in dating Ryan?"

"Possibly."

"What if you and Ryan joined me and my roommates for a hike?" Zana suggested. "That could break the ice."

Alexia smiled and said, "Sure."

The two women ran down Monsarrat Avenue to their cars.

"A hui hou!" Zana said before Alexia drove out of the parking lot.

Instead of heading home, Zana plugged in her headset and ran a lap around Kapiolani Park listening to tunes from her favorite playlist. Her stride matched the beat of the songs as she turned down Paki Avenue. She hardly noticed the sparse traffic on the road next to her—until she saw a red Ferrari. It was unmistakably Jerry's. The car was going so fast she only caught a glimpse of the back of his head as he drove by. Despite the upbeat music, her pace slowed and she wondered whether he had noticed her.

Even though she had tried to stop thinking about him, there were times when she couldn't get him off her mind. He had been texting her everyday with discreet Xs and Os until she stopped responding on New Year's Day.

At first it was hard to have no contact with him, but as time went on, it seemed to get a bit easier. Thoughts and images of him still popped up—especially in her dreams.

Last night, Zana dreamt that she was sitting in the Jerry's Other-Half director's chair at the studio and Annabelle was next to her, wearing a completely transparent blouse showing a huge baby bump. Annabelle looked smug and said she was naming her first born after his father. Jerry then began acting out a wedding scene in front of a green screen, which was supposed to be a church. He grabbed Zana's hand and pulled her into the scene. She was wearing a white lace and tulle wedding dress.

And then, Zana woke up, wishing her dream were reality, except for the bits about Annabelle.

Seeing Jerry's car reminded Zana of her dream and how she wished things had turned out differently. If she hadn't been assigned Ryan's case, they would still be together.

As she picked up her pace again, she wondered if he would take her back if she quit her job at the firm. Who knows, maybe she could get an offer somewhere else. She then realized the foolishness of the idea. A few friends had been searching for jobs with no success, because no law firms were hiring. Besides, Jerry was now with Annabelle who was—according to the rumors—most likely pregnant with their child.

Zana decided to cut her run short and head home. It was close to 8 p.m. and she needed to get some sleep if she was going to get an early morning swim in at the UH pool before work. After she returned home and showered, she cooked some rice and added leftover teriyaki chicken and bok choy, poured a half glass of Chardonnay and slumped down on the couch to relax before bed. As she flipped through the channels, she landed on the latest episode of "Fighting in Paradise". Jerry Ho was using capoeira against Brazilian hoodlums.

"Are you sure you want to watch that?" Kelly asked as she entered the living room and joined her roommate on the couch.

"It's probably not the best idea," Zana said, taking a bite of chicken with chopsticks.

"You still love him, don't you?" Kelly asked in a soothing tone.

"Yeah." Zana admitted, her mouth full.

"Have you tried talking to him?" Kelly gently squeezed her shoulder with her hand.

Zana swallowed hard. "It's not that simple."

"If there's a baby involved, I can understand that."

Zana sighed. "It's more complicated than that." She clicked the channel to "Hawaii 5-0".

"I'll listen if you want to tell me," Kelly said, rubbing her friend's shoulder.

With eyes glued to the T.V., Zana said, "Maybe, someday."

They sat in silence and watched the show. Zana finished her wine and half of her dinner. Before she could protest, Kelly poured some more into her glass.

"Do you want to go out on a blind date?" Kelly broke the silence.

"Are you kidding me?" Zana said and turned to her roommate.

"Andrew's best friend from New York will be here for a few days before he boards a cruise ship with his family," Kelly said.

"Are you suggesting that I go on a date with Andrew's friend?" Her eyes widened. Since they'd known each other, Zana had consistently told her roommate that she despised set-ups.

"He's a great guy. Stuart is cute, single and age appropriate."

Zana played along and asked, "What does he do for a living?"

"He's a stockbroker. You must be considering it, if you're asking."

"It sounds like a really bad idea," Zana said, setting her dinner bowl down. She'd lost her appetite.

"What's a bad idea?" Andrew asked as he walked into the living room, carrying a newspaper.

"I was thinking that Zana could meet Stuart when he comes to town."

"Oh, you mean like a blind date?" He raised an eyebrow.

"Sort of." Kelly shrugged.

"I'm not interested," Zana said.

He sat down on the Lazy Boy. "You and Stuart might hit it off."

"I'm sure we have nothing in common," Zana said.

"Well, let's see—Stuart is as Type A as they get. Kind of like you, Zana. He's super ambitious and he's making big bucks at his firm. Sounds like the perfect guy," Andrew said. "He doesn't drive a red Ferrari, but he does have a black Porsche."

Zana shook her head. "I'm not after a guy's money."

"That would be a first. Ever since Stuart bought his Porsche and started wearing a Rolex, he's hounded by women wherever he goes."

"Are you saying that Stuart couldn't get a date until he started making money?" Zana asked. "He must be homely."

Andrew laughed. "Not at all. What I'm saying is that you women want men who drive fancy cars and have money. Average guys like me don't stand a chance," he said, winking at Kelly.

"You've done very well," Zana said.

"I know—I'm the luckiest guy in the world," he said, reaching to hold his fiancé's hand. "Zana, you can meet Stuart, but he's not much different than Jerry. There are Annabelles waiting in the wings to snag him, too."

"So, what's your suggestion?" Zana raised her eyebrows.

"If I were you, I would date nice, average guys who aren't flashy or rich," he advised. "You'll find someone nice who you feel comfortable with. To tell you the truth, ever since you started dating Jerry you've been a nervous, jealous wreck. You were much happier before you met, when you were just fantasizing about him while watching him on T.V."

"Those are interesting observations, Andrew," Zana said, feeling her face heat up.

"He doesn't mean it," Kelly said.

"I meant every word. I'm not trying to be critical," he said. "You're our friend. Kelly and I want you to have the same happiness we have. We'd like to go to your wedding and have our children play with yours. This won't happen if you continue to date men like Jerry."

"Maybe, you're right." Zana frowned and pulled a pillow to her chest and sunk back into the sofa. She imagined a future with children, but couldn't imagine their father being anyone other than Jerry.

Chapter Twenty-Eight

@ZLaw Living up to my reputation for exciting depositions. I had no idea I had a reputation. #Proud

Zana had made it a policy to avoid asking Lucas for help. It wasn't that she didn't think he was a talented attorney. He was. It felt strange and risky delegating to the boss's son. She let Lucas come to her if he wanted to assist on the Schubert case or any other case. However, today was different. Her hand shook as she knocked on his closed door.

"Come in," a male voice called.

Zana was startled to see Dennis sitting where she expected to see Lucas, his desk piled high with neat stacks of documents. *Did I miss something? Did Frank fire his own son?*

Her eyes scanned the room. "Oh, sorry. I didn't realize you were in here. I'm looking for Lucas."

"It's strange how everyone who stops by is looking for him," Dennis said. "It makes me feel unpopular."

"Was he fired?" Zana stammered.

Dennis laughed. "Nah, he moved offices."

She frowned. "Okay, I'll take a look down the hall." There were always a few empty offices vacated by recently terminated attorneys.

"He's in Michael Lee's old office," Dennis offered.

"Are you sure?" Zana stared at the new associate in disbelief. "He's newer than me. I heard that Michael's old office is quite posh."

Dennis shrugged. "I've only been here for a month and I'm amazed at the confusion. No one seems to know where anyone is, and they're always fighting over office space. Sometimes, I wonder whether I should have taken the job with the Public Defender."

"I'm sure you made the right decision," Zana said and then added, "We should ask Libby for a regularly updated directory."

"Good idea."

"I'll let you get back to work." Zana turned and headed down the hallway towards the Makai wing.

She had never been in Michael's former office before, but knew it must be large with a magnificent view, considering he was a partner. As she entered the hallway, she noticed it was much quieter. The secretaries were dressed more professionally and talked in hushed tones compared to the loud chatter amongst the staff in the low rent district. Christine, a paralegal who she had only met once, directed her to an office with a partially open door.

Zana entered without knocking and was stunned by the breathtaking view of the ocean and Diamond Head. It looked like a penthouse living room with its red Italian leather love seat, glass coffee and end tables, modern lamps, and a small wet bar, complete with a dorm refrigerator. Lucas sat behind a black lacquer desk with a three-screen computer.

"Nepotism is alive and well." Zana raised an arched eyebrow.

"What can I say? I was offered the office, so I took it," Lucas said, turning away from his computer screens.

She shook her head. "This isn't fair."

"You know what isn't fair, Zana? I grew up without a father. Frank wouldn't admit that I was his son until I worked at his law firm for many months. My parents lied to me throughout my whole shitty childhood. That's what's not fair."

"Still—don't you think that someone like Andrew, Tom, or one of the associates who has been here longer should have been given this office?" Zana said with hands on hips.

"No. Frank finally decided to do something for his son. He didn't spend time with me or give me gifts when I was growing up," he said. "This partially makes up for all of that."

She shrugged. "Okay, I'll drop it."

"Thanks." He relaxed his shoulders and leaned back in his chair.

She sat down on the red leather love seat and gazed out the window at the sparkling ocean. "I can see why you've kept this a secret. It's amazing enough to make even partners jealous." She reached out and touched the tropical floral arrangement on the coffee table—surprised it was made of silk. She smiled.

"I do love it. But, it's getting old having to defend my right to be here," Lucas said. "You know, Zana, you seldom came to my office when we shared the same Dole pineapple view. What are you doing here today?"

"I need your help," she said, again feeling her hands tremble. "I've got a deposition for the Schubert case tomorrow."

"That's a dog case." He scowled. "We don't stand a chance."

"I understand what you're saying," she said. She wasn't in the mood to try to sell her arguments as to why Ryan should prevail.

"Who's being deposed?"

"Ryan and Terry's swim coach," she said.

"What's he supposed to say?" Lucas leaned forward.

She shrugged. "I have no idea. He hasn't returned my phone calls."

"Then, how can you prepare?"

"That's why I'm here talking to you."

"Let's see your outline," he said.

Zana handed him a thumb drive and he pulled the document up on his computer. He went through it line by line while she relaxed on the sofa and closed her eyes, sipping a San Pellegrino sparkling blood orange soda from the wet bar. She could get used to this.

"Okay, all done." He smiled. "Take a look." He turned one of his computer screens so it faced her.

She moved from the sofa to a black, modern chair next to the desk and examined the changes. After a few minutes, she nodded and said, "Nice. That looks better."

"I think you should offer the one million dollar policy limits. It you don't, Ryan is on the hook for some big bucks," Lucas said. "No one will win a trip to Paris at the Freewheel Movement tri."

"He didn't do anything wrong," Zana protested.

"It doesn't matter. You've got to protect your client's assets. He's making big money now. His race series and sponsorships are huge. Schubert is a greedy son-of-a-bitch and won't think twice about going after everything Ryan has worked for."

"If it doesn't go well tomorrow, I'll talk to Alexia about paying," she said. "Do you have time to come to the deposition?"

"Are you sure you want the spoiled boss' son there with you?" Lucas grinned as he gazed out the window.

"Yes." She nodded, seeing a cruise ship in the distance. "I'd really appreciate it." When she looked down, her hands were no longer shaking.

***

Zana and Lucas walked a half-mile to the First Circuit Court building where Gary Moretti's deposition was scheduled. As planned, Ryan was waiting for them just outside security. The men took off their belts and she put her briefcase and purse through the x-ray machine before they all walked through the screening arch. Ryan was the only one who caused the machine to buzz and had to be scanned a second time by the security officer's hand held wand.

"Why did you set off the buzzer?" Zana asked, after he was cleared.

"I have some hardware in my wrist from a bike accident. It happens all the time," Ryan said, holding out his wrist with its long faded scar.

A loud buzz came from the x-ray machine. Zana raised her eyebrows when she saw Bud Schubert, wearing a sport jacket and slacks, walking through and then hugging one of the security guards and high-fiving another. He then joined Preston, and they walked together towards the elevator.

"How did he get away without a second screening?" Zana whispered to

Lucas.

"It's Hawaii. Schubert is probably related to them, or they went to school with his son," Lucas whispered as they followed their opponents.

The elevator opened and Bud and Preston stepped in, and the doors snapped shut. Zana put her hand on Ryan's arm and said, "Let's take the stairs—I'll race you to the top." Even with her two-inch heels, she wanted to get her blood flowing. "Are you in, Lucas?"

"I'll take the elevator. You triathletes are crazy," Lucas said.

Ryan and Zana ran up the four flights of stairs and waited for Lucas outside the elevator.

"I can't believe you beat me and you're not even out of breath," Lucas said after he stepped out of the elevator. "You're animals."

Zana grinned.

Bud and Preston were already seated at the long conference room table when they entered the room.

"Is the witness here yet?" she asked as she set up her laptop.

"We haven't seen him," Preston said.

She recognized the court reporter, Trish—a favorite of the partners of her firm.

"I think I saw the witness in the hallway," Trish said. "Do you want me to get him?"

"That's okay, I'll go," Lucas said, rising quickly from his chair.

Moments later, Lucas came in with a tall, athletic-looking man wearing a green UH Rainbows ball cap. He smiled and nodded at Bud and Ryan, and then sat down across from Preston and next to the court reporter.

Preston quickly went through his preliminary questions, learning that Gerardo Pietro Moretti, Jr., who had been called Gary all his life, was born in Italy, but his parents immigrated to San Diego when he was a baby. His family later moved to Los Angeles where he attended high school and then UCLA on a swimming scholarship. He had competed in the Olympic trials twice for the 100 and 200 meter freestyle events and had succeeded in earning a slot as a member of a USA relay team at the 1976 Montreal Olympics, and the team won a bronze medal.

He moved to Hawaii in 1984 to serve as the University of Hawaii's swim coach. He also had side jobs, one of which was privately instructing Terry Schubert from ten years old until his death. Coach Gary, as everyone called him, also coached the UH Masters swim program, of which Ryan Peterson belonged to for the past two years.

"Do you mind if I take a break to use the restroom?" Gary asked.

"No problem. Let's go off the record and take ten minutes," Preston said.

Zana, Ryan and Lucas walked out of the room together and stepped into a courtroom alcove so they could talk privately.

"Is there any way you can ask Bud Schubert to stop staring at me?" Ryan asked.

"Yeah, I noticed he's been giving you stink eye," Lucas said. "It's good that he's not armed, because if he were, I'd be worried for you, buddy."

"Ryan, it might be a good idea for you to leave," Zana said, biting her lip.

Ryan ran a jerky hand through his hair and stammered, "No, I want to stay. I just wish he wasn't staring at me."

"Let's switch places and you can move your chair so that you're sitting at an angle, facing the witness and not Schubert," Lucas said. He then turned to Zana and asked, "Are you sure Bud's not armed?"

She shook her head. "No, but Preston and I had a long chat about it, and he agreed to talk with his client. Besides, he can't bring a gun in here."

After they returned to the conference room and Ryan re-positioned himself, Preston continued his questioning, which Zana read on her laptop.

Q. (Preston Farnsworth, III) Did you attend the Paradise Lagoons Triathlon in March?

A. (Gerardo Moretti, Jr.) Yes.

Q. In what capacity did you attend the race?

A. As Terry Schubert's coach.

Q. Were you aware that Ryan Peterson was participating?

A. Yes.

Q. How did you know that?

A. When I was helping Terry set up for the race, I saw Ryan's bike next to Terry's.

Q. Did you talk to Ryan before the race?

A. Yes.

Q. What did you say?

A. I wished him good luck and he thanked me.

Q. Had you ever heard Ryan threaten Terry?

The witness paused.

Q. Mr. Moretti, I need an answer. Did you ever hear Ryan threaten

Terry?

A. Not directly.

Q. What do you mean by that?

A. Well, Ryan liked to blow off steam. I did hear him talk trash about his competitors.

Q. What do you mean by 'talk trash'?

A. He'd say stuff like, 'I'm going to kick his ass'.'

Q. Did Ryan ever say the words, I'm going to kill Terry?

The witness paused.

A. Yeah.

Before Preston could ask his next question, Bud reached into his suit jacket and pulled out a gun and aimed it at Ryan, who raised his hands and slowly stood up. Zana grabbed Trish's arm and pulled her under the table where they laid flat against the ground next to Preston.

"I didn't kill your son!" Ryan shouted.

"You're a fucking murderer!" Bud said, cocking the pistol. "You'll get what's coming to you."

"This is between you and I," Ryan's voice shook. "Let everyone else go."

"You're the only one who's getting a bullet, you God-damned prick!" Bud took a step in Ryan's direction.

"Now wait a minute, Bud," Gary said, standing up. "You haven't heard the whole story."

"I know enough," Bud said gruffly and moved even closer to Ryan.

"If Terry were here, he'd want you to hear who really caused his death," Gary said.

As Bud momentarily lowered the gun and stared at the coach, Lucas took a running leap, slamming Bud against the wall and holding him there with the weight of his body. The gun fell to the floor and tumbled in Gary's direction. Gary bent down, picked it up, put the safety on and opened the chamber.

"It's empty," Gary said, tossing the gun on the table.

"What the fuck?" Lucas pushed Bud against the wall and then released him.

Zana, Preston and Trish stood up slowly and stared at Bud.

"Bud, this is absolutely unacceptable," Preston said in a loud, gruff voice. He began pacing.

"I didn't want to hurt anyone." Bud slumped into a chair. "Losing my son has destroyed me." He sobbed into his hands.

Preston grabbed a box of tissues from a side table and placed it with a thud on the table in front of his client. After a few moments, Preston sat down and the others followed his lead.

Gary broke the silence. "Do you want me to continue?"

Preston looked at Zana. She then whispered in Ryan's ear, "Are you okay?"

Ryan nodded and then whispered back, "Let's get this over with."

"I can ask questions," she said.

Preston gave her a wave of his hand and said, "Be my guest, counselor."

Zana motioned for Gary to sit across the table from her and she pulled up the outline on her computer and examined it for a few moments.

Q. (Zana West): Had you ever witnessed Ryan and Terry have any interactions with each other?

A. (Gerardo Moretti, Jr.): Yes, many times.

Q. Were they cordial?

A. Always. Terry and Ryan were friends.

Q. Have you ever witnessed Ryan and anyone else have any non-cordial interactions?

A. I'm not sure what you mean by non-cordial, but I have seen Ryan in an argument with someone before.

Q. When was that?

A. Let's see—probably about a week or two before the Paradise Lagoons Triathlon.

Q. Who was the argument with?

A. This guy named Rockstar. I don't remember his real name. He owns a bike shop called Freewheel.

Q. What was the argument about?

A. I remember it well, because it happened at the UH pool. Ryan was about to get into the water for the evening workout when Rockstar showed up and started swearing at him.

Q. Do you know what he was swearing about?

A. Yes. Ryan had just started his charity and Rockstar was angry at him for naming it the Freewheel Movement. He threatened to sue Ryan.

Q. How did Ryan respond to his threats?

A. Ryan told him to calm down and that the pool wasn't the place to have this discussion.

Q. Then, what did Rockstar do?

A. He went ballistic. He started throwing kick boards. Ryan dove into the pool and I called security.

Q. Then what happened?

A. Rockstar heard me report the altercation. He knocked my iPhone out of my hand, causing it to fall to the ground and break.

Q. Then what happened?

A. Rockstar pointed at Ryan in the water and said, 'I'm gonna kill you'. He then pointed at me and said, 'Watch your back'. Then, he left.

Q. Let's go back to the morning of the Paradise Lagoons Triathlon, did you have any other interaction with Ryan Peterson that day?

A. Only to wish him good luck.

Q. Did you see how Terry's and Ryan's gear were set up in the transition area before the race?

A. Yes. They both had their bikes in their assigned slots, with their towels and water pans to wash the sand off their feet after running out of the water. They both had their helmets on their aero bars with their sunglasses in them. They had the same set up—like most triathletes.

Q. Were you coaching anyone else that morning?

A. No.

Q. Was your attention focused only on Terry?

A. Yes.

Q. Did you walk with Terry to the swim starting line?

A. Only part way.

Q. Why was that?

A. Terry forgot to put some Body Glide on, and I told him I'd run back to the transition area and grab it. He told me to hurry, because he wanted to get a warm up in.

Q. What was the Body Glide for?

A. It was for rubbing on his skin so it doesn't chafe from the salt water.

Q. What happened when you got to the transition area?

A. From about 30 feet away, I saw only one person in the closed area and he was standing next to Ryan's and Terry's bikes. I think he heard me coming and walked away before I got there.

Q. How would you describe the person?

A. Well, I recognized him.

Q. Who was it?

A. Rockstar.

Q. Did you observe anything about him?

A. He was wearing gloves and carrying a knife. When he saw me, he gave me a nasty look and made a motion with the knife.

Q. What kind of motion?

A. Threatening—like he would cut my head off.

Q. So, then what did you do?

A. I heard the fifteen-minute warning announcement, so I grabbed the Body Glide and ran as fast as I could to the swim start to give it to Terry before he got in the water.

Q. Did you see anything amiss with Terry's or Ryan's equipment when you were getting the Body Glide?

A. I saw that both of their helmets had toppled to the ground, but that was all.

Q. Did you do anything to move them?

A. No. I didn't have time. I figured that the guys were professionals and could simply reach down and pick up their helmets.

(Pause)

Zana West: Here's some tissue, Mr. Moretti.

Preston Farnsworth, III: Would you like to take a break?

A. (Gerardo Moretti, Jr.) No, I'm okay. (Pause) I was hired to help Terry get the fastest swim possible and I was focused on that. I needed to give Terry some coaching before the race.

Q. What did you do when you met up with Terry?

A. I helped him apply the Body Glide and then I got in the water with him and finished the warm up with him.

Q. Did you tell him about Rockstar?

A. No. I didn't think there was anything to tell and I didn't want to disturb his concentration before the race.

Q. When you saw Rockstar in the transition area, was there anyone else there?

A. No.

Q. Were any transition security personnel there?

A. Rockstar was the only one.

Q. What do you mean by that?

A. Rockstar was the bicycle mechanic for the race and had volunteered to watch the transition area while everyone left to watch the swim start.

Q. How do you know that?

A. I asked the race director why no one stopped me when I went back into the transition area.

Q. When did you ask him that?

A. After Terry had finished the swim and went off on his bike.

Q. What did he say?

A. He said that Rockstar had volunteered to watch T-1.

Q. Did you tell him what you saw when you approached it?

A. At the time, I didn't know what I saw. Rockstar was standing by the bikes holding a knife with a gloved hand. Maybe, I thought he had been working on a bike. I don't know. The only thing that bothered me at the time was his threatening gesture. Do you mind if we take a break? I just need to walk around a little bit.

Zana led Lucas and Ryan back to the courtroom alcove.
"It sure sounds like Rockstar cut your helmet strap, Ryan," Lucas said.
"The problem is that Gary didn't actually see him do it," Zana said.
"A jury would probably infer that he cut it and at least conclude that you weren't at fault," Lucas said to Ryan.
"I hope so. I had no idea that Rockstar was a murderer. He was clearly out to get me—but killed Terry," Ryan said, tears forming in his eyes.
"You're shaking," Zana said as she put her hand on Ryan's shoulder.
"Did you notice that when Gary told his story about Rockstar, Bud took his cowboy hat off and put his head in his hands?" Lucas asked.
"Yeah. Maybe, he finally gets that Ryan didn't do anything wrong," Zana said.
"I hope so," Ryan said, wiping his eyes with the back of his hands.
When they walked back, six sheriff deputies in brown uniforms were standing outside the conference room with guns drawn. One of them motioned for them to back away as Bud was led out of the room with his hands in cuffs. Preston followed with his cell phone to his ear.
After the men had left, Zana led Ryan and Lucas back into the room so she could retrieve her laptop. Trish was packing up her machine.
"What happened?" Lucas picked up a chair that had fallen over and set

it upright.

"My boss called and I told him that Mr. Schubert pulled a gun on us. He must have called the Sheriff's office," Trish said.

"But it wasn't loaded," Ryan said, raising his eyebrows.

"When he was arrested, one of the deputies said it's illegal to bring firearms into the Courthouse—whether it's loaded or not is irrelevant. Plus, he threatened us." Trish closed her case and walked to the door. "Zana, my boss said your depositions are usually quite exciting. He was right."

Lucas laughed and looked at Zana, "Apparently, you have a reputation."

Zana rolled her eyes.

Chapter Twenty-Nine

@FreewheelMV When #hiking in Hawaii, always be prepared. See our website FreewheelMovement.com for a full list of gear. #EagleScout

Zana wheeled her bike into the garage, leaning it against the wall next to Kelly's Infinite, and threw her gear bag into the plastic bin with her name written in Andrew's sloppy handwriting with a black permanent marker. He was sick of her triathlon gear being scattered all over *his* garage, so he gave her two large stacked bins in the corner. She pulled off her bike helmet and was too tired to lift a lid. Instead, she hung it on an empty hook reserved for Andrew's ball caps. *Maybe he wouldn't notice.*

It was already past noon and so she would barely have time for a quick shower—if she were lucky—before their planned hike. Her roommates were waiting for her in the kitchen.

"We've got to get going. Stuart just texted from the lobby of the hotel," Andrew said, reaching into the refrigerator for Zana's Camelback she filled with water the night before.

"What time are we picking up Alexia?" Kelly chimed in.

"I think I said one-thirty," Zana said, grabbing some string cheese from the fridge. "I've got to take a shower and eat something."

Andrew shook his head. "There's no time. You're going to get dirty on the hike anyway."

"Okay, I've been riding my bike for three hours and then I ran six miles in the hot sun. I'm disgusting." Zana smelled an armpit.

"You should have come home earlier." Andrew handed Zana her backpack.

"I'm wearing bike clothes for God's sake. Text your friend that we'll be there in a half hour."

Zana rushed to her room, grabbed the hiking clothes she had tossed onto her bed in the morning and then popped into the bathroom where she took a record fast shower and brushed her teeth. She returned to the kitchen ten minutes later and said, "If you're serious about setting me up with Stuart, you'll give me more time to put on some makeup."

"You look fine," Andrew said, without a glance.

She wasn't interested in impressing his friend and pulled her wet hair into a ponytail. As they walked into the garage, Zana grabbed a UH Rainbow Warriors cap from a hook and asked, "Can I wear this?"

Andrew squinted at her and pulled his New York Yankees cap off a hook. "Wear this one. At least you'll score some points with Stuart."

Zana had no interest in scoring points with any guy except Jerry, but changed hats anyway. They headed to her SUV, because hers was the only vehicle roomy enough for all of them. Andrew and Kelly climbed in the back, leaving the front passenger seat vacant for Stuart.

"I feel like I'm your chauffeur," Zana said as she backed out of the driveway.

Kelly laughed. "You are."

"Does your friend know you're trying to set us up?" Zana asked as she pulled up to the Palm Hotel, where Kelly worked as a front desk manager and had gotten Stuart a comp room.

"Not exactly," Andrew said.

Zana smiled. "Good." Her shoulders relaxed a bit.

And then she saw him approach their car. Stuart's brown hair looked blow dried to perfection and he was wearing aviator sunglasses, a pink polo shirt, white shorts and gleaming white tennis shoes, a Rolex watch, a thick gold chain around his neck and was carrying a large bottle of Coke in one hand and his iPhone in the other.

"Hey, Stuart—lookin' good, buddy," Andrew said, then he awkwardly fist-bumped Stuart's open hand.

"Aloha," Stuart said in his heavy Brooklyn accent and then "Hey there" to Zana after he took his seat next to her. She gave him a weak smile and drove towards Alexia's house in Makiki.

Andrew and Stuart chatted about the Super Bowl and the upcoming baseball season while Stuart took a few pictures out the window with his phone.

"How's your hotel room?" Kelly leaned forward in her seat to ask their guest.

"It's okay—nothing to write home about." Stuart laughed heartily. "It's small, but everything works. And, if I stand on tiptoes by the window, I can see the ocean."

Zana looked at Kelly through the rear view mirror and saw her grimace, sit back in her seat and fold her arms in front of her.

Alexia was waiting outside when they drove up. Even with her khaki hiking shorts, plain olive green T-shirt, and long blonde hair in a high ponytail held in place by a navy ball cap, she looked stunning. She and her backpack with large water bottles in the side pockets squeezed into the backseat with Kelly and Andrew. Stuart's eyes were glued to Alexia from the instant he saw her and he turned around to say, "What's up, sweetheart?"

Alexia ignored him and began a conversation with Kelly about stand up paddling.

When they finally made it to the trailhead, with detailed instructions from her iPhone navigation, Zana realized she had done this same hike with Jerry. Before she could protest and suggest another option, she saw Ryan waiting for them next to his mountain bike and a huge backpack.

"Did you bring a sleeping bag in that thing, buddy?" Andrew asked after they all piled out of the car.

"Nah. I like to be prepared in case something goes wrong." Ryan opened his pack and showed them his extra water bottles, rain gear, socks, a towel, whistle, waterproof matches, small shovel, first aid kit, sunscreen, bug repellant, Swiss army knife, and black nylon rope.

"What's the rope for?" Kelly asked.

"Lassoing women?" Stuart chuckled.

Ryan ignored him and said, "It has many uses in an emergency situation. A few months ago, I needed rope to help rescue a hiker who slipped and fell about thirty feet."

"Good for you," Alexia said, smiling at him.

"Let's get moving," Zana said, walking onto the trail and signaling with her hand for them to follow her. "We're losing daylight."

Ryan and Alexia fell in step with Zana. The first part was only a modest incline and the others stayed close behind.

Ryan turned to Stuart, offering him a bottle of water.

"No, I'm good. I only drink Coke," Stuart said, raising the bottle in his hand.

Zana rolled her eyes.

"Suit yourself," Ryan said and put the bottle back into his stuffed backpack.

Every time Stuart sidled up to Alexia, she'd cling more to Ryan's side. When Zana noticed her apparent discomfort, she positioned herself so Alexia was safely in between her and her client. Since all three were extraordinarily fit, they kept up a fast pace even as the trail became steep. Kelly and Andrew, who exercised regularly, playing Ultimate Frisbee, were only a few steps behind, but after about thirty minutes, Zana could see Stuart's bright white shorts trailing about 50 yards. They stopped intermittently to let him catch up, but he always waved them on and took another sip from his Coke or took pictures with his phone.

When they reached a large rock with a view of the valley below, Zana saw some other hikers in the distance. The man was a dead ringer for Jerry and his companion wasn't Annabelle, but looked like the other woman he was with on New Year's Eve. Zana shook the thought out of her head. She always mistook people for Jerry. She pulled out a Kind bar from her pack and ate it while Kelly, Andrew, Stuart and Ryan posed for selfies. Alexia drank from her water bottle away from the group, refusing to be photographed.

Ryan looked at his watch. "Our turnaround time is three-thirty, so let's get going." He had explained earlier that in order to return safely back to the car before sunset, they had to impose a strict schedule. They resumed their fast pace in silence—with Ryan, Alexia and Zana leading.

"Hey Zana, did you read anything about Bud Schubert in the news yesterday?" Ryan asked after they began hiking through a wooded area.

"No. I even bought the paper, thinking the story of his arrest would be featured prominently. I thought it would be front page news," Zana said, positioning herself next to Ryan as they walked through the narrow path lined with tall trees.

"Yeah, I thought it was weird that one of the most well-known businessmen in our city was arrested and there wasn't a single mention," Ryan said, raising his eyebrows. "I even googled his name and found nothing about it."

"Caron said Schubert runs this town, so the press wouldn't dare report anything negative. I wonder if he owns controlling shares in some of the media outlets," Alexia said in a low voice.

Ryan frowned. "I wouldn't be surprised."

Alexia put her hand on his shoulder and said, "Maybe, we should enjoy our day and not talk about the case."

"Good idea." Zana smiled at her plan to bring Ryan and Alexia together on the hike and as an added bonus, the "double date" with Stuart and her roommates was less awkward.

As they hiked up the incline, the trail grew wider, but was still surrounded by trees. Zana glanced back and saw Kelly and Andrew walking hand-in-hand together ten feet behind and Stuart, now covered with dirt, was aiming his phone at a Java finch.

"Did you hear that?" Ryan asked.

Zana paused to listen. "It sounds like a dirt bike. I've been on this trail before and saw some guys riding down."

The sound grew louder. Then a dirt biker emerged onto the trail, driving straight for them.

"Look out!" Ryan yelled and grabbed Alexia by the arm and stepped off the path.

The biker, who was wearing a black helmet with a black shaded visor concealing his identity, picked up more speed as he approached and drove straight for the lead group.

Zana jumped onto some thick underbrush, just in time. Kelly and Andrew climbed onto a large rock.

"That was a close one," Andrew said, helping his fiancé off the rock.

"Crazy!" Alexia said, putting her hand on Ryan's arm for balance as she stepped back onto the trail.

"Shit! He's coming back," Ryan shouted, and they all jumped off the trail again.

This time, they saw the biker more closely as he sped past. He was holding a machete and waved it towards Alexia, Zana and Ryan. They watched the biker ride past and then he slowed, turned around and raced directly towards them again.

Ryan lifted Alexia up onto a solid tree branch, and Kelly and Andrew flung themselves behind the large rock. Zana ducked behind a tree, feeling her heart pound as she heard the engine grow closer.

"Get the hell out of here!" Ryan yelled, grabbing a hanging tree branch and swinging away from the biker, just in time as he waved his weapon in Ryan's direction.

Zana peeked out from behind the tree and saw Ryan grab his backpack and search for something. *Does he have a weapon?*

"Zana! Grab this," Ryan shouted.

She stepped out and caught the end of the long, black nylon rope he had thrown.

"Tie it to that tree," he said, pointing to a small, but sturdy tree on her side of the trail.

Her hands were shaking as she tried to tie a knot, but the sound of the bike was getting louder.

Ryan leaped across the trail and grabbed the rope from her hand, and quickly tied a secure knot so the rope stretched across the path. He motioned her to take cover and then he walked into the middle of the trail, standing beyond the nearly invisible nylon cord—facing the deafening noise of the dirt bike, which was fast approaching.

"Get down!" Zana shouted.

But it was too late.

The dirt biker rode straight towards Ryan with his machete brandished, aiming it at him.

The gold medalist stood still in the middle of the trail looking more like an athlete waiting for the starting gun to fire than the target of a crazed killer.

Zana watched as the biker hit the rope and was suddenly flung backwards off his bike. His body flipped, and fell violently to the ground, falling chest first onto the machete.

Zana screamed. Blood oozed on the ground encircling the fallen biker, who lay completely still. The sound of the bike smashing into a nearby tree was loud in her ears.

"Oh, my God!" Kelly shrieked.

"You set up a trip wire, dude," Andrew's eyes were like saucers. He then called, "Stuart! Where are you?"

"Hey, guys," Stuart yelled as he ran up the path. "I called the police. I wasn't sure exactly where we are, but they said they were able to determine the location of my phone."

Ryan helped Alexia down from the tree and she gave him a wordless hug, her body was shaking. He then walked over to the biker and felt for a pulse, shook his head and stepped away.

"Who is he?" Zana asked.

Ryan wiped the sweat off his brow. "I think I know."

"Was he after you?" Kelly asked.

Ryan nodded.

"I wouldn't be so sure," Andrew said. "It looked like he was after either you, Zana or Alexia."

"Why would he target Alexia?" Stuart asked.

Alexia slunk down to the ground and put her face in her hands and Ryan bent down to comfort her.

"She's a claims adjuster. They're not exactly popular. And, of course Zana's an attorney." Andrew smirked. "Some say knocking her off would be a good start."

Zana punched him in the arm. "What about you?"

Andrew was about to punch her back and then looked up. "Do you hear them?"

Zana nodded. She could hear sirens from the valley below.

"It's going to take them awhile to get up here," Ryan said. He was sitting on the ground with his arm around Alexia.

"Do you think we'll get into any trouble about the trip wire?" Kelly wrinkled her brow.

"It was self-defense," Zana said. "The guy was going to kill us."

"Me—at the very least," Ryan said, his head down.

"Or, me." Alexia wiped tears from her face with her hand, leaving a streak of dirt on her cheek.

Ryan pulled out a blue bandana from his pack and wiped Alexia's cheeks. He said, "We have six witnesses."

"And I recorded it." Stuart held out his phone.

All of them, except Alexia, crowded around him and watched footage of the biker speeding on the trail towards them, holding the machete in a black, gloved hand. It looked like he came close to hitting Ryan and Alexia in one scene.

"Don't touch anything," Andrew warned. "Let them investigate."

They all sat in silence, waiting for the police to arrive. Andrew embraced Kelly and Ryan and Alexia clung to each other. Zana sat on the ground leaning against a large rock with her eyes closed and Stuart sat on a tree stump, recharging his phone with its auxiliary charging case.

Soon, they heard heavy footsteps on the trail and saw six police officers and four firefighters make their way towards them.

"Stuart Levine?" one of the officers asked.

"Yes, sir," Stuart said, standing up—his white shorts were now a blotchy brown.

Most of the men made a beeline to the dead body, but two detectives watched the video.

"Good work," Officer Wong said to Ryan. "This could have turned out badly."

Ryan nodded. His eyes brimmed with tears. He looked towards the body and put his arm tightly around Alexia, who buried her face in his chest. The officers took the helmet off the deceased man's head.

Ryan put his hand to his mouth.

"Did you see who it is?" Zana asked.

Ryan couldn't meet her eyes. "It's Rockstar.

Chapter Thirty

@ZLaw If you wear shoes lined with barbed wire, at least bring a few bandages. #bloodyfeet

Zana froze in place when she saw three black suited young women sitting side by side at the conference room table quietly writing on firm issued legal pads.

"Hmm, am I in the wrong room?" she stammered.

"Are you here for the litigation meeting?" the woman wearing blue-framed glasses asked. She then smiled, revealing a full mouth of metal braces.

"Yeah." Zana paused. "Are you new?" She didn't dare add the word "attorneys". They were probably law clerks or paralegals. Frank had never hired more than one token female associate at a time.

The striking blonde nodded. "This is my first day. I'm Isabelle Christianson, but my friends call me 'Izzy'".

Kim McCall, Brian Ching and Michael Lee walked in.

"So you've met our new associates?" Michael grinned.

Zana nodded. "Well, Isabelle just introduced herself."

"Izzy just moved here from Boston. She graduated from Harvard Law," Kim offered with sparkling eyes.

Zana raised her brows. The young woman looked more like she should be strutting the runway during New York Fashion Week rather than walking the halls of justice.

"This is my cousin, Gwen," Brian said, pointing out the young woman wearing glasses and braces. Zana could see their resemblance.

Gwen said, "Nice to meet you, Zana."

"And this is Jade Aoki, who just finished her law clerkship with Hawaii Supreme Court Justice Nancy Lum," Michael said, waving a hand in her direction.

"Are you any relation to Judge Aoki?" Zana asked.

"He's my dad," she said, her eyes boring into Zana. "It's a pleasure to finally meet you. I've heard *so* much about you."

Like what? Never having a dull moment in my life?

"Where's Dennis?" Zana asked, trying to ignore her comment.

"I'm in his office," Gwen said. "I heard he was let go."

Zana frowned.

"You're next door neighbors," Brian said with a toothy smile.

"It looks like most of you are here," Frank said as he walked in, followed closely behind by Lucas, who was wearing a gray Armani suit and purple power tie.

Did Lucas get a raise? Zana slumped into a chair as far away from the new associates as possible. Now, there were "attorney girls" she had to keep an eye on. *Why did Frank hire women all of a sudden? Did this mean she was being replaced?*

After George Tao, Andrew and a half dozen attorney-boys and junior partners joined them, Frank cleared his throat.

"As you know, our litigation meeting is generally held on Saturdays. This week, I changed it to Monday morning so you could meet our new associates—Gwen, Isabelle and Jade—all of whom have promising futures at the firm." Frank looked directly at Zana when he said "promising". She stared down at her legal pad, feeling a wave of nausea.

Frank beamed at the young women. "You'll have plenty of time to talk with our new dream team, as I call them. But first, we need to discuss a problem case." Again, Frank's eyes were on Zana.

She looked up and noticed everyone was staring at her. She put a hand to her face, self-conscious about the two-inch scratch on her cheek, most likely caused by a branch when she had leapt out of harm's way the day before. She looked across the table at Andrew who also had some visible scrapes.

"I'm not going to go into the details of yesterday's…" Frank paused, "… situation. Why don't you tell us your strategy for the Schubert v. Peterson case? We're all ears, Zana." Frank sat back in his chair and rested his hands in a steeple position.

"I filed a motion for summary judgment, which is scheduled to be heard tomorrow," Zana said. "I'm hoping the court will dismiss the case."

"On what grounds?" Lucas asked. He was leaning back in his chair with his hands in the same position as his father's.

"Well, uh…," Zana stammered. "Our expert opined that Schubert's chin strap was intentionally cut, which caused his helmet to fall off, leading to traumatic brain injury and death. Terry's coach saw a bicycle mechanic called Rockstar wearing gloves and holding a knife near the helmet the morning of the race. And, you may have heard—Rockstar tried to kill Ryan yesterday. Our client had nothing to do with Terry's death." As she explained the facts, she could see from the eyebrow lifts and cocked heads that no one was convinced of her arguments.

"You can't win on a motion for summary judgment," Lucas said. "There are remaining issues of material fact. The court will deny the motion and the case will have to go to trial."

Frank patted his son's shoulder. "I agree."

"The insurance company gave me authority to file the MSJ," Zana said. She looked at Andrew, hoping he'd weigh in. He focused on his legal pad and began doodling.

The room was noiseless as everyone, but Andrew, stared at Zana. No one was shaking their knee, clicking their pen or sipping a coffee. They were all still looking at her.

George interrupted the silence. "I agree with Zana. Filing a motion made sense. Sure, she might lose, but at least it might move the case forward."

Although it wasn't a complete endorsement, at least someone was on her side. Her eyes met George's and he gave her a warm smile.

"We're far too busy to have associates spend time on nonsense. Zana, I suggest you win the motion," Frank said, leaning forward in her direction. "Human Resources tells me there are hundreds of newly sworn in attorneys who submitted their resumes just last week."

Zana looked at the three young women who wore doll-like smiles on their pretty faces. There was not a hint of fear in their eyes. She searched her memory for a day when she felt as confident, but could think of none.

***

The sky was cloudless and the sun beat down on Zana as she walked to court the next morning alone. Lucas refused to go, claiming he had deadlines, but it was clear to her that he wanted no part in her impending failure. Andrew admitted to agreeing with the others and suggested she withdraw the motion to save face and preserve her job. *How could she back out now?*

After yesterday's meeting, she had called Alexia, who said, "You should at least try. What do we have to lose?"

Zana couldn't tell her about Frank's veiled threats or the vulture-like wanna-be attorneys waiting for her to stomp out of the office with her tail between her legs and a bankers box full of barely hung framed diplomas in her arms. F.I.M. would only lose the cost of attorney's fees for the motion, but Zana stood to lose her reputation and job in the few minutes it would take for her to explain her lame arguments to Judge Banks and the courtroom of attorneys who were waiting for their turns to argue.

Kelly rolled her eyes last night when Zana slumped in front of the T.V., downing an extra glass of wine to help numb her worry. "You're always anxious about being fired and then you win and end up being a hero. Tomorrow will be the same, you'll see." Zana ignored her and took another gulp of alcohol. Andrew educated his fiancée by explaining the reality of the situation. They both took turns suggesting non-legal jobs Zana could apply for, including stevedore, flight attendant, and hotel concierge. They were only trying to help.

Zana could feel the back of her shoes rubbing her heels as she reached the intersection across from the courthouse. She wished she would've driven, or at the very least, had a few bandages to cover the bloody sores she could feel developing. The shoes were new and not broken in, but she had thought wearing them would make her feel better today. She grimaced. It wasn't the first time she'd made a bad shoe choice on a court hearing day.

She looked at the time on her phone, and with only four minutes until her meeting time with Ryan and only nineteen minutes until the clerk would call the court calendar, Zana ignored her raw heels and picked up her pace.

Ryan was waiting for her on the bench beyond security. He was freshly shaven and wore black slacks and a long sleeved gray dress shirt, opened at the collar. He smiled brightly as if there was a chance his case would be dismissed and he'd walk into the sunset in an hour's time.

She smiled back at him. He would surely notice there was no matching joy in her eyes—only dread.

"I'll race you up the stairs," he said, bouncing up from the bench.

She grimaced. "Let's take the elevator."

"If you're going to win your age group on Saturday, you have to get your legs moving," Ryan said, taking a step towards the stairs.

"I don't want to get sweaty before this motion," she lied and walked gingerly towards the elevator.

When they reached the courtroom, a half dozen sheriff deputies were milling around outside. It wasn't until they walked in and saw more deputies surrounding Bud Schubert that Zana realized the plaintiff posed a threat after wielding a gun in court the week before. Just as she feared, the court was filled with attorneys who, according to the calendar posted outside the courtroom, would argue their cases after her motion and bear witness to her likely defeat.

Preston, wearing a navy suit and yellow bowtie, was already seated at the right hand counsel table next to Bud Schubert. Next to him was a woman Zana recognized as his wife, Sandy, from the dinner at Preston and Kenny's house, which now seemed a distant memory. She looked younger than Bud, with her pageboy style auburn haircut and a more youthful face, likely due to strategic Botox injections.

Zana led her client to the left hand counsel table and busily unpacked her briefcase, trying to ignore the buzz of conversation from the galley. Their case was scheduled first and the audience was no doubt wondering why Schubert, who wasn't wearing handcuffs and a leg iron, was surrounded by deputies.

She took a deep breath as the clerk called their case. Her voice was shaking as she identified herself and her client.

Preston rose to his impressive height when he noted his and his client's presence, and introduced the court to Sandy Schubert seated next to her husband. Zana voiced no objection to her presence before the parties took their seats.

"I'm inclined to deny the motion," Judge Banks said without wasting any time. "Ms. West, do you have anything to add?"

"Your Honor, the decedent's swim coach testified that he saw a man with a knife close to the triathlete's helmets shortly before the race, and our expert has opined that the helmet chin strap was cut, ultimately leading to Terry Schubert's death. We also have testimony regarding Howard Hara's AKA Rockstar's motives to kill or hurt Ryan Peterson. We believe there is sufficient evidence to dismiss Mr. Peterson from this lawsuit," Zana managed to say. She held onto the table to steady her hand, but she could hear her voice quivering.

"Your Honor, there are many remaining issues of fact, including whether Defendant Peterson was negligent in crashing into Terry Schubert's bike on the race course," Preston bellowed.

"Plaintiff won't be able to meet his burden of proof on negligence." Zana shot out of her seat. "My client will testify at trial that he held his line while riding and that Schubert hit his bike while attempting to pass. There's no evidence to refute my client's testimony."

"While I appreciate the points raised by both parties, it's all in your briefs. I'm not convinced by Ms. West's argument. The court denies Defendant's motion for summary judgment."

Zana heard the gavel pound and felt the room spinning.

Then, she heard a voice asking if she was okay. When she opened her eyes, she was lying on the floor between counsel tables with Ryan and a few deputies leaning over her. Her first thought was relief that she'd worn pants rather than a skirt. She'd finally given up on her relationship with Jerry and there was no one else for her to dress to impress.

"Are you okay?" Ryan asked.

"Uh huh," she said and then slowly lifted herself off the ground.

"Do you need an ambulance?" a pot-bellied deputy asked.

"No, I'm okay," she said. "Just a little light-headed, I guess." She felt the heat on her face. She was absolutely *not* okay. The word of her fainting would spread through town like wildfire, and after she was canned later that day, she'd have no choice but to submit applications for work at Matson, Kokua Airlines, and the Hilton as her roommates suggested.

The crowd around her slowly dispersed. Ryan helped pack her briefcase and she walked shamefully past partners and associates busily texting the story to their colleagues. She and Ryan wordlessly rode the elevator down to the first floor, both staring up at the numbers as they counted down—4, 3, 2, 1 and then the door pinged open.

Opposing counsel was waiting for them outside the elevator.

"My client and his wife would like to have a word with you," Preston said. "Don't worry, Mr. Schubert isn't armed."

Zana shrugged and looked at Ryan, who said, "Sure."

Preston led them up the stairs one floor and down a hallway to a small Hawaii State Bar sponsored attorney workroom. A few deputies were posted outside. Bud and Sandy were seated at a table, and Preston gestured for Ryan and Zana to sit opposite them.

Preston nodded to Bud, who looked down at the empty table.

"Go ahead, dear," Sandy prodded.

"My wife," Bud paused, "and I…have decided to dismiss this lawsuit."

"We don't blame you for Terry's death," Sandy said, looking at Ryan. "Until today, I didn't know that Terry was wearing Ryan's helmet or that Rockstar had cut the chinstrap."

"It's my fault. I wanted to protect my wife from this litigation, but in doing so…" Bud's voice cracked. "I haven't been able to rely on her for support. Things have gotten out of hand."

Sandy looked at her husband expectantly and placed a hand over his.

"I'm sorry I pulled a gun on you last week. It wasn't loaded—I don't even know why I did that," Bud said, wiping a few drops of sweat from his brow.

"And—" Sandy said, tugging at Bud's shirtsleeve.

"Zana, I'm sorry I interfered with your relationship with Jerry. Please accept my apology," Bud said, looking her in the eyes.

Zana nodded and swallowed hard. His apology was months too late. The case cost her relationship with Jerry and her job, but Ryan would be able to move on with his life and F.I.M. wouldn't have to pay. She smiled weakly at the positive outcome for her client and the insurance company.

"Are you agreeable to dismissing this action with prejudice, Mr. Peterson?" Preston asked.

"Absolutely!" Ryan smiled. "Mahalo."

"Very good. My staff will deliver the stipulation for dismissal to your office this afternoon," Preston said to Zana.

After she and Ryan shook hands with the opposition and made their way to the ground floor, she popped into the bathroom while her client busied himself with texting.

When she came out, Ryan was grinning from ear to ear, humming the song "Happy" by Pharrell Williams.

"Congratulations," Zana said, now smiling warmly at her client. "How are you going to celebrate?"

"Alexia agreed to go out with me!" Ryan said. After fist bumping and hugging, Ryan headed to the parking garage and Zana hobbled back to her office to pack up her boxes. The case's dismissal would surely be overshadowed by the news of her fainting after losing a motion.

Chapter Thirty-one

Zana's walk back to the office was slow and excruciating. She regretted not asking Ryan to give her a ride, but decided not to for fear he'd insist on parking and coming up. She didn't want him to witness her being sacked. The moment she stepped into the building, she took off her offending shoes and walked barefoot onto the escalator, onto the elevator and then down the hall to her office. She shut the door and sunk into her chair, staring out at the pineapple in the distance. She watched the sun rise higher in the sky and shadows of nearby buildings shift. She didn't bother to turn on her computer or check her phone for messages. There was nothing for her to do, but wait for the inevitable.

After what seemed like hours, Frank appeared in her office as expected, carrying some papers in his hand. She probably had to sign a termination agreement or something. At least he wasn't going to throw a thick legal brief at her like he often had at her former colleagues. Instead, he sat down facing her.

"I heard you lost the motion," he said, gruffly.

She nodded slightly.

"I also heard you fainted," he said.

She nodded again.

"What you did calls for your termination," Frank said.

"I'll pack my stuff," she said, standing up.

He tossed the paper on her desk. It was the Stipulation to Dismiss with Prejudice of the Schubert vs. Peterson case.

"Have a seat," Frank said. "I just got off the phone with Mr. Peterson."

"Oh?" she said as she returned to her chair.

"He raved about your performance and said he called Caron Rossi at

F.I.M. to thank her personally for appointing you as his attorney."

"Really?" Zana said, wondering if Ryan had guessed her job was in jeopardy.

"He expressed concern for your health and mentioned that you're competing in the Freewheel Movement Triathlon on Sunday," Frank said, rubbing his chin.

"Yeah. It won't interfere with work. I'll get my billable hours in and be at the Saturday meeting," Zana stammered.

Frank shook his head.

Was he going to fire her anyway?

"I want you to go home and take the rest of the week off to rest before the race," he said with a smile that was almost warm.

"Are you serious?" Zana asked. *Did he mean she could take time off? Or, was this his way of firing her?*

"Yes. It wasn't exactly my idea. Mr. Peterson suggested it and I agreed. You should be rewarded for your hard work. If there's anything that needs to be done in your absence, let Lucas know. He's agreed to cover for you while you're out. You can also take Monday off to rest, and we'll see you first thing on Tuesday morning."

Zana's eyes widened. "What about the Saturday meeting?"

"You're excused," Frank said. He rose out of the chair and turned to walk out the door.

"Thank you," Zana stammered, willing herself not to cry from happiness. While she was dating Jerry, she had unsuccessfully begged Frank for a few three-day weekends and now he had suddenly bestowed an unsolicited four days off. She was stunned.

He then turned back and said, "Good luck!"

Zana quickly reviewed and signed the stipulation for dismissal, and gave it to Sylvia with instructions to deliver it to Preston. She filled out her timesheets, grabbed her handbag, and headed to the elevator so her unexpected mini-vacation could begin. As she drove home, she pulled out her iPhone to call Ryan.

"Thanks so much, Ryan," Zana said the instant he answered the phone.

"Who's this?"

"Zana West."

"Just kidding," Ryan laughed. "I knew it was you. Frank must have given you a few days off like I suggested."

"It's amazing. I can't believe I have four days off. It'll be great—I can bike fifty miles today and then go for a long run," she said into the speakerphone.

"Hold up, Zana. The time off is for you to catch up on sleep. You looked like the walking dead today."

Zana turned on her blinker to switch lanes to pass a slow car. "I need to get some training in before the race."

"You're already in great shape," Ryan said. "Promise me that you'll stay off your feet and get lots of sleep. I forbid you to do anything, but very short swims or slow jogs."

"Okay, coach." She would at least give him lip service. She sped up thinking about her planned bike ride.

"I don't even want you to get on your bike unless you're checking to make sure the gears are working and the tires are pumped. Got it?"

"Can't I just go for a twenty mile ride?" she whined.

"Zana, I won a gold medal in the Olympics for the same distance triathlon you're doing on Sunday. I know what I'm talking about," he said.

"What will I do for four whole days while I wait for the race?" She slowed her car to the speed limit, realizing that she no longer had to get home quickly to train.

"You'll sleep a lot, eat healthy food, drink lots of water, binge watch *Orange is the New Black*, and go for some easy swims and short jogs. You can also do some yoga and meditation."

"Okay, that gives me something to do," Zana said, relaxing her shoulders. "How many people are entered in my age group?"

"Ignore your competition." Ryan sighed. "It's you against yourself, Zana. You told me that your fastest time for this distance is 2:14. Well, Megan Alexander has raced a 2:07, which is in the ballpark for qualifying for the US Olympic Team. Just focus on your own race."

"Thanks for the encouragement." Zana frowned. "I don't understand why Megan isn't competing in the elite category. It doesn't seem fair that I have to race against her."

"The winners of each age group get a trip for two to Paris. I broke it down only by age group. It's just how this race is."

"Okay, I get it." Zana sighed. She didn't have a shot of winning against Megan.

"If you hadn't filed the motion and explained the facts in court today so Sandy could hear, the case might have gone to trial. Who knows, I could have lost everything," Ryan said. "If you don't win the Paris trip, I'll take you there myself. You deserve it."

"Ryan, that's a nice offer, but I'd rather win it. There's nothing else going on in my life. I could at least go to Paris and stroll along the Seine and try to speak the French I learned in high school," Zana said as she took the 6th Avenue exit off the freeway.

"*Trés bien,*" Ryan said in his perfect accent honed from years of cycling in France.

"*Merci beaucoup* for your advice and for talking to Frank." Zana smiled. "I'll see you at the race on Sunday."

"*Bonne chance!*" Ryan said.

It was almost 1 p.m. by the time Zana returned home. Andrew and Kelly were at work and the house was eerily quiet. She decided to follow Ryan's advice and take a much-needed nap.

When she woke up, she saw on her digital clock that it was 3 p.m. If it hadn't been so bright from the sun shining through her bedroom windows, she would have thought it was close to midnight, because sleeping during the day was something she never did.

It took her a few minutes to remember that she had been awarded a reprieve from her arduous schedule. She started to pull herself up out of bed, but then fell back onto her pillows to enjoy the comfort of her mattress for a few minutes longer. Out of habit, she grabbed her phone off the nightstand and saw that Ryan had texted her to call him.

"Ryan?" Zana croaked.

"You sound like you just woke up," he said.

"Yes," she yawned. "I had a luxurious nap."

"Good to hear! I have surprise for you," he said. "It will give you the edge you need to get your PR at the race."

"I'm sure I'll set my personal record no matter what with all of my training," Zana said, switching to the speaker function on her phone and stretching her arms above her head.

"That's the spirit. My surprise is that I've booked you a suite at the Ala Moana Hotel for the next five days."

"You're kidding me, right?" Zana froze and stared at the phone.

"I'm totally serious. Before a race, I try to stay at a nice hotel as close to the starting line as possible. Otherwise, there are too many distractions and I lose my focus," Ryan explained. "The Ala Moana Hotel is across the street from the starting line and you won't have to bother with parking on the morning of the race."

"Oh, my gosh! That's so cool!" Zana squealed. "You've already done enough for me. I don't understand."

"I didn't explain to you earlier, but the only reason Alexia is going out with me tomorrow night is because of your glowing recommendation," Ryan said. "From her texts, I get the impression that she's open to something more than friendship."

Zana smiled and walked with the phone to the kitchen. "Wow, that's awesome."

"I want to show my appreciation by giving you the best opportunity to have a great race," Ryan said. "You have to promise me one thing, though."

"What's that?" Zana opened the refrigerator and grabbed a bottle of water and a yogurt.

"When I meet you at the hotel this afternoon for check in, you'll have to hand over your phone to me and you have to promise you won't bring an iPad, laptop or touch the business center computer in the hotel until after the race."

She shook her head. "I don't think I can do that."

"Then I don't think you're serious about winning," he said.

She could hardly comprehend what it would be like to be totally out of touch for almost four days. What would she do without her cell phone, texts, Facebook, Twitter, Instagram, Pinterest, or the Internet, Google, Youtube, and Amazon.com? She took a bite of yogurt and contemplated how empty her life would be without social media.

"Are you there, Zana?"

"I was just thinking. What if the office needs to get in touch with me or there's an emergency?" She noticed her hand holding her phone was actually shaking. *How could she do without it for so long? It was like a beloved pet.*

"No worries. I'll keep your phone with me and if anyone texts or calls, I'll let them know where you are," Ryan said. "If it's important, they can call you at the hotel on the landline in your room."

"I'm not sure I can be without my phone." Zana felt her chest constrict.

"Yes, you can. You'll have plenty to do. You can watch movies in your room, shop at the mall and go for swims and slow jogs at Ala Moana Beach Park across the street. I also highly recommend watching the sunset."

Zana took a long drink from her water bottle. "I'll do it. This will be like a real vacation—except alone."

"Being alone will give you the peace and serenity you need before a big race. Believe me, you'll feel much stronger after a few days of clearing your head."

"So—should I pack all my gear for the race and bring it with me?" She tossed the yogurt carton in the trashcan under the sink and headed back to her room.

"Yeah. I'll meet you there at five."

Zana had no idea what all she'd need for her mini-vacation and the race, so she stuffed her suitcase with workout clothes and gear, toiletries, underwear, sleep and relaxation clothes, a few books and magazines, and each item on her pre-race check list. She grimaced when she parked her laptop and iPad on the desk—not to be touched until after her return. She wouldn't need her knock off Coach bag and began emptying its contents into her backpack. She unzipped each pocket—and there inside was the small ring-sized box with the maneki-neko Jerry had given her months before.

She opened it and pulled out the tiny good luck cat, which seemed to be waving at her. She stashed the box in her purse and tucked the tiny cat into her bike toolkit so it would ride with her during the race. *She could use all the luck she could get.*

***

After checking Zana in at the front desk, Ryan helped her move her race gear filled gym bags, racing bike, and suitcase all in one load to her suite on the 23rd floor facing the ocean.

"Wow! Look at this amazing view," Zana said after she opened the door with the key card. "There's a little kitchen and a dining table. It even has a living room. This is so cool! It's like a little apartment. I would totally *live* here."

Ryan raised his eyebrows. "Have you never been in a hotel suite before?"

"I stayed in a really nice hotel—a Marriott—when I went to Minnesota for a deposition trip last year, but other than that, no, I've hardly ever stayed in hotels. Nothing like this—just Motel 6s. Places like that," Zana said, exploring each room.

"I'm glad you like it," Ryan beamed.

"What's this basket?" Zana said, touching a large basket of fruit, nuts, and healthy snacks wrapped in cellophane and a large pink ribbon.

"Read the card," he said.

"It says: 'Race Fuel for A Winner! Aloha, Ryan.'" Zana smiled. "Thank you so much, this is amazing."

"I stocked the refrigerator with bottled water, Greek yogurt, some ready to eat salads and other healthy food. You can also order anything from room service or eat at any of the hotel restaurants and charge it to the room," Ryan said, opening the refrigerator to show her.

Zana peered into the fridge. "Thanks, but that's not necessary. It's way too extravagant."

"No, it's not nearly enough. Enjoy your room and spend this time reflecting on what you want to do in the race, and maybe *even* what you want in life."

"This is so perfect," Zana said, looking out the floor to ceiling window and gazing at a tiny catamaran sailing toward the harbor below.

"Now—hand it over," Ryan said, holding his hands out.

"My phone?" Zana pulled it out of her backpack and gave it to Ryan. "Here's the charging cord. Make sure you keep it with you at all times. I still don't understand why this is necessary."

"Look, there's a phone by your bed, next to the sofa and there's one in the bathroom. Don't worry. If someone needs to reach you, they'll call you here. If they leave a message, the little light on the phone will blink."

"See, I'm already getting tremors from giving up my digital life." Zana held up a shaking hand.

"You're fine. One more thing before I go," Ryan said, handing Zana an envelope. "Here's something I want you to open the morning of the race."

"What is it?" Zana asked, holding the sealed envelope in her hands.

"You'll see. Now, enjoy yourself. I've left my phone number on the pad next to your bed so if you need anything, give me a call."

She set the envelope down and gave him a hug. "Thanks, Ryan."

***

Zana spent the next few days enjoying every moment of her blissful, pre-race vacation. She slept in until she could sleep no more and then ordered an egg white and veggie omelet, a bowl of mixed berries and herbal tea from room service. Her mid-morning jog around Ala Moana was so late that the park was filled mostly with tourists and none of her triathlete friends. She cooled off with an easy 500 yard swim and then walked back to the hotel for an afternoon nap and to watch talk shows on television. In the late afternoons, she wandered through shops in the mall and returned to the hotel for a room service dinner of salmon, wild rice and vegetables while she watched movies.

Normally, she would have gone to the pre-race meeting to pick up her race packet on Saturday morning, but Ryan had it delivered to her room. He also included a print out of all of the information on the Internet about the race, a map of the course and a one-page reminder of the rules that would be enforced by officials.

There were some temporary tattoos in the race packet, one of the Freewheel Movement Logo and another of the Eiffel Tower. Zana washed and dried her face and pressed a tattoo onto each cheek.

She was so relaxed by Saturday night that she felt oddly peaceful about the race the next morning. She pumped up the tires on her bike, checked the brakes and gears, and filled her backpack with a swim cap, a few pairs of goggles, running shoes, hat, sunscreen, race belt with number, sunglasses, water pan, Power Bars and gels, towel, I.D., a $20 bill, and some other items that were on her pre-race checklist. She remembered to place the sealed envelope Ryan had given her next to her backpack to read the moment she got up in the morning.

Zana couldn't remember ever being relaxed the night before a race. She wondered if she needed to take an Ambien or whether she would fall asleep naturally as she had since she checked into the hotel.

As she lay in bed at 9 p.m., after she had called the front desk to ask for wake up calls every fifteen minutes starting at 4 a.m., it occurred to her that for the first time in years, she had spent several days in almost total silence except for her requests to the hotel staff. There was no gossip on the phone with Shelby or Moana, and no complaining to Andrew about work. There were no conversations about triathlon races or training, and there was no hashing over what went wrong with her and Jerry's relationship. Her focus was the present, rather than the past or future. She was calm.

Chapter Thirty-Two

@ZLaw The secret to life? #Sleep. Binge watching fave T.V. shows ain't bad either. #FeelingStrong!

Zana opened her eyes a few minutes before the first hotel wake-up call sounded. She felt refreshed from another good night's sleep and wasted no time popping out of bed and pulling on her skin tight racing suit. After bending her body into some warm up yoga poses, taking a few bites of bagel and banana, she tore open Ryan's envelope while sipping coffee. Inside, was a typed sheet of paper from him.

Zana,

Today, you will enjoy how rested and relaxed your body feels. You are fueled by good food and fresh water. Your muscles are well-trained and strong. As you ride your bike across the street, feel confident that you are well-prepared. Enjoy every moment of the race and pay special attention to how fast your body moves, its strength and power. Today, you are racing against yourself. The measure of success is whether you've improved and grown, and not how you compare to others.

Go out and have fun!

Aloha,
Ryan

She grinned as she tucked the letter into her backpack. If she had read it two days ago, she would have completely ignored his advice and would instead be focusing on chasing down Megan. Now that she was well-rested and had regained her health after such a brutal work and training schedule, she understood his message. She sat back in her chair and took a deep breath. He was right—she did feel strong and powerful. This was a new sensation for her body, which was usually sleep and nutrient deprived.

After finishing breakfast, she rolled her bike out the side entrance of the hotel where she paused to gaze up at the crescent-shaped moon surrounded by twinkling stars in the night sky. She closed her eyes and breathed in, letting her body relax.

She stretched her calves, slipped on her bike shoes and helmet, and rode across the street and into the entrance of the transition area where race officials were checking bicycles and helmets for safety and rule compliance. After her gear passed inspection, she made her way through the transition area and racked her bike, carefully arranging her towel, water pan, helmet, and other bike and run items.

As Zana made her way past rows and rows of bike racks to the restroom, she passed a few of her training buddies and wished them good luck.

After she emerged from the restroom, she noticed the transition area was now packed with athletes from the US mainland, Japan and other countries. The morning of a big race, she was usually oblivious to T-1, except for the location of her bike.

Today, she felt relaxed enough to soak in the atmosphere. There was French pop music playing from the loud speakers and all the banners were decorated with Eiffel Towers, wine bottles and other symbols of French culture. There was a long table covered in a red-checkered tablecloth with plates of baguette pieces and coffee for athletes and volunteers. American and French flags flanked the run finish line, transition area and swim finishing chute, and the race volunteers wore bright yellow T-shirts with the Freewheel Movement logo and images of the Eiffel Tower on them.

"It looks cool, doesn't it," a voice said from behind her.

Zana turned and saw Ryan wearing a blue polo shirt with the Freewheel Movement logo.

"It's fantastic!" Zana said, giving him a hug.

"Are you ready?" he asked.

She beamed. "I can't wait."

"That's the spirit." Ryan winked at her. "I've got to help sort out some timing chip problems. Go get 'em, Zana!"

After Ryan headed towards the timing chip table, Zana walked towards the beach. The sun hadn't risen, but in the moonlight she could see the water lapping at the shore. A lifeguard was setting a buoy and a few athletes were swimming.

She took a deep breath, closed her eyes and stretched her arms above her head, surprised at how relaxed she felt. Her stomach wasn't churning with pre-race butterflies, and for the first time before a race, she didn't have stress-induced diarrhea.

She took her time walking down the beach, goggles and swim cap in hand, and hummed along with the classic French tune she heard playing in the distance. By the time she reached the race start at the far end of the beach, the sun was peeking out from behind the clouds in the distance, illuminating the water. She barely noticed the chill of the ocean when she stepped in to warm up with long freestyle strokes.

Zana was aware that the first wave of athletes were gathering between two surf boards to start the race, but she continued her warm up, paying more attention to her breathing than the blare of the starting gun or the crowds of triathletes waiting for their turn on the beach. When her wave was a few minutes from starting, she lined up in the front with the other women in her age group, not even looking for Megan Alexander or her friends. This was *her* day and she would focus on her own race.

The instant the starting pistol sounded, Zana launched into the 1.5-kilometer swim in a westerly direction, around a large orange buoy and then against the current towards the rising sun. Each freestyle stroke felt strong as she propelled her body through the water at a controlled rapid pace. Her breathing was steady and she intermittently raised her head to glance forward so she didn't veer off course. When she spotted the end of a concrete wall on her left and coral on her right, she increased her speed in an effort to catch the trailing, younger swimmers from the wave before hers.

She sensed that she was swimming alone with none of the women in her group within her sight line, yet she made no effort to check for competitors in her wake. Her sole focus was to emerge from the ocean as quickly as possible. When her hands touched the sandy bottom, she pulled herself up into a standing position and ran out as quickly as the calf deep water and sand would allow.

As she reached the beach through the swim finishing chute, she heard voices yelling "Go Zana", "Looking good, Zana", but she didn't look on either side to see who might be cheering her on.

Once she reached the pavement, she immediately located her bike and swiftly dipped her feet in the water pan and stepped on the carefully laid out towel to dry them before slipping on her bike shoes. She popped her bike helmet on her head, buckled the chinstrap, and put her sunglasses on—all in a few quick and practiced movements. She pulled her bike off the rack and ran with it until she reached the mount line, where she swiftly straddled it, clipped her shoes in the pedals and began the 25-mile ride.

She rode alone for only a few minutes before she caught up with a half dozen slower athletes, passing them with little effort. She made sure to keep within the allowable three bike lengths from the cyclists in front of her and to execute each pass within fifteen seconds, so she wouldn't be penalized by the course officials.

For the first 10 miles of the race, Zana rode on her aero bars, systematically passing athletes in front of her. It wasn't until she almost reached Hawaii Kai when some of the older, faster men zoomed past.

She felt strong and powerful as she reached the turn-around point just before Hawaii Kai. When she was riding back on Kalanianaole Highway, she sensed a cyclist drafting on the back of her rear wheel. The space between the other cyclist and her couldn't have been the required three bike lengths, and clearly the other triathlete was gaining an advantage by riding in her slipstream.

Zana sped up, but the cyclist continued to draft. Finally, she decided to ignore the other rider and focus on her own race as Ryan had advised. She returned to the zone, pedaling fast and strong and paying close attention to maintaining an aerodynamic body position.

As she rode towards Kahala, she heard the race marshalls on their motorcycles driving by periodically, but never looked up at them. Instead, she focused on the road in front of her.

After Zana made the turn into Kahala, the cyclist behind her continued to draft until she reached the back of Diamond Head and began to climb the hill. The cyclist made a move to pass and then, Zana saw that the athlete who had been drafting was Megan Alexander!

Zana made sure she stayed three bike lengths behind Megan as they rode down the steep hill and around Kapiolani Park. She focused her efforts on keeping up with her rival at precisely the permitted space allowed under the rules. Before they rode into the transition area, she was still following Megan, but dropped back to almost four bike lengths so there would be no question about her rule compliance.

The cheers were deafening as Megan and Zana made their way through T-2.

Zana quickly racked her bike, dropped her helmet and replaced her bike shoes with running shoes. She grabbed her run hat and placed it on her head as she raced out of the transition area, just behind Megan. She heard her name being called and people yelling, "Go Zana", but she didn't look to see where the cheers were coming from.

As she ran in Megan's wake, she remembered Ryan's words. 'Enjoy every moment of the race and pay special attention to how fast your body moves, its strength and power.'

She then relaxed and began to feel how effortlessly her leg muscles propelled her forward. She got into a rhythm, moving her arms and legs in sync. Without realizing it, Zana pushed ahead of Megan at mile 4. She decided to continue focusing on her own race and not to look back. Her rival was probably running on her heels and there was nothing she could do about it. Better to follow Ryan's advice.

As Zana reached mile 5, she continued to hear Megan's footsteps and breathing immediately behind her. A half-mile from the finish line, Zana realized that Megan's breathing was more labored than her own.

Again Ryan was in her head. 'Focus on your own strength and power,' she heard him say in her mind.

By mile 6, she heard the crowd near the finish line roar, which drowned out the sounds of Megan. Zana kicked into high gear and sprinted as fast as she could through the long finishing chute, expecting her competitor to pass her at any moment. As she crossed the finish line, she realized that Megan was still a step behind.

Zana looked up at the timing clock and saw 2:08:49. She had improved her previous personal best by more than 5 minutes. She felt her knees buckle and so she put a hand on a volunteer's shoulder while another slipped a kukui nut lei over her head and handed her a bottle of water. Zana grinned broadly and gazed up at the sky, wishing her mother was there to share this moment.

"Congratulations!" Ryan said as he gave her a sweaty hug. "I knew you could do it."

"You're so awesome, Zana. Great job!" Alexia said, enveloping her in a hug. Zana noticed that Alexia was wearing a Freewheel Movement polo shirt that matched Ryan's.

"Did you notice my time, Ryan?" Zana asked and then took a gulp of water. "I just barely beat Megan."

"Actually, you beat her by more than four minutes. She got two drafting penalties and the race officials added two minutes to her final time for each penalty," Ryan said.

Zana smiled.

"You don't look surprised."

Zana put her hands on her hips. "Guess who she was drafting."

"You go girl!" Ryan said, giving her a fist bump. "You're amazing."

Ryan grabbed Alexia's hand and pulled her in for a kiss.

Zana's eyebrows shot up and just when she was about to comment, Alexia nodded at someone behind her. "It looks like someone's waiting to talk with you."

Zana turned around and saw Jerry standing there. He wore cargo pants and a T-shirt that said "Go Zana!" On his head was a beret and he was holding a baguette and a single red rose.

Her knees felt weak. She hoped she wouldn't faint again and put a hand on Jerry's muscular arm to steady herself.

"Congratulations!" Jerry beamed.

He leaned over and kissed her tentatively on the mouth, and then handed her the rose. He turned to Ryan and Alexia. "Can I steal her away?"

"Sure," Ryan said, and he and Alexia walked away holding hands.

"Zana, I'm so proud of you," Jerry said as he led her away from the crowd towards the shade of a tree next to the ocean. "Ryan let me ride one of his course marshal's motorcycles and I got to see the entire race. You're such a star."

She bit her lip. She wasn't sure how to feel or what to say after not talking with him for almost two months. She felt the butterflies in her stomach that she'd expected to feel that morning before the race.

"Bud Schubert called me and apologized for interfering with our relationship. He said that he would do anything he could to make it up to us," Jerry said. "Kenny apologized, too."

Zana hung her head and whispered, "It's too late."

"I was afraid you'd say that," Jerry said.

She noticed a tear sliding down his cheek.

"You need to focus on your baby," Zana said.

"What baby?" Jerry's eyes widened.

"Yours and Annabelle's."

Jerry laughed. "Oh, shit! You must have read the tabloids from New Year's Eve. Annabelle was joking that she was going to have my baby. She's obnoxious. Some tabloid reporter heard it and the rumor instantly spread."

Zana shook her head. "I saw you on T.V. with her. She had her hand on your ass."

"Yes, and as soon as that happened, we decided to leave." Jerry sighed.

"You and your date?"

"My date was my sister, Jennifer," Jerry said. "We were at that party for about ten minutes before we left and went to our parent's house to spend the evening with them. I guess there was a lot of damage done in such a short time."

"I had no idea—I thought Annabelle was your date and that she was pregnant," Zana said. Now, *she* had tears streaming down her face.

"Sweetheart, I'm so sorry this happened," Jerry said, pulling her close.

"I'm all sweaty," Zana protested.

"I don't mind," Jerry said. "I've missed you so much."

"Me, too," Zana said, resting her head on his chest.

"I've been calling and texting you since Bud called to apologize. Finally, Ryan answered the phone. At first I thought maybe the two of you had gotten together," Jerry said.

"Are you serious?" She pulled away and looked at the hurt in his eyes.

"He then told me you were in hiding, getting ready for the race."

"That snake—he was supposed to have people call me at the hotel," Zana said, frowning.

Jerry held her hand tight and looked into her eyes. "He was just looking out for your best interests. He told me that the chances of you beating Megan were less than zero."

"I surprised everyone, didn't I?" Zana said, grinning.

"You sure did," Jerry said as he leaned in to kiss her again.

"You're wearing a beret. And, you have a baguette," Zana said between kisses.

"I bought you an apology present," Jerry said.

"What's that?"

Jerry reached in his cargo pants pocket and pulled out a travel folder and handed it to her.

She opened the folder and laughed. "A trip for two to Paris!"

"But now you've won your own trip," he said, smiling.

"*Oui*," Zana giggled.

He then put his hand on Zana's cheek with its temporary Eiffel Tower tattoo and looked into her eyes.

"I love you, Zana," Jerry said softly.

The words, the ones she had longed to hear for almost a year, drowned out everything around her. Her heart was no longer beating fast from the race, but from the feelings inside her.

"*Je t'aime*," she said back in her best French accent and held onto him tightly.

Haley O'Neill's teeth chattered as she pressed her body even closer against Sean's. The ground was hard and damp. Their moth-eaten tent purchased at Goodwill with the last of their money provided little protection from intermittent heavy rain showers, not uncommon for February on Oahu. She had finally dozed off on her bed of Hefty bags, a thin army blanket and makeshift pillow of balled up athletic wear when the announcement startled her awake. She nudged Sean, who was bundled up in his University of the Pacific sweatshirt and matching sweats.

"Did you hear that?" she said.

"What?" he groaned.

"We have to move. They're kicking us out of the park," Haley said, sitting upright.

Sean rubbed his eyes. "Now?"

"By noon, the guy said." Haley rummaged around the tent and found her Ironman watch. "It's after seven. If you're going to shower at 24-Hour Fitness before your interview, you've got to get moving."

Sean pulled Haley to him, kissed her and slipped his hands under her over-sized T-shirt.

"Your hands are cold." She giggled. "I'm serious, Sean. We're out of money and we only have one energy bar left. You need to get a job."

Sean closed his eyes and moaned.

"If you don't get up, I'll go. I wish both of us could work, but one of us has to watch our stuff," Haley said, looking up at their triathlon racing bikes, helmets, suitcases and gear piled at their feet.

"I'll go." Sean sat up slowly and then fished in his suitcase for his last clean clothes he'd been saving for the interview.

Haley clutched her small, ragged stuffed bear. *Tessie*, she called it. The little brown bear with its faded blue dress had given her comfort when it traveled with her to every swim meet, from age six years old to college, and to every triathlon, from age-grouper to pro. She enveloped Tessie in her arms and willed herself not to cry. If Sean landed a barista job at Starbucks, they could save money for plane tickets to leave this expensive island. They couldn't go home to Sacramento where the tent cities of homeless and unemployment was much worse, but there were some US cities with opportunities for newly minted college graduates with liberal arts degrees.

Haley watched her boyfriend carefully place his interview clothes into his backpack along with his toiletry pouch and topsider shoes—his only non-athletic pair. He changed into shorts and a T-shirt for the quick bike ride to the gym to use a free 3-day pass to shower and shave.

"I'll be cutting it close," Sean said, reaching into his bag for the last protein bar and handing it to Haley.

She passed it back to him. "You'll need your energy to answer their questions."

Sean tore open the bar and carefully split it in half, handing Haley her breakfast. They silently chewed their small portions.

Haley took tiny bites, not knowing when they might be able to scrape up some food again. The night before when they had shared a Cliff Bar for dinner, Sean had commented that people throw perfectly good food away in trashcans. She knew what he was getting at and shook her head. Tonight, they might have no other choice.

"I'll pack everything, but will you promise to be back by eleven o'clock?" she said, after taking the last bite.

"I should be back well before then." Sean leaned down to kiss her. "We'll be okay."

She nodded and gave him her most reassuring smile.

He smiled back, unzipped the tent and wheeled his bike out.

***

After Sean rode off, Haley folded up the Hefty bags and their only blanket, and squeezed them into her big suitcase stuffed with almost everything she owned, save for a few boxes left with her mom in Sacramento. They also had their bike case, used to fly their bikes to Honolulu for the Freewheel Movement Triathlon last week. She grimaced as she thought of their failed plan. They had used the last of their frequent flyer mileage earned from years of traveling to triathlons, swim and track meets with the hope of one of them winning the trip for two to Paris offered to the winner of each age group. As professional triathletes, they were sure they had it in the bag. How could they lose? They hadn't counted on stiff international competition, a few flat tires (him) and a stomach ache (her).

Haley had thought Sean's idea of winning the all-expenses paid Paris trip was the perfect way to celebrate their college graduation, and instead of flying back to Sacramento, they could fly to Houston, Atlanta, Miami or whatever city Monster.com led them to for their first *real* jobs. Ever since Freewheel Movement founder Ryan Peterson announced the prize, they had envisioned biking south of Paris to explore the French countryside for a few weeks. Thoughts of *foie gras*, baguettes and wine picnics had motivated Haley to finish up the five credits needed at the University of the Pacific, where she attended on a swimming scholarship.

Haley sipped the last water from her Hydro Flask and felt the urge to pee.

She zipped the tent and carefully placed a U-Lock she used for her bike through some thin nylon rope Sean had strung through the tent's zippers. This would only delay thieves from getting to her expensive triathlon bike, their gear and suitcases, but she had no choice.

Wearing running shorts, an oversized T-shirt and flip flops, she walked across the street and then another two hundred yards to the public park bathroom with working drinking fountains and stall doors. Her Oakley sunglasses protected her eyes from the bright sun and her long, wavy auburn hair was pulled high into a ponytail, which she had threaded through a white Nike hat.

When she reached the restrooms, she drank to quench her thirst and then filled the two water bottles she'd brought with her. While she waited in line, Haley heard some shouting and the sounds of trucks in the distance, but thought nothing of it. The park had its share of crazy people who awakened her at night with their screaming, fighting and loud chatter. After finally taking her turn in a grubby bathroom stall, she again drank from the fountain before heading back.

As she walked across the street, she didn't see their tent where she'd left it. Shaking her head in disbelief, she sprinted towards the palm trees where they had tied a line across to hang wet clothes. The tent was gone. The only thing left was her pink T-shirt blowing in the breeze on the line.

Haley grabbed the shirt and wailed, "Oh, my God!" She scanned the park. The other tents, filled to the brim shopping carts and tattered rolling suitcases littering the park only twenty minutes ago were also gone. She then heard the rumbling of a large truck in the distance near the Honolulu Zoo.

"They got your stuff, too?" a man with a toothless smile said.

Haley could only nod. Her insides felt like they were going to burst.

"Every few months they haul our stuff to the dump like rubbish." He swatted at a few flies with his hand. "It took me weeks to collect my newspapers and bags. Now, I've got to do it all over again."

"Where did they take everything?" Haley swallowed hard.

"The dump, on the other side of the island. Even if you can get there, they won't let you in," the man said, shaking his head.

Haley slumped to the ground and put her face in her hands, letting the tears flow down her cheeks.

"Is this yours?"

Haley looked up and saw the man bend down to pick up something. It was Tessie. She reached out and enveloped her little stuffed bear in her arms.

If you enjoyed Freewheel, you may enjoy these other mysteries from Written Dreams Publishing.

Death Nosh

A Noshes Up North Culinary Mystery

Mary Grace Murphy

Released in Autumn 2016

Someone is sneaking into houses, committing murders, and escaping without a trace. Can Nell Bailey convince the police to take her seriously?

The police chief thinks it's the normal passing of senior citizens when people start to turn up dead. But Nell Bailey, food blogger and restaurant reviewer, has a different opinion.

To further complicate her life, Sam, her gentleman friend, isn't acting very gentlemanly. Plus, his plans don't include Nell investigating any more murders.

Can she hold her own against two men, Sam Ryan and Chief Vance, who are so accustomed to doing things their way?

Parts Unknown

An Alaskan Mystery

Toni Niesen

To Be Released in Summer 2017

*Can Beri Quinn find the answers she's searching for, or
will she have to close shop on her flight instruction school?*

As Beri Quinn, a flight instructor in the wilds of Alaska, searches for answers about her missing student, Ken Abbott, she questions his reason why he flew into a storm alone and how he went missing?

When Ken's mother visits Beri and presses the issue, Beri takes matters into her own hands and begins her own search for Ken.

What she discovers is startling and could jeopardize Beri's family, her business and her life.

Acknowledgements

Thank you to My Heavenly Father for His many blessings. Mahalo to my boyfriend, Bill Touth, for his encouragement and listening patiently as I read early drafts aloud.

Aloha and Mahalo to my biggest cheerleaders, my brother, Kim Nohr and his wife (my sis-star) Hannah Nohr. And, thank you to the wind beneath my wings—all of my family: Gerrie Nohr, Ed Haney, Jill, Gordy and Drew Gradwohl, Jeff Iversen, Jay Iversen, Sandy Crouse, Wendy Monette, Kelly and Rick Shewey, Sharon Beals, Shane and Joyce Sullivan, and my extended Christensen family—Paul and Lois Wilson, Christian Wilson, Marsha Fu, Kelly Graves, Todd Graves, Melissa Fu, Oli Fu, Elliot Fu, Emily Fu, Kiana and Kalin Uluave, Lucie Poehere Wilson, Krystle Kendrick, Ed Kendrick, Rachel Kendrick, and my other aunts, uncles, cousins, their spouses, and their children.

Special thanks to my editor and publisher, Brittiany Koren, who made this project a reality with her skill and enthusiasm. Thank you to my writers group, Brian Malanaphy, Steve Novak, Karin O'Mahony, who have provided feedback, encouragement and support from day 1 of *Freewheel*, and to our new members and friends, Nathalie Pettit and Doug Corleone. A special thank you Kelly "Rae" Monet and Rick Shewey for their patient support and work on my author website.

A special thank you to my *Land Sharks* launch team for showing me that I'm not in this alone: Tamara Gerrard, Jill Gradwohl, Kristina Selset, Ramona Emerson and Lesia Schafer. And mahalo to Tamara's family for hosting me during my book launch: Don Hubner and triplets Sophie, Tess and Gina Gerrard. Mahalo to all of my cheerleaders, friends and family who attended my Seattle book launch, including: Cindi John, Gerrie Nohr, Jeff Iversen, Jay Iversen, Gordy Gradwohl, Drew Gradwohl, Margie Person, Steve Pearson, Cheri Huber, Marilyn Bontrager, Keith Schafer, Leslie Baldwin, Paul Buckingham, Lisa Peterson, Dana Cline, Tracy Nelson, and others.

My first year of being a published fiction author would not have been as special without supportive friends: Mary, Del and Athena Alexander, Dianne Johannson and Brian Rosa, Dr. Kristie Byrum, Donna Good,

Cheri Moore, Lisa and Jim Ghahramani, Debra Stevens, Prebah and Ivan Covetz, Melissa Deats, Heather McVay, Winston Dang, Angela Hayslett, Dr. David Samsami and Elizabeth Samsami, Aysa Demir, Daphne Barbie-Wooten, Deborah Blackman, Jennifer Papastephanou, Dr. Kose Abdusselam, Colleen Graham, Amy Nelson, Chay Samalay and so many others. Mahalo to my fabulous friends and staff: Lenore Ogawa, Emmy Nation and Celeste Moore. And a shout out to my loyal and lovely Facebook friends, who put up with so many mentions of *Land Sharks*. You know who you are.

Writing fiction is not for sissies and requires a team of patient friends to slog through first drafts. Mahalo to those who patiently did so: Mary Alexander, Donna Good, Dianne Johannson; Emily Schmit, Teresa Tico, Ruth Chun, Debra Stevens and Angie Sullivan. And thank you to my advanced readers of Land Sharks: Siri Lindley, Doug Corleone, Teresa Tico, Lesia Schafer, Emily Schmit, Nathalie Pettit, roz horton, Roy Tjioe, Donna Good, Tamara Gerrard, Ralph Rosenberg, Dianne Johannson, Murphy Reinschreiber, Steve Novak, Mary Grace Murphy, Angie Sullivan, Karen O'Mahony, and Stefan Reinke.

Thank you to all of my fabulous HAIP and IAIP friends: Julie Kirk, Tracy Adams, Cindy Prud'homme, Angie Sullivan, roz horton, Jane Densch, Mitula Patel, Maria Carvalho, Robin Fawkes, Mariah Williams, Chenise Blalock, Danny Douglas, Linda Ipsen, Gayle Nakasone, Renee Fazeli, Freeda Koopmans, Sandy Malone, Kathleen Schumate, Annette Ing-Firmeza, Kimberly Shattuck, Deb Oldfield, Diane Martell, Fay Evans, Sue Cutter, Regina Lemanowicz, Pat Park, Ali Holmes, Kim Cameron, Rae Lynn Zachary, Nancy Hudson and many, many more.

And, last but not least, purrs to my late kitty, Bucky, and my feline children, Tashi and Ninja.

About the Author

Katharine M. Nohr is the author of *Managing Risk in Sport and Recreation: The Essential Guide for Loss Prevention* and her first fiction novel in the Tri-Angles Series, *Land Sharks.* She speaks internationally on Olympic Games and professional athlete risk management. Ms. Nohr served as Regional Coordinator of Officials, appellate hearings officer and member of the Pacific Northwest Council for USA Triathlon. Ms. Nohr served as a Judge (per diem) of the Honolulu District Court and continues to practice insurance defense litigation in Hawaii. Ms. Nohr is a past Regional Vice President for International Association of Insurance Professionals and was awarded Insurance Professional of the Year in 2012. She is a principal of Nohr Sports Risk Management, LLC and Claim Crazy, Inc. and the owner of the Law Offices of Katharine M. Nohr, LLC.

Currently, she is writing her third book in her legal mystery series. Visit her websites at KatharineNohr.com, nohrsports.com; or claimcrazy.com. She's also on social media on: Twitter: @TriathlonNovels, Linkedin: Katharine Nohr, and on Facebook: Katharine Nohr.

www.ingramcontent.com/pod-product-compliance
Lightning Source LLC
Chambersburg PA
CBHW031236120726
47905CB00002B/620